The
and the Pagan Beauty

Mahlon and Ruth were very much in love. Yet there was an invisible barrier that kept them apart— they worshiped different gods. . . .

"Ruth, there is only one God . . . the God of Israel," Mahlon pleaded.

"But Chemosh and Ashtar have been my gods since childhood! I can worship no other!" she cried.

"Let me tell you about our God, Ruth," he begged. "Then you can decide for yourself whether the things He teaches are important."

She sat very quietly as he spoke. "When Moses led the children of Israel out of Egypt many years ago," Mahlon began, "He spoke with the God we call the Most High on the mountain called Sinai. And God gave Moses the Ten Commandments, by which we live. My people call it the Law. . . ."

THE SONG OF

RUTH

A LOVE STORY FROM THE OLD TESTAMENT

by

FRANK G. SLAUGHTER

A KANGAROO BOOK
PUBLISHED BY POCKET BOOKS NEW YORK

Distributed in Canada by PaperJacks Ltd., a Licensee
of the trademarks of Simon & Schuster, a division of
Gulf + Western Corporation.

THE SONG OF RUTH

Doubleday edition published 1954

POCKET BOOK edition published May, 1977

With the exception of actual historical personages identified as such, the characters are entirely the product of the imagination and have no relation to any person in real life.

This POCKET BOOK edition includes every word contained in the original, higher-priced edition. It is printed from brand-new plates made from completly reset, clear, easy-to-read type.
POCKET BOOK editions are published by
POCKET BOOKS,
a division of Simon & Schuster, Inc.,
A GULF+WESTERN COMPANY
Trademarks registered in the United States
and other countries.
In Canada distributed by PaperJacks Ltd.,
330 Steelcase Road, Markham, Ontario.

ISBN: 0-671-80965-2.
Library of Congress Catalog Number: 54-6247.
This POCKET BOOK edition is published by arrangement with Doubleday & Company, Inc. Copyright, 1954, by Frank G. Slaughter. All rights reserved. This book, or portions thereof, may not be reproduced by any means without permission of the original publisher: Doubleday & Company, Inc., 245 Park Avenue, New York, N.Y. 10017.
Cover illustration by Robert Berran.

Printed in Canada.

ACKNOWLEDGMENT

Moving pictures are frequently filmed from novels, as well as from original screenplays. Occasionally, the latter have been adapted for publication in novel form, but usually after the story had been filmed and the picture released. To my knowledge *The Song of Ruth* represents the first time that novel and screenplay have been written simultaneously. The first book of this novel was written in first draft in the Beverly Hills Hotel in California as part of a screenplay. The second was completed a few months later, after my return from Hollywood. The third book and final revisions upon the entire story were made following completion of the "shooting script" for *The Song of Ruth*.

The idea for a moving picture based upon the Book of Ruth in the Old Testament originated with Mr. Herbert Kline. The original screenplay was prepared by Frank and Doris Hursley in collaboration with Mr. Kline for Chas. K. Feldman Group Productions. Later scripts were also prepared for Mr. Charles Feldman by Mr. Noel Langley, Mr. Maxwell Anderson, and myself.

I wish here to acknowledge my indebtedness to Mr. Kline and Mr. Feldman for suggesting that I write this novel, and particularly to Mr. Feldman for making available to me the publication rights in my own and all other scripts for the film, *The Song of Ruth*, necessary for the purposes of the book. His suggestions and criticisms have also been invaluable to me. I am also grateful to the other authors who helped produce the screenplay from which a portion of this novel is adapted, Herbert Kline, Frank and Doris Hursley, Noel Langley, and Maxwell Anderson.

AUTHOR'S PREFACE

Biblical authorities do not agree upon the exact status of the Book of Ruth. One group, with considerable evidence, considers it to be a work of fiction, a very beautiful and tender short story composed by a Hebrew writer about 500 B.C. Its purpose was twofold: first to place a foreigner in the ancestry of David, in this instance Ruth, broadening the appeal of the Israelite faith to others; and second, to teach a lesson of tolerance and love which might lessen racial antagonisms and intense nationalism, at a time when the Jews were coming out of exile to resume their place as a separate people. Others believe it a true tale from Israel's past, set down at a much later date, as were most of the Old Testament accounts.

The action of the book takes place much earlier than its authorship, probably about 1,000 B.C., toward the end of the reign of the Judges and near the selection of Saul as Israel's first King.

For whatever purpose it was written and at whatever time, the Book of Ruth remains a gem of ancient writing and prose rhythm. It is also an eloquent and effective sermon on tolerance and racial prejudice fully as applicable today as it was some twenty-five hundred years ago. It is my sincere hope that *The Song of Ruth* may in some small measure approach the beauty and eloquence of the original.

Jacksonville, Florida
October 1953

CONTENTS

BOOK ONE

THE PLACE OF REFUGE

Now it came to pass in the days when the judges ruled, that there was a famine in the land. And a certain man of Bethlehem-Judah went to sojourn in the country of Moab, he, and his wife, and his two sons. And the name of the man was Elimelech, and the name of his wife Naomi, and the name of his two sons, Mahlon and Chilion, Ephrathites of Bethlehem-Judah. And they came into the country of Moab and continued there.

RUTH 1:1–2

i.

THE NOONDAY SUN BURNED DOWN FROM A GLASSY SKY UPON the little caravan, as if angry at this small band of puny humans who dared to cross the desert wastelands west of the river Jordan and north of the strange sea that knows no life. Centuries later the prophet Jeremiah was to characterize it as "a land of deserts and of pits, a land of drought and the shadow of death." So it had been when the children of Israel wandered through it during those forty perilous years while they sought the promised land of Canaan. And so it remains to this day.

More than just the shadow of death hung over the land today, however. Death itself was there, both to see and feel in the bleached white skull of an ox lying beside the faint path marked by the caravans that plied occasionally between Moab and Israel. Far ahead, too, it waited where a flock of vultures wheeled in the brassy sky above what had been a living thing, perhaps a mule, killed mercifully when it could go no farther, or a sheep being driven hopefully from the parched fields of Israel toward the green plains of Moab, but doomed when a hoof had cracked upon the rocks.

Or it might even be a man, dying of thirst because a thorn had slit his waterskin and he could stagger no farther toward the tumbling waters of the Jordan River ahead and the springs of Ain-et-Tabeah that formed a fertile oasis of the "Place of Refuge," or "Meeting Place" on the border between Moab and Israel. Here the river that formed the dividing line between two countries split to enclose a small island. According to custom, two traditionally enemy people could meet on the neutral ground to trade peacefully, but in reality each kept his hand on his dagger and looked as much behind as before him.

The wings of the angel of death hung close over the little caravan plodding across the sands and particularly above the mule upon which an old man rode. His beard was long and his body shriveled from sickness and from the heat. His eyeballs were yellow beneath closed lids, and he could not always repress the moans of pain that arose to his lips.

3

The woman riding a mule beside him heard one of them and moved closer, reaching out with a gentle hand to touch his shoulder. "Only a few more hours, Elimelech, my husband," she said softly, love and pity shining from her fine eyes.

"I thirst, Naomi," the old man managed to gasp. "Give me to drink or I die."

"Mahlon!" Naomi called peremptorily to the tall young man in the dusty, patched robe trudging at the head of the five mules and two camels that made up the caravan. "Stop for a moment while I give your father to drink. Chilion," she went on, "come hold the cup."

The second son, a plump young man with a cherubic face, handed the reins of the animals he led to his brother Mahlon and hurried back to hold the cup beneath the waterskin. His mother untied the neck spout and filled it carefully, lest a drop of the precious water be spilled. She gave the old man a drink, holding the cup tenderly to his lips, then filled it a second time for her son Chilion, who drank greedily. The waterskin was flabby, for they had come a long way since it had been filled and there was little enough to last through the long dusty miles to the river crossing.

"There is enough for you, Mahlon," Naomi called.

The elder son had been staring reflectively toward the horizon where the vultures still wheeled in the sky. He smiled now and shook his head. "Take some for yourself, Mother," he said. "It is not far to the Meeting Place and I am not thirsty." With the strong sensitive hands of the artisan Mahlon beat dust from the dingy robe that covered his slender, wiry body and wiped sweat from his face. Hunger had deepened his eyes and sharpened his features, but it was still the face of a dreamer, although the anvils, forges, and hammers piled upon the backs of the two camels betrayed the occupation of the family as that of metalsmiths.

Naomi tied the strings about the opening of the waterskin and helped her husband move in the saddle a little to relieve the cramp in his limbs. She did not drink, however, although her thirst was as great as Mahlon's. Naomi was the rock to which the members of her little family anchored themselves in times of stress, the real leader of her flock. For Mahlon, in spite of his strength of character, was too much the gentle artist ever to be a real leader, and Chilion had always followed his elder brother.

"I see tracks here on the path," Mahlon said. "Two horses, ridden fast, came this way not more than two days ago."

"Moabites!" Naomi caught her breath. She did not need to voice her fears. The men of Moab were enemies of Israel, and this was the borderland where raids from either side were common.

"They were but two and they rode from Judah toward Moab, ahead of us," Mahlon said reassuringly. "Perhaps others of our tribe are fleeing from the famine."

Naomi drew a long breath of relief. "Let us push on and cross into Moab. Then we can claim the right of refuge for workers in metal."

"I have heard that Zebushar is a just king, even though he serves a cruel god," Mahlon said, and added hopefully, "Surely he will respect the ancient right of metalsmiths to refuge in any land."

Late that afternoon the spirits of the little caravan were heartened by the sight of green trees on the horizon ahead where the road to Moab crossed the river of Jordan at the Place of Refuge. Mahlon did not mention his fears to the others, but he had been troubled for some time by the sight of the vultures circling over the trees. Where they hovered so long, he knew, something that had been living was close to death.

Concerned at what might lie ahead, he did not even notice the cloud of dust on the path behind them, or hear the thunder of horses' hoofs being ridden rapidly, until Naomi cried suddenly, "Mahlon! Look there behind us!"

The elder son turned quickly, shading his eyes with his hand. "It is a small party of horsemen," he reported. "They ride as if the devil himself pursued."

"Do they look like robbers?"

"They come from Judah," Mahlon assured her. "So they must be of our own people." But his fingers tightened upon the spear in his right hand and he loosened the dagger in its sheath at his belt, signaling to his brother to do the same. In a time of famine a man could not always trust his fellows.

Then a smile broke over Mahlon's face. "It is Boaz! No one else in all of Israel sits so tall and straight in the saddle."

"And I recognize my friend Joseph," Chilion added. "He rides beside Boaz."

The horsemen, over a dozen in number, were upon them in a few minutes. They reined in, swords and spears uplifted, until there was mutual recognition. "Elimelech! Naomi! Mahlon and Chilion!" the leader cried. Boaz was older than Mahlon. His greater height and breadth of shoulders, coupled with the sternness in his face and a bleak light in his eyes, made the difference in their ages seem much greater than it really was. "Why are you here upon the road to Moab?" he asked.

"We are leaving Israel," Mahlon said quietly.

Boaz stared at them incredulously. "Leaving Israel? Why?"

"My father is ill and there is famine. Unless we find food soon, he will die and all of us with him."

"Many of us are hungry, but we stay in our own country," Boaz said sharply. "Where are you taking Elimelech?"

"To Moab."

"Moab!" the young man beside Boaz, whom Chilion had called Joseph, cried. "Are you mad?"

"We are starving," Naomi said sharply. "And that is worse than madness."

"But the Moabites are the sworn enemies of our people," Joseph protested. "They will surely slay you all."

"You forget that we are metalsmiths," Mahlon reminded him. "An ancient right gives metalsmiths and sorcerers safe conduct."

"Have the Moabites ever respected our rights?" Boaz demanded grimly.

"Metalsmiths are entitled to safe conduct in all nations," Mahlon pointed out. "It is not a question of our being Israelites."

"And famine is no respecter of rights either," Naomi added.

Boaz raised his hand. "Nay, kinswoman, we shall not quarrel. The same blood runs in our veins. In Bethlehem only Tob is closer kin to you than I am. Besides, Mahlon and I swore to be as brothers when we were yet striplings."

"A vow I still keep," Mahlon said quietly.

"And I," Boaz agreed. For a moment he seemed lost in thought, as if he were remembering the days when he and Mahlon had been youths in Bethlehem together and had sworn, as young men have done since the beginning of time, a pact of blood brotherhood. And for that moment the harsh lines softened in his face and the bleak misery in his eyes lightened.

"Did you see anyone on the road these last several days?" Joseph inquired.

"From Moab?" Mahlon asked.

"From Judah."

"The tracks of two horses go ahead of us." Mahlon pointed to the caravan track. "You can see them there in the sand."

Aroused from his reverie, Boaz spurred his horse a few yards ahead of Mahlon's mule and stared down at the road. The others gathered around him, reading the story so plainly written in the sandy tracks.

"Two horses," Boaz said, his voice suddenly hard. "And one rider light in the saddle."

At the pain in his voice Naomi looked up. "What has happened, Boaz?" she asked quickly.

"The woman who shared my couch left in the night with another man," Boaz said heavily. "While I strove in the councils to save Israel, a Moabite took my place in her arms."

"A Moabite," Mahlon cried. "Are you sure?"

"They were seen leaving Bethlehem. Cheb, son of the madwoman who dwells near the gate, trades with Moab. He recognized the man."

"Cheb is a liar and a thief!" Naomi cried indignantly. "It is well known among the women that he gives short weight and sells shoddy merchandise."

"Nevertheless, he spoke truth this time," Boaz said quietly. "Others saw them too."

"If she left of her own will," Naomi asked, "why do you ride after her?"

A spasm of pain crossed the tortured features of Boaz. "Would you deny me the life of the man who took her?" he demanded angrily.

"No," Naomi admitted. "That is the Law. Suppose you find Tamar, what will you do?"

"If she is alive, I will return her to Bethlehem and the council."

"But they will stone her."

"It is the Law," Boaz reminded her. "We will ride with

you to the Meeting Place and stop for the night, Mahlon. Tomorrow I will pursue them into Moab."

Mahlon nodded, but his eyes lifted to the vultures circling in the sky ahead. And he wondered what they would find at the Place of Refuge.

ii.

In the days of Zebushar, Moab was ruled from the capital of Heshbon by the King, who also bore the title of "Heavenly Son of Chemosh," the god whose mortal counterpart he was. The southern tribes of the neighboring Edomites were in general a peaceful people, tending their flocks and herds, but the Moabites of the north were cruel and warlike, skilled in the use of sword, spear, and the iron chariots of war.

On the same day that Naomi and her family met Boaz on the road to the Place of Refuge, a party of eight were riding along a faint path that followed the Jordan and the eastern shore of the Dead Sea from Edom to Moab. The leader was a giant with pale blue eyes that revealed little of the thoughts behind them. He was superbly muscled, every inch a fighting man. His face was craggy, but not unhandsome in a very musculine way, and a livid scar across his cheek spoke of at least one close call in battle. He sat his sleek black horse as if he were a part of the animal itself. Around his neck was a gold chain identifying him as a prince, for Hedak was captain of all the armies of Moab and second only to the King in power.

Even Hedak's spirited charger moved listlessly, however, for the day had been long and they had ridden many miles through the heat and the dust. Behind the Moabite leader rode a slender, graceful figure, wrapped to the eyes in a cloak against the dust.

"How much farther today, Prince Hedak?" a girl's voice demanded petulantly from the depths of the riding cloak. "I am tired."

"We will camp at the Place of Refuge, Ruth," the leader promised. "Maybe some more Israelites will be there."

"More?" the girl echoed. "What do you mean?"

"A very beautiful Israelite woman was at the Meeting Place with her Moabite lover when I came this way yesterday," Hedak explained, turning in the saddle to look with unmistakable interest at the slender girl riding almost at his stirrup. "We killed them both."

Ruth loosened the cloak from her face. She was startlingly beautiful, with dark red hair, high cheekbones, and warm eyes, filmed a little now by weariness. "Why kill them? Our men have captured Israelite women before. They make fine slaves."

"The man was an officer in my army. She might have talked him into revealing our secrets to Israel."

Ruth laughed. "Is it a secret to Israel that you will attack them as soon as you are certain your army surpasses theirs?"

"Perhaps not." Hedak shrugged. "But I want no spies in Moab. When my plans are ready, I will move against the Israelites, but it will be with the advantage of a surprise attack."

"Why fight them at all?" she asked. "Our country is far more prosperous and fertile than theirs."

Hedak lowered his voice. "I will tell you something I have told no one else before, Ruth, not even the King."

"Why tell me, then?"

"Because you are a part of it."

Ruth looked startled. Before she could speak, Hedak went on, "It should be no secret to you that I desire you for one of my wives. After all, you must have seen it in my eyes."

"I saw something in your eyes," Ruth said spiritedly. "But I was not sure until now that it was a desire for marriage."

Hedak threw back his head and roared with laughter. "Well spoken, daughter of Abinoth!" he cried. And then in a lower voice, "But even I do not delude myself that you would come to me on any other terms."

Ruth smiled. "Now that we understand each other, proceed to reveal this scheme of yours."

"The kings of Moab have sought for centuries to control the cities and ports along the Great Sea," Hedak confided, "but without success. Were it only the followers of Yahveh that I wished to conquer, I might be able to do that tomorrow, for they have become like sheep and do not listen to their leaders, not even such a man as Boaz. But when the armies of Moab move westward across the Jordan into Judah, we will not stop until the print of our feet can be seen in the sands of the sea."

"How long will it take to get ready?"

Hedak shrugged. "Five years. Ten. What does it matter? When so much is at stake, I can be patient."

"Then I should be flattered that with so much on your mind you stopped in Edom to escort me back to Heshbon," Ruth said mockingly. "Or is that, too, a part of your scheming?"

Hedak grinned admiringly. "Your mind is as keen as your face and body are beautiful, Ruth," he approved. "The Edomite tribes are proud that one of their daughters is the favorite handmaiden of the god Chemosh and his Heavenly Son, Zebushar. Besides, your father was a great warrior of Edom. The tales of his exploits are still told about the campfires."

"So by coming for me yourself, you make a favorable impression upon my people, against the time when you may need their men for your march to the sea?"

Hedak smiled at her acute perception. "Of course I enjoy your company, too," he assured her, and moved his horse nearer to hers. But Ruth, without appearing to do so, managed to draw her own mount away.

"I have heard my people call this man Boaz the Lion of Judah," she said. "What is he like?"

Hedak's fingers went to the scar on his face and a hot light burned momentarily in his pale eyes. "Boaz gave me this scar in battle several years ago, which is one reason why I hate him, I suppose. He is a fine soldier, though—for an Israelite."

"But still an enemy of Moab."

"Naturally. When a man of Moab meets an Israelite, he kills first and bids peace upon his corpse afterward."

"Even at the Place of Refuge, where every man is supposed to be safe?" Ruth asked dryly.

Hedak gave her a startled glance, but the girl's eyes were upon the green ribbon of trees lining the riverbank ahead. "Even upon the Neutral Ground." he admitted. "Still, it is just as well if you don't mention that to Zebushar, Ruth. Some of his ideas are—well, old-fashioned."

iii.

Shortly before sundown the now augmented caravan of Israelites reached the Place of Refuge, where every man was supposed to have sanctuary from his enemies. The river bed had divided here long ago to form an island perhaps an acre in extent. It was shady, green, and cool under the trees. There were pools between the rocks, too, where clear, fresh water could be dipped for drinking, and a shallow place down river for watering the animals.

Today it was obvious that death had visited even the Place of Refuge. At the sight of the overturned tents and the bodies lying on the ground Boaz hurried across the stream, followed by Joseph and his men.

Mahlon stopped to steady Elimelech while the mule stepped across the rocky bottom over which the cold waters of the Jordan dashed. He lifted his father from the animal and carried him over to the shade of a spreading tree where Naomi had placed cushions for his body. Only when his father was comfortable did Mahlon hurry over to where Boaz and Joseph stood, with the armed Israelites who accompanied them in the background.

The body of a young woman lay sprawled in death amidst the wreckage of a tent. Even in death she was beautiful, as beautiful as Mahlon remembered her three years before, when at sixteen she had become the bride of Boaz. The girl's arms were still around the young man who lay beside her, as if in death she had tried to protect him from the swords which had cut them both down. Her lover was a handsome youth with the beard hardly yet dark upon his cheeks, and the tattooed circular mark of Moab upon his forehead.

Gently Boaz touched his dead wife's face and hair, doubtless remembering the times that he had done so in life. For a moment it seemed that he was going to kiss the cold lips that once had turned to fire beneath his own. Then he appeared to notice for the first time that her arm was still about the dead lover at her side. He pushed the body of the lover away roughly then and all memory of their love seemed suddenly to go out of his face. With a quick movement he slipped the gold ring from the dead girl's finger and stood up.

"Take them away and bury them, Joseph," he commanded harshly. "Bury them together . . . forever together in their shame and their sin." On the last word, however, his voice almost broke.

Mahlon reached out and touched his friend's arm in sympathy, but Boaz shook off his hand, as if pride and anger would not let him betray his sorrow and his need for sympathy in the loss.

"Master . . . master." It was only a whisper, but they could tell that it came from a little way down the stream. Picking their way over the rocks, Boaz, Mahlon, and Joseph soon came to where the crumpled body of another woman lay almost in the stream, as if she had been trying to reach the water in her agony. Her dress was that of a servant.

"It is Sarah," Mahlon said quickly, "Tamar's maid . . ."

"Speak not that name again, Mahlon." Boaz's tone was sharp. But when he knelt beside the stricken woman, his hands were gentle. He dipped the corner of his riding cloak into the cold water and bathed her bruised face as tenderly as a woman cares for the sick.

The servant's eyes opened, but the film of death was already upon them.

"Master . . . master," she gasped.

"Who slew them, Sarah?" Boaz asked gently.

"Moabites from across the Jordan," she whispered.

Boaz exchanged a swift glance with Joseph. The men of Moab had occasionally violated the Place of Refuge before. But the dead man was a Moabite, and it was a strange thing indeed that fellow should slay fellow.

Already the rattle of death was in Sarah's throat. When her fingers groped toward him, Boaz took her hand and held it in his own strong one to give her strength in the hour of death. "The God of Israel will bless you, Sarah," he said with his head bowed, "for you were faithful, even unto death."

When the dying woman had ceased to breathe, Boaz folded her hands and closed her eyelids, even though she had been a slave. He stood erect then and, oblivious of the others, raised his arms to the brassy sky. "May the Most High God deliver into my hands him who——"

His prayer was interrupted by an alien sound, the jangle

of a soldier's harness. All eyes turned to the group of horsemen who were approaching on the other side of the river.

"Moabites! Into the trees." Boaz snapped a quick order to Joseph and the dozen or more soldiers who accompanied them. Gripping their spears and loosening their daggers, the Hebrews moved behind the protecting boles of trees, but Mahlon stood firm in the open beside Boaz, and Chilion did the same.

Hedak, Ruth, and the Moabite soldiers rode into a clearing across the stream. Hedak pulled up his horse and rose in the saddle. "Israelite sheep!" he shouted contemptuously. "What do you here on the border of Moab?"

Suddenly the Moabite captain's hand went to his sword. "Boaz!" he cried happily, drawing his weapon. "We meet at last!"

Boaz did not put his hand to his sword and the sons of Elimelech did not lift their spears as Hedak spurred his horse into the stream, shouting, "Kill the Israelites!" The Moabite soldiers were following him when, at a word of command from Boaz, the Israelite warriors behind him stepped forward. Realizing then that he was outnumbered by more than two to one, Hedak pulled up his horse in the midstream, an ingratiating smile upon his broad face.

"I was overly anxious to return this present you gave me years ago, Boaz," he admitted, fingering the livid scar upon his cheek. "Of course, we of Moab respect the Place of Refuge as you do. You need fear no harm from us."

"The soldiers of Israel fear no Moabite," Boaz snapped. "But if you respect the Neutral Ground, why did you kill two defenseless ones here?"

Hedak shrugged. "Where is proof that we of Moab violated the Place of Refuge?"

"Here." Boaz pointed to the tent and the bodies still lying in its shreds. "Come and see."

"Have I your word upon the name of the God you worship that you, too, respect the Neutral Ground?"

"You have my word," Boaz assured him.

Hedak ordered his soldiers to remain on the other side and rode across the stream to join the Israelites. Nobody seemed to notice that Ruth, so hidden by the cloak that she seemed a mere youth, followed the giant Moabite across the river.

Hedak dismounted and walked over to where the two bodies lay. "Who are these?" he demanded.

"The woman was my wife," Boaz said. "The man I did not know. But he is a Moabite. See, the mark of your god is upon his forehead." He pointed to the small blue circle of Moab tattooed on the dead man's forehead just beneath the hairline.

"It seems you have been betrayed, Boaz," Hedak said contemptuously. "Even if I had slain them you should thank me for avenging you."

" 'Vengeance is mine, saith the Lord,' " Boaz snapped. "But this time I reserve it to myself when no Neutral Ground lies between us."

"As you wish." Hedak shrugged. "This man I would have slain anyway. We want no Israelite spies brought into Moab, not even women."

"Do you still deny that you killed them?" Joseph cried, unable to restrain his indignation any longer. "A slave was dying when we reached this place. She named Moabites as the killers."

Hedak's hand dropped to his sword hilt. "Do you dare give me the lie on the word of a dead slave, O youthful firebrand?" he demanded angrily. "Yonder, in Moab, is no Neutral Ground. We will settle it with swords or spears, whichever you prefer."

Joseph reached for his spear, for only Boaz among the Israelites carried a sword, but Boaz stopped him with a word. "Hold, Joseph," he said quietly. "This is between Hedak and myself. We will settle it another time."

Hedak looked about him. Seeing the family of Elimelech, with their loaded camels and mules, he said, "These are no warrior band. Who are you?"

"Peace be upon you, noble Prince," Mahlon said courteously, stepping forward. "This is my father, Elimelech, and my mother Naomi. My name is Mahlon and Chilion here is my brother. We are on our way to your capital of Heshbon."

"Would you have dared to cross into Moab?" Hedak demanded incredulously.

"We are metalsmiths by trade," Mahlon explained. "And we claim the right of safe conduct guaranteed to followers of that trade."

"Are you sorcerers, too?" The traditional right of safe conduct was granted to sorcerers as well as smiths, for ordinary people regarded the ability to temper metal as a form of magic.

Mahlon shook his head. "Our sorcery lies in the bellows and in the coals, in the mixing of earths and the tempering of the metal, not in any works of magic."

Hedak pursed his lips. "Can you temper a sword so the blade will hold an edge?"

"I am accounted the best swordmaker in Israel," Mahlon admitted. "But I prefer to make plowshares and hoes."

Hedak spat contemptuously at the younger man's feet, so that dust spurted up on his leggings. "The metalsmiths of Moab forge swords for warriors." He drew his own sword and held it up to the waning sunlight. The weapon was long and heavy, the metal rough, with the marks of the hammers which had fashioned it plainly visible. "I will pit my weapon against yours, O Maker of Swords," he boasted, "since you are so proud of your work."

Mahlon smiled and shook his head. "A slave can wield a sword, but only a skilled artisan can fashion it and temper the edge."

Hedak's eyes narrowed. He was accustomed to having people cringe before him, but this tall Israelite in the dingy robe showed no fear, even though he refused combat. "Show me one of these swords of yours," the Moabite prince challenged him.

Mahlon, however, seemed not to hear, for he had just become conscious of Ruth's presence on her horse at the edge of the clearing in which they all stood. She had loosened the voluminous hood that covered her head and unwound the transparent blue veil from about her face. And as she shook out the coppery masses of her hair, she was a beautiful enough sight to make any man stop, even in battle, to look at her.

High cheekbones proclaimed that the blood of the proud Edomite tribes who lived in the southern part of the Kingdom of Moab flowed in her veins. The soft mouth and the violet eyes, warm with life and excitement, were those of a young girl of about twenty. As with all Moabite women, her eyelids were shadowed with some dark tint and her long eyelashes black with kohl. The white of antimony strove to hide the youthful flush of her cheeks, but failed, and no touch of carmine gave those lips their moist redness.

"Show me one of your swords, Israelite," Hedak com-

manded the woman-struck young smith again. But it was
Boaz who answered.

"I carry a sword forged by Mahlon," he said, drawing
his own weapon. Everyone could see how much slenderer
the blade was than Hedak's, even though it was as long.
And the metal showed few marks of hammers upon its
shining length. Ruth leaned forward to see it better, her
veil floating out before her face upon the evening breeze
that stirred the trees.

Even Hedak was impressed by the weapon. "When can
you reach Heshbon, if I grant you safe conduct?" he
asked Mahlon.

The young metalsmith looked to where Naomi knelt
beside Elimelech. "My father is sick and starving," he
said. "Give us food and we will travel as fast as we can."

"My steward will supply you and I shall leave word
along the road that you may pass unmolested," Hedak
promised. "You have a week to reach the city, no longer,
so see that you do not dally along the way."

It was not of forges, fires, swords, or even food that
Mahlon thought, however, as he went about setting up the
tents for the night. His daydream was of a girl whose hair
rivaled the sun in its fire, and whose slender loveliness of
form even a rough traveling cloak had not been able to
conceal.

iv.

The cooking pots had been scoured and the fires were but
glowing coals when Mahlon went to look for Boaz, for
the Israelite captain had not come even for food. As he
picked his way along the riverbank in the faint light of a
rising moon, he heard a sibilant whisper.

"Swordsmith!" The voice was that of a woman and
Mahlon's heart leaped at the sound.

"Swordsmith." It came again and he saw her now in
the faint brilliance of the rising moon sitting on a broad
rock across the stream dabbling with her bare feet in a
little pool.

He came down to the water's edge. "Did you call me?"
he asked in the same whispered tone that she had used.

"Come here, I would speak with you."

Slipping off his worn sandals, Mahlon waded across the shallow pool to the rock on which she sat. She had been scrubbing her cheeks with a cloth and the white of antimony no longer covered the soft skin.

"I am looking for Boaz," Mahlon explained. "He did not come to the evening meal."

"He is on the other side." She pointed downstream to where Boaz sat at the edge of the water, like a statue carved from the hardest rock.

"He has not moved for a long time," Ruth added. "What is wrong with him?"

"The woman who lay dead there was his wife."

"Oh! Did he love her dearly?"

"She was his wife," Mahlon repeated as if that answered the question.

"Then he must not have loved her very much," Ruth said matter-of-factly. "Else she would have stayed with him."

"I know nothing of love," Mahlon admitted. "My eyes have been only for the coals and the iron in the forge."

"Always?" she asked in a mocking tone.

"Until today," he dared to say.

She giggled. "You are forward, but I like it. What is your name?"

"Mahlon."

"I am called Ruth. If you are coming to Heshbon, perhaps we may be friends."

"I hope so," he said fervently.

She smiled. "Thank you, Mahlon." Her eyes turned to the solitary figure across the stream. "Why does he sit like a rock by the river, telling himself that because one woman betrayed him he hates them all?"

"I hope he will soon see how wrong he is," Mahlon said. "Boaz is a fine leader, although a little too stern. He deserves happiness."

"Only another woman can bring it to him," Ruth said in a tone of vast assurance. "And he must love her so much that he will not doubt her, ever."

"You are very wise to be so young."

"Women are smarter than men," she assured him. "Much smarter."

"You may be right." Mahlon grinned. "I have never known many women. And no one like you."

She put her hand upon his arm. "We may see each

other again, Mahlon, if you are coming to Heshbon. I serve in the Temple of Chemosh as a handmaiden to the god." Ruth's expression grew more serious. "Hedak will not like it if he sees us together, so listen carefully to what I have to say. He is letting you come into Moab because your swords are better than those of the Moabite smiths. When you get to Heshbon, don't go inside the wall to live. Take one of the caves on the hill outside the city, near the statue of Chemosh."

"I don't understand."

"You will know it when you see it," she assured him.

"Mahlon!" It was Naomi's voice.

"Yes, Mother."

"Come and help me move your father into the tent. The air grows cold."

"I am coming," Mahlon called. "Peace be upon thee, Ruth of Moab," he said hastily.

"And upon thee, Mahlon of Israel." She watched his tall form as he waded across the stream and stopped to put on his sandals before striding away into the darkness toward his father's tent.

v.

The pain in Boaz's heart was more than just the ache of a man for the woman who had been his wife. He had realized for months that Tamar was not happy, but had not known how to bring to her eyes once again the sparkle that had been in them those first few weeks after they were married, or the warm color that had risen in her cheeks when he returned home in the evening, weary from training the troops with which he hoped to protect his own tribe of Judah, at least, from the ravenous beast of Moab across the Jordan to the east.

Perhaps that had been the trouble from the start, he thought now as he watched the dark surface of the pool, too disturbed in his mind even to notice the gnawing pangs of hunger. If he had not been so bound up with the work of trying desperately to arm a complacent and unwarlike people he might have given the time to Tamar that he should. They had grown up as children together with Mahlon, Chilion, and Joseph. But Boaz had always been the eldest and the leader in childish games, the strongest who always won the maiden in the mock wars they staged. The maiden had always been Tamar, Tamar of the dark hair and flashing eyes, Tamar of the slender limbs and lovely body. And so they had drifted into marriage as naturally as they had given up the childish pleasures of their games.

From the beginning, however, he had been unable to bring to their union the gaiety, the lack of reserve, and the warmth that Tamar had possessed. Even at the ceremony of the winnowing, when the grain was separated and sacked, the feast eaten, and everyone warm and ardent with wine, he had not been able to enter freely into her embrace, although others around them were giving themselves unreservedly in this traditional celebration when the restraints of ordinary living were cast aside for one night of the year and the maidens were free to choose the men whose cloaks would cover them for the night.

He groaned aloud now as he remembered the emptiness in his heart when he had returned home two nights before and found her gone. But anger once again pierced even his hurt at the thought that she had chosen a hated Moabite with whom to betray him.

Tamar deserved death, he told himself sternly once more, as he had a hundred times since he had stumbled to this stone beside the pool to brood over his unhappiness and his anger. She deserved the stoning that would have been hers if he had found her alive and had taken her back, as the Law ordered, to be judged. The God he worshiped, the Most High, whose word was law and whose commandments must be obeyed unquestionably, had made it plain that the penalty of adultery was death.

While he watched the pool the picture of Tamar being stoned took form upon the mirror-smooth surface of the water. He saw himself, as was the duty of the betrayed, casting the first stone, and the pain that twisted his heart was almost beyond bearing. In spite of his anger and hurt he realized now, as he never had before, that somehow love was not something to be hedged about with hard and fast rules, that under its influence even the pronouncements from Sinai could sometimes be modified.

Yet such a thing was in itself a sin, his stern Israelite conscience insisted. For did not the edicts of the Most High brought by Moses plainly say that his people could have no other gods? And to deny even one divine edict was to deny the One who had made them all.

In his sorrow and shame Boaz did not hear Ruth when she waded across the stream, for she was barefooted and her feet made no sound on the ground. When she struck a small stone that went rolling down into the pool to shatter the picture he had been watching there, Boaz looked up and saw her standing nearby. Even in his perturbation, he could not help noticing how beautiful she was.

"Would you," she began hesitantly, "would you accept the sympathy of a Moabite?"

"You Moabites killed my wife," Boaz said savagely. "Why should you sympathize with me?"

"I am a woman," she said simply.

Boaz did not speak, but turned to look again at the water.

"Tell me something," Ruth continued. "If she were alive, would you take her back to your house?"

"I would take her before the council," Boaz said harshly. "To be judged for her crime against the law of God."

"And then?"

"She would be stoned."

"Stoned because she loved someone!" Ruth cried. "That is cruel."

"It is the Law."

"Then I hate your law," she flared.

"The laws of Israel are of no concern to you, woman of Moab," Boaz said coldly.

"But I have a heart!" she said hotly. "And I hate to see anyone warped by hate. Mahlon says you are a leader of your people," she continued. "But how can you be a wise leader when you have no compassion for others?"

"What would you have me do? Take them both in my house?"

"When a decent interval has passed, take another woman to wife," Ruth said earnestly. "Learn to love and trust her unreservedly and you will find yourself again. She may even give you strong sons—"

Boaz leaped to his feet. In his anger he lifted his hand as if to strike the girl for her presumption, but she did not cringe and his hand dropped to his side. He stared at her for a moment, then turned suddenly and stumbled through the darkness to his tent.

"Good night, troubled one," Ruth called softly to his retreating back. "Try and learn to love again, if you can."

The Moabite party departed at dawn, when the Israelite camp was just beginning to stir. True to Hedak's promise, the steward left food for Mahlon and his family, and gold with which to buy more on the way if they needed it. Boaz came up as Mahlon was securing the pouch containing the gold to his belt.

"You can still turn back to Judah, where your people are, Mahlon," he said abruptly.

"I have given my promise," Mahlon reminded him.

"To the Moabite woman?"

Mahlon looked at him in surprise. He had not realized that Boaz had even noticed his conversation with Ruth beside the stream the night before. "No," he said. "To their leader, Prince Hedak."

"Hedak's promises mean nothing. I know him from old."

"But *my* promise means I will carry it out. You have your flocks and your fields, Boaz," he added. "The famine is bad for you, of course, but you will survive it. For smiths there is no hope, since the people have no money to buy our hoes and our axes and plowshares. And the council will buy no spears for the army, so we have no money to find grain. Unless we move our forges to Moab, we will all perish."

"Your own people may perish if you make swords for the Moabites."

"I did not promise to make swords," Mahlon insisted. But even as he spoke he remembered Ruth's words the night before when she said Hedak was letting them come to Moab because of the quality of his swords.

"You know I would stay in Judah, Boaz," he continued, "if I could only find food to keep my father and mother from starving. But I have no skill save with the hammer, the forge, and the anvil. I must sell that to whoever will buy it."

"What will your father say when you become a Moabite?" Boaz demanded. "When you forsake your people to marry a Moabite woman and worship Moabite gods."

"There is no God save the Most High," Mahlon said

quietly. "Neither I nor my family will ever bow down to another. And as for forsaking my people, may God's punishment be upon my head alone if He does not approve my actions. You are the one who sins, Boaz," he added, angered a little by his friend's unreasonableness.

Boaz jerked up his head, his eyes hot with anger. "How?" he demanded.

"You are leader of Israel, capable of siring other leaders for the future. If you let—what has happened—turn you against all women, you will produce no sons and your line will die."

Boaz stared at him coldly. "This is strange talk, indeed."

"It is sensible talk. You are not the strong and kind friend of our childhood and youth any more, but an embittered man, filled with hate."

"Who put these words in your mouth?" Boaz asked. "Was it the Moabite woman? You say Moab will not change you, but you are changed already by one glimpse of a pretty face." He turned on his heel and walked a few steps away, then suddenly came back and seized the younger man by the shoulders, his face ravaged with pain and grief. "We have been as brothers, Mahlon," he said in a choked voice. "And I would not have us part in anger. May God protect you and yours, for only grief can come of this."

vi.

As the little caravan struggled across the wastelands of desert and stone that separated the Dead Sea and the Jordan from the fertile valleys of Moab, Mahlon found that Prince Hedak had been true to his word in guaranteeing them a passage from harm.

At the occasional oasis they passed food could now be purchased with Moabite gold to keep the spark of life burning, however faintly, in the frail body of Elimelech, and assuage the belly cramps of hunger that tortured the others. Here, too, as in Judah, the strong rock in the troubled sea of sand and stone was the mother, Naomi. She slept little, for Elimelech needed care at nearly every hour of the day. Her tongue was often so dry with thirst that she could not speak because she secretly pretended to take water but did not, so the skin would not empty quite so swiftly. And always her voice was lifted in encouragement, helping the others to carry on.

As the women of Israel had walked the dusty trails, driving the sheep before them and leading or carrying their little ones on that long trip of forty years from Egypt to the land of Canaan, much of it through these same wild wastelands, so Naomi both drove and led her little flock, looking always to the green fields and the ripe fruit that might give life again to her husband and the father of her children.

Hedak could guarantee them safe conduct and thereby make the way easier, but he could not control the heat, the dust, and the thirst. Nor could he warm the chill nights that stiffened the joints and brought sickness, ease the rubbing of a worn leather sandal upon tortured skin, or stop the torture from flies that swarmed over the oases.

Tragedy they carried always with them in the person of Elimelech, racked with pain, and weakening daily. And new tragedy came upon them when the mule carrying the waterskin stumbled and broke its leg, falling to the rocky path and thrashing in pain so that the skin itself was torn before Mahlon could hasten to remove it and much precious water was lost. After the skin was removed, they could only stand and stare numbly at the stricken animal, until Mahlon took the dagger from his belt and mercifully slit its throat.

Wearily they sewed the waterskin as best they could and put it upon another of the mules, distributing the things the mule had carried upon the backs of the other animals, although this loaded the other animals almost to exhaustion. They could not throw aside the instruments and the tools of the metalsmith's trade, for without them there would be no way of making a living in Moab and no reason for the Moabites to make them welcome.

Again the little band pushed on, but when Mahlon looked back at the body of the mule lying beside the path, he sent the others on ahead, and returned to build a cairn of stones over it. For it was not right to leave to the tearing claws and cruel beaks of the vultures the body of one who had served them so well, even if it were only a mule.

The week that Hedak had given them to reach Heshbon was almost up, when late one afternoon a long dark line of mountains appeared from the haze ahead.

"Mother! Father! Mahlon! Look!" Chilion cried excitedly. "The mountains that ring the valley of Moab."

They made camp that night in the shadow of the mountain range. Elimelech was very ill, and by morning all of them were taut from weariness and lack of sleep. Looking up at the peaks towering above their heads, Naomi began suddenly to weep.

"What is it, Mother?" Mahlon asked quickly.

"You and Chilion will have to go on and leave us to die here," she sobbed. "Your father and I can never cross such mountains."

"But you don't have to cross them," he assured her. "There is a pass into the valley. Cheb, the son of the madwoman who dwells by the gate of Bethlehem, trades with Moab. He told me about it."

Naomi managed to smile then and her shoulders straightened. "Let us push on," she said. "Perhaps we can find fresh fruit for your father before nightfall."

It was not yet noon when they entered a narrow defile that penetrated the mountains with a burbling stream running through it beside the roadway. Pausing for a little while, they drank of the cold clear water from a mountain spring and let the animals drink and crop a little grass beside the path.

The walls of the pass were high on each side and the way narrow. Mahlon looked about him uneasily, for if they were attacked in such a narrow place, there would be little chance to defend themselves. Wishing to be first to contact any danger, he pushed on with the camel he was leading until he was perhaps a hundred paces ahead. Suddenly a guttural cry sounded from above his head and a spear thudded into the roadway almost at his feet, an unspoken command to halt, fully understandable in any language and in any country.

Mahlon stopped suddenly, his body rigid, waiting for another spear, or an arrow to strike him. But it did not come. Instead a Moabite soldier with a drawn sword dropped from a rocky overhang where he had crouched out of sight, watching the path.

"Whence come ye?" he demanded.

"From Bethlehem," Mahlon answered. "In Judah."

The soldier took a step toward the young smith, his sword raised as if to strike. "The life of all Israelites, except Cheb, the merchant, is forfeit in Moab."

"Prince Hedak granted us safe conduct to Heshbon," Mahlon said resolutely. "Were you not told of it?"

"Are you the Israelite swordsmiths we were told to expect?"

"We are smiths and we come from Israel. The others are just behind me."

"We had given you up as lost," the soldier told him. "At the end of this course of the sun, your week of safe passage would have been up, and any hand in Moab would have been raised against you."

Mahlon smiled wanly. "There was a sandstorm . . . and we lost a mule."

"I must examine your packs," the soldier said importantly, "so I can be sure that you are really the metalsmiths."

Weary as they were, Mahlon and Chilion were forced by the officious Moabite soldier to unpack the anvils, forges, bellows, hammers, tongs, chisels for cutting iron, and every smallest tool of the metalsmiths. He even inspected the swords, spearheads, and reaping hooks they carried as samples of their skill. When he finished, Mahlon and Chilion had the laborious job of packing them again. Altogether it was over an hour before they were allowed to move on, but their hearts were lighter already, for the breeze was cool here and around every turn lay still another promise of the fertile land ahead.

Then suddenly they were through the gorge and there were no more mountain walls on the left, but a broad fertile valley shining green and rich in the afternoon sunlight as far as they could see. Orchards, vineyards, and fields dotted the broad sea of green, and the lowing of cattle and the bleating of fat sheep rose to their ears from the pastures.

Eagerly the Israelites surveyed the valley before them, for it was like nothing they had ever seen. Only a few miles away was a great city which they knew must be Heshbon, with a great circular building near the center whose dome glowed as if it were made of gold. Cheb, the merchant, had told Mahlon of this city, and he recognized the great golden building as the Temple of Chemosh, the pagan god of the Moabites.

"May the Most High forgive us," Naomi said contritely. "We should have given thanks to God when our eyes first beheld the valley."

"Surely He will understand, Mother," Mahlon said. "Let us thank Him now." With great tenderness he lifted the shrunken body of Elimelech from the mule. The old man was barely conscious, but when Mahlon said, "Look, Father. We have reached the land of Moab," he opened his eyes and a smile broke over his face.

"Put me upon my knees, Mahlon," he said. "And hold up my hands in supplication, for I am too weak to lift them."

Mahlon knelt beside his father with Naomi and Chilion. "Let us give thanks unto God for our deliverance," Elimelech whispered. "Let us praise the Most High for His mercy and loving kindness."

And when the prayer was completed they repeated the timeless words of assurance from the God of Isaac and Jacob, to the children of Israel:

> *"Be strong and of good courage:*
> *be not afraid, neither be thou*
> *dismayed; for the Lord thy God*
> *is with thee, whithersoever thou*
> *goest. Amen."*

vii.

The little caravan, revitalized now, descended the road that wound down the mountainside toward the distant city in the lush green valley of Moab. People working in the field and vineyards looked up at them curiously, but no one challenged them, for they had been passed by the border guards. Most of those who stirred the fertile soil were using tools of wood, Mahlon noticed. And he saw no plowshares at all made of iron.

Chilion, too, had noticed this. "We have come to a good place, Mahlon," he said. "When we show the people of Moab the tools we make of iron, they will rush to buy us out."

Mahlon smiled. "The Most High has favored us by

sending us where there is a market for our wares. It is a good omen."

"How will we know where to find Prince Hedak in such a great city?"

"We will not go inside the walls today," Mahlon decided, remembering Ruth's warning. "The hill before the city is pocked with caves. Let us choose one for our home and set up our forge."

A few hundred paces outside the city walls they turned off the road and climbed a hillside to where the mouth of a large cave yawned. Naomi went inside to inspect it. When she came out her face was beaming. "It is roomy and the floor is dry," she reported. "Let us stop here. This is a good place."

"I see a spring nearby from which we can carry cool water for the tempering tub," Mahlon agreed. "There is shade and plenty of dead trees upon the hillside to furnish wood for the forge. We will set up our shop here, but first we must build the altar to the Most High." He lifted his father's frail body down from the mule and carried him just inside the cool mouth of the cave. "Come, Chilion," he told his brother. "Help me gather stones from the mountainside for the altar."

Chilion looked toward the city and the golden dome of the temple. "We are in an alien land," he said doubtfully. "Perhaps . . ."

"The people of Moab serve a heathen god," Naomi said firmly, "but we worship the God of Isaac and of Jacob. Go build the altar, my sons. When we have made a thank offering you may set up your forges."

The two young men started up the hillside searching for flat stones. A few moments later Chilion came running down the hillside, his face pale and his eyes wide with fear. Mahlon's hand went to the dagger, which was his only weapon, since he had left his spear before the cave. "What is it, Chilion?" he asked. "You look as if you had seen a ghost."

"A horrible statue stands upon the hillside."

"What is it like?"

Chilion shivered. "The body is made of stones, like a fat old man squatting on his heels. The face is hideous with two clear flints for its eyes."

"Ruth, the girl who was with the Moabites back there at the Place of Refuge, warned me not to go inside the walls of the city," Mahlon said. "She told me to make our dwelling in one of the caves on the hillside, near the image, and said I would know it when I saw it. This must be the place she meant."

Chilion shivered. "It is an evil omen, Mahlon. I am afraid."

Mahlon laughed and clapped him on the back. "If the idol is an omen, it must be a good one, for it came through Ruth."

"She is very beautiful," Chilion agreed. "I could see that. But she is a Moabite."

"And we are living in Moab, O my brother," Mahlon reminded him. "Go find a flat stone for the altar while I strip the dry bark from one of these dead trees to make tinder."

The altar was the most important part of the furnishings of any Israelite home, whether palace, tent, or a cave upon an alien hillside such as this. This one was soon made, of rough stones piled up and a flat one laid across them. When it was finished, Mahlon knelt and stripped away the dry bark from an armful of dead branches he had picked up on the mountainside. He broke the branches into short lengths and piled the fagots beside the altar, then turned to the bark and began scraping away the dry inner layer until he had a small pile of brown powder upon the stone. This was the tinder.

Next he took from their baggage a piece of flint such as metalsmiths carried always with them and a short length of tempered metal. When he struck the metal upon the flint with a skilled glancing blow, a shower of sparks flashed upon the tinder. He repeated the action several times until a dozen tiny spurts of smoke showed where the sparks had caught. Then, dropping the flint and the iron, he blew gently upon the tinder until it glowed and burst into a tiny flame.

Upon the flame he put small strips of bark, placed across each other, and as the fire began to lap at them, added the sticks he had broken from the dry branches, one upon the other. Soon a fire was crackling merrily upon the flat stone.

"The altar is ready, Father," Mahlon called to Elimelech. Only the head of the family or a priest could make a sacrifice wholly acceptable unto the God of Israel. "What shall we use for the sacrifice?"

Elimelech opened his eyes. "The first fruits are the Lord's," he whispered.

"We have no fruits save some figs we gathered in an orchard beside the road."

"Surely they will be acceptable unto the Lord," Naomi suggested. "And soon as we can afford it, we will buy a lamb and sacrifice it, too, as an offering of thanksgiving to the Most High."

Mahlon nodded. "Tomorrow morning Chilion and I will set up our forges and grinding stones. There are always hoes and knives to be sharpened, so we should soon earn enough to buy the lamb." He took three ripe figs from a basket and carried them upon a plate to where his father lay in the cool, shady mouth of the cave. Kneeling before the old man, he held them out.

"Bless these first fruits of our coming to this new land unto the Lord, Father," he said. "And I will place them on the altar as a burnt offering."

Elimelech spoke the words of blessing and a prayer that their sacrifice might be acceptable. Reverently Mahlon took the figs and put them upon the fire crackling on the stone altar.

When the flames had consumed the fresh fruit, they busied themselves with the work that must be done. From the altar Naomi took a blazing fagot to light a fire for cooking and to warm the pain-racked bones of Elimelech against the chill that was settling over the valley with the coming of night. The mules and the camels were watered at the spring that gushed from the rocks nearby, and staked out where they could graze on the green grass growing on the banks of the brook that drained the waters of the spring. Chilion and Mahlon carried the meager family belongings into the cave, the woven sleeping mats, and the cloaks of homespun that served a double purpose as garments by day and covering by night.

While they worked, Naomi set up her pots and cooking tools. She was very proud of them, for they had been fashioned by Mahlon from iron and were easily cleaned. There were metal hooks from which to hang pots over the cooking fire, and spoons with long handles to stir the savory stew, when there was meat for the pots, or the gruel of barley and meal when there was not. Tonight there was no meat, but they had fruit in abundance and Naomi happily stirred into the pot the last of the barley meal she had been saving, confident that the Lord was favoring them in this new venture and that they would find food for the morrow.

Being craftsmen, Mahlon and Chilion wasted no time in setting up the forges and the grinding stones, placing the tubs for tempering beside the forges, where they could be filled quickly with water in the morning, ready to temper the first blade. They labored long after dark to gather wood, and after the evening meal was finished they worked upon the bellows skins, rubbing and kneading them with oil to soften the hides that had become hard and dry from the long journey, so they would be pliant and flexible for the pumping tomorrow.

Mahlon, as befitted the elder son, stretched his sleeping mat across the entrance to the cave with his dagger at hand and a spear lying beside him. But it was not of attack or battle that he thought as he lay there looking out upon the city below them, nor of the metal heating in the forge and the shining tools that would take form under his skilled hands. Instead his thoughts were of the girl who no doubt lay sleeping somewhere there in the city, the girl whose name was Ruth.

His heart quickened at the thought, for he could picture her in his mind, her hair tumbled upon the pillow, and perhaps one lovely bare arm thrown across her face. Of the loveliness of the body beneath the coverlets he dared not let himself dream, for she was a maiden, he was sure. And unless she were betrothed to him, he could not even think such thoughts, lest he lust after her in his mind and thereby break the stern laws of Israel.

If they were betrothed, however . . . The thought sent a sudden warmth flooding through him. But then cold logic reminded him that he was an Israelite with not even a second pair of sandals for his feet, or a robe of rich cloth for the wedding garment, while Ruth must be a person of some importance in Moab, for Prince Hedak himself to escort her.

Still he reminded himself proudly he was of the people chosen by God as His own. And he was descended directly from one of the sons of Jacob, whose names designated the twelve tribes of Israel, of the tribe of Judah, from which had come stalwart leaders for Israel and from which, according to tradition, would yet come a king.

viii.

The sun had barely risen when Mahlon came out of the cave. He looked with approval at the forges with the tempering tubs beside them, the anvils set up close by with the hammers ready, and the pile of dry wood ready to be turned into coals by the blast of the bellows. Already the long journey and the privations they had endured were only a faint memory before the reality of the great city lying before him and the promise of the future. From hundreds of chimneys wisps of smoke were rising into the sky and the sound of people moving about, of cocks crowing, and dogs barking came to him across the walls. Surely, he told himself, with the favor of an important man like Prince Hedak already obtained, they must prosper as smiths in this new land.

And then he frowned, for he remembered that Boaz had accused him of coming here to make swords and that Ruth had said almost the same thing. But he had made no agreement with Hedak to make them, although the forging of a slender, well-tempered blade, such as the one Boaz carried, gave him greater pleasure than anything else he did.

Chilion came out of the cave yawning and stretching. "First you get me up when it is still night," he grumbled. "And then you stand mooning. I'll wager you were thinking of Ruth, the Moabite?"

Mahlon shook his head. "Not just then, but she is much in my thoughts. Did you ever see anyone so beautiful?"

Chilion shrugged. "I prefer a little more meat on a woman."

Mahlon laughed and punched him affectionately upon the shoulder. "Get some figs and a piece of bread and go stand by the city gate. When the people come out to till the fields, cry out that we will sharpen their hoes and make them plowshares and pruning hooks. If you talk well, there will be meat in the pot tonight."

"And on my ribs, too, I hope." Chilion pulled out his loose robe. "I look like a walking tent." He disappeared into the cave and came out a few minutes later carrying some figs and munching a chunk of the cold barley gruel that Naomi had cooked the night before. "Have the fires hot in case I lure any of the Moabites up here," he advised his brother as he started down the hill toward the road leading to the city.

While he worked around the forges, Mahlon could see Chilion's stocky form where he had taken a stand outside the gate of Heshbon. From experience he knew the very words his brother was intoning in a merry singsong:

"Hear ye, O good people of Heshbon! I have good news."

The people coming out the gate stopped to listen. They carried hoes and pruning hooks, and a few pulled plowshares. Most of these were of wood and those that were of metal were dull.

"We are a band of metalsmiths." Chilion addressed the people leaving the city for the fields. "Granted safe conduct by Prince Hedak to sharpen your hoes, your scythes, and your pruning hooks. And to forge plowshares for you of metal that will not break."

He lowered his voice to a confidential tone. "We will sharpen your knives, too, if perchance you would slit the throat of an enemy, or a husband."

The crowd roared with laughter at the sally. Some of them turned aside to the path leading up the hill to the cave and the forges. Chilion continued his singsong announcement until perhaps a dozen people had gone up the hill, then he climbed the steep path, panting with the effort.

A small group of peasants was standing around the forges, watching Mahlon as he pumped the bellows with one hand and steadied a pruning hook in the flames with the other. Chilion came over and took the handle of the bellows. "I pump air down there to get people up here so I can pump some more," he grumbled. Then he grinned. "But maybe there will be meat to cover my poor ribs." And he started to sing as he pumped up and down on the lever of the bellows:

"Oh I pump and I pump."

Mahlon swung the hot iron to the anvil and, lifting the hammer, struck it in rhythm to the merry ditty as he sang:

"While I pound and I pound."

Chilion took up the next line:

"And when the iron is cherry hot,"

Mahlon ended with:

"I'll dump it in the tempering pot."

"It's just a tub, you know," Chilion explained glibly to the onlookers. "But what rhymes with tub, except maybe glub?"

As the roar of laughter subsided, he began again merrily:

"Oh I pump and I pump."

They were busy for a while, Chilion pumping the bellows to keep the coals glowing and Mahlon hammering the iron into form and tempering it at just the right moment by dropping it into the tub of water. Neither realized that anything was wrong until they saw the peasants around the forge suddenly scatter as if threatened by a lion. Mahlon looked up then to see Prince Hedak, his face black with anger, riding up the path, followed by a cruel-faced man wearing a lion skin and by several soldiers.

Mahlon felt a sudden cold chill of apprehension, but he stood his ground and said courteously, "Peace be upon thee, Prince Hedak."

"Who gave you permission to set up a shop here? Enticing people from the fields with the promise of sharp hoes?"

"You gave us safe conduct at the Place of Refuge," Mahlon reminded him.

"I gave you safe conduct upon your promise to forge swords for my soldiers. And a week to reach Heshbon. Yet here I find you sharpening hoes and hammering plowshares and the week is already passed."

"We were delayed by a sandstorm," Mahlon explained, "and almost lost our lives."

"You are Israelite spies seeking a new road into Moab," Hedak accused.

Mahlon shook his head. "We did not leave the road.

Except when a mule died and I dragged it aside to bury it."

"That convicts you out of your own lying mouth," Hedak snapped. "No man of sense would bury a mule on the desert."

"Our God teaches kindness, even to the beasts of the field," Mahlon said proudly.

"Your god!" Hedak looked around and saw the altar. "I have seen such as this in Israel. Do you dare worship an alien god in Moab?"

"The God of Israel cannot be alien, because He is everywhere," Mahlon explained. "We worship Him wherever we go."

"And spy upon those who are fools enough to trust you," Hedak said savagely. He turned to his lieutenant, who rode behind him. "Seize them, Nebo, and bring them before the King."

Nebo rode forward, but Mahlon stepped quickly in front of Elimelech, who lay in the mouth of the cave where the morning sun could warm him. "My father is ill and my mother is in the city buying food," he said. "Take me with you, but leave my brother here to care for my father."

"Take them all," Hedak ordered savagely. "We grant no boon to Israelite dogs in Moab."

Mahlon made one last desperate effort to save his father and Chilion. "You have seen one of my swords, Prince Hedak," he said. "And you know one man with such a weapon is the equal of two armed by your own metalsmiths. Touch my father and I will forge you no swords, not even if your king himself declares us innocent."

Hedak's own sword was out of its sheath in an instant. Death might well have come before Mahlon drew another breath, for Hedak was quick to anger, but Nebo intervened. "The old one is dying, Prince Hedak," he said. "And the young one a mere babbler of childish words. We know that what the smith says of his swords is true. Let Chemosh decide this matter which concerns the armies of Moab."

The Moabite chief reluctantly sheathed his sword. "As you say, Nebo, this is a matter of some importance to the people of Moab," he admitted. "We will let the King

decide. Tether this Israelite dog to your stirrup and we
will return to the city."

As Mahlon was led through Heshbon to the temple
with his wrist lashed by a thong to Nebo's stirrup, he
could not help noticing the teeming pagan life of the city,
the magnificence of its buildings, and particularly the
presence of armed soldiers upon almost every street corner. Nor could anyone miss the fear in the eyes of the
people who crowded the streets, and the frantic way they
made room for Hedak and Nebo, who slashed with the
backs of their swords at those too feeble or too slow to
get out of the way. There was no real love for Hedak in
Heshbon, Mahlon saw, even if he were a prince and next
in importance to the King.

The most startling thing to an Israelite in this pagan
city of the Moabites, however, was the large number of
women on the streets. In Israel, women rarely left their
houses except to work in the fields, to buy food for their
families at the market place, to carry a jar of water upon
their shoulders from the well, or to purchase a lamb, a
dove, or a kid for the sacrifice. And when they appeared
in public they wrapped their bodies in shapeless robes of
dark homespun material and covered their heads and their
faces, often to the very eyes, with dark shawls, hiding
their beauty, lest any man be tempted to lust after them
in his heart and thus break the law of God.

In Heshbon, however, women went openly in the streets,
and the sound of their gay chatter was like the twittering
of birds in the trees. Sometimes they wore veils of some
thin stuff wrapped around their hair and faces, but as
often their heads were bare. Kohl dripped from their
eyelashes, galena shadowed their eyelids, and the paste
of antimony whitened their cheeks, while the red of the
dye used sometimes to color the skins of rams tinted full
lips. Many wore robes of clinging soft materials so that
a man could easily see the shape of their bodies through
the garment. Their ankles were often bare and through
the open leatherwork of the sandals they wore toenails
could be seen, dyed as red as their lips. Upon their necks
and wrists ornaments of every kind jingled as they walked
with a swaying movement that took a man's eyes and
held them in spite of himself.

Mahlon was glad he did not see Ruth in the crowd, for
he would not have wanted her to see him like this.

Stumbling and prodded by Nebo's spear, he entered the great circular temple and climbed the steps to a broad platform upon which sat the towering, hideous statue of the god of the Moabites.

Chemosh was in human form, but with a gross, strangely misshapen form like a fat man squatting on his heels, as Chilion had described the idol upon the mountainside yesterday. He was of stone and therefore inert and harmless, Mahlon told himself, but there was nothing harmless about the raging fire burning in the bellow furnace that made up the belly of the god, or the swords in the hands of the guards who flanked the altar platform upon which stood the throne of Zebushar, King-Priest of Chemosh and absolute ruler of Moab.

"Prostrate yourself before the Son of Chemosh, Israelite dog," Nebo ordered, releasing the thong by which he held Mahlon and thrusting him forward so that he stumbled and went down on his knees to keep from falling. Half stunned by the unexpected blow, Mahlon staggered to his feet and found himself staring into Ruth's startled eyes.

She stood upon a short flight of steps leading up to a narrow platform running back of the body of the idol and twice a man's height above the level of the floor below. Her dress was the rich clinging robe of a temple priestess, and the headband of Chemosh with its short silver plume was about her hair, which fell in all its bright beauty about her shoulders. Noticing how the thin stuff of Ruth's garment clung to her body, Mahlon quickly looked away. But he did not miss her nod of recognition or the smile of encouragement she gave him.

The King-Priest Zebushar was a great hulk of a man upon a throne of hammered copper covered with rams' skins dyed in scarlet and blue, and flanked on either side by guards with drawn swords. The royal face was cruel and dissipated, with sagging pouchy cheeks and bulges beneath the eyes, plus an unhealthy sallow color that spoke eloquently of too long attendance at the wine cup and the banquet table. And for all his royal splendor the King-Priest was almost bald.

Hedak's eyes were cruel and their pale glare masked his thoughts, but the King's were inscrutable, yet somehow amused, as if while ruling a great nation and serving as its god in human form he still found time to look upon the foibles of humankind and find them amusing, perhaps even sometimes deserving sympathy from one whose earthly power was unlimited.

Nebo cuffed Mahlon again, pushed him to his knees. "Grovel, Israelite!" he ordered harshly. "Grovel in the dirt before Zebushar and the Great God Chemosh."

Mahlon held his head erect, even under the buffetings of the Moabite, until Zebushar raised his hand. "Leave him be, Nebo," the King-Priest commanded. "The Israelites are a stiff-necked people, bowing only to their god." Turning to Hedak, he asked, "Who is this man?"

"He is called Mahlon, O Heavenly Son of Chemosh," Hedak said unctuously. "As you can see from his features and his dress, he is an Israelite."

"How did an Israelite reach Heshbon? Are my soldiers blind that they let him cross the border?"

"I met him, with his family, at the Place of Refuge, when I was escorting Ruth back to Heshbon," Hedak explained. "He is a swordsmith and I was able to see one of his weapons."

"Where is the sword?" Zebushar demanded.

It was Hedak's turn to squirm now. "It was carried by Boaz, sire," he admitted. "He claimed the right of refuge at the Neutral Ground."

"Prince Hedak forgets, O King," Ruth said quietly from the background. "He would have attacked the Israelites upon the Neutral Ground until he realized that Boaz and his men outnumbered him."

Hedak's face was red, but he controlled his anger. "Boaz let me examine a sword made by this man," he explained stiffly. "I thought his skill might be of value in Moab."

"Why do you bring him before the god to be judged, then?" Zebushar demanded.

"Because they dallied on the way from the Place of Refuge," Hedak explained. "And being friends of Boaz, our enemy, they may have been sent here as spies."

"You have spies in Israel," the King reminded him.

"But I will have no Israelite agents in Heshbon," Hedak snapped angrily. "Today I found this man and his brother sharpening hoes and pruning hooks for the people who work in the fields. No doubt they are trying to learn our secrets."

"It is time someone sharpened hoes in Moab," Zebushar

said dryly, "perhaps even at the price of learning some of your precious secrets. The people complain that our smiths are always busy forging weapons and have no time to make tools."

"You have laid on my shoulders the task of defending the kingdom," Hedak said haughtily. "Am I to be censured because I do my work well?"

"Not because you do your work well, Hedak," Zebushar said calmly. "But perhaps because you warn us of dangers that may not exist. Are your people preparing for war against Moab, swordsmith?"

"We ask only to live in peace in the land that the Most High has given us," Mahlon assured him.

"Much of that land once belonged to Moab," Hedak objected. "Besides, I found them with an altar before their cave. They had been worshiping their god here."

Zebushar frowned. "This is a serious charge, although Israelites have worshiped Yahveh before in Moab, when they passed through on the way to Canaan." He turned to Mahlon. "Speak in your defense, swordsmith, if you can."

Mahlon looked directly at the King, for he had already sensed that Ruth and Zebushar were his only possible champions here. "We are workers in metal, not spies, O King," he said simply. "And we claim refuge under the ancient right that gives protection in any land to metalsmiths."

"There is such a tradition for metalsmiths and sorcerers," Zebushar agreed. "But not for spies."

"We are not spies," Mahlon repeated. "Before the God of Israel, I swear it."

"He blasphemes in Moab," Hedak shouted angrily.

"Nay," Zebushar said. "A man can only swear by the gods he believes in. Continue, swordsmith."

"My father is ill unto death, O King," Mahlon continued. "So we were forced to travel slowly. Besides a mule broke his leg and had to be killed. I stopped to erect a cairn——"

"An obvious lie," Hedak snapped. "Who would stop to bury a mule?"

"Our God created animals before man," Mahlon explained with simple dignity. "So we believe He values even the beasts of the field. This mule had served us well, I could not leave its body to be torn by vultures." He glanced to where Ruth was standing and saw that she had moved down the steps beside the image of the god and was now only a few yards from the King's throne. There was a puzzled light in her eyes, as if she were seeing him for the first time. When his glance met hers she gave him another quick smile of encouragement.

"You are an eloquent advocate of your own cause, Mahlon of Israel," Zebushar said, not unkindly. "But what of Prince Hedak's charge that you worshiped the god you call Yahveh in Moab?"

"Wherever we go, we worship the Most High," Mahlon explained. "It is the Law of Israel."

"He admits his guilt," Hedak cried triumphantly. "I claim his life as the accuser."

"It is your right, Hedak," Zebushar said reluctantly. "The Israelite admits worshiping another god in Heshbon, a right that only Chemosh could give him."

Hedak drew his sword and moved toward Mahlon, while Nebo stepped closer in case he tried to run. But a voice stopped them both before the sword could touch Mahlon.

"It is well known that all metalsmiths are sorcerers as well." Ruth's voice was a little shrill with excitement. "Does Prince Hedak dare to risk the curse of Yahveh?"

"I fear no Hebrew sorcery," Hedak snapped contemptuously.

"In Edom we know how powerful is the curse of Yahveh," Ruth insisted. "These people have claimed the right of refuge granted to all metalsmiths and sorcerers. If you shed innocent blood here, the curse may descend upon the entire city."

"What is this curse, Ruth?" Zebushar asked curiously.

"I am not familiar with all the words," Ruth admitted. "But the swordsmith should know them."

"What is it?" Zebushar repeated, turning to Mahlon.

"The curse of Yahveh is an ancient curse, put upon those who opposed the children of Israel by our God," Mahlon explained. "I learned it as a child; perhaps I can remember it now." He began to recite:

"*Cursed shall you be in the city and
cursed shall you be in the field. Cursed
shall be your basket and your kneading trough.
Cursed shall be the fruit of your body, and*

the fruit of your ground, the increase of
your cattle and the young of your flock.
Cursed shall you be when you come in, and
cursed shall you be when you go out."

Hedak looked a little discomfited by the list of curses prescribed by the Israelite God. He shifted the sword from his right to his left hand. Zebushar's quick glance did not miss his chief captain's discomfiture. "These are powerful curses, Hedak," he said. "And it is well known that sorcerers are protected by powers stronger than any gods."

"I fear no Israelite gods," Hedak said contemptuously. "Let this be decided in the way of Moab, with the test of the sword." He turned to Mahlon. "Have you no sword, Israelite, when you boast of your prowess as a sword-smith?"

Mahlon looked at the King, but he did not ask for mercy, although he knew he would have no chance in battle against Hedak.

"Prince Hedak has demanded a test by the sword," Zebushar said. "Under our custom it cannot be denied. Will you select a sword from one of my soldiers, Israelite?"

Chilion spoke from where he was standing just behind Mahlon. "We brought only one sword to Moab, O King, as a sample of our work. The soldier there in the leopard skin"—he pointed to Hedak's lieutenant, Nebo—"took it just now when we were arrested."

Nebo stepped forward and handed the sword to Mahlon, no little embarrassed by the laughter of his comrades at being caught. Zebushar leaned forward to examine the weapon more closely and a faint smile came over his face. Even at a distance anyone could see the superior smoothness of the weapon Mahlon held and the absence of hammer marks upon its shining length.

With a flamboyant gesture Hedak knelt and seized the shaft of his own sword with his left hand near the point, holding it above his head. "Strike down upon my blade, Israelite dog," he commanded. "If your cause be just, you will split my skull in two."

Mahlon looked around the room. If he did not accept the challenge, he knew, death for both him and Chilion, as well as Naomi and Elimelech, would follow.

"If you would live and prosper in Moab," Hedak taunted. "Strike as I command."

Mahlon raised the sword and deliberately swung it so as to miss Hedak. For a moment the Moabite chief was disconcerted by the gesture, then he got to his feet, smiling grimly. "You missed me, fool! Now it is my turn."

Mahlon took his own blade in both hands, as Hedak had done, and knelt on the stone floor of the altar platform. As he tensed himself for the blow of Hedak's sword, he pressed upon the ends of his own weapon so that it bowed upward just a little. His face was strained, but he did not flinch as Hedak twirled his own heavy weapon about his head, preparatory to striking.

Then, with a triumphant grunt, Hedak brought the sword down, striking the slim arc of steel which alone protected Mahlon's head from the heavy Moabite blade that could easily split his skull.

There was a crash of metal upon metal, there a cry of surprise from the onlookers as Hedak's blade split down the shaft and the pieces clattered to the floor, leaving the Moabite prince staring stupidly at the hilt that remained in his hand. For a moment Hedak was too stunned at this unexpected happening to move, then with a curse he cast the shattered sword aside and jerked a spear from the hand of a soldier standing nearby. He was raising the spear to stab Mahlon's unprotected back, when the voice of Zebushar, the King, rang out over the assemblage.

"Hold, Hedak! No blood will be spilled here until I command it!"

Even Hedak dared not defy the authoritative ring in the King-Priest's voice. Reluctantly he lowered the spear and handed it back to the soldier from whose grasp he had torn it.

"Advance, Israelite," the King commanded. "I would examine this blade of yours closer."

Mahlon approached the throne and handed the weapon to Zebushar, who surveyed it admiringly, balancing it in his hands. "Moab has need of such mysteries as this," he said thoughtfully.

"There are no mysteries, O King," Mahlon assured him. "The arts we know are those of the smith, and the secrets only in the mixing of earths and powders to harden metal. This knowledge is passed on from father to son, I learned it from Elimelech my father."

"Can you make spearheads?"

"Yes, O King. But I prefer to make scythes and reaping hooks."

"What say you now, Prince Hedak?" Zebushar asked dryly. "May not these smiths remain in Moab with their family as they have requested?"

Hedak hesitated, then bowed his head. "If it is the will of Chemosh, sire."

"You are right," Zebushar agreed. "Let the god decide, since they worship Yahveh."

Mahlon had paid no particular attention to the image of the Moabite god after one glance at it when he had been dragged into the temple. But when all eyes turned to Chemosh now, he followed their gaze. The fire burning in the great iron maw of the image was a mass of brightly glowing coals. High up beside it, at the top of an incline that ascended to some higher level back of the god of Moab, stood a priest arrayed in ceremonial robes. The sun shone through an open window in the wall of the temple, bathing the throne upon which Zebushar sat in bright light and moving on to caress Ruth's dark hair.

"O my father, Chemosh, God of Moab," Zebushar intoned. "Judge for us this day whether the Israelite Mahlon and his family come in peace. Send forth thy fires, O my father, if they are to be granted the refuge they claim of us, and the right to worship their god in peace."

All eyes were still on the fire, and no one noticed when Zebushar moved his hand so that the sun took hold of the great seal ring on his finger. Something inside the stone of the ring, perhaps a mirror, or one of the facets of the jewel itself, caught the light and sent a beam darting upward to where the priest stood beside the highest level of the platform beside the image. It struck the wall beside him, breaking into a tiny band of color like a miniature rainbow.

The priest looked at the small rainbow with startled eyes, then darted back of the image to a small room in which stood a great bellows made from a whole oxskin. When he pumped upon the bellows, a blast of air struck the glowing coals in the iron furnace in the image of Chemosh that housed the sacred fires.

"Speak, O God of Moab!" Zebushar shouted. "Tell us thy will."

As if in answer to his plea the fires began to rise in the glowing maw of the god and Mahlon heard a gasp from the onlookers. The tentacles of flame seemed almost to be reaching out to seize him, and he staggered back as a sudden gush of fire burst upward from the furnace.

"Chemosh has spoken!" Zebushar shouted. The others in the temple took up the cry, prostrating themselves upon the floor of the altar platform. Over their bodies Mahlon looked across at the King and saw that he was laughing silently, his great belly shaking.

"The god has indeed favored you, Mahlon of Israel," Zebushar announced. "You may live in Moab and forge swords for our warriors. And you may worship your god in peace."

Mahlon bowed his head. "It is the will of Yahveh," he whispered. Just how his life had been spared Mahlon did not know. But he sensed that it was somehow through human intervention and not by an idol which obviously had no life and no power, save that attributed to it by those who worshiped the god of Moab. He did not question the method, however; it was enough that he was alive and free.

"Forge swords for us, Mahlon," Zebushar said dryly, "and you will earn favor in the sight of Prince Hedak, who captains my armies. But think not that by letting you worship your god unmolested Chemosh has given you the right to teach false doctrines to my people. Convert even so much as one Moabite to your faith and the favor of Chemosh will be withdrawn."

"I understand, O King," Mahlon said quietly. "We will cause you no trouble."

Zebushar turned to Hedak. "See that the family of Mahlon have food and clothing sufficient for their needs," he ordered, "as well as iron for their forges."

As he was leaving the temple, Mahlon heard someone call him, and turned to see Ruth hurrying down the steps. She took his arm and drew him around the corner of the building, where there was a small garden.

"The god saved you," she said breathlessly. "But you have made a bitter enemy in Prince Hedak."

"But for you," Mahlon said warmly, "Chemosh would never have had the opportunity to speak in my behalf."

Ruth shook her head. "It was the way you defended yourself and the temper of your sword that pleased the god. But Prince Hedak hates you now, so be very careful of what you do."

"I will stay at my forge, where I can offend no one," Mahlon promised. "If you will come to visit us there."

"You are obviously a favorite of the God of Moab," Ruth said demurely. "As his handmaiden, I cannot go against his will."

"Then I will see you soon?" he asked eagerly.

"Perhaps Chemosh will speak again," she said enigmatically. "We can only wait and see."

ix.

More than just the need to gather wood took Mahlon up the hillside above the cave one afternoon a few days later, but he used it as an excuse. More than anything else, he needed time to consider what had happened in the Temple of Chemosh when he had apparently been saved from death by the favor of a heathen god. Surely, he thought, the Most High had intervened to save him. And this could only mean that his own God smiled upon his work even though he was obligated now to fashion swords for the Moabites that one day might be used against the people of Israel.

The ways of the Lord of Hosts, he knew, were inscrutable. Again and again in stories told around the campfires of Israel the Lord had moved in a roundabout way to accomplish what was best for the people He had chosen as His own from among all those on earth. But could the favor of God, Mahlon wondered, extend to the girl, Ruth, who had been so much in his thoughts since that night at the Place of Refuge? The laws of Israel forbade marriage between Israelites and the women of other countries, but these rules had been relaxed more than once when there were no maidens available for marriage among the women of Israel.

Mahlon knew his friend Boaz would say that he had been bewitched by the girl and was a traitor to his people when he put into the hands of the Moabites weapons with whose use the warriors of Judah and the other tribes of Israel were not familiar, and against which their spears and daggers would be pitifully inadequate. But Boaz was a man of a steadfast uprightness and harsh passions. Constantly in the councils of Israel he strove to convince the old men that they could not live peacefully with the armed hosts of Moab on their borders, pretending that the state of armed neutrality existing between the two countries could long remain.

Boaz had fought Hedak on more than one occasion, and he knew the tremendous ambition and greed of the man who stood second only to Zebushar in Moab. Knowing Hedak's ambition and greed, Boaz never ceased to argue that the Israelite tribes should arm themselves with swords and train their young men with every manner of weapon and every type of fighting, against the time when the Moabites dared to attack.

Now that he had seen Heshbon, the Moabite stronghold, with soldiers upon every street corner, and had heard the Moabites complain that all their substance was eaten up by taxes to finance even more military preparation, Mahlon was sure that Boaz was right. Unless Israel listened soon to his counsel, they would indeed be lost.

But if this were true, he thought in a sudden rush of self-doubt, was he not, as Boaz had termed him, a traitor in making swords for the enemy? The answer would seem inescapable, and yet that day in the temple when the Lord God could easily have let him be destroyed, He had intervened. It was a hard thing to understand, but the only answer seemed to be that, however complicated it all might be, this was the will of God. And since it was God's will, Mahlon assured himself, he could do nothing except follow where his best judgment seemed to lead him.

Mahlon had been walking idly along a faint path near where he and Chilion had gathered the wood on the day they arrived. And now he found himself face to face with the idol Chilion had discovered and which had frightened him so. Having seen Chemosh, Mahlon recognized the statue upon the side of the hill instantly. It had the same gross body, the same round head, and the same squatting posture, even the depression in the stone belly where, in the huge statue inside the great temple, burned the eternal fires of Chemosh. Unlike the parent idol, however, the height of this image was only about twice that of a man.

Standing before the image, Mahlon looked out across the city of Heshbon and shivered a little when his eyes fell upon the gilded roof of the temple. Now that he and his family were safe, he could appreciate the beauty of the city, with its luxurious palaces and temples, the shops along its streets that displayed all manner of fine fabrics and objects of silver and gold, even the bright colors worn by the women. But he still could not look at the temple without remembering the harsh clang of metal upon metal and the long, suspense-filled moment before he had felt Hedak's sword split upon his own tough blade.

The magnificence of Heshbon made Bethlehem seem a mean city indeed, with the flimsy wall that ran an irregular course around it, and the simple homes and buildings lining the dusty streets. The most splendid house in all of Bethlehem had been that of Mahlon's nearest kinsman, Tob the merchant. Tob bought and sold, trading with caravans from Moab and Philistia, and shipping the produce of Judah even as far south at times as Egypt. Yet for all his wealth, Mahlon realized now, Tob's house was less magnificent than almost the meanest dwelling inside the walls of Heshbon.

From the city Mahlon's eyes turned to the valley, with the mountains towering above it and ringing it around, save for the gorge through which they had entered, the only ready means of access to the stronghold of Moab. The road from the gorge and the pass ran only a few yards below the spot upon which Mahlon stood now. He could almost reach down now and touch the towering packs of a caravan that was moving along the road toward the city. It had come a long way, he knew, for both packs and camels were powdered with dust, and the leather harnesses which had dried out on the long journey across the desert wastes creaked in protest with every step of the animals.

"You, up there," a shrill voice called from below. Mahlon looked down and saw a small man, wrapped in a voluminous cloak, moving up a path from the road, scattering gravel and stones down upon the caravan in his haste. His cloak was powdered with dust like that on the camels' packs and his sandals were worn from the trail. He clambered over the edge of the rocky outcrop and squatted, panting for breath, a few yards away from Mahlon, tearing open the breast of his cloak to give himself air.

The newcomer was short and swarthy, with a thin wiry body and bright black eyes. He wore a beard and his features were those of an Israelite rather than a man of Moab. His left hand was missing, having been cut off at the wrist. In place of it he wore a metal hook secured to the stump by a cuff and a buckle of hammered brass.

Mahlon recognized the cuff and the hook at once, for he had made them himself. The man was Cheb, son of the madwoman of Bethlehem. Alone among the Israelites, Cheb had the right to trade with Moab, and Mahlon had seen him more than once, loading and unloading the camels at the storehouses of his kinsman, Tob, in Bethlehem. Cheb was well known in the city, although never well liked by the people, partly because of his traffic with foreigners, and partly because of his long absences, during which his mother roamed about the streets, screeching and grimacing like the poor mad creature that she was.

"You must be a stranger here or you would know the meaning of that image," Cheb continued, still panting. "This is forbidden ground."

"No ground is forbidden save that set aside by the Most High, Cheb," Mahlon said quietly.

Startled, the caravan leader got to his feet and peered at Mahlon "Who are you?" he demanded.

"Mahlon, son of Elimelech and Naomi. The sun burned me black while we were crossing the desert, else you would have recognized me at once as I did you."

"Crossing the desert?" Cheb repeated unbelievingly. "Only Cheb in all of Judah has been granted safe passage into the land of the Moabites."

"Nevertheless we are here; my mother, my father, and my brother Chilion. We live in a cave just below."

"Does Prince Hedak know of this? He has sworn to kill any Israelite found in Moab, except myself."

"Hedak granted us safe passage when I promised to forge swords for the Moabites," Mahlon explained. "And Zebushar himself has given us immunity and the right to worship the Most High unmolested."

Cheb shook his head slowly. "Nothing like this has ever happened before. I can't understand it."

"The Moabites had never seen swords such as mine."

"I remember now that Boaz carries one of them. It is a fine blade."

"Poor Boaz," Mahlon said. "Has he recovered from the shock of his betrayal by Tamar?"

"Boaz is not the same since his wife shamed him with a Moabite," Cheb said. "He stays much to himself and speaks but little, except to argue in the councils."

"Does he still urge our people to arm?"

"More than ever, but they do not listen. And why should they? You have seen yourself that Moab sends no warriors against Israel."

"I have seen soldiers upon every street corner," Mahlon said shortly. "And Hedak is overly anxious for my swords. Take this word back to Boaz when you return, Cheb. Tell him Mahlon, his friend, says his warnings against Moab are true and should be heeded."

Cheb shrugged. "For arming there must be taxes, and already a man can hardly make a profit on what he buys and sells. Israel need have no fear of Moab. But why are you in this place cursed by Chemosh?"

"The God of our people has shown us His favor," Mahlon said confidently. "We fear no curse."

"This is Moab, not Israel." Cheb shivered. "Shun this idol, Mahlon. Or you will die of its curse."

"No man hopes to live forever," Mahlon said quietly. "When my time is appointed, it will come."

"Never say that I did not warn you, then. I would not touch that statue at the risk of my life."

"Come down to our cave for a moment," Mahlon invited the caravan driver. "We can offer you some refreshment, and my mother may want to send a message by you to our kinfolk in Bethlehem."

Naomi was laying out the sleeping mats in the sun at the front of the cave and Chilion was bringing water from the spring when Mahlon came down the side of the hill with Cheb. "Here is a countryman of ours—Cheb, the leader of caravans," he announced. "He has just come from Bethlehem."

"Shalom, Cheb." Naomi gave him the courteous greeting of Israel. "I remember your mother. How is she?"

"As mad as ever," Cheb said blithely. "She harms no one, but sometimes she is noisy and must be locked up for a while. It is a surprise to find you here in Moab, Naomi. Tob will be glad to know you are well."

"We are not well," Naomi said sadly. "Elimelech grows weaker daily, although we have plenty of food. Is there famine still in Judah, Cheb?"

"Yes. The rich give alms, for such our God commands. But there is no food to be bought with the money. If it does not rain soon, we are lost."

"Then we did right to leave," Naomi said, "else we would all have perished."

"I am sending a message to Boaz by Cheb when he returns," Mahlon said. "I thought you might wish to send one to Tob, our kinsman."

"I will be carrying goods for Tob on the return trip," Cheb added. "Anything you wish to tell him will be faithfully repeated."

"Tell Tob that Elimelech grows weaker," Naomi said, and added in a low voice so her husband could not hear, "and that I fear he is sick, even unto death."

"Your messages will be faithfully delivered," Cheb assured them. "Peace be upon the family of Elimelech the Just, and may God restore him to good health."

"And peace be upon you," the others called out in farewell. But when he was gone, Naomi shook her head. "It is an ill omen that Cheb should come here. Where he goes, there is evil."

x.

The fires were lighted early in the forges each morning and the brothers were hard at work even before the sun rose over the mountains. Obeying the command of the King, Hedak had sent a plentiful supply of metal, as well as food for the family. They had no need to leave off work for anything except to gather wood on the mountainside when the supply was burned out, and to carry water from the spring below for the tempering tubs.

The people came, as they had on the first day, bringing hoes to be sharpened and tools to be brought to a tempered edge again. But Mahlon was forced to turn them away, for his orders had been to make swords alone. They departed grumbling, not against him, but against Hedak. All seemed to know that the insatiable ambition of the Moabite general had saddled them with the heavy load of a large army and high taxes. Now he would not let them have the sharp tools of metal they needed, yet none dared protest loudly enough to reach the ears of Hedak himself.

Chilion had gone to the spring one morning and was kneeling beside it to drink when he heard a footstep and looked up to see a plump, pretty girl in Moabite dress standing nearby. He scrambled to his feet and stared at her, his eyes popping with astonishment.

"Have you never seen a woman before, O Israelite?" the girl asked in an amused tone.

"None so beautiful as thee in Moab," he said promptly.

The girl laughed. "You are quick of tongue for an Israelite. My name is Orpah. You must be Chilion."

"How did you know?"

"Ruth described both you and your brother to me."

"Are you Ruth's sister?"

"No. We are companions. And she is much more beautiful than I."

"Not in my eyes," Chilion said eagerly.

"You should have been a singer of songs and a teller of tales," Orpah retorted. "Lies come easy to your tongue. Where is this brother of yours?"

"Up there at the forge fashioning a sword. Why?"

"I have a message for him."

Chilion led the girl up the path. His eyes did not miss the gentle sway of her hips as she walked or the opulent grace of her body.

Mahlon was putting the rough outline of a sword through its early heating in the forge, pumping the bellows slowly with one hand and watching the metal glow as it took up the heat. Intent upon his work as always, he did not know he was observed.

"Mahlon," Chilion called. "We have a visitor. This is Orpah, companion to Ruth."

Mahlon stopped pumping the bellows and wiped the sweat from his face. "Peace be upon thee, Orpah," he said courteously, "and upon Ruth as well. We have little refreshment to offer a visitor, but such as we have we will share with you."

Orpah smiled and shook her head. "I bring you a message from Ruth. Tomorrow is the Festival of Ashtar. Ruth invites you and your brother to come and witness the ceremony."

"We live outside the gates, and they are closed at nightfall."

"Not on this day," she assured him. "People will be coming into the city for the festival. The gates will stay open."

Mahlon hesitated. As a devout Hebrew, he doubted

the propriety of their witnessing a pagan celebration, but the opportunity of seeing Ruth again was very alluring, and Chilion was busy making signs to him that he should accept.

Hearing voices outside the cave, Naomi came out. "This is Orpah, Mother," Mahlon said, "companion to Ruth. She came to invite Chilion and me to a festival!"

"Shalom, Orpah," Naomi said, but with little warmth.

The girl sensed the hostility in Naomi's voice and flushed. "And upon thee be peace, O Mother of Mahlon and Chilion," she said politely. "I must go now. Ruth charged me to return quickly." She turned to Mahlon. "Will you come?"

"Yes," he told her. "We will come. And thank Ruth for me."

Chilion quickly emptied the buckets he had brought from the spring into the tempering tubs. "I will go with you as far as the spring, Orpah," he said quickly. "We need more water."

"Why didn't your mother like me, Chilion?" Orpah asked as they walked down the path. "I spoke courteously to her."

Chilion grinned. "She thinks Mahlon and I are still children and distrusts any girl who attracts our interest."

"Do I attract your interest?"

"My eyes should speak it," he assured her boldly.

"They speak more than interest," Orpah said a little hurriedly. "I had better go back to the city. But you will come with your brother to the festival tonight, won't you?"

"Could I refuse you anything?" Chilion asked, smiling. "We will be there, if I have to carry Mahlon on my shoulders."

Mahlon allowed the fires of the forge to cool an hour before sunset on the day of the festival, but he might as well have let them die earlier. Chilion had puffed and sighed at the bellows all afternoon, his thoughts only of Orpah, so the heat was not constant enough to insure the even temper of the metal that was vital, if the sword edge was to hold both its toughness and sharpness. By the time darkness had begun to fall both were dressed in their best robes, their hair and short beards combed well, and their bodies clean after a bath in the tempering tubs.

Chilion was on tenterhooks to leave for the festival, but Mahlon stopped to talk to Naomi, who disapproved strongly of their going into the city.

"Ruth has been very kind to me, Mother," he protested. "Hedak would have cut me down that day in Heshbon if she had not frightened him with the threat of sorcery."

"We are not sorcerers," Naomi said sternly. "It is a sin to pretend that we possess evil powers."

"I did not pretend," Mahlon assured her. "So long as we know in our hearts there is only the one, the true God, nothing we hear or see in Moab can harm us."

Naomi looked at him fondly, but there was sadness in her gaze, too. "The love of a man for a woman is sometimes stronger than family bonds or even his duty to God, my son. Remember the man of Israel and the woman of Midian."

"I have only seen Ruth twice, Mother," he protested. "She is of Moab and I of Israel. Our customs and everything about us are different. Would you have me affront her by refusing to go when she was kind enough to invite me to witness a festival?"

"Go, then," Naomi agreed reluctantly. "But watch Chilion, for he has not your strength of will. He is forward with girls and easily bewitched."

At the gates Mahlon and Chilion were drawn into a stream of people pouring into the city for the festival. There was a festive air about everything and much laughing and talking as the crowd moved toward the temple area. These people were not so different from their own, Mahlon thought as they walked along, even if they were heathen and worshiped idols and images instead of the only true God.

The crowd before the temple was far too large for the building to accommodate, and the great doors had been thrown open so that what happened inside could be seen from a distance by those unable to enter it.

Orpah found them in the crowd. She was dressed in a colorful robe of thin stuff, as were most of the Moabite women, with a heavier cloak thrown around her against the chill of night. Her sandals were dainty and thin-soled, with narrow straps to hold them upon her feet.

"You metalsmiths are supposed to be sorcerers," she said gaily, taking them by the arm. "But you wouldn't see much out here. I will take you closer. This is the Temple of Ashtar," she explained as they made their way to an area which had evidently been set aside for special guests, for it was guarded well. The sentry passed them through without question into a balcony overlooking the altar platform and the image of the goddess.

"Do the Moabites worship more than one god?" Mahlon asked. "I thought Chemosh was your deity."

"Ashtar is the goddess of love," Orpah explained. "She is the bride of Chemosh and their dwellings are side by side. The festival reaches its climax tonight, when the people celebrate the giving of life by Ashtar and Chemosh to everything that grows, to the trees and the flowers . . . and to human beings."

The goddess of love, immobile in stone, silver, and gold, squatted, as did her divine husband, upon a stone platform. Her waist was relatively slender, like the body of a woman, but her hips were exaggerated out of all proportion to the size of her waist. And her great bulging breasts were gross caricatures of the normal beautiful fullness from which the nursing mother gives life to her child through her body. The face, too, was hideous, fully in keeping with that of her marital partner in the adjoining temple.

"Ashtar!" Orpah said proudly. "Goddess of life."

From wall to wall the temple was packed with people, their upturned faces tense and eager, fired with an orgiastic fever by the ceremonies they were witnessing. In the belly of the goddess a smaller fire burned than that which roared in the maw of her divine husband. And in front of the image was an altar of pure white stone, raised above the broad stone platform on which the goddess herself stood to the height of a man's waist.

Behind the altar stood a woman of great beauty in a jeweled headdress so tall that she towered above the two priestesses on either side of her. These were nude to the waist, their loins covered by a white cloth held just below the navel with a jeweled clip. They too were exaggeratedly full-breasted, as if they had been chosen because of their similarity to the goddess. Beside the altar, upon a small gilded pedestal, lay a long knife with a shining blade, its handle set with precious stones.

People were packed to the very edge of the platform, where three empty chairs of hammered brass, evidently positions of great honor, faced the altar and the goddess. Zebushar, with Hedak beside him in full armor and drawn sword, occupied an elevated throne.

A handsome trio now ascended the steps leading up to the altar platform. All were richly dressed and the father led by the hand a beautiful young girl of perhaps fifteen or sixteen. The parents carried themselves with pride, and the girl moved as if in a trance, her glowing eyes uplifted to the hideous features of the Goddess Ashtar.

"She is the virgin, for the sacrifice," Orpah whispered.

"Do you mean she will be killed on the altar?" Mahlon asked.

"Of course. A virgin is always sacrificed to the goddess at the Festival of Ashtar."

"I cannot watch it," he said. "We must go, Chilion."

"Ruth will be hurt if you leave without seeing her," Orpah protested.

"Where is she?"

"Over there, back of the King. He trusts her and has her hold the wine cup so he can be sure no one will poison him."

Mahlon looked at the figure of the bored King. As Orpah had said, Ruth was standing just behind the throne, with the golden wine cup in her hands. She saw his eyes upon her and smiled.

"See! She knows you are here," Orpah told him. "If you left now, it would offend her."

"Will I see her tonight?"

"Of course. When the festival is over, Zebushar will release Ruth. The four of us are going to have supper together in the garden."

In the face of that exciting prospect, Mahlon decided that Orpah was right. It would not be courteous to leave without seeing Ruth. Besides, since he was only a spectator here tonight, it was not as if he were actually worshiping Ashtar, or Chemosh.

When the young girl and her parents had taken their places in the seats of honor, a strange compelling music began, played by a hidden orchestra of musicians. The tones were low and barely audible at first, played mostly upon flutes and harps, with none of the harsh, clanging notes that the Israelites were accustomed to hear from the shofar, or ram's horn, and the drums and cymbals used in the music characteristic of their native country.

A troupe of scantily clad dancers ran out on the platform to carry out graceful but intricate evolutions in honor of the goddess, symbolizing in the dance the age-old miracle that repeats itself over and over with the passage of the seasons. First was the quickening of life in the seed, the bursting from the soil, and growth of the plant. Then came its fruiting and the formation of the seed, and, finally, its dropping to the ground, there to lie dormant until the seasons' magic, by some strange alchemy, set the hidden life stirring once more to repeat the cycle. At the conclusion of the dance the troupe of dancers prostrated themselves in honor of the beautiful family honored by the goddess. The father and mother were obviously greatly pleased, but the girl herself stared at the idol with the same trancelike glow in her eyes, caught up in a spell that nothing seemed able to break.

One of the priestesses now lifted a golden bowl of grain that stood beside the altar and held it before the tall priestess who was the bride of Chemosh. Taking the bowl in her hands, the earthly counterpart of Ashtar intoned a few ritual words over it, then tossed the grain into the fire burning in the image of the goddess. Next the priestess brought her a basket of fruit, which also was consumed by the fire, and afterward a baby lamb, not yet able to stand upon its own legs. This, too, was blessed and cast, still alive, into the flames.

During the ritual a tension had been rising within the crowd, as they anticipated the next scene in this striking drama. And when a second priestess walked over to the handsome trio at the edge of the platform, a deep hush fell over the crowd. She held out her hand and the young girl took it unhesitatingly, nor did her steps falter as she was led across the platform to the altar itself, even though she was going to her death. The girl must be in some sort of trance, Mahlon decided, but could not figure out how it had been brought about.

Orpah's grip upon Mahlon's arm warned him that in this assemblage any protest against this, the culminating rite in the age-old ritual worship of Ashtar and Chemosh, would mean instant death. Nor, in spite of his revulsion, could he take his eyes off the scene before him.

The tall priestess stared for a long moment into the

eyes of the virgin destined for the sacrifice and spoke a
few low words that Mahlon could not hear. He could see
that the girl's body was gripped by a strange rigidity,
however, presaging the final spasm of death. Then with
a slow deliberate movement, the priestess passed her
fingers down across the young girl's eyes, closing them.
She stepped back to the small pedestal, upon which lay
the ritual knife with its gleaming blade and richly jeweled
handle, while two of the priestesses seized the girl's body,
as rigid now as if it were a statue of stone, and lifted her
to the altar. Lying there with her eyes still closed, the
girl did not move or show any fear of what was to come.

Gripped in the hand of the high priestess, the knife
rose, then flashed down.

A great "A-h-h!" of indrawn breath rose from the
crowd, but there was no sound from the girl, even as the
blade pierced her breast. A tiny red fountain rose momentarily around the knife, then collapsed, staining the
altar and trickling down upon the stone floor of the platform. Before the first droplets of blood struck the floor,
the husky priestess seized the still-rigid body and, with
a practiced movement, hurled it into the fiery maw of the
goddess. And as if ravenous for the gift they were receiv-
ing, the flames gushed upward and licked from the furnace.

Wave upon wave of sound rolled through the temple
as the people, prostrating themselves upon the floor,
shouted, "Ashtar! Ashtar! Bless us, O Ashtar!" While
they groveled before the repulsive image, the voice of the
high priestess, the fleshly counterpart of the goddess of
love, reverberated through the temple:

"Ashtar gives her blessing once again to the people of
Moab, and to her divine spouse, Chemosh! Let joy be
unrestrained!"

Instantly the mood of the crowd changed. Shouting
and laughing, they surged forward and lifted to their
shoulders the mother and father of the girl who had been
sacrificed, carrying them in a triumphant procession from
the temple.

"The people will drink and worship the goddess of
love throughout the night," Orpah said hurriedly. "Come
quickly lest you be noticed as not being of Moab. There
is food and wine in the garden."

She led the brothers through a door at the back of the
temple opening upon a garden in which a small summer-

house stood. A low table was set in the center, covered
with fruits and several kinds of meats and other viands,
with tall silver goblets and jugs of wine, cooled by damp-
ened cloths.

"By the tents of Israel," Chilion cried. "Moab receives
us well." He accepted a filled goblet from Orpah and took
preserved figs from a dish.

Mahlon hesitated momentarily, wondering if it were
right to eat and drink alien food and wine.

"Ruth will be here in a moment," Orpah said, mistaking his hesitation. "As soon as the King has left the temple."

He decided to sample the wine then and found it excellent. "Is—is Ruth a priestess of Ashtar?" he asked.

"We are only handmaidens. Later, if we wish, we may
become priestesses." Orpah turned to Chilion. "Come,
merry one, I will show you the garden."

Ruth came into the summerhouse a few minutes later,
her eyes still shining from the excitement of the evening.
She wore a clinging robe, like most of the women of
Moab. Mahlon glanced at her, then looked quickly away,
but not before he noticed how the thin stuff of her robe
clung to the sweet lines of her body.

"Did you like the festival?" she asked shyly.

"It—it was like nothing I had ever seen before," he
admitted truthfully.

She did not miss the note of reserve in his voice, or
the way he had glanced at her quickly and then looked
away, lest he be tempted to sin in his heart by lusting
after her. "What didn't you like?"

"I—I suppose it will take me some time to become accustomed to the ways of Moab."

"What particular custom?" Her eyes danced mischiev-
ously. "The way we dress, perhaps?"

"Well, yes," Mahlon admitted, flushing with embarrassment.

"Our poets say the body of a woman is the most
beautiful thing on earth," she said with disarming frank-
ness. "Do you disagree?"

"You are more beautiful than I ever dreamed a woman
could be," Mahlon said with sudden fervor, and could have
said nothing that would have pleased her better.

"Then let us be happy," she cried. "As Ashtar commands on the night of her festival." She lifted her cup to touch his own, but Mahlon drew back.

"I do not worship Ashtar," he explained. "It would be a sin for me to drink to any god but my own."

Ruth looked at him with a puzzled frown, not knowing whether to be hurt or not. She had been attracted by this tall Israelite that night when he had come upon her sitting beside the stream at the Place of Refuge with her feet in the water, watching the strange man of turbulent passions called Boaz. Had she troubled to analyze her feeling, she might have realized that one reason she had been drawn to Mahlon was because he was gentle and kind, yet strong, so completely different from the other one, who repelled her, yet attracted her, too, in an odd sort of way that left her unsure and troubled.

"But Ashtar is the goddess of love," she explained, a little hurt by his refusal. "Do you not love in Israel?"

"Of course. We are men and women, like you of Moab."

"Do you thank your god for the bursting of the seed in the spring?"

"Our celebration is at the harvesting." Mahlon's eyes kindled. "We call it the Festival of the First Fruits."

"You sacrifice the first fruits of the harvest to your god then?"

"Yes. We burn them upon an altar, fruits and grains and even a young lamb."

"We are only doing the same," Ruth protested. "You saw that tonight."

"But you sacrifice to Ashtar. And to Chemosh."

"We honor our gods as you honor yours. What is the difference?"

"We believe there is only one God," he explained. "He teaches that we must not kill a fellow being."

"Is not the young lamb you sacrifice the fruit of its mother's body?"

"Yes."

"Why not sacrifice a human first-born, then?"

"We do not kill our fellow man save in defense of our lives," Mahlon explained. "Besides, think how the father and mother of that child felt tonight."

"They were happy," Ruth cried indignantly. "And honored."

"Happy at the death of their child?"

"It is an honor to the father and mother when their child is sacrificed to Ashtar. Parents vie with each other to be selected. They have the highest place at the feast and are honored throughout the year until the next festival. How could it be wrong when the parents wish it, and so does the goddess?"

"The Most High says, 'Thou shalt not kill,'" Mahlon said simply. "That commandment was given to Moses many years ago."

"I have heard about the man you call Moses," Ruth said bitterly. "He killed thousands of people in Canaan."

"But only in war."

"In a war made by you Israelites. The people of Canaan were living peacefully until the Israelites came from Egypt. They took whatever they wanted, and killed the people who resisted them. Do you wonder that we Moabites hate the people of Israel?"

Mahlon knew the history of that exodus from slavery in Egypt. And it had been just as bloody as Ruth was saying, according to stories told around the campfires of Israel and Judah. But he had never before considered just how the people of Canaan must have felt.

"How could Yahveh justify such killing?" she demanded.

Mahlon half expected her to be stricken down with the dread name upon her lips, for no Israelite dared mention his God by name. But nothing happened.

"He had promised this land to us," he explained a little lamely.

"But it belonged to somebody else."

"Ours is the one true God and above all others," he explained; "everything belongs to Him, so He can give it to anyone He desires."

"Chemosh does not claim the land of Israel!" Ruth jumped to her feet. "What right does Yahveh have to intrude upon other gods?"

"There is but one God, Ruth . . ."

"Yours?"

"Yes."

"Then I will have nothing to do with him!" she cried. "He would have made your friend Boaz let his wife be stoned. And now you tell me he takes property from anyone he wishes and gives it to others! Chemosh is a better

god than that, and so is Ashtar! At least they teach people
to love and cherish each other!"

"But, Ruth——"

"You had better go, Mahlon," she said quickly. "Perhaps when you have learned more about the customs of
Moab, you will find that we are not completely wrong
about everything." Before he could stop her or try to explain any further, she ran from the summerhouse, leaving
him alone.

Walking back to the cave with Chilion, who babbled incessantly of Orpah, Mahlon still thought of Ruth, even if
she had left him in anger. And as he lay wrapped in his
cloak at the mouth of the cave, he was forced to admit
that he had thought of almost nothing but her since he
had first seen her that day at the Place of Refuge.

And now he knew what that meant. He was in love
with Ruth of Moab, a hopeless love, for he could see no
ground upon which they might meet on even terms in this
strange pagan land to which he had brought his family,
unless he renounced his own God. And that he would
never do.

xi.

The palace of Hedak, leader of the warriors of Moab,
and second-in-command to the King-Priest, Zebushar, was
only a little less magnificent than the Temple of Chemosh,
where dwelt the King. It was certainly an odd place for the
Israelite caravan driver, Cheb, to approach as confidently
as if it had been his own home.

At the gate a sentry barred the way. "Begone, herdsman," he said contemptuously. "This is no place for such
as you."

Cheb bared his teeth in a snarl, then thought better of
it and smiled ingratiatingly. From his wrist he slipped the
metal hook he wore and tossed it to the soldier, who caught
it on his sword and held it up to the light.

"What is this?" he demanded, but at the sight of the
inscription engraved inside the band his manner changed
instantly. "I will send word to Prince Hedak that you are
here," he said deferentially, and called to a servant who

ushered Cheb into the house, carrying the arm band with him.

Hedak was lying on a couch eating the roasted leg of a hart. A dozen women, wives and concubines, reclined on cushions around him, hanging upon his every word, and a beautiful Egyptian girl, wearing only a tiny girdle, writhed in a sensuous dance before him.

When the servant approached, the Prince of Moab looked up and took the band. Then with a sudden push of his foot, he tumbled over the harpist who sat nearby playing for the dancer, breaking off the music abruptly.

"Outside! All of you!" he barked. When one of the girls pouted at his tone, he kicked her viciously, so that she sprawled upon the floor, whimpering with pain as she scrambled out of the reach of her master's foot.

Roaring with laughter, Hedak tossed the cuff and hook to Cheb, who caught it expertly upon the stump of his left wrist and locked it in place. "Well, Cheb," he said, "I see you haven't lost your head yet. They must have become softhearted toward thieves in Judah."

The merchant grinned and held up his good hand. "Nor have these fingers lost their cunning, master. I leave in the morning with a load of goods for Bethlehem."

"Upon which you will make a good profit because I let only you trade with Moab."

"In return for news of Moab's enemies," Cheb reminded him.

"What news of them, then?" Hedak demanded impatiently. "Out with it."

"The Edomite tribes are pleased that you personally escorted one of their daughters named Ruth back to Moab."

"Tell me something new. I was in Edom myself only ten days or so ago."

"The woman you slew at the Place of Refuge was wife to Boaz."

"That I know also, from the lips of Boaz himself."

"But not that he has vowed to repay you in blood?" Cheb said slyly.

"I know Boaz." Hedak picked up a piece of meat and bit into it wolfishly. "The debt will be paid in blood, but his, not mine."

"When?"

Hedak spat out a piece of bone and grinned. "When I am ready. And don't expect me to tell you, so you can take pay from both sides."

The Israelite spy turned a little pale. "But, master, you know my loyalty."

"I know it can be bought by the one paying the best price," Hedak said bluntly. "Now, tell me about the inner councils of Israel."

"They are still not willing to prepare for war," Cheb reported. "Of the chiefs only Eliab stands with Boaz when he urges them to arm."

"Is Boaz as eloquent as ever?"

"More, since you slew his wife. He hates you and all Moabites with a consuming passion."

"But Israel is ruled by old and timid men, not by firebrands like Boaz."

"That is true," Cheb admitted. "Nathan and Zadok and Tob are your greatest weapons against Israel. In the shops they tell the mothers how their sons will be killed if Boaz is allowed to lead them into war against Moab. And in the shop of the wine seller the old men shake their heads over the taxes they must pay if Boaz is given the arms he demands."

Hedak grinned. From his belt he detached a purse. "Keep your eyes and ears open, then," he ordered, tossing it to the merchant. "And come to me again when you return."

"One other thing, master. A few days ago I met Mahlon, the son of Elimelech, on the hill outside the city. He asked me to tell Boaz that he is forging swords for Moab and that Israel should arm."

"By Chemosh!" Hedak started up angrily from his seat. "I will have his head for this."

"Mahlon is the finest swordsmith in both Israel and Moab," Cheb reminded him shrewdly.

"And what good is a dead swordsmith, when Moab needs weapons?" Hedak relaxed. "Mahlon shall live, but only on my sufferance."

"And the message to Boaz?"

Hedak grinned. "Tell Boaz that Mahlon is happy and well, sharpening hoes and fashioning plowshares for the peaceful people of Moab."

xii.

In the days that followed the visit of Mahlon and Chilion to the Temple of Ashtar the forges roared upon the hillside and the anvils clanged with the pounding of hammers, while the grinding stones turned until far into the night. There was food and wine in the cave and Elimelech seemed to gain a little strength. Yet Naomi's heart was heavy as she went about caring for her family. For Mahlon and Chilion hardly ever laughed and sang at the forge any more, pushing each other about while the iron sizzled in the tempering tubs, or dousing each other with the pails of water from the spring kept ready to fill the tubs.

Instead both brothers went about with long faces much of the time doing their work, but with little zest. On the third day Naomi took Chilion aside and learned how Ruth and Mahlon had quarreled on the night they had visited the city for the Festival of Ashtar. Chilion had seen Orpah furtively once since then, when he had gone into the city for more iron, but Ruth had sent no message to Mahlon and there was no sign that she had relented. "Orpah says Ruth is moping, though," Chilion added, "just like Mahlon."

"I have seen the girl only once," Noami said. "Is she beautiful?"

"Yes, but not so much as Orpah in my eyes."

"You are young," his mother told him sharply. "Your eyes may still be those of a fool."

Chilion laughed. "On the other hand, Mother, they must be the eyes of a man, for they notice things that boys think nothing of."

The next morning Naomi went into the city, ostensibly to buy food. She did not stop at the market, however. Instead she went on to the temple, but was stopped outside by a guard. "No common woman is allowed inside the Temple of Chemosh," the soldier told her pompously.

"I am no common woman," Naomi said proudly. "Send word to the young woman called Ruth that Naomi, mother of Mahlon, would speak to her."

Ruth had been walking in the gardens of the temple and came at once. "Will you come into the garden?" she asked

Naomi politely. "I remember seeing you at the Place of Refuge."

"Why have you bewitched my son, Ruth of Moab?" Naomi asked when they were seated upon a bench.

Ruth flushed. Her immediate reaction was one of anger, but, being a woman herself, she understood something of what was torturing Naomi. "I have cast no spell upon him," she protested. "By Chemosh, I swear it."

"Swear to me by no alien gods! It is enough that my son thinks of nothing but a girl of Moab."

Ruth was startled at Naomi's vehemence. But the news that Mahlon was thinking as much of her as she was of him made her happy for the first time since the night she had sent Mahlon away. "Why is it so wrong for him to think of me?" she asked.

"You are of Moab and he is of Israel," Naomi pointed out.

"But you are all living here now." The quiet sincerity of the Moabite girl shone in her lovely eyes and in her graciousness and earnestness. Had Ruth been an Israelite, Naomi admitted to herself, she could not have found reason to disapprove of her, even as a daughter-in-law.

"Do you love my son, Ruth of Moab?" Naomi asked suddenly.

Ruth's eyes went wide. She had not even asked herself that question yet. "I—I don't know," she admitted. "He is very gentle and kind. I have never known a man like Mahlon before, except my father."

"Is your father dead?"

"He died when I was a little girl. But I remember him well, and your son, Mahlon, is very much like him."

"Do you love my son, Ruth?" Naomi asked again.

"I think I do," Ruth admitted. "I have been very unhappy since we quarreled. But I cannot understand your religion."

"Why?"

"Your god is so stern. Is there no joy in serving him?"

Naomi considered the question for a moment. When she spoke her voice was quiet and certain. "The joy in serving the Most High is in loving and trusting your fellow man," she explained. "And in refraining from the things He forbids because doing them brings only hurt to others."

"Then you can have no joy in this day, Naomi," Ruth

said quietly. "Because you have brought hurt to my heart by doubting that I am worthy of your son."

It was Naomi's turn to look startled. Before she could speak, Ruth said impulsively, "Forgive me, please. I spoke harshly and now I have brought pain to you."

The older woman shook her head. "You have taught me something again that I had forgotten, Ruth. Humility . . . Every mother hates to think she may one day lose her son to another, even though she knows it is the will of God that the seed must go on." She paused, then went on. "Long ago, a man of Israel loved a woman of Midian from near your home."

"I know the land."

"He brought her to the camps of Israel and into his tent. But Moses ordered the grandson of Aaron, the high priest, to thrust them through with a javelin as they lay in the tent asleep, and it was done."

"It was a cruel decision." Ruth shivered.

"But one that every woman not of our land must risk who marries an Israelite."

"Would you approve my loving your son and his loving me, if I were willing to take that risk?" Ruth asked.

"I would have to ask you another question," Naomi said. Sitting there on the bench, she seemed to the young woman a somehow regal figure, instead of only an old woman of Israel with a patched shawl over her head and worn sandals upon her feet.

"You said you had a question to ask me," Ruth prompted.

"When the children of Israel were on the way from Egypt to the Promised Land, there were not enough wives for the men. And so when they conquered a people in battle, the men were allowed to choose women for wives, provided they were virgin. Such has been the custom of Israel ever since." She stopped, her eyes holding those of the Moabite girl.

Ruth's gaze did not fall, although the color rose in her cheeks. "I have never known a man, in the way that you mean, Naomi," she said firmly. "Is that your only question?"

"If my son should wish to take you as his wife, would you worship our God?"

A spasm of pain went over Ruth's face, but she did not hesitate. "No," she said. "I cannot do that."

"Then I cannot give you my blessing," Naomi said harshly before Ruth could give any explanation.

"Are you asking me not to see Mahlon again?".

Naomi shook her head. "The old cannot stand in the way of the young. We are in an alien land and if my sons choose to marry women of Moab, I cannot prevent them."

A few afternoons later Ruth and Orpah came up the hillside from the city. Naomi was outside, kneading bread for the evening meal. She looked up as the girls stopped before the cave. "Peace be upon thee, Ruth and Orpah," she said quietly.

"And upon thee, Naomi," they said.

"How is your husband today?" Ruth asked.

"For a while he seemed to grow stronger. But now he is weaker again."

"If there is anything I can do," Ruth said gently, "you have only to tell me."

"It is the will of God. We cannot go against it or change it." Ruth sensed that Naomi was speaking as much of the relationship of herself and Orpah to her sons as of her dying husband.

Mahlon was working at the forge. He was stripped to the waist and the sweat shone upon his body as he stared down into the bed of coals where the metal of a new sword was already taking on a cherry-red glow. Chilion was pumping the bellows, and both were so intent upon their work that they did not see the girls.

"In a moment he will thrust the iron into the tempering tub," Orpah whispered, for she had seen them at work upon her visits with Chilion. "Then the work will be finished for a while."

Ruth noticed two small baskets beside the open mouth of the cave, and her eyes brightened. "There are many berries on the mountainside," she said. "Perhaps we can pick some for Naomi."

Naomi did not hear their whispered interchange, for she had gone into the cave, leaving the two girls alone with her sons.

The coals in the forge glowed more and more brightly as Chilion pumped furiously upon the bellows. Intent upon the blade, for it must be exactly the right color if the temper were to be hard enough to furnish a sword of the correct quality, Mahlon studied the flame. Suddenly, with a shout of elation, he lifted the cherry-red iron with a pair of heavy tongs and tossed it into the tub.

Steam gushed upward as the water bubbled from the heat of the iron, but Mahlon paid no attention to it. Turning to the second tub, he doused his head in it, for the afternoon was warm and the heat of the forge even warmer. Obeying an impulse to mischief, Ruth moved quickly. As Mahlon rose from the tub, she put her hand on his head and shoved it down again before he could get his breath.

Strangling, coughing, and blowing water, Mahlon rose from the tub, shouting brotherly imprecations at Chilion as he reached blindly for a cloth to wipe his head and shoulders. In the midst of his toweling he saw Ruth and his eyes popped with amazement. "You!" he cried. "You tried to drown me."

"If you could have seen yourself." She was gasping with laughter.

"Then in you go," he shouted with mock anger, and seized her by the shoulders, as if to thrust her shining head into the tub too.

Laughing, not quite certain that Mahlon would not do as he said, Ruth struggled against him, until, suddenly conscious of her strong, young body in his arms, he flushed and turned her loose. She ran a few yards away until she was safely out of reach, then turned and hooted derisively, "Coward! Are you afraid of a girl?"

But the look in his eyes, and the consciousness that her own pulse was racing from that moment in his arms made her stop. To mask her confusion, Ruth picked up one of the baskets. "Go with Orpah, O Blower of Bellows," she said, tossing one to Chilion, and puffing out her cheeks in imitation of the inflated skins that were his own particular tool. "And remember, berries don't grow in caves."

Chilion's round face flamed, but he picked up the basket and started up the hillside with Orpah. Mahlon quickly pulled his robe up around his shoulders—the top part had been hanging from the cord that girdled it about his waist —and smoothed his dark hair with his hands. Then, calling to his mother that he would be back later, he took the other side of the basket Ruth was holding and they started along the mountainside toward the clumps of berry bushes dotting it here and there.

Now that they were together, both Mahlon and Ruth

were shy. As they picked the rich, dark berries and dropped them into the basket, their hands touched occasionally. And each time the contact was a little longer than necessary, until one of them would suddenly draw away. Finally, when the basket was almost filled, each put in a handful simultaneously and, as their hands touched, Mahlon seized Ruth's fingers in his own and drew her close to him.

She looked up into his eyes and her breath quickened at what she saw, for she knew he was about to kiss her. But when he dropped the basket to put his other arm around her, she looked down at the intertwined hands which had been filled with berries. The juice from the crushed fruit was slowly dripping between their fingers, and at the sight of it she could not keep from laughing. Mahlon, too, laughed and for the moment the spell that had almost sent them into each other's arms was broken.

They unclasped hands then. When Mahlon stopped to wipe the berry stain from his dripping fingers on a bush, Ruth turned and started running down the mountainside, laughing back over her shoulder at him. He seized the basket from the ground and followed her, but she was light of foot and when he caught up with her, panting from the effort, she was already in a small glen from which a spring gushed, washing her hands in the cold clear water.

Mahlon knelt beside her, washing the stain from his own fingers. Then he dipped up water from the spring in his hands and held them for her to drink. Both were silent now, knowing that they had been nearly in each other's arms up there on the hillside, and wondering what would happen next.

Their thirst satisfied, they moved, still holding hands, to a grassy spot against an upright rock overlooking the stream, and sat down, but not yet very close together. The city lay before them, for the glen occupied a cleft in the mountainside, and in the distance stretched the green valley of Moab in all its beauty.

"This is a beautiful place," Mahlon said. "I have been too busy to explore the mountainside before."

"I used to come here often when I first came from Edom to serve in the temple. Hedak is pleased with your swords," she continued. "I have heard the soldiers speak of it in the city."

"I would rather be forging tools for the farmers. But we have enough to eat for the first time in many months, so I should not mind."

"Do you?"

"Yes," he admitted. "A sword has no purpose except to kill another. It seems there should be enough room in the world for everyone, without killing."

"Yet your own people left Egypt."

"They were slaves. If they had been allowed to live in peace, they would have stayed."

"I know how you feel," Ruth said. "My people among the Edomite tribe shun the cities and stay in their own land. But Hedak wants Moab to rule even as far west as the Great Sea."

Mahlon looked startled. "Have you heard him admit this?"

"Of course. It is no secret in Moab."

"Then Boaz is right in urging Israel to arm. And I am wrong to be making swords that will be used against my own people."

"If you didn't make them someone else would," Ruth pointed out practically. "Besides, you make tools, too. Maybe someday the people will see how important they are, and be less interested in swords."

"I hope you are right. But I can do nothing else, anyway, as long as Hedak controls us."

"I had never seen you at the forge before, Mahlon. How do you know when the iron is ready to temper?"

"It is something you feel," he explained. "Sometimes I make Chilion pump the bellows until his eyes are bulging."

"You need a bellows like the great one at the back of Chemosh. When a priest swings on the lever, it makes the flames gush out as they did the day the god favored you."

"So that is what happened!" Mahlon cried. "I thought there must be a bellows somewhere. Chilion would like to know that," he added excitedly. "I wonder where he and Orpah are."

"Somewhere up on the hillside making love," Ruth said matter-of-factly.

"Making love! When they are not even betrothed?"

"Don't men and women make love in Israel until they are betrothed?" Ruth asked in surprise.

"Certainly not! And usually not until they are married."

"You do have strange customs. In Moab, when a girl thinks she would like to be a man's wife, she goes to live in his house. If she is happy, they marry."

"What if they are not happy together?"

"Then they go their ways and no harm is done."

"No harm! In Israel a man cannot even desire a woman without breaking the Law! Unless he is betrothed or married to her."

Ruth frowned. "Is this the same law that would have made Boaz take his wife back to Israel to be stoned, just because she found out that she loved someone else?"

"She was married to Boaz in the sight of God," Mahlon said. "When she left him, she broke the Law, and the penalty is death."

"Would your god have her stay with Boaz even if she didn't love him?" Ruth asked incredulously.

"He teaches that."

"Then I will have none of such a god," she cried angrily. "He is cruel and unjust."

"The Most High does not demand human sacrifices," Mahlon reminded her a little tartly. "Like Chemosh and Ashtar."

"But they teach us to love and we can see them. Has anyone ever seen your god?"

"Only Moses, when He spoke to him on the mount."

"Chemosh speaks to us every day," she cried triumphantly. "He speaks through the King, who is his son. And we can see him whenever we wish to, just by going into the temple."

"I was in the Temple of Chemosh," he reminded her, nettled by what he considered her unreasonable attitude. "And I saw nothing but an idol of stone and mortar, with a bellows to make the flames gush forth."

Ruth's anger evaporated before her concern lest Chemosh strike Mahlon dead for this blasphemy. For they were in full sight of the great shining temple in the center of the city below them, where the lights were just beginning to glow with the coming of dusk. "Kneel and ask forgiveness from Chemosh," she cried, seizing him by the shoulders and trying to force him to his knees. "Beg forgiveness before the fire descends from above to destroy you."

Mahlon looked at her and his eyes softened. She was very beautiful in her concern. "Are you worried for me, Ruth? Or lest I should be telling the truth about your god?"

She burst into tears and turned away from him, by which he knew that she had already begun to experience some doubts about the divinity of the god she worshiped.

"I will show you that I am in no danger from Chemosh, when there is no priest nearby to act in his stead," Mahlon told her. He walked to the edge of the grassy plot where they had been sitting, facing the city and the great temple whose dome shone in the late afternoon sunlight. "There is but one God," he shouted, "the God of Israel, and of Isaac and Jacob. If I do not speak the truth, may the fires of Chemosh strike me now and consume me."

Ruth crouched against the rocks, her face white with fear as she waited for the god of Moab to strike the blasphemer dead. But nothing happened and Mahlon turned to her. "You see, Ruth," he said. "If Chemosh were not simply an idol, a thing of stone and metal and wood, he would have destroyed me for daring to speak as I did. There is only one God; let us kneel here and pray together that you may soon know Him in your heart."

"Chemosh and Ashtar have been my gods since childhood," Ruth cried. "I can worship no other." She turned and started to run, but her eyes were blurred by tears, making her stumble before she had gone more than a few steps. Mahlon caught her easily. When he put his arm about her shoulders, she clung to him like a frightened child. Nor did she resist when he led her back to the place where they had been sitting against the rock.

"Let me tell you about our God, Ruth," he begged. "Then you can decide for yourself whether the things He teaches are important. And I promise not to press you to believe in Him."

She sat very quietly as he began to speak, but they were not as close as they had been before, for the invisible barrier was between them.

"When Moses led the children of Israel out of Egypt many years ago," Mahlon began, "he spoke with the God we call the Most High, because we must not utter His name, on the mountain called Sinai. And God gave Moses the Ten Commandments, by which we live. My people call it the Law...."

xiii.

Darkness had fallen before Mahlon finished the story of
how the first set of rules by which men could live in peace
were given to the world. Ruth's eyes were bright now and
she had moved closer to him. His arm was around her and
her head was resting against his shoulder. In the city below them torches were blazing upon the walls where the
guards kept their nightly vigil. And in the streets other
lights were bobbing as the people moved about.

"You see, Ruth," Mahlon said quietly. "If people would
only live by the laws of our God, there would be no wars.
And no man would be unkind to another."

"Your god always seemed harsh and unfair before,"
Ruth admitted. "But I can see now why you love him and
want to obey his laws." She turned to look up at him.
"Why did you tell me all this today?"

"Because I love you, Ruth. And I hope someday you
may come to love me."

She smiled and touched his cheek tenderly. "Why do
you suppose I came to the forge this afternoon if not
because I could not sleep since we quarreled the other
night? Why have my thoughts been only of you?"

He held her tighter, too much overcome to speak by
this wonderful, this incredible thing that had happened to
him.

"Is that love, Mahlon?" Ruth asked. "Thinking always
of the same person, and wanting to be with him because
he is kind and good and sweet?"

"It's the way I feel about you, Ruth," he said gently.
"So it must be."

"Hedak asked me to be one of his wives," Ruth told
him. "And many men have wanted me. But I have given
myself to no man."

Mahlon's arms tightened about her and he kissed her
shining hair.

"But I will give myself to you this night." Her voice
faltered a little. "If you ask me."

"I ask nothing, beloved," he told her gently, "except the
right to love you and the hope of being loved in return.

But I would be the happiest man on earth if you would betroth yourself to me here, tonight, as we do in Israel."

"Oh, I will," Ruth cried. And then she added softly, "They say a first wife is the most beloved. I am glad you have no others yet."

"Nor will I have," he promised. "We will vow to live together and cherish each other, not just for a night or a year, but for all of our days."

"Did your friend Boaz take the woman who betrayed him with those vows?"

"Yes. I heard him speak the words."

"And yet he would have let her be stoned," Ruth said thoughtfully. "Would you do the same, Mahlon, if I were unfaithful?"

"Don't ask that, Ruth," he cried. "It is a sin for a man to love a woman more than he loves his God. And yet . . ."

Before he could say more, she put her fingers to his lips, silencing him. "I wonder if I will ever really understand the god called Yahveh, Mahlon," she said. "But I do know that you are dearer to me than even my father was. Let us become betrothed, as you do in Bethlehem."

Mahlon stood up. "I must first build an altar. Wait here until it is finished."

There were plenty of stones at the edge of the glen and it took him only a short while to erect two small piles of them and place a long flat stone across them. When he finished he led Ruth to the altar, where she knelt beside him. Holding her hand tightly in his, Mahlon lifted his eyes to the heavens where the stars were just beginning to burn brightly.

"I, Mahlon, of Bethlehem-Judah in Israel," he said slowly and clearly, "vow before the one true God that I will take thee, Ruth of Moab, to wife. And that I will honor, love, and cherish thee, whatever may happen, through all the years of my life."

"And I, Ruth, a woman of Moab," she began in a voice that was clear and sweet, if a little tremulous, "promise to take thee, Mahlon, for my husband, in honor and obedience and love, until death shall part us."

"My beloved." Mahlon lifted her from her knees. "Tomorrow we will go before the King and ask him to approve our marriage, since we are of different countries. Then I can bring you to my cave and to my couch."

"But I can kiss you now, can't I?" Ruth asked tremulously. "Or would that be breaking . . ."

His lips found hers, putting an end to words. And for a long moment there was no need of speech. Finally she pushed him away. "I must go now," she said breathlessly. "They may want me in the temple."

"Tomorrow you will cease to be a handmaiden of Chemosh," Mahlon promised. "We will go before the King when he holds audience for the people in the morning."

"I think Chilion and Orpah will want to go with us," Ruth said. "Orpah has told me they love each other."

Mahlon started down the hillside toward the cave, but Ruth drew back. "The gates of the city are closed," she said. "I cannot go back that way."

"You can stay here until morning. Mother will not mind if you spend the night in our cave."

"There is a gate back of the temple called the Priests' Gate," she told him. "Only those of us who serve in the temple know how to open it." She stood on her toes and kissed him again. "Until tomorrow, then, beloved."

Mahlon watched her as long as he could see her in the darkness, then he turned back toward the hillside and the cave. Chilion and Orpah met him coming down the hillside. The girl went on after Ruth, and Chilion walked back to the cave with Mahlon.

"Mother!" Mahlon called happily when they came to the mouth of the cave. "Ruth and I are betrothed."

Naomi came out and they saw that her face was drawn with grief and wet with tears.

"What is wrong?" Mahlon cried, putting his arms about the thin shoulders upon which he had leaned so many times as a child. "Do you mind that much?"

Naomi shook her head. "Your father is dead, my sons," she said, her voice breaking in a sob. "I found him just now when I took food to him. The Lord was merciful and took him in his sleep."

Mahlon's eyes filled with horror and grief. "He died while I was on the hillside, babbling of love," he whispered. "I who am the elder and should have been here to close his eyes in death." Clutching his mother, he suddenly began to sob like the little boy he had been not so long ago. Chilion, too, knelt beside her, burying his face in her skirt.

"Love, my sons," Naomi said softly as she comforted them, "is for the young. For through it life has a beginning. But death is for the old." Her voice broke again. "And the end of everything."

In the room that she shared with Orpah in the temple Ruth blew out the flame in the dish of olive oil that served as a lamp, and stretched herself upon her couch in the darkness. "Did you and Chilion kiss each other this afternoon, Orpah?" she asked.

"Of course." Orpah laughed. "Why else did we go into a cave?"

"Do you feel a great tenderness when he kisses you?"

"Oh yes, I feel that."

"Wh-what else?"

"What you always feel when a lover kisses you," Orpah said matter-of-factly. "As if your very bones had turned to water and you wanted nothing else save to stay in his arms and let him have his will with you."

"Oh!" It was almost inaudible, but Orpah sat up. "You really love this Israelite, don't you, Ruth?" she asked anxiously. "It will mean unhappiness for you if you betroth yourself to him without being sure you love him."

"Of course I love him, Orpah." Ruth spoke in a rush as if trying to convince herself. "Whatever gave you the idea that I don't?"

Satisfied, Orpah lay back down and was soon asleep. It was a long time, however, before Ruth stopped tossing and turning on her couch, unable to sleep. And when she did, it was strange that she dreamed, not of her betrothed, but of her father, and how tender and kind he had been to her as a little girl.

xiv.

The death of Elimelech removed any immediate plans Ruth and Mahlon had for asking the King's permission to marry. Ruth learned of it through a messenger sent her by Mahlon, and early the afternoon following the death of her betrothed's father she came with Orpah up the mountain from the roadway, carrying platters of food and stone jugs of wine.

Mahlon was busy digging a grave on the hillside. There was no one else of the Hebrew faith in Moab save themselves, and nowhere seemed more fitting to bury Elimelech than on the mountainside where they had made their first home in this new land.

Both Ruth and Orpah wore their usual bright-colored robes, for here death was not considered deserving of any particular sorrow. To the Moabites the dead were transported to the underworld, where, in company with other jovial spirits, they spent most of the time in singing, drinking, and making love, pleasures which they had not always been able to afford on earth.

Ruth knelt beside the grave. "Your grief is our grief," she said to the lonely family gathered around it. "Chemosh console you."

And Orpah repeated, "Your grief is our grief. Chemosh console you."

Naomi frowned at the name of the alien god and Mahlon looked questioningly at the trays of food and jugs of wine. "What are these for?" he asked.

"For your father's spirit to take with him on the long journey into the underworld," Ruth explained. "We put them in the grave."

"Will you let them desecrate your father's resting place with their offerings to idols?" Naomi cried. She seized the trays and threw them against a stone, then ran into the cave where her husband's body lay and threw herself sobbing on the ground beside it.

When Ruth started to follow Naomi, Mahlon put his hand upon her arm. "Let her be, Ruth," he said. "She will feed differently tomorrow. Today she is overcome with grief."

"What did I do to make her accuse me of desecrating your father's grave, Mahlon?"

"My father has not gone to the underworld, Ruth. He was a good man and obeyed the Law, so he has returned to the God who created him and gave him life."

"But where? Where is he?"

"Somewhere up there." Mahlon pointed to the sky.

"On the mountaintops?"

"Above them, even above the clouds. It is a place we call Heaven where the Most High God dwells. My father will live with Him."

"Is it a happy place?"

"There is none happier."

"Then why are you sad?" she asked. "Why does your mother not rejoice that your father has gone to this happy place you call Heaven, since he was so sick and in pain here on earth?"

Mahlon could not answer, because there was no answer. "I shall never understand your God, Mahlon," Ruth said sadly then. "Sometimes I think I don't even understand you. And your mother hates me. You saw that just now. Come, Orpah," she called. "We must return to the city before the gates are closed."

"My mother did not mean to hurt you, Ruth," he protested. "She is distraught."

"For a while I thought we had come to understand each other a little," Ruth said sadly. "But now she will never think of me as anything but an enemy who desecrated your father's grave. She will never believe that even though I cannot understand why you do it. I can still grieve with you for your father, and feel pity and love, even for her."

"If you could only tell her that," Mahlon said, "it might make so much difference."

Ruth shook her head. "She would only see the circle on my forehead and look at me as if I were a crawling thing, fit only to be stamped beneath her foot."

"Give her time, dearest," Mahlon pleaded. "My mother is no longer young and my father was very dear to her. Now she feels that she is losing Chilion and me also."

Ruth turned back, sorry for her outburst, and kissed him quickly on the forehead as he stood in the almost completed grave. Then she turned and hurried down the path toward the road and the city gate before he could see that she was weeping.

Two weeks after the death of his father Mahlon asked his mother if he could take Ruth before the King and beg permission for them to marry. She had been sitting in the cave staring out at nothing for the long days since her husband had been taken by death, stirring herself only to prepare the food, and then returning to her hopeless immobility. When she did not answer, Mahlon kissed her gently on the forehead and went down to the city, accompanied by Chilion, for it was the younger brother's intention to wed Orpah at the same time if the King approved.

Zebushar received them in his private apartment, where he gave daily audience to the people. Mahlon and Ruth approached and knelt before the King with Orpah and Chilion beside them.

"Do you kneel to me, Israelite?" Zebushar asked with a cynical smile.

"I give you the honor due to a king," Mahlon said quietly.

"But not to the Heavenly Son of Chemosh?"

"Your god has given me the right to worship my own God," Mahlon reminded him.

Zebushar smiled. "So he did! So he did. What boon do you beg of me, Mahlon of Israel?"

"I ask permission to take Ruth as my wife," Mahlon said. "And my brother asks the same for Orpah, her companion."

Zebushar looked first at Ruth and then at Orpah. "And you, Ruth and Orpah, do you ask this boon of me also?"

"I do, O Heavenly Son of Chemosh," Ruth said firmly.

"I do, O Heavenly Son of Chemosh," Orpah repeated.

Zebushar looked down at the four young people kneeling there. For a moment there was a faraway look in his eyes, as if he were remembering when he, too, had been young. "If you, Ruth, and you, Orpah, are sure that your hearts persuade you to turn away from your people and marry an Israelite," he said finally, "I will put no barrier between you. But I must warn you that it is not a good thing for people of different religions to marry."

The King raised his hand. "May the blessings of Chemosh be upon this union of Ruth to Mahlon and of Orpah to Chilion. You may rise and go in peace." Then he smiled. "I will even give you a wedding present. There is a house just inside the city gates, Mahlon, with a yard where you can set up your forges, and a spring to furnish water for your tubs. See that you move there tomorrow."

As they climbed the hill to the cave, Ruth's grip upon Mahlon's hand grew ever tighter and she held back unconsciously until he almost had to pull her along. Chilion and Orpah were well behind them, giggling as they walked along arm in arm. "I'm afraid, Mahlon," Ruth whispered as they rounded the last turn and saw the open mouth of the cave.

Naomi knelt in the doorway of the cave, kneading the bread for the evening meal as she always did. And her face, as it had been for weeks, was set in a mask of suffering.

"Mother," Mahlon called. "Come greet your daughters."

Naomi looked up. Seeing the utter loneliness in her eyes, Ruth ran quickly and fell on her knees beside the older woman, putting an arm about the frail shoulders. "I have not taken him away, Mother Naomi," she cried. "We will stay together, always."

For a moment Naomi's body remained stiff and it seemed that she was going to push Ruth roughly aside. Then the resistance seemed to go out of her. When the words came they were hardly more than a whisper. "I could forgive you everything, Ruth, except that you will not take our God as yours."

"But, Mother," Mahlon cried. "The King has forbidden anyone of Moab to acknowledge the Most High, or me to sway them, on pain of death. If Ruth takes Him as her God, both she and I will die."

Naomi looked at Ruth for a long moment. And at what she saw in the younger woman's face she began to smile. "What is it your friends call you, Ruth?" she asked. "I heard them speak of it in the market place."

"The 'Steadfast One.' It is a name my father gave me when I was a child."

"And I give it to you again," Naomi said, kissing her son's new wife. "Can you ever forgive me for not being able to understand?"

"You have my forgiveness," Ruth told her softly, "and my love."

Naomi's mouth worked, but no words came. Then she pushed the kneading trough over to Ruth. "There is a saying in Judah," she said, "that a man's bread should be kneaded by the woman he loves."

But Ruth moved the trough until it was between them and, taking Naomi's hand, pushed it into the dough again with her own.

"Then both of us will knead, Naomi," she said through her tears. "For both of us love him. We will share his love between us."

BOOK TWO

THE FIRES OF CHEMOSH

And Elimelech, Naomi's husband died; and she was left and her two sons.

And they took them wives of the women of Moab; the name of the one was Orpah, and the name of the other Ruth: and they dwelled there about ten years.*

RUTH 1:3–4

---

* An arbitrary period, often used by oriental writers to describe the passage of a number of years. It may have been less than ten.

i.

IN THE DAYS WHEN ZEBUSHAR RULED THE PEOPLE OF MOAB, east of where the turbulent waters of the river called Jordan tumbled down to the strange sea that knows no life, there was peace of a sort between Moab and the Israelite tribes. But it was an uneasy truce, in which both sides raided herds, flocks, and groups of travelers who came too close to the border marked by the course of the river.

Only at the Place of Refuge was there a meeting place, in which both sides were committed to strict neutrality. But such trade as was carried out there was small and of little consequence, although the men of Israel eyed with longing the pots, knives, and pruning hooks of the Moabite smiths, while the men of Moab rubbed bellies hungry for the meat of the Hebrew flocks. Only the caravan of Cheb, son of the madwoman of Bethlehem, traded regularly between that city and Moab, both in goods and information for Hedak about the affairs of the Israelites.

Moab and Heshbon had not been unkind to the sons of Elimelech. They had acquired moderate wealth in their adopted country, as well as brides from among the loveliest maidens in Moab. Although Ruth was the more beautiful of the two, and Naomi loved both her daughters, the older woman was drawn to Ruth with an affection equaled only by the young Moabite woman's love for her mother-in-law.

By all obvious standards the metal-working establishment of Mahlon of Israel in Heshbon should have been a happy one. Not a forge was cold, not a hammer idle, and the large courtyard of the house near the city wall that served as both living quarters and shop was a scene of marked activity from dawn to darkness. Slaves pumped the bellows while smiths watched the metal grow cherry red in the flame before lifting it from the fire to be pounded into shape on the anvils and tossed into tubs of water for tempering. Outside the gate eager purchasers waited, ready to bid for the occasional pruning and reaping hook, or iron plowshare that came from the forges when the number of swords allotted for that day had been finished.

An air of troubled apprehension hung over the metal-working shop today, however. Chilion's normally cheerful round face was grim with concern as he walked about between the forges superintending their operation. It even showed upon the features of Orpah, who had grown slightly plumper with marriage, but was still as pretty as ever. She came out of the house now and surveyed the activities in the courtyard, but with no pleasure.

From the ovens came the savory smell of baking bread, spread in a thin layer on the inside of huge earthen jars that served as ovens, each resting in its bed of coals like a hen upon her nest. The aroma of a whole calf turning on the spit over a bed of coals assured everyone that meat would be plentiful for the evening meal. But even these familiar sights did not bring a smile to Orpah's face as she sauntered across the corner of the yard to the shade of a large olive tree where Ruth and Naomi knelt before a kneading trough, working the dough into a consistency that would allow it to be spread inside the huge jars for baking.

Naomi's face showed the deeply etched lines of one who has known care and sorrow. But Ruth was as serenely beautiful as ever, slender and lovely of form, with warm dark eyes. "Don't worry, Mother Naomi," she said, pushing the dark red hair back from her forehead with her arm. "Mahlon knows what he is doing."

Orpah came up just then, the expression of discontent still upon her features. "Why do you still knead the bread?" she asked. "There are plenty of slaves to do your bidding."

Ruth looked up and smiled. "There is a saying among our husbands' people that a man's bread should be kneaded by the woman he loves."

"I love Chilion," Orpah said a little tartly, looking over to where her husband was showing a smith exactly how to fashion the curve in a pruning hook. "But he doesn't want me doing a slave's work."

Ruth's face became grave. "Mahlon is so concerned lately I don't believe he notices what any of us are doing."

"Why waste your time, then?" Orpah asked.

Ruth looked at Naomi fondly. "It is not for Mahlon alone that we knead together, Orpah," she explained. "Naomi and I love to do it, just as you like to dress up and please Chilion."

"As long as my husband likes what I do, I see nothing

wrong in my wanting pretty things." Orpah tossed her head and moved over to where Chilion stood by the forges. He smiled and put his arm about her waist.

"How many years has it been since you came to Moab, Mother Naomi?" Ruth asked thoughtfully. "They go so fast that I lose track of them."

"Years are of no importance," Naomi said with a smile, "when you are happy and beloved."

A shadow passed momentarily over the younger woman's face. "I have tried to make Mahlon happy," she said. "But sometimes I wonder if he might be more contented about making swords for Hedak if I were able to give him a child."

"Mahlon agreed to make swords for Moab because we had been starving in Bethlehem," Naomi said. "He has always known that they might be used one day against Israel. It was bound to prey on his mind, Ruth."

"But he seems to get worse instead of better." She looked up at the sun, now almost directly overhead. "The King's audiences never last longer than noon; we ought to hear from Mahlon soon."

"Let us hope Zebushar agrees with him that a permanent peace between Israel and Moab is possible," Naomi said. "I think that is the only thing that will really make Mahlon happy."

"I still wish I could bear him a son," Ruth said unhappily. "The women of my family have always been fruitful. Why should I be barren?"

"The gift of life comes only from God, Ruth. But the ways of love are as many as the moods of a woman."

Ruth looked startled. "What are you trying to tell me, Naomi?"

"Sometimes we cherish the child-to-be in the men we love, just as your father cherished you. That is one face of love."

"And the other?" Ruth asked almost in a whisper.

"The other is a burning flame that takes of your lover's strength through his passion, while yielding utterly."

Ruth looked away to where Orpah was leaning against Chilion, whose arm was about her shoulders. "Orpah told me once that when Chilion made love to her it was as if her very bones turned to water and she had no will of her own."

"It is like that . . . sometimes."

"Can no woman know both?" Ruth asked almost in a whisper.

"Blessed above all women is she to whom such a boon is granted," Naomi said quietly. "For she is happy beyond expression."

"But I love Mahlon," Ruth protested. "And I have been happy with him. Very happy."

"Your happiness is in serving those you love, Ruth, like mine. We don't call you the Steadfast One without reason."

"I would be content to be called steadfast if only Mahlon were truly happy. No woman could ask more than the kindness and love that Mahlon has given me."

A shout came from the gate opening into the courtyard from the street. They looked up to see Mahlon coming up the walk. Happiness shone from his face. Seeing it, Ruth ran to meet him, wiping the dough from her hands upon her apron. "Is it good news?" she cried. "Did Zebushar agree?"

All work in the courtyard had stopped at Mahlon's shout. The years had been as kind to him as they had been to Ruth. Tall and slender still, with the wiry grace of an artisan and the deep-set eyes of a dreamer, only the deepened maturity of Mahlon's face showed the passage of time.

"What did Zebushar say?" Chilion demanded. "Quick, Mahlon, tell us the news."

"The King promised to think seriously about my suggestion that we invite an emissary from Israel to talk of peace."

"Was he angry because you have stopped making swords?" Ruth asked quickly. This was what had been troubling them most since Mahlon had left that morning to see the King.

"I was so carried away with my own eloquence arguing for peace between our peoples that I forgot to tell him," Mahlon admitted. "But that is not important. Soon there will be a treaty of peace between our people and Moab, and then we will make no more swords. Our forges can turn out tools of iron by the hundreds for both Moab and Israel."

Chilion rubbed his chin, which was covered by a short beard. "It is true that we would make more money forging tools," he admitted. "But Hedak will be angry when he returns."

"The people want hoes and plowshares," Mahlon cried. "They complain because of the heavy taxes. If the King stops this making of arms, Hedak will have no choice but to give in." He looked at the others and saw the doubt in their faces. "Don't you believe me?" he demanded. "Don't you all feel as I do that it is wrong to make weapons of war?"

Ruth gave Mahlon's arm a quick squeeze. "Of course we feel as you do, dear. But Prince Hedak is a powerful man and he may not approve. It is just that we don't want you to get your hopes too high."

"Even the King rules only on Hedak's sufferance," Chilion added dourly. "He could be King himself whenever it suits him to take the throne."

"Maybe you are right," Mahlon conceded, his enthusiasm beginning to wane now. "But when I think what peace between our peoples would mean to everyone, I see nothing else. Send the men back to work, Chilion. I will rest for a while and see if I can think of some way to persuade Hedak that my proposal is better than conquest."

Ruth followed Mahlon into the house and brought him a cool cup of wine. "We will think of some way to persuade Hedak, dear," she assured him, smoothing his dark hair gently with a soothing hand.

"The people want hoes, pruning hooks, and plowshares, not swords and spears," he insisted. "You have only to see how they wait outside the gate to buy every tool we make to realize that."

"Perhaps the King would let you forge tools while the other smiths make swords," she suggested.

Mahlon shook his head. "That is not the answer, Ruth. Only a few generations ago the people of Moab were friendly with the Hebrews. Your own people among the Edomite tribes still trade with Israel, but they are herdsmen and shearers of sheep, like the Israelites. Here in Heshbon we make tools of metal, the very things that Israel needs and could have freely if there were only peace and free trade between our two countries. And Israel has plenty of hides and wool to sell to Moab." He walked to the window. . . . "What does Hedak plan to do with all these swords we have been making, if not to wage war upon Israel?"

"He plans to extend the borders of Moab to the Great Sea," Ruth agreed.

"But if the King and the people do not follow him, even Hedak is powerless."

"The people do not rule Moab," Ruth reminded him. "And the King is old and tired. Hedak wields the power, Mahlon. It would be dangerous to forget that for one moment."

"Zebushar is still the King," he protested. "He told me today he tires of the people continuously crying out against taxes. Yesterday there was a riot; ten soldiers and fifty people were killed. Tomorrow there will be another and the next day another. It cannot go on like this."

"Hedak will return any day now," Ruth pointed out. "He will put down the rioting as he did before, by claiming that Israel has violated the border again, so the people will be angry and forget their grievances."

"Then I must stop him before he can find an excuse to make war."

"But how?"

"By arranging a treaty of peace between Israel and Moab."

"We have never had such a treaty," she pointed out.

"And never will unless someone has the courage to make the first move."

"Why must you do it, Mahlon? You are a metalsmith, and not even one of the King's advisers."

"My anvils and my forges have produced weapons that can destroy Israel," he said firmly. "It is my duty to see that they are not used against my people, even if it costs me my life."

"Don't, Mahlon!" Ruth cried out in a sudden panic at his words. "Don't say that!"

He took her face between his two hands and kissed her. "You are a wonderful wife, Ruth. Far better than I could ever deserve. . . ."

"Then give up this idea," she begged almost hysterically. "We will move somewhere else, back to Bethlehem, or down into Egypt. There you can make tools and plowshares in peace."

"No. The guilt is mine for building this threat against my people. I must do everything I can to try and save them from it."

"Suppose Hedak will not let you?"

"I believe the people and the King will follow me. That is why I must act before Hedak returns. I will go to the King again tomorrow and suggest that he invite an emissary from Judah to talk of peace."

"You Hebrews have no king," she pointed out. "Who would come?"

"Boaz is the strongest man in all of Judah. If he would come to Heshbon, I know we could work out a treaty."

"Would Hedak let him? You know they are bitter enemies."

"Hedak will know better than to oppose a move for peace when the people and the King want it." Mahlon's confidence was returning again. "The treaty is as good as written already."

"I hope you are right, dear." Ruth leaned over and kissed him gently. "With all my heart I hope it."

But deep inside her she could not still the sense of foreboding that had gripped her ever since Mahlon first broached this idea of making peace between Moab and the Hebrew tribes to the west. For, being a Moabite now herself, she knew how easily Hedak could arouse the people against the Hebrews with tales of border atrocities and promises of plunder when the cities of the Israelites were sacked by a victorious Moabite army. And that army would be victorious, she knew, because Mahlon's swords gave them an almost insuperable advantage over the simple spears of the Hebrew tribes.

ii.

Returning from a trip to the northern tribes, Hedak heard before he reached the city that his chief swordsmith was no longer fashioning weapons of war, for a courier always rode out to greet him with the news so that he would be forewarned against anything that might arise upon his arrival in Heshbon.

The Moabite chief never made the mistake of leaving anything to chance. He had been preparing a long time for an attack upon the Hebrew tribes, patiently building up the vast stores necessary for the great army he planned to take into the field. And what Mahlon planned, Hedak recognized instantly, could defeat him before he began.

"By the fires of Chemosh!" Nebo snapped when he heard the news. "Mahlon should be killed for this."

"Eventually," Hedak agreed. "But since the people cry out and riot against taxation, it will give them something else to talk about if they think there may be peace. Meanwhile we can make our own plans."

"Which will be?"

"I don't know yet," Hedak admitted. "But when the time comes, I will think of something."

Actually Hedak had almost enough swords stored away in the armories of Heshbon to equip the army he planned to put into the field soon. Already there were more than enough to conquer the Hebrew tribes who had not been able to join closely enough together to make a solid front against their enemies since the days of Joshua. Together the tribes of Israel outnumbered those who might try to make war against them, but they had ceased to become a warlike people during the years they had been living in Canaan. And had not an occasional leader arisen, such as the judges who periodically managed to consolidate the quarreling groups long enough to defend themselves against their enemies, the Israelites would long since have been destroyed.

Boaz and a few others had continued to argue in the council of Israel through the years while Hedak had been building his strength, urging that the young men be armed and trained against the day when Moab would descend upon them. But few listened, as has happened since men have lived together in villages and tribes. The old, the unsure, and those whose wealth would be decreased by war were in the places of power. The people harkened to councils of weakness and complacency instead of to the voices of strong men warning against a certain doom if they did not bestir themselves and make the necessary sacrifices to forestall it.

In Hedak's plan to extend the borders of Moab to the Great Sea the Israelites were actually no more than a steppingstone, since little booty would be gained from conquering them. The long famine that sent Elimelech and his family to Moab had also impoverished the Hebrews, and only in recent years had they begun to recover from it. Besides, the tribes of Israel were a pastoral people, living with their herds and flocks, tilling the soil for barley and fruits, and rarely accumulating great wealth.

To the west of the Israelites, however, lay Hedak's real goal, the Philistine cities of the coast, where the working of iron and other metals had progressed even beyond that of either Moab or Israel, and where great treasures had been accumulated through trade. With these in Hedak's hands and the skilled artisans of the Philistine cities at his command the Moabites would be a great power, capable even of threatening the might of Egypt to the south.

Then the hated Israelites would be slaves and the shame of Moab would be erased from the clay tablets of their history. Baal would be cast down from his temples in the Philistine cities and Chemosh with his flaming maw would rule. It was a prospect to gladden the heart of a ruthless and ambitious man, particularly when his plans included getting rid of the old King and eventually putting himself upon the throne of one of the most powerful nations in the world of that day.

Mahlon's first intimation of Hedak's arrival in the city came when a trumpet blast sounded outside the gate of the courtyard and a herald shouted pompously, "Make way for Hedak, Prince of Moab and Captain of its armies."

Mahlon hurried out into the courtyard to greet his visitor, but Hedak's bodyguard had already thrust open the gate and the Moabite leader was striding into the court. Long ago Hedak had begun to dress more magnificently even than Zebushar, whom he was supposed to serve. His robe was of a rich woolen cloth, dyed a deep blue with scarlet rosettes around the hem and the facing of short sleeves that barely covered his muscular shoulders. At his waist was a broad girdle, richly embroidered, with a brace of daggers stuck into it.

Over the robe he wore an outer garment like a loose jacket, but as long as the robe, which came to just below his knees. His boots were of soft leather, laced up his muscular calves. And upon the outer cloak were elaborately embroidered patterns in flowers of all kinds, with gold and silver trimmings. The buttons that held it together were each a separate precious stone. A single large jewel shone in the center of the cone-shaped tiara of striped woolen material that encircled his forehead, and the sheath of his sword was also heavily jeweled. With his handsome features, thick sensuous lips, and dark, curling hair the Moabite prince was a picture of wealth, arrogance, and barbaric magnificence.

Behind Hedak were ranged a dozen or so soldiers of his bodyguard, wearing conical helmets of metal fashioned in Mahlon's forges, with a short crest, also devised by Mahlon, jutting over the forehead and serving as a protection for the face. Their torsos were covered by jerkins of leather, closely set with overlapping plates of metal, thick enough to turn the points of arrows except at a close range, but not a spear hurled by a man of some strength. A short waistcloth fell to their knees. Beneath this were close-fitting breeches extending to high leather boots. A sword swung in a leather sheath from the left hip of each soldier, and a long dagger was thrust into the girdle on the opposite side.

Each soldier carried, also, a six-foot lance, with a short metal blade terminating the shaft. The lance could be used both as spear and sword, a truly murderous weapon against ill-trained soldiers or those not protected by some sort of armor. Each man also bore a shield of wicker, faced with metal.

Hedak spoke abruptly, without any greeting. "You have prospered in Moab these past ten years, swordsmith. But only on my sufferance and because of my favor."

"No one knows this better than I, Prince Hedak," Mahlon said courteously. "Have I not made swords enough for any army you are likely to need?"

"That is for me to decide. When I need your advice on military matters, I will ask for it."

"Then it is true that you plan to march to the Great Sea and attack the Philistine cities?"

Hedak looked startled. "Who has said such a thing? You must have contact with Israelite spies."

"Nay." Mahlon shook his head. "I have seen no one from among my people since I left the Place of Refuge, where we first met, except Cheb, the merchant. But it is common talk in Moab that you will not be satisfied until your horse's hoofs are wet from the waters of the Great Sea."

"What I plan is no concern of yours," Hedak snapped. "Now toss these hoes and pruning hooks out of the forges and get to work making shields and swords."

Mahlon shook his head firmly. "I have talked to many

people. All agree with me that it would be a good thing if there were peace between our two peoples."

"Peace! Bah!" Hedak spat on the ground at Mahlon's feet. "There has been nothing but an uneasy peace between Moab and Israel since Moses led your accursed people into Canaan." He stopped. "Or is your real purpose to make us slaves again, Israelite?"

"We who serve the Most High want no gain through bloodshed, for our God counsels that we live in peace when we can. There is room enough in this land for all of us," Mahlon continued earnestly. "If you must go against the Philistine cities, why not march north, around Israel?"

"So now you have become a military leader as well as a statesman?" Hedak's voice was heavy with sarcasm. "Tell me the whole of this plan of yours, so I may have the full benefit of your wisdom."

"If you will but enter the house," Mahlon suggested, "Ruth will be glad to serve you refreshment while I explain it to you."

"My wives cry out because their lord has been so long away," Hedak said impatiently. "Tell me this silly plan of yours quickly and let me go."

"I would have the leaders of Moab and of Israel sit down in peace and talk together," Mahlon explained. "The King agrees with me that it would be a good thing for both nations if there were free trade between Moab and Israel. And the merchants favor it, too, for they would prosper."

"At the expense of admitting Israelite spies to Moab?"

"Only one man need come from Israel," Mahlon demurred. "A leader who could speak for the people. Surely you are not afraid of one man?"

"I am afraid of no man," Hedak snapped. "But who could speak for the Hebrews? You have no king."

"The people respect Boaz. He is the leader of the young men who would defend my people if they are attacked."

"Boaz!" Hedak's cheeks purpled at the name and Mahlon thought for a moment that the Moabite captain was going to attack him in the heat of his fury. Then Hedak's expression changed slowly and his anger seemed to fade as his hand left the hilt of his sword and began to stroke his elaborately curled beard.

"I, too, respect Boaz," he admitted finally. "And something good might come of our meeting together."

"I know it will," Mahlon agreed eagerly, not stopping to wonder at the sudden change in Hedak's manner. "The people will hail you as a great leader for assuring peace and free trade between the Israelite tribes and Moab."

"Do you think Boaz would agree to come to Heshbon?"

"Cheb, the merchant, is here," Mahlon said quickly. "I saw him only today. Let a clay tablet be prepared with the King's seal, giving safe passage to Heshbon for Boaz. Cheb can carry it with him to Bethlehem and Boaz can return with the next caravan. Together you can work out the details of a treaty for peace between our countries. Then Israel can trade its hides and cheese and its barley for the things made by the artisans of Moab." Carried away by enthusiasm, Mahlon rushed on. "You might even arrange for caravans from this country to go all the way to the Great Sea and trade with the Philistines who sail upon it in ships as the northern tribes of Israel do."

"It is a fine prospect," Hedak admitted with an alacrity that Mahlon, had he not been so eager to put his plan into effect, might have found surprising.

"Boaz and I were like brothers in our youth," Mahlon continued eagerly. "I will give Cheb a tablet written in my own words, telling Boaz that he can safely accept the invitation of the King. Then there should be no doubt in his mind."

"You make it all sound very simple," Hedak observed. "But then you may be right."

"You will send the tablet?"

Hedak nodded. "I will speak to the King and if he approves, the letter will be given to Cheb this night." He turned toward the gate, while Mahlon walked along a few steps behind him. Nebo seemed to be enjoying a private joke, but he did not share it.

At the gate Hedak said genially, "You should be a statesman, Mahlon. Meanwhile you need not make swords, if it troubles you. As you say, the people will be happy to know that there will be peace, so you will have a fine market for your hoes and pruning hooks."

Ruth had been listening at an open window. When Hedak had gone, she turned away thoughtfully. There was no point in planting a doubt in Mahlon's mind now about what he had accomplished, when he was so sure that he had done a great thing for both his native and his adopted country. But deep inside her she was not at all sure about Hedak's sincerity. She had known the Moabite chief longer than had Mahlon and she understood how intense was his ambition for conquest. Just why he had agreed so easily to the peace conference she did not yet know, but she was quite sure that the reasons were Hedak's own and that they had nothing to do with peace.

Late that night Cheb the merchant came to the palace of Hedak in answer to a summons from the man he served as a spy and courier. The Moabite chief was drinking wine with his lieutenant Nebo and both were in high spirits. Before the divan upon which they sat a naked dancing girl postured in the age-old dance of invitation to love, but neither paid her much attention. At the moment a more interesting matter claimed their attention.

Cheb's eyes gleamed at the sight of the girl's tawny, oiled body, but Hedak ordered everyone from the room except Nebo and the merchant. When the doors were closed, he poured a goblet of wine and handed it to Cheb, who drank it greedily.

"I am honored by your summons, master," the Israelite caravan driver said obsequiously.

Hedak laughed. "You will be even more honored when you leave for Bethlehem tomorrow, Cheb, for you will be carrying a message to your Council of Elders from the King of Moab. It is on this clay tablet, sealed with the royal seal." He handed Cheb a tablet of clay secured against damage by an outer case of the same material.

"A tablet?" Cheb took it in his good hand and rubbed his cheek with the hook that served him in place of the left. "I have carried nothing like this before."

"The writing gives safe conduct to a leader of Israel," Hedak explained. "Boaz is to return with you on your next visit."

"Boaz!" Cheb almost dropped the tablet. He clutched it frantically to the breast of his stained robe. "But Boaz is a bitter enemy of both you and Moab, master."

"He will be coming here to talk of peace," Hedak explained, his face creased with a broad grin. "It is an idea of his friend Mahlon."

"Surely you jest, master. Mahlon knows how Boaz hates you."

"This is an affair of state," Hedak explained. "A conference between the heads of nations."

"I—I still don't understand."

"It is simple," Hedak said with a malicious smile. "When there is peace, I will not need spies among the Israelite tribes to tell me what they do and say. Then you would have no job, Cheb, except driving your caravan. And even that would bring you little profit, for then anyone could trade between Moab and Israel."

Nebo guffawed at the dismay on the caravan driver's face. But Cheb was no fool. He sensed that there was more to this than he was being told, and suddenly he thought he saw the answer. "The way to Heshbon is dangerously narrow in places," he said with a knowing grin. "If a horse were to stumble accidentally and go over the mountainside, I would be desolate over the loss of a valuable animal. And no one would wail louder than I at the death of Boaz."

"Don't be a fool!" Hedak snapped. "If I simply wanted Boaz killed, I could hire a dozen Hebrew assassins to slip a dagger between his ribs while he lay asleep. I want him safely here in Heshbon. Do you understand?"

Cheb paled. "B-but . . ."

"And your life shall be forfeit for his safety."

"As you command, master," Cheb whimpered. "I am your slave."

"Another thing," Hedak continued. "The swordsmith is also sending a clay tablet to Bethlehem, assuring Boaz that the summons from the King is given in good faith. Before you leave tomorrow, stop by Mahlon's house and take this tablet with you. It is important that both of them reach the council and Boaz."

"I obey your every word, master," Cheb mumbled miserably, backing away from Hedak's presence, but the Moabite chief stopped him with an uplifted hand.

"You have served me well, Cheb," he said, his good humor restored now. "So I will not torture you. You are to bring Boaz safely to Heshbon because something important is going to happen when he arrives. Something for which our friend Boaz is going to take the blame, and which will so anger the people of Moab that they will beg me to make war."

Cheb's face was wreathed in smiles now. "Have no fear, master," he said. "I will serve you faithfully in this matter."

"See that both tablets reach the council," Hedak warned,

"and that you bring Boaz safely back with you from Israel. No one else will do."

True to his instructions, Cheb came to Mahlon's shop the next morning to collect the tablet upon which he had written the message assuring Boaz that the invitation from Zebushar was genuine. "You can tell Boaz you talked to me, Cheb," Mahlon added. "He will surely come now and between us we will save Israel from destruction."

Cheb held up the tablet that Hedak had given him. "The King has put his seal into the clay," he agreed. "Boaz cannot but believe the messages I carry. I will bring him safely to Moab, Mahlon, have no fear. Hedak has made my life forfeit if I fail."

"Tell Boaz he will stay in my house and that I hold myself personally liable for his safety," Mahlon said as Cheb was leaving the courtyard.

Ruth had been watching for Cheb's arrival since early morning. When he came into the courtyard, she slipped out another gate to wait. As Cheb approached the city gate at the head of the string of mules, she stepped quickly out and signaled him to halt.

"I am Ruth, the wife of Mahlon," she explained hurriedly. "Be sure and tell Boaz that I do not trust Prince Hedak entirely in this matter. It would be wise if he took precautions for his own safety, in case this is a trap to get him to Heshbon."

Cheb's eyes gleamed. He looked away quickly, lest she see the guilty knowledge mirrored within them. "It is unusual to carry opposite messages," he said with some show of hesitation.

"Here is something to repay you for your trouble." Ruth gave him a gold coin. "Don't fail to warn Boaz, Cheb, if you value his life and the welfare of Israel."

The merchant transferred the coin to his purse with a quick movement. "I will personally give him your message, noble lady," he assured her. "You need have no fears."

As he led his caravan toward the gate, Cheb rubbed his cheek reflectively with the metal hook, debating whether or not he should delay his departure long enough to warn Hedak that Ruth, wife of Mahlon, the silversmith, suspected his real intention in bringing Boaz to Heshbon. But then he decided to keep this knowledge to himself. Someday, he sensed, it might be valuable to him, for

Cheb was an opportunist and quite willing to trade in blackmail as well as to spy upon his own people and carry word of the things he learned to their bitterest enemy.

As Ruth was preparing for bed that night, Mahlon came over to where she was sitting in her thin nightdress before a dressing table of rich wood, brushing the lustrous masses of her hair. He put his hand on her shoulder and she reached up to press it against her breast.

"You will be proud of me, Ruth," he said confidently, "when I make peace between Israel and Moab."

She stood up to kiss him. "I am proud of you already, darling," she assured him. "Now go to bed and I will blow out the lamps."

He lay on the couch, watching her as she went about the room. Each lamp consisted of a bowl of olive oil in which a small wick dipped. And as she stood on tiptoes to blow out the flames, the light filtered through the thin nightdress, outlining the sweet contours of her body, even more lovely in its early maturity than on that night when he had watched her dance in the Temple of Ashtar.

When Ruth lay down on the couch beside him, Mahlon drew her close. "I was thinking of the time we first met at the Place of Refuge," he told her. "Do you suppose our coming to Moab may actually have been part of a pattern, Ruth?"

"What do you mean?" She turned to face him in the glow of the moonlight flowing through the open window.

"Perhaps the Most High sent us here from Bethlehem so that one day I might be the agent who would bring about peace between Israel and Moab."

"Oh, I hope so," she cried, holding him fiercely close to her in a sudden rush of apprehension. "I hope so."

He smoothed the rich masses of her hair with his hands, and noticed that she was trembling. "What is wrong, Ruth? You were never like this before."

"It's just that . . ." She stopped, not wanting to reveal her apprehension to him, and not knowing how to keep from doing it if she continued. "Have you ever regretted coming to Moab, Mahlon, and leaving your own people?" she asked, to change the subject.

"Never," he said at once. "For then I would not have had you. And having you makes me the happiest man in the world."

She buried her face in his breast to hide the tears, and felt ardor beginning to warm his body. "But I have given you no child," she protested. "Why should you love me when I am barren?"

"The fault could not be yours. Such a lovely body could not be barren in itself, Ruth. It must be . . ." He stopped and did not go on.

"What were you going to say?"

"I have thought more than once lately that the reason my seed has not stirred within your womb may be because God is punishing me for making the swords."

"But that would be cruel. You agreed to make them so your family could live."

"The Most High is always just, Ruth. If I deserve punishment, I would not want to escape it."

"But you are atoning for that sin, if it is one, by trying to bring about peace."

"Then perhaps . . ." He stopped and when he spoke again the words tumbled over each other in his excitement. "Then perhaps the Most High will grant us a child after all, Ruth."

Some of his excitement was communicated to Ruth's body now and they clung together, drawn perhaps closer than they had ever been before by the thought that at last they might be given a child. "Naomi says the gift of life comes to a woman from God," she whispered.

"And if my seed should quicken to life within your body, it would be an omen that God has shown favor to me in this, and in my plan for peace." He swept her eagerly to him.

Ruth's greatest happiness in their love-making had always come through holding him tenderly to her breast until his passion was spent. But now there was a fierceness, an urgency that had never been present before. She yielded herself utterly to it and felt her body respond in a way that she had rarely known in the years that they had been married, a burst of ecstasy that seemed to promise the conception they both so devoutly wished.

Her happiness was only momentary, however, and long after Mahlon was asleep, his ardor spent, Ruth lay awake in the darkness, unable to resist the sense of foreboding that had been with her ever since Mahlon had announced his decision to make no more swords for Moab.

iii.

Cheb reached Bethlehem with his messages and went at once to the house of Tob, to whom he sold his goods. In addition to being the nearest of kin to Naomi, Mahlon, and Chilion, Tob was also an important man in Judah. Not only did he deal in goods from caravans, but he also consigned the products of Israel to merchants in other countries. And, in addition, he was president of the Council of Elders of Judah, and therefore the logical one to receive the tablets that Cheb carried.

Tob's house was one of the most pretentious structures in Bethlehem, as befitted its owner's position. It was of two stories, built from sun-baked blocks of mud, with a flat roof upon which rushes were laid out to dry. Israelite families spent their evenings on the roof tops in hot weather, taking advantage of the cooling breezes that blew across them after nightfall. And here Cheb found Tob with his slave girl, Adah, a beautiful sultry young woman whose attitude toward her master was wholly proprietary, and whose relationship to him was that of a wife in every sense except the legal one.

Boaz was next of kin to Tob, but there was little love lost between the two men. For while Boaz tried to arouse the people of Judah and the other tribes to the danger of Moab, Tob preached conservatism, fearing, now that the Israelites were prospering after the long famine, to disturb the exceedingly profitable trade that he carried on with Moab by way of Cheb's caravans.

The merchant had been eating his evening meal, a very luxurious one, when Cheb was announced. He frowned his displeasure when the caravan driver entered, and did not offer him food and wine, as Israelite courtesy required. "Why did you not come to my shop in the morning, Cheb?" he asked pompously. "You know I conduct no business at home."

Cheb glanced at the slave girl Adah and grinned. He knew well her function in this household and the influence she had over the plump merchant. On occasion she had even helped him cheat her master, for a portion of the profit.

"Out with it," Tob commanded. "What is your business here tonight?"

Cheb took the clay tablet Hedak had given him from his robe. "I had good reason to come to you immediately, Tob, since I carry a message from the King of Moab to the Council of Elders, and you are at the head of the council."

"A message?" Tob asked, startled. "What kind of a message?"

"From the King of Moab, as I told you. It is an invitation for a leader of Judah and Israel to come to Heshbon and talk of peace."

"Peace! Surely you jest."

"Just what I told Prince Hedak, and he gave me a tongue lashing. Mahlon has convinced them that there can be peace between Moab and Judah. And if we make a treaty, the other tribes will follow."

Tob pursed his lips. "That is true," he admitted. "Judah is the leader."

"Mahlon thinks that if Boaz——"

"Boaz!" Tob exclaimed. "Why should he go? Why not I?"

"Boaz and Mahlon are friends. But if you wish to go . . ." He shrugged. "Still I must warn you that it is not an easy journey. Sometimes, in the sandstorms, I wander for days . . ."

"I must think of this," Tob said abruptly. "Leave the tablet with me and I will take the matter up with the council tomorrow."

"I also have a letter from Mahlon to Boaz, guaranteeing to him that the offer of the King is made in good faith."

"Leave that with me, too," Tob said. "I will give it to Boaz in the morning."

Cheb handed over the tablets. As he was leaving the room, he managed to signal Adah and she joined him a few moments later outside the house. "Tob must not go," he said urgently. "They want Boaz."

"Why?"

"Prince Hedak told me that something is going to happen in Heshbon, and that Boaz will be blamed for it."

"You mean he will not return?" Adah asked quickly.

"I am sure of it."

"But without Boaz to lead them the armies will be like sheep before Hedak's swords."

"You forget that Boaz is next of kin to Tob and if he does not return from Heshbon, Tob will inherit a fortune."

"Will it do him any good if Hedak conquers Israel?"

"Hedak is aiming for larger game," Cheb explained. "The Moabite cities on the coast. Someone must govern Judah and perhaps all of Israel for him. Why not Tob? I could tell him how Tob co-operated in getting Boaz to come to Heshbon."

Adah smiled. "You are clever, Cheb. I am sure I can persuade my master that Boaz should go to Heshbon instead of him."

"And when Tob inherits Boaz's property, you will not forget how Cheb helped you to bring this thing about?"

"I will not forget," she promised with a smile. "You shall be well rewarded."

It was the custom of the Council of the Elders of Judah to meet in the morning under a shady arcade near the gate, close to the well from which most of the town obtained its water. Word had been carefully spread by Tob and by Adah and Cheb that a matter of much importance concerning the tribe would be discussed, so a considerable crowd had gathered well before the eleven elderly men who made up the council filed slowly into their seats behind a long narrow table.

Only one seat was empty, that of Boaz, when Tob stood up importantly to begin the meeting. The opening prayer was hardly finished, however, when the thudding of horses' hoofs sounded from the direction of the fields that surrounded the city and two horsemen appeared, riding hard. One was Boaz, the other his lieutenant, Joseph.

Before the well Boaz pulled up his horse and dismounted. His expression was stern as he strode across the open space and into the arcade where the elders were meeting. The years and his sorrow had etched their lines deeply into his face, but his body showed the lean strength of the soldier, and his skin was burned dark from the sun. Joseph tied the horses to a rack before the well, then hurried closer so he could hear the discussion of the council.

"Peace unto thee, Boaz, mighty warrior of Israel," Tob greeted his kinsman effusively.

Boaz shrugged impatiently as if to throw off the oily words of the merchant. "Why call a meeting of the council when I am busy in the fields, Tob?" he demanded. "You could have met without me, since you never listen to what I say anyway."

"We listen, Boaz," one of the old men spoke placatingly. "It is just that we are not sure war is inevitable as you claim. We have lived at peace with our neighbors for many years now. If we make a show of arms, they may begin to fear our intentions."

"You will be sure enough of Hedak's intentions when his army is upon us," Boaz said bluntly. "Then it will be too late and we will be slaves." He looked around the council, and turned to the people, silently watching. "Do you want your young women ravished by the soldiers of Moab?" he demanded. "Your elders killed and your young men driven off as slaves?"

A babble of excited denials came from the people and Boaz turned back to the council. "How long will you continue to keep Judah weak while you pull your beards and argue in the council?" he demanded rudely of the ruling group. "In olden days the Lord raised up a judge when Israel was in danger to lead us against the Philistines. You should be praying for one now to show you the error of your ways."

"Boaz!" the people outside the arcade shouted. "Give us Boaz as a judge."

"Nay." Boaz raised his hand. "I am but a voice crying in the wilderness of what is to come. The prophets have promised that a leader to Israel shall yet rise up from my seed. I would like to be sure that there are people left for him to lead when he comes."

"Boaz!" the people shouted again, and became quiet only when Tob held up his hand, signaling that the business of the council was about to begin.

Tob knew how popular his kinsman was, particularly among the younger element, and the knowledge pleased him not at all. Like all small-souled men, he was jealous of his position and power as chief of the Council of the Elders of Judah and a member of the larger body, the Council of Israel, that ruled the loose federation of the Hebrew tribes which remained as the only relic of the tightly knit group who had been led to this land by Moses and Joshua.

Tob waited until the shouting died away, although he was seething inside with anger against Boaz and those who would have him elected a judge, thus placing him over the council and almost in the position of a king.

"Israel is indeed honored this day," he said, and held up the tablet Cheb had brought from Hedak. "Upon this tablet of clay is imprinted a writing which bids a leader of our people come to Heshbon to talk of peace with Zebushar, King of Moab."

A hush fell over the crowd at this unexpected news. None was more startled than Boaz. "What drivel is this?" he demanded. "For a whole generation the Moabites have killed every Israelite who has come into their hands."

"See for yourself." Tob handed him the tablet. "It is plainly written here."

Boaz took the tablet and studied it for a long moment. "It is what you say, Tob," he admitted. "A guarantee of safe conduct for one to be chosen by us, and an invitation to come to Heshbon and talk of a treaty of peace between our peoples. But how did it come into your hands?"

"Cheb, the caravan driver, brought it only last night from Moab," Tob explained. "He is here to vouch that the tablet came from King Zebushar himself."

Cheb stepped forward. The son of the madwoman was not well liked in Bethlehem. People instinctively distrusted him because only he was allowed to enter and leave Moab freely. The women claimed that he brought shoddy goods, but his caravans were always sold out within a few hours of arrival. Many of the men, too, envied the caravan driver the opportunity to visit places of which they knew nothing. His stories of Moab, particularly the painted women and naked dancing girls, were eagerly listened to in the wineshops.

"It is as the noble Tob says," Cheb verified. "Just before I left Heshbon, I was called to the palace and the tablet was put into my hands with strict orders that it be delivered to the Council of the Elders."

"Do you still doubt its authenticity, Boaz?" Tob demanded.

Boaz turned the tablet over in his hands. "I recognize the seal of Chemosh," he admitted, "having seen it before when I went into Moab to seize animals stolen from my flocks. But why would Zebushar suddenly send out a dove of peace?"

"Cheb bore another tablet for you alone, Boaz," Tob

said, "given him by your kinsman, Mahlon. Perhaps it may explain the one from Zebushar."

Boaz took the second tablet and studied it. "This is from Mahlon," he agreed. "He says the invitation of the King is genuine. And Mahlon's message is marked with a sign we used as children, which no one else would know."

"Then it must be genuine," Tob said promptly.

"Mahlon says it is his idea that we can have peace and free trade between Moab and Israel," Boaz continued. "And that both the King and Hedak agree. He suggests that I come and makes himself personally responsible for my safety."

"Mahlon of Israel is highly regarded in Heshbon," Cheb confirmed. "I have personally seen his metal-working establishment. It is the largest in all of Moab."

"He makes the finest swords outside the cities of the Philistines on the coast of the Great Sea," Boaz confirmed. "If we are ever destroyed by Moab, it will be with Mahlon's weapons."

"They say in Heshbon that lately Mahlon is sorely troubled because he has made swords for the soldiers of Hedak," Cheb added. "Perhaps this is his way of making amends."

"You may be right, Cheb," Boaz agreed. "The family of Elimelech would not have left Israel except for the great famine. No doubt Hedak forced Mahlon to fashion swords as the price for their lives, so he is not really to blame."

"Do you doubt any more, Boaz?" Tob asked.

Boaz looked around the group of elders, then back at Tob. Under the scrutiny of his grave dark eyes the older man flushed. "I can understand *your* wanting me to go to Moab, Tob," he said deliberately, "since you are the next of kin and I am childless." He turned to the others. "What have you decided, O my elders? Since I know you waited to call me until you had agreed among you before the meeting what you would say."

Some of the men looked away, unable to meet Boaz's accusing gaze. But a visitor from the neighboring tribe of Benjamin, a tall man with iron-gray hair and amused eyes, said quietly, "I have agreed to nothing, Boaz."

The Israelite leader smiled and for a moment all the harshness and mockery left his face. This was the Boaz who was loved by those who served him—kind, sincere, generous, deserving respect, and earning it by his acts. "I do not need to be told that, Eliab," he said simply, then turned back to the others. "Well," he demanded, "what is your decision?"

Only the throbbing beat of the pulse at his temples betrayed Tob's pent-up anger at Boaz's manner. "Naturally we have discussed such an important matter between us," he admitted. "After all, others besides yourself are concerned for the welfare of Israel, Boaz."

Boaz shrugged but did not speak. "You are the leader of our armies," Tob continued. "Who else could speak for us but you?"

A murmur of approval rose from the crowd. "Boaz should go," one of old men agreed. "Have not the prophets foretold that a king shall come from his seed?"

"Suppose I do go to Heshbon," Boaz said. "And suppose Zebushar is so old and addled with wine that he claims to want peace. What will have been accomplished after all?"

"Our sons will not be killed in battle by the swords of the Moabites." It was Nathan, an old and respected member of the council.

"And we will all grow prosperous through trade with them," Tob pointed out shrewdly. "Our hides and tallow will bring twice their present price in the markets of Heshbon."

"Each time I go to Heshbon the people cry for more of our leather," Cheb confirmed.

"But Hedak will still have swords," Boaz reminded them bluntly. "And his armies will still be twice the number of ours."

No one argued, for these facts were well known.

"The children of Israel will be lulled into believing that all is well when it is not," Boaz continued. "And one day the Moabites will fall upon us with their swords when we are defenseless."

"We all know Boaz has good reason to hate Moab," Tob said impatiently. "But none of us can afford to let personal feelings come ahead of the good of Israel."

It was a shrewd move, for it was common knowledge among the onlookers that ever since Boaz's wife had run away with a Moabite years before and been killed at the Place of Refuge he had been unrelenting in his hate of the neighboring nation.

"When *you* put the welfare of anything ahead of your own interests, Tob, I will willingly become your slave," Boaz said. "But never let it be said that I overlooked any chance to keep us free. If the Moabites attacked today we would be defenseless, so I might as well go to Heshbon and gain as much time as I can. At least I can count their swords."

A hum of approval rose from the council and the onlookers gave ungratified endorsement. "Boaz!" they shouted. "God preserve Boaz, the Lion of Judah."

"When do you return to Heshbon, Cheb?" Boaz asked the caravan owner.

"Within three days," Cheb said promptly, "for I know how anxious Mahlon is to see you. He bade me say that you will live in his house and his wife also joins her welcome with his."

"I will be ready, Cheb," Boaz told him. "Joseph and Eliab will accompany me to the Place of Refuge and wait my return there."

"And if you do not come back," Eliab said grimly, "Cheb had better not show his face in Israel again or my spear will find his heart."

iv.

Four days later, in the early morning, Boaz stood with Eliab and Joseph at the Place of Refuge and watched Cheb's caravan cross the river into Moab. A group of soldiers from his own picked bodyguard waited behind him under the command of a grizzled man in the leather jerkin and metal cap of a soldier.

Boaz's face was troubled as he watched the caravan. Suddenly he turned to Eliab. "I have changed my mind," he said decisively. "No one must follow me."

"Why?" Joseph asked.

"You know that I believe this to be a trap baited by Hedak to entice me into Moab," Boaz explained. "But if the offer is genuine, I would be guilty of treason against my people not to go to Moab."

"And if it is not?" Eliab asked dryly.

"Then I must be the only one to die. You, Eliab, and you, Joseph, know my plans for defending Israel. If I am killed in Heshbon, even the sheep of the council can no longer doubt that Hedak means to make war against us. And with both of you alive Israel will have two leaders at least."

"But, Boaz," Joseph protested. "Ram here"—he nodded toward the grizzled soldier standing behind them—"knows a way into Moab through mountain passes which are not guarded. We will hide in the hills outside Heshbon. If you do not return, we can capture some Moabite soldiers from the border guard. In their clothing and armor we could easily enter the city to rescue you."

"It is too risky, Joseph." Boaz shook his head. "You will remain here until I return. Those are my orders. If I am not back in ten days, return to Bethlehem and rally every man who can bear arms, whether the council agrees or not. Set watches in the hills and try to trap the Moabites in the narrow passes where their swords are of little value against our spears. It is the only hope for Israel."

"*You* are the only hope of Israel," Joseph said bluntly. "I cannot let you go to your death alone."

Boaz smiled. "We have always ridden together, Joseph, but today our paths must separate. If it comes to a fight in Heshbon I will not be alone. Mahlon and Chilion will stand beside me." He bestrode his horse in one lithe movement and sent the animal splashing into the stream. As he rode up on the other bank, he raised his hand in a gesture of farewell.

When Boaz had disappeared, Joseph turned to Eliab.

"You are the leader now," he said. "Are you going to let him go to his death alone?"

"My heart tells me to follow," Eliab admitted. "But my head tells me he is right. Some of us who know his plans must stay behind. We all know his way is the only one that can possibly save Israel."

"You know his plans and are already a leader," Joseph pointed out. "But I am only a lieutenant and not necessary to the army. Let me ride with Ram over the mountains by the secret passes and wait outside Heshbon in case Boaz needs us."

Eliab looked at the younger man keenly, then smiled and slapped him on the shoulder. "I will not stop you, Joseph. But you heard Boaz's orders. If you go into Moab and Boaz does return safely, he will be angry. The decision is yours to make, not mine."

"We will follow Boaz, then," Joseph said decisively, and turned to the soldier standing behind him. "How close can we get to Heshbon, Ram, without being seen?"

The grizzled man smiled. "If we are luckly enough to surprise two soldiers of Moab, I could put you at the feet of Chemosh himself, but we had best be content with a cave overlooking the city. There are many such from which we can see without being seen, and I have even heard of a secret way into the city, if we can find it."

"A cave will be close enough," Joseph approved. "We will ride at dawn tomorrow."

Boaz's cloak and cap were dusted with white when Cheb's caravan emerged from the pass leading into Moab, the same pass through which the family of Elimelech had come years before. As the lovely green valley opened out before them, with the gleaming city in the distance, Boaz reined in his horse beside the path and allowed the rest of the caravan to pass. Slowly he surveyed the perspective before him, the mountains ringing the valley, the people and flocks in the fields, and the walls of the city.

Ever since they had entered Moab, the stern lines in Boaz's face had slowly etched themselves deeper as he noted the state of military preparedness that was obvious everywhere. The patrol stations along the road were staffed with soldiers carrying swords whose secret of manufacture Mahlon had brought with him into Moab. Heavily fortified strong points guarded the mountain passes. Everywhere he saw evidence of full military preparations strangely at variance with the invitation to talk peace which had brought him here.

Only when he looked at the city in the distance, with the green fields and orchards surrounding it, and the domes of the great Temples of Ashtar and Chemosh gleaming in the afternoon sunlight, did Boaz's face soften a little. For there was great natural beauty in the fertile valley where lay the great city of Heshbon. And Boaz, the landowner and farmer, could appreciate it, even though Boaz, the military leader, was more concerned by the implications of the military strength he had seen. As he scanned the whole scene before him with intent eyes, he etched into his memory every detail of what he saw against a possible future need.

Cheb grinned and wiped the dust from his face with his sleeve. "See how wrong you were to doubt me, Boaz?" he said genially. "There is Heshbon and I have brought you safely to it. A courier rode ahead of us from the pass and even now, I'll wager, great preparations are being made for your arrival."

"I will thank you properly when I return to Bethlehem." Boaz's eyes flicked up to the idol on the mountainside where Mahlon had first set up his forges. "What is that?" he demanded.

Cheb looked up quickly, then down again, as if the very sight of the idol terrified him. "The Moabites regard that statue of their god as holy," he said hurriedly. "The ground around it is sacred."

"Why? They have a great temple there in the city."

Cheb shrugged. "I don't know. The people of the city say the whole place is cursed and few of them go there."

Boaz looked up again at the hideous statue of the God of Moab. "Chemosh is evil enough looking at that," he admitted. "I can hardly blame them."

"Hush!" Cheb cried. "You must not speak disparagingly of the Moabite god in his own country."

Boaz looked keenly at the caravan driver. "You still cling to the beliefs of Israel, don't you, Cheb? Although you trade with Moab?"

"Of course." Cheb shot him a quick glance, conscious that he had made a slip. "But I am careful not to offend the gods of the people with whom I trade. And you would do well to do the same while you are in Heshbon."

"There is but one God, the Most High," Boaz said curtly. "I will make obeisance to no other. And neither should you."

They were almost to the gates of the city when a trumpet blared from the ramparts, and a group of horsemen rode out at full gallop, swords unsheathed. Boaz's hand went to his own weapon as the horsemen circled the caravan until the leader, Hedak's lieutenant Nebo, reined in his animal.

"Welcome to Heshbon, noble Boaz," Nebo greeted him. There was an undertone of impudence in the Moabite officer's voice that brought a wary light to Boaz's eyes. "Prince Hedak is occupied, but he sent me to escort you to the house of Mahlon, the swordsmith, who will entertain you until tonight."

"I am honored," Boaz said simply.

"A mighty feast has been ordered in your honor this evening," Nebo continued. "The King and Prince Hedak will greet you then."

Boaz bowed courteously, but none of the wariness left his eyes. "I am overwhelmed by the magnificence of your city and my reception into it," he admitted.

Nebo's eyebrows lifted. "Prince Hedak says you are the finest swordsman in all of Israel. If there is time, it would be an honor to cross weapons with you merely as an exercise."

Boaz carefully refrained from letting his misgivings show in his face. "I come on an errand of peace," he reminded Nebo. "But if the occasion should arise, I may be able to accommodate you."

Nebo shot him a wary glance before he wheeled his horse and rode to the head of the group. The Moabite cavalrymen ranged themselves upon either side of the Israelite leader, and thus they rode through the streets of Heshbon to Mahlon's house.

Boaz's alert gaze did not miss the fact that armed soldiers stood at almost every street corner in Heshbon, or the listlessness reflected in the faces of the people who crowded the city, scurrying aside fearfully as the military escort rode through the street, not caring if those unable to move quickly enough were trampled under the horses' hoofs.

In the few short minutes required to traverse the distance between the gate and Mahlon's home Boaz decided that there was little love between the armies of Hedak and the people of Moab. But he did not delude himself that this necessarily meant any weakening of Hedak's hold upon them, for he knew very well how easily the emotions of a people can be swayed to fit the purpose of an unscrupulous leader.

The most startling thing about Heshbon to an Israelite was, as it had been to Mahlon and Chilion years before, the large number of women on the streets. In Israel women remained at home, except to go to the well for water, or to shop for food at the market. Here they were everywhere, dressed in bright-colored fabrics, their faces painted almost as brightly as their garments. Bracelets, anklets, and neck chains jingled as they walked and many wore precious jewels openly on the streets.

In Israel, too, when a woman left her house, she covered her body completely, so that not even her feet showed, unless she stumbled over a stone in the street. And her head was covered with a shawl, lest a man see her hair and face and lust after her, breaking the Law. Here in Heshbon, however, a filmy robe managed usually to reveal a trim ankle and toes, the nails often painted scarlet, as were the straps of the flimsy sandals they wore on their feet. Some of those whose charms best stood masculine inspection had even adopted the Egyptian fashion and went with one breast, or sometimes both, bare, the nipples painted scarlet. Others added a cloth tightly bound beneath the breasts to make them more prominent.

Cheb's eyes met those of Boaz, and he grinned slyly. "Didn't I tell you there would be much to see in Heshbon? And when they fête you tonight . . ." His eyes rolled suggestively.

Boaz had heard about the magnificence of Heshbon, but today he was seeing it for the first time. And the reality dwarfed even the tales of Cheb. From the gate by which they had entered the city a broad road led to the Temples of Chemosh and his divine wife, Ashtar, skirting a wide square that teemed with people. Upon one side of it stood a strongly fortified building, with soldiers upon the ramparts and at every door.

"The palace of Prince Hedak," Nebo announced proudly, nodding toward the citadel. "Headquarters for the armies of Moab."

The two great Temples of Chemosh and Ashtar stood on either side of the square, facing each other with the large image of Chemosh used for outdoor ceremonies at one side between them. From the square a series of terraces, reached by a short flight of stone steps, led upward to the magnificent façade of the Temple of Chemosh, carved with images of the God of Moab and of bulls battling with men and women. The walls on either side of the terraced staircase were of black basalt, into which had been chiseled a continuing story of the courtship of the divine Ashtar by Chemosh, their marriage, and even their mating.

At each terraced level was a landing, set into the wall, in which stood exquisitely carved statues of the Moabite god and his bride, encompassed by the winged disk of the sun that was the emblem of divine kingship everywhere

in this land. Where the steps opened out upon a wide
veranda before the brass-studded doors of the temple-
palace, huge lions carved from black basalt supported
the corners of the first story above.

Across the façade of the temple a carved frieze de-
picted the victories of Zebushar, King and living embodi-
ment of Chemosh. Chariots drove over the prostrate
bodies of the enemy, identifiable at close range as Israelites.
Soldiers carried pikes upon which were spitted the heads
of defeated foes. And in another panel the officers cast
offerings of booty at the feet of the King-God.

The Temple of Ashtar was smaller, but no less magnificent. The figures of the frieze across the face of her
home were those of the non-warlike activities of the
people. Children played with lambs and other animals.
Youths and maidens danced before the altar as the fruits
of the harvest were offered upon it. In one panel was a
realistic depiction of the sacrifice of a girl, which Mahlon
had witnessed on the night when he had come to the
temple during the Festival of Ashtar.

At either side of the entrance to Ashtar's temple the
statues were of beautiful girls, quite nude. But so realistic
was the sculpture and the colors of bright enamel with
which they had been painted that they seemed at first
glance to be alive. The plain limestone walls of the lower
floor were surmounted with an ornamental brickwork
enameled in yellow with blue and red flowers.

All this Boaz saw as his eyes moved from point to
point, overlooking nothing against the day when his
knowledge of the city of Heshbon might be important
to him and to Israel. Prepared as he was by the magnificence of the city, he was not startled by the richness of
Mahlon's house in the busy courtyard where the forges
glowed and the anvils rang with hammers pounding upon
metal.

It was a large villa, surrounded by an open porch,
under whose shelter the manifold activities of the household were carried on. Slaves moved about, carrying water
from the well which stood in the midde of the courtyard,
tending the ovens in which bread was baking, turning
the spit upon which the meat for the evening meal was
slowly cooking, or stirring pots of savory stew. Others
worked with stones, sharpening the tools that came from

the forges. Everywhere was an atmosphere of busy activity and prosperity.

At the gate of the courtyard Nebo and the military escort took leave of Boaz. Mahlon had been warned of his friend's coming and rushed out to meet him.

"The years have been good to you, my friend," Boaz said as they embraced. "It is obvious that you have prospered."

"I would gladly give it all up to undo the damage I have done, Boaz. You came through the city, so you saw how things are."

"All Moab is an armed fortress. This does not look to me like they want peace."

"But the King desires it," Mahlon said eagerly. "And the people. You will see that when you have been here a while."

"Where are your children?"

"Alas, we have none."

"Then the Moabite woman you married does not want them?"

"Both of us want children, Ruth even more than I do," Mahlon protested. "But the Most High has not seen fit to favor us."

"Are you happy with this woman you married, Mahlon?"

"With Ruth?" Mahlon looked at him incredulously. "Of course I am happy. She is the loveliest thing ever created by the Most High, and the kindest. Wait until you see her. You will love her as much as we all do, Boaz."

"I would have thought it the wife's place to welcome her husband's guests."

"Ruth is at the palace," Mahlon explained hurriedly. "Before we were married she was a handmaiden of Chemosh, and Zebushar has always been fond of her. Like me, she is anxious for this peace conference to be a success, so she is superintending preparations for the feast tonight. You will see her after it is over."

"Your wife came from the Edomite tribes, didn't she?"

Mahlon looked startled. "Yes. How did you know?"

"It is my business to know much of what happens in Moab," Boaz said matter-of-factly. "We in Israel have little quarrel with the Edomite people or with the Ammonites. But they would all fight on the side of Moab if war comes."

"Then you still consider all Moabites as enemies?"

"Yes. And I have seen nothing since I came here to change my opinion."

Mahlon smiled. "You will change it when you see Ruth. If all the people of Moab were like her, there would be no reason for war."

"Hedak will make his own reasons when he is ready," Boaz assured him. "And from what I see in Heshbon the time will not be far off."

"Can't you at least give him credit for wanting peace?"

"Why should I? Every other man I have seen in Moab carries a sword, many of them from your forges. I can still recognize your trademark in a weapon, Mahlon. No others are as light, or as keen in the blade as yours."

"I almost wish I had never developed that skill. But if we had stayed in Bethlehem we would have starved."

"You could have gone to Philistia."

Mahlon shrugged. "Are they any the less our enemies than Moab? Hedak gave us safe conduct to Heshbon, but he would have killed us all if I had not forged swords for him. What else could I do, Boaz?"

The older man put a hand on his friend's shoulder. "I am not censuring you, Mahlon. A man must live and protect his family. But I am curious to know how Hedak talked you into sending for me."

"It was my idea from the beginning," Mahlon protested. "In fact, Hedak was very angry when I first mentioned it. But he saw reason when I explained how peace would benefit Moab."

"Hedak sees reason only in what will work to his advantage. I still wonder just why he agreed to your plan."

"I had already spoken to the King while Hedak was away," Mahlon explained, "and convinced him that the people wanted peace. You should have heard them cheer when it was announced that I was trying to negotiate a treaty between our two countries."

"They will shout as loudly for your blood and mine when Hedak stirs them up to war," Boaz said bluntly. "I tell you, Mahlon, you have been made a partner in a clever trick to lure me here to Heshbon. I thought so when I received the tablet from Zebushar, and I am sure of it now. But you were sincere and if I am betrayed, it will at lease serve to force Israel into arming."

Mahlon shook his head. "You have little reason to

trust Hedak, I know, Boaz. But Zebushar is a just man. As long as he is King, the promise of Moab is as good as a treaty."

Boaz smiled and punched Mahlon affectionately upon the arm. "For my own sake and that of Israel I hope you are right, my friend. And now may I have water to wash the dust of the desert from my body?"

"Of course," Mahlon said, instantly contrite. "Ruth would be angry if she knew I had been so discourteous to a visitor in our home. Your room is close to ours."

Mahlon went out to order water brought, leaving Boaz alone in the room. He studied the rich draperies at the windows, then went to examine the construction of a delicately wrought metal pot that served as a lamp, with a wick projecting from the olive oil to be lighted at the fall of darkness by a slave with a torch from the fire kept burning always in the courtyard.

The door opened and Boaz turned to see Naomi standing on the other side of the room. A smile broke over his face and he went quickly to kiss her upon the forehead.

"Welcome to this house, kinsman," Naomi said warmly. "What news do you bring of Bethlehem and our people?"

"The rains have come and bread is plentiful in the land." He smiled. "Your kinsman Tob is as contentious as ever and perhaps so am I. I still argue with the council and they pull their beards and refuse me." He took her by the shoulders and looked deep in her eyes. "Are you happy here in an alien land, Naomi?"

The older woman met his eyes without wavering. "Who ever leaves the place of childhood and does not long to return? But even here in Moab the Most High has been kind, although He took Elimelech from me. I have two strong sons who have prospered and there is no lack for bread in this house."

"You get along all right with their wives, then?"

"They are as my own daughters, especially Ruth."

"This Ruth must indeed be a paragon," Boaz said a little sarcastically. "I hear nothing but praise of her."

"Nor will you hear anything else in this house," Naomi avowed. "Had I a daughter of my own body, I would not want her to be different from Ruth."

"Even though she is a heathen?"

"Zebushar has been kind to us and he is very fond of

Ruth," Naomi explained. "Although she pretends to believe in Chemosh, she knows that the Most High is the one true God, and worships Him in her heart."

"One cannot pretend allegiance to one god while worshiping another, Naomi. The customs of Moab have seized hold of you and your sons. I am sorry to see it."

Naomi looked at him for a moment. When she spoke her voice was low, but it brought a flush to his cheeks. "Because you were betrayed once, Boaz, must you refuse to believe that any woman can be true? It is you who sin by continuing to hate, not we who keep the God of our fathers foremost in our hearts, even in an alien land."

v.

The feast given by Zebushar in honor of the emissary from Israel, preparatory to the peace talks scheduled to begin on the morrow, was of a magnificence unusual even in Heshbon. It was held in the private dining chamber of the King, a magnificent room about a hundred feet in length and half that in breadth. The guests gathered around a low table upon which food was served upon plates of beaten gold and silver, with goblets of similar material for the wine.

Boaz sat at the right hand of the King, with Hedak on the left, and Nebo beside him. Farther down the table Mahlon sat beyond the high priest of the temple. Behind each guest a slave waited to serve his immediate needs, while others wielded huge fans to keep the air stirring in the long room.

Course after course followed, with the wine cups filled as soon as they were half empty. Boaz ate heartily, for, being an outdoorsman, he was hungry, and food of this kind was not often available in Bethlehem. First was the flesh of wild hart, next fat pheasants, and then a whole roast of yearling bull, borne on a great iron spit carried in by slaves. With the meat came steaming vegetables from the lush fields of the valley of Moab, ripe fruits and nuts and sweetmeats of every kind, limited in their number and variety only by the ingenuity of the slaves who manned the kitchens and the skill of a cook imported from Egypt.

Musicians played soft music while the meal was being served, and scantily clad girls teased the guests with special delicacies, preserved fish from the beautiful lake to the north out of which the Jordan tumbled on its way to the sea that knew no life, candied fruits and melons spiced with fragrant herbs, and many others. Groups of dancing girls postured before them between the courses, their lovely bodies almost nude.

Mahlon had become accustomed to the plenitude of food and drink at the feasts of the King during his stay in Moab. He ate and drank steadily, his face becoming more and more flushed from the wine and from his happiness that his beloved plan seemed now to be going into effect. Boaz, however, drank but little. Instead he watched the other guests as if seeking to discern their real thoughts beneath the mask of courtesy, which indeed he was, for he wanted to discover as quickly as possible just why he had been lured to Moab.

From the beginning of the ceremony Hedak and Nebo had not been particularly courteous. As the evening progressed and they emptied goblet after goblet of a sequence of wines, their laughter grew more and more boisterous, their manner more and more openly contemptuous of their guest. The King was already drunk; occasionally the slave at his back had to pick up the wine cup when it fell from his fumbling fingers.

Ruth did not take part in the feast, but directed the slaves in serving the succession of courses that followed one upon the other. And since she was very anxious that this first meeting between the representative of the Israelite tribes and the King of Moab should go well for Mahlon's sake as well as for the benefits of peace between the two countries, she was genuinely relieved when the feast came to an end.

Hedak broached the purpose for which the elaborate entertainment was intended for the first time during the evening when he proposed a toast.

"Let us drink to peace between Moab and Israel! And to our illustrious guest, Boaz."

All glasses were lifted and Zebushar roused enough to mumble, "May we find common ground when we talk together of peace on the morrow."

"To peace!" Mahlon cried, lifting his glass.

"To peace!" Boaz agreed.

From their end of the table Nebo and Hedak joined in. But their enthusiasm had such a false ring that Boaz looked at them keenly for a moment. "To peace!" they chorused heartily.

Zebushar had grown steadily drunker as the evening progressed. He had managed to remain upright until the feast was over, but now the King's head dropped upon his chest and a great snore filled the room.

Hedak gave his sovereign a sharp glance and got to his feet, lifting his cup. "To our guest." It was the customary toast at the end of a feast. "And to Israel."

They drank the toast, but when the King did not interrupt his snoring, Hedak observed with a smile, "The Heavenly Son of Chemosh seems to have taken too much wine. Shall we leave him to his slumbers?"

At the door Mahlon stopped to look back at the figure of the King. Zebushar had slumped almost out of his chair, and the slave behind his chair was holding him by the shoulder to keep him from tumbling bodily to the floor. As Mahlon watched a rigor seemed to grip the pot-bellied figure on the throne.

"The King!" he cried. "Something must be wrong with him."

"He is drunk." Hedak laughed loudly and so did Nebo. "Even kings cannot drink what he did tonight and keep their wits."

"Shouldn't we carry him to his quarters?" Mahlon asked.

"Nebo will attend to that." Hedak turned to his guest. 'Will you accept my apologies for our sovereign, Boaz? His earnest desire for peace seems to have overcome his better judgment tonight."

Boaz looked at the Moabite chief sharply, sensing the undertone of amusement, but as yet unable to fathom its reason. All evening Hedak and his lieutenant had seemed vastly amused by a private joke which they had not shared with the others. "It has been a long evening," he agreed. "You will forgive me if I seek my rest?"

"Of course." Hedak bowed with exaggerated courtesy. "Until tomorrow, then."

Ruth had told Mahlon she would go directly home from the palace, since they did not know how long the feast would continue. As Boaz and Mahlon walked through the streets to the metalsmith shop, the swordsmith was jubilant over the lavishness of the feast and the atmosphere of friendliness which had characterized it. "I never saw Zebushar so drunk before, though," Mahlon admitted. "He would not ordinarily be so discourteous as not to bid a guest farewell."

Boaz shrugged. "If the armies of Moab were as weak as its King. Israel would have little to fear. We are so poor that the women must glean in the fields, lest a single head of barley or wheat is lost, yet enough food was wasted tonight to feed all of Bethlehem."

"When the treaty of peace is signed, our people can sell hides and wool to buy food. And tools of metal will make the reaping more efficient."

"So that less remains for the widows and the poor?"

"When people are prosperous, they give alms. There are no poor and needy."

"I have yet to see such a land," Boaz said. "Even if it exists, I believe people should work for what they get. Still," he admitted, "it might be as you say, if there were no people like Hedak in the world."

"You misjudge him," Mahlon protested. "I am sure he has realized at last that Moab can gain more from peaceful trade than by conquest."

"I saw few omens of peace tonight," Boaz said soberly. "Hedak is too smug and it is obvious that he, not Zebushar, is the real power in Moab."

When they reached the courtyard of the house and shop, Boaz went inside, while Mahlon stopped to inspect the supply of iron to be sure there would be plenty for tomorrow's work. Ruth came from the back of the house as Boaz entered. Since she had been at the palace that evening, she wore the fashionable robe of thin material favored by Moabite women for court wear. One lovely shoulder, as well as both arms, was bare, and her graceful figure was well outlined by the soft folds of her dress.

"Shalom, Boaz," she said courteously, using the Israelite greeting. "Welcome to this house."

"Peace be upon the wife of Mahlon, son of Elimelech the Just." His tone was cold with disapproval and she looked at him with surprise.

"Don't you remember me? From the Meeting Place when Mahlon and his family were coming to Moab?"

"I remember."

"Mahlon tells me you have never married again," she said with a smile, thinking to put him more at ease. "When you are old and lonely, you may be sorry you did not take my advice, Boaz."

"I am sorry now for your husband,' 'he said abruptly.

"Why?"

"Because he has so far forgotten the customs and laws of his people that he allows his wife to go half naked."

Ruth flinched and her hand went involuntarily to her breast, although she was as fully dressed as the women of Moab usually went. "I am not half naked," she cried indignantly. "Women here always dress like this."

"In Israel women are modest, as becomes them," he said severely. "They cover even their faces. Only hussies display themselves in the company of men."

"I seem to remember that your wife's body was seen by another man," Ruth cried, thoroughly angry at the unjustness of the accusation. "And taken by one, too."

The instant the words were spoken she regretted them. For she saw in Boaz's eyes that the years had not really dulled the pain of what had happened back there at the Place of Refuge, when he had found the body of his young wife, Tamar, in the arms of another man. And she understood now why he would feel antagonistic toward her, for she was of the same people as the man who had betrayed him.

Sorry now for her angry retort, Ruth took a quick step toward Boaz and touched his arm. "Forgive me," she pleaded. "I spoke in anger, and it was not fair to remind you."

He shook her hand off roughly, refusing to accept her apology. "You spoke the truth; such is my shame," he said harshly. "No forgiveness is needed." And without looking at her he strode from the room.

"Where is Boaz?" Mahlon asked when he came in a few moments later and found Ruth alone. "We were going to drink a final cup with you."

"We—we quarreled. And he went to his room."

"Quarreled? Over what?"

"He accused me of being half naked, because I dress like the other women of Heshbon."

He smiled. "Boaz is not accustomed to our ways here, Ruth. I remember how different everything seemed to me when we first came to Heshbon." He put his arm around her. "But I like the Moabite dress now, especially on you."

Ruth glanced down at herself and saw how the thin fabric clung to her body. "I suppose I was a shock to Boaz, after the women of Israel. Tomorrow I must ask him to forgive me."

"For being beautiful enough to turn any man's head?" he asked fondly.

"I was very rude, Mahlon. When Boaz accused me of being half naked, I reminded him that his wife's body had been seen and taken by another man, a Moabite."

"Boaz still distrusts all Moabites because of Tamar," Mahlon agreed. "I realized that as soon as I met him again."

"But why would I say a thing like that?" Ruth asked. "I never hurt people, if I can possibly help it. But I wanted to hurt Boaz."

"You two are like flint and metal," he said, smiling. "Whenever you come together, sparks seem to fly. But you will learn to like Boaz when you know him better, Ruth, I am sure of that. He is fine and sincere. And he would give up his life for Israel gladly, if he thought it would make our people safe."

"You should be very happy that the peace conference got off to such a fine start tonight," Ruth said giving him a quick embrace. "Now we had better go to bed. You and Boaz will be busy tomorrow at the peace conference."

Mahlon stretched out on the coach with his head on a pillow, watching Ruth as she sat before her dressing table, brushing the lustrous masses of her hair with an ivory-handled brush that had come from Egypt. "I am happier than I've been since the night we were betrothed on the hillside, Ruth. Who knows? This may be the beginning of a long era of peace and prosperity for both Israel and Moab."

"I am glad, Mahlon. Glad for you and for Israel."

"Have you felt any stirrings of life yet?" he asked casually.

Ruth laughed. "Don't be so impatient. I wouldn't know for another month at least. But I do hope to bear your child," she rushed on happily. "A man-child who will look just like you and be as good as you are."

"And I would be content with a girl," Mahlon said. "If

she had her mother's beauty and spirit." He got up and went to listen at the window.

"What do you hear?" Ruth asked.

"It sounded like people shouting, but this is not a feast day and there is no celebration that I know of."

Ruth moved to the window and stood beside him. The noise was much louder now and its nature could no longer be doubted. A large crowd of people was moving through the city, shouting something they could not yet understand. And since the sound grew steadily louder they could not doubt that the crowd was moving toward them.

While Ruth and Mahlon watched at the window, torches appeared in the street and the noise of the crowd rose to a roar. Then the jangle of military harness could be distinguished and the sound of horses' hoofs ringing upon the stones.

"They are coming here," Ruth said quickly. "Oh, Mahlon, I am afraid."

"Why? We have done nothing." He had taken off his robe when he lay down and wore only the loincloth that the men of Heshbon used under their robes and also as a sleeping garment. Now he reached for his robe, but before he could gird it about him, the sound of peremptory knocking came from the front of the house.

"I am coming," Mahlon shouted, opening the door. "Put on your robe, Ruth," he said hurriedly. "I don't know what this means."

Before Mahlon could reach the door, a voice he recognized as that of Nebo, Hedak's chief lieutenant, shouted, "Open up in the name of Hedak, Prince Regent of Moab."

"Prince Regent!" The color drained from Ruth's cheeks. "Then the King is——"

"Zebushar is dead!" Nebo shouted. "Long live Akton, King of Moab, and Hedak, Prince Regent."

With trembling fingers Mahlon unbarred the door and opened it. Nebo strode in, followed by two guards with drawn swords. "Where is Boaz, swordsmith?" he demanded.

"Wha-what has happened?" Mahlon asked.

"Are you deaf? Zebushar is dead. His son Akton reigns in his stead with Prince Hedak as Regent."

"Dead? But how? We left the King only a short time ago."

"Poisoned. While he sat at the table tonight." Nebo turned to the guards. "Search the house. The Israelite must not escape."

"Why do you seek Boaz?" Mahlon was still stunned by the news that the King was dead.

"He has been here ever since the dinner was over," Ruth added.

Just then the door of Boaz's room opened. He was a commanding figure, even in this hurly-burly. "Who called for me?" he asked.

"Search the room," Nebo ordered one of the guards. "The Israelite has not yet had time to rid himself of the poison he used to kill Zebushar."

"Poison?" Boaz said sharply. "What mummery is this, Nebo?"

"Boaz could not have poisoned the King," Mahlon protested. "You were with us this evening, Nebo. He handled no wine or food."

Nebo shrugged contemptuously. "Search the room," he commanded the soldiers. "Make no move to escape, Boaz, or I will cut you down."

Boaz smiled grimly. "Since Hedak has gone to so much trouble to get rid of the King and me at one time, your man will no doubt find the poison you seek. . . ."

"Then you admit it," Nebo started to say, but Boaz stared him down.

"In his own pocket." He completed the sentence. "Where it was all the time."

The soldier who had been sent to search Boaz's room rushed out with a show of triumph holding a small vial in his hand. It was half filled with a green fluid.

"The poison!" Nebo cried. "Boaz stands convicted of murdering the King! Seize him!"

"Keep your hands from me, Moabite dogs," Boaz said curtly. "Would I have any chance to escape with such a well-organized plot against me?"

"Kill the Israelite!" The crowd outside began to shout as word was passed quickly back to them that the poison had been found. "Kill the murderer of Zebushar!"

"Tell your master, Hedak, the people are calling for him," Boaz said contemptuously to Nebo. "And get on with this farce." The guards surrounded him then and he was marched from the house.

When the room was clear, Mahlon stood staring dumbly at the doorway, as if unable yet to comprehend the swift unraveling of what had undoubtedly been a carefully planned plot. "Zebushar tricked me," he mumbled finally. "I believed him sincere in wanting peace."

"It isn't your fault, Mahlon." Ruth tried to comfort him. "Hedak used your desire for peace to remove Israel's leader and gain control of Moab."

"But there will be no treaty now," Mahlon said hopelessly, "and the swords from my forges will cut down my own people."

"You acted in good faith, so none of the guilt is yours." She seized his shoulders and shook him, trying to bring him out of the trancelike state. "Get control of yourself, Mahlon," she urged desperately. "We must think of some way to get Boaz out of Hedak's hands and back to Israel."

But Mahlon only dropped to the couch, holding his head between his hands. "Boaz trusted me and I let him be betrayed," he mumbled. "The Most High is punishing me for my sins in making the swords."

It was over an hour before Ruth could persuade Mahlon to lie down. And long after he was asleep, she lay wide-eyed in the darkness trying to think of some way by which Boaz might still be saved. But it seemed utterly hopeless, for the whole strength of Hedak was against them. And Hedak was now King of Moab in everything but the name.

vi.

Heralds rode through the wildly excited city the next morning, announcing that during the ceremony of the new King's coronation, three days later, the Israelite Boaz, who had murdered Akton's earthly father, would be consigned to the fires of Chemosh as a sacrifice. Having taken the first step in his long-planned campaign to conquer Israel and move on to the Great Sea, by ridding himself of Boaz and Zebushar at one stroke, Hedak's second, and logical, move was to inflame the people against Israel, by emphasizing the alleged guilt of Boaz for the death of the King. That he was himself guilty of the actual murder made no difference.

Ever since Boaz had been taken away, Mahlon had been in a half stupor, sitting or lying down in his room, his face expressionless except when tears rolled down his cheeks. When he spoke, it was in a monotone, and the words were always the same: "My swords will destroy Boaz and Israel. Have mercy upon me, O God, for my sins."

At first Ruth tried to reason with her husband, pleading with him to arouse himself and help her devise some plan to free his friend. But all her entreaties had no effect. Mahlon had withdrawn to a place deep within himself, where no one else could reach him. She had no choice, therefore, save to try and help Boaz herself in whatever way she could devise.

Attempts to visit the Israelite leader in prison were of no avail, for Hedak had secreted him in the dungeons beneath the temple. Akton was a mere boy and long subservient to Hedak's will, so no help was possible from the new King.

The rest of the family were too stunned by the sudden tragedy of Boaz's betrayal to be of any help. Chilion had always followed Mahlon's leadership, and now that his brother was in a daze both he and Orpah turned to Ruth for guidance. Her heart went out to Mahlon in his disappointment and his obsession with guilt for what seemed inevitable death for Boaz, but there was nothing she could do to help him, it seemed.

When Chilion and Orpah could give her no help, Ruth turned to Naomi, but her mother-in-law could suggest nothing that might save Boaz.

"We can't sit by and see him burned to death in the fire," Ruth cried. "Boaz came to Heshbon because he trusted Mahlon; we must do everything we can to save him."

"Can we open prison gates?" Naomi asked quietly. "Or change the mind of Hedak? Sometimes we can only trust in God to do what seems best, Ruth."

"Would He want us to fold our hands? I have heard you tell how the children of Israel were freed from Egypt, Naomi. But it was Moses' rod that struck the stone to bring water, and it was Joshua's trumpets that sounded against the walls of Jericho. We must do something ourselves."

"What?" Chilion asked. "'Tell me what to do and I will do it, Ruth."

She put her head in her hands. "I don't know," she admitted. "Perhaps, when the time comes, God will show us the way to help Boaz. Until then. . . ."

vii.

Noami was kneeling before the simple altar in the court-yard where she and her sons worshiped, when Ruth came out of the house shortly after darkness had fallen on the night of the coronation ceremony. Her face was drawn with worry and fatigue.

"Mahlon is asleep," she said. "I think it will be safe for me to go now."

"I will watch him," Naomi promised.

"If only there were some hope," Ruth said dejectedly. "It hardly seems worth-while to go to the coronation ceremony."

"We cannot understand the purpose of the Most High, Ruth. We can only obey His voice when He calls us, and do what He commands."

"If only some miracle would free Boaz. Once clear of the city, he might be able to make his way back to Bethlehem through the mountains."

"Perhaps God will show you the way," Naomi said simply. "I will stay here and pray that He does."

Ruth bent to kiss her mother-in-law, then went quickly out through the courtyard toward the street leading to the great temple square, leaving Naomi to pray before the altar to the God whose favor alone, it seemed, could save Boaz and Israel from Hedak.

Occupied with her prayer, Naomi did not realize that Mahlon was awake until she heard the door open and saw him standing there. "Wh-where is Ruth?" he asked dazedly. "I thought I heard her talking out here just now."

"She had something to do, my son." Naomi went to him and put her arm around his shoulders. "Come and lie down again. You have been ill and need rest."

"I thought I heard Ruth say something about Boaz," he mumbled.

"Ruth went into the city on an errand." Naomi assured him. "She will be back soon."

Mahlon let himself be guided back to his room. "Help Boaz," he mumbled. "Must help Boaz."

"Boaz will be all right." Naomi said reasuringly. "Ruth will—" She stopped, aghast at having almost blurted out the truth.

"Has Ruth gone to help him?"

Naomi hesitated. It went against her deeply grounded religious beliefs to lie. "She went to the temple," she admitted finally. "We will find out what happened when she returns."

Mahlon looked at her for a moment, as if he did not believe her. Then his shoulders dropped hopelessly and he seemed to be deep in a stupor once more. "Try to lie down and rest, my son," Naomi pleaded. "All this has been a great shock to you, but God will surely protect Israel and Boaz."

Under the soothing pressure of her hands and her reassurance Mahlon grew quiet. When she was satisfied that he was asleep, Naomi left the room. But hardly was she outside when he sat up again. He seemed to have thrown off his lethargy, for the moment at least, and his movements showed more purpose than they had for several days. Stealthily he slipped from the room and opened the door to the inner court. He was hidden from Noami's view as he stepped into the court and she had no way of knowing that he was not sound asleep on the couch where she had left him.

Quickly Mahlon went to a great chest at one side of the inner court and opened it. Rack on rack of newly finished swords were inside, gleaming like silver in the moonlight. From among them he selected two polished blades, thrusting them beneath his robe. No one in the household saw him as he crossed the court with a stealthy tread to where a great tree towered over the walls, and climbed quickly up into its branches. Only a faint thud sounded when he landed on the grass outside the wall and disappeared into the shadows toward the temple.

There was naturally a great deal of excitement in Heshbon over the crowning of the new King, and it was heightened by the news that the culmination of the day-long event would be the casting of the Israelite Boaz, who had poisoned the young King's father, into the fiery maw of Chemosh. Long before darkness fell thousands had gathered in the great open square between the two temples, in spite of a black thundercloud that had hung over the city for several hours, and occasional light gusts of rain. A roaring fire burned in the great iron belly of the giant image of Chemosh that stood to one side of the square, and the metal glowed brightly from the heat. Like all important ceremonies, the coronation was to be held in the open air.

Ruth did not try to push through the crowd, but made her way back of the temple and entered it from the garden. She was familiar with the maze of passages beneath the building and soon came out upon a landing near the altar platform where the coronation and the sacrifice would take place. Orpah and Chilion were waiting, for both of the women knew the temple well from their service as handmaidens of Chemosh before their marriage.

"We thought you would never come," Orpah whispered. "They are almost ready to crown Akton."

"I had trouble getting Mahlon to go to sleep," Ruth explained.

"More than once lately I've wondered if he doesn't know more of what is happening than we think he does," Orpah said. "Maybe he suspects why you left the house."

"He was sound asleep," Ruth assured her. "And Naomi is watching him. Have you noticed anything that might help us?"

Both Orpah and Chilion shook their heads. "It is hopeless," Orpah said. "You can see how they have stoked the fires. The instant the flames touch his body Boaz will be dead."

"At least God will be merciful to him, then." Ruth looked about her. The whole colorful panorama of pagan ritual was being enacted tonight in honor of the new Heavenly Son of Chemosh, the title Akton would henceforth bear. On the open space of the altar platform before the god a huge throne had been set up, larger and more luxurious even than that from which Zebushar had ruled Moab for so many years.

A chorus of dancing girls, forming a riot of color in their bright diaphanous costumes, was posturing before the throne, while Akton looked on eagerly. Slender and boyish, the new King was almost dwarfed by the magni-

ficence of the throne and its appurtenances. His head
seemed far too small to support the great jeweled crown
on a pedestal beside the throne, awaiting the final act of
the coronation ceremony. Scores of the nobility and the
richer citizens of Heshbon lounged on divans at the feet
of the new King, and a double row of guards stretched to
either side of him, each in full military equipment, with
drawn swords. Akton might be technically the King but
it was quite obvious that he was also a prisoner of Hedak's
army.

Beside the royal throne was another. Only slightly less
magnificent than that of the young King, it was occupied
by Hedak. The Moabite chief was dressed in a rich robe
chased with an intricate pattern of gold and silver em-
broidery. A necklace of heavy gold links hung from his
neck, and jeweled bracelets were piled upon his muscular
arms. He had put off the helmet of a soldier for tonight
and wore a band of silk about his dark hair instead, set
thickly with jewels.

Robed in all the barbaric trappings of his office, the
high priest of Chemosh stood on the other side of the boy
King, his hands hidden in the flowing sleeves of his brocaded robe. A tall conical cap was upon his head, thickly
crusted with jewels set in the bull's-head pattern that was
the eternal symbol of the god of Moab and the lesser
Baals that served the neighboring tribes as deities. As the
music rose in a crashing beat and the dancing girls prostrated themselves before the boy King, the high priest
raised his hand and the clang of a mighty cymbal, struck
with a bronze hammer, filled the room.

While the sound died away, the girls scampered from
the platform, disappearing through doors on either side
of the huge image of the god. A great bed of coals completely filled the iron maw of Chemosh and the heat of
the flames swept out over the crowd, bringing perspiration
to the faces of those sitting close to the great idol.

"Where is Boaz?" Orpah asked in a whisper. "I have
seen nothing of him."

"They must be holding him just outside the altar platform," Ruth said. "Hedak likes to be dramatic. He will
probably wait and bring Boaz in at the last moment."

Once again the high priest raised his hand and the clang
of the great cymbal filled the temple. A hush fell over the
audience as he held out his hand to the boy on the throne.

Akton rose, a satisfied smile upon his thin, vulpine features. The stories of his cruelties both to servants and animals had caused much comment, even in Heshbon, where such things were commonplace. This weak and vicious child of a king would fit easily into Hedak's scheme of things. The leader of the Moabite army had laid his plans well, plotting so as to be rid of the main obstacle to the conquest of Israel, Boaz, and, at the same time, remove Zebushar, who had begun to listen to the cries of the people against taxation and war.

Led by the high priest, the King-to-be stepped down from the throne and walked across the altar platform to the feet of the giant image of Chemosh. Hedak lifted the jeweled crown from the small table, and followed just behind Akton and the priest carrying it before him upon a brocaded pillow.

Again the great cymbal boomed out and the boy knelt before the image and the glowing furnace in the belly of the god.

"Akton, son of Zebushar, bows before thee, O Mighty God of Moab, asking to receive his father's crown," the priest intoned. And when the great cymbal sounded once more, the priest took the crown from Hedak and lowered it to Akton's head as he knelt there, looking small, insignificant, and far from kingly in his robes.

As the crown touched the boy's head, Hedak drew his sword and shouted, "Hail Akton, Heavenly Son of Chemosh and Ruler of Moab! Hail the King!"

The crowd joined in the salutation with a mighty roar. As their shouting died away, Nebo's voice was lifted, obviously by prearrangement, in another great cry of "Hail Hedak! Prince Regent of Moab, Protector of the People!"

Once again thunderous applause came from the people who, a few days before, had been cursing Hedak because of the taxes imposed upon them to support his vast military machine. This, however, was a night for pageantry and blood lust, after which there would be wine for everyone and an unrestrained orgy in honor of the crowning of the new King. In the face of such an inviting prospect previous grievances were forgotten for the moment.

Akton turned to face the people, looking oddly topheavy with the crown upon his head. He lifted his arms, and piped in a thin boyish voice, "Let joy be unrestrained this night. Wine will be poured from the royal stores for all the people."

Another roar of approval went up from the crowd. "Hail to Akton!" they shouted. "Heavenly Son of Chemosh and King of Moab! Hail to Akton!"

When the acclaiming voices died away enough for him to be heard, the King announced in tones shrill with expectancy and excitement. "My Heavenly Father demands a human sacrifice this night, that my reign may be long and profitable. Bring the Israelite prisoner, Boaz, to the altar!"

Ruth found that she was trembling from the tension of the moment, although she still had no idea how she might help Boaz. In fact, here with the crowd around them and the fires leaping in the iron belly of the image, as if anticipating the gift that would soon be tossed to them, she could see no hope any more.

"Ruth," Orpah whispered, "I am afraid."

"So am I," Ruth admitted. Chilion's round face was pale and his forehead was wet from the tension of the moment.

"What are you going to do?" Orpah asked.

Ruth shook her head. "I don't know," she admitted. "We can only wait."

As four burly guards led Boaz out upon the platform before the boy King and the great idol with its glowing furnace, the square rocked with the cries of the people for the blood of the man they had hailed a few days before as an emissary of peace. And as if the very elements concurred in this homage to a new King, a rumble of thunder came from the dark clouds that had hung low over the square for the past hour or more.

Boaz carried himself with courage and an obvious determination not to cringe at the horrible and painful death that lay before him. Only a loincloth covered his magnificent body, but as he stood proudly before the throne he was a far more regal figure than the puny youth who had been elevated to kingship by his father's murder. Akton seemed to realize this, for he screamed angrily, "Kneel, Israelite! Kneel before the God Chemosh and his Heavenly Son!"

Boaz stared contemptuously at the puny figure on the throne, ignoring the command. "The men of Israel bow to none save the Most High God," he said in a loud clear voice. "Be sure He will seek you out, Akton, and strike you down for the treachery of Moab and the poisoning of your father."

A startled look came momentarily into Akton's eyes. "You murdered my father as you sat at the table with him! What greater treachery could there be?"

Boaz turned accusing eyes upon Hedak, who stood beside the King. "Ask Prince Hedak that question," he suggested. "Ask him who really poisoned Zebushar."

Involuntarily Akton turned to the Regent. For a brief moment his guilt showed in Hedak's face, but he recovered himself quickly. "It is a lie!" he snapped. "The Israelite lies to cover his guilt."

"Let us settle who tells the truth, as fighting men should, then," Boaz challenged. "I will fight Prince Hedak with swords, daggers, or both. If I win, I go free. If I lose, you may do with me as you will."

Shouts of approval came from the crowd. A battle to the death between the champions of Moab and Israel would be far more than they had expected.

It was no part of Hedak's plans, however, to risk his life in this hour of triumph by fighting Boaz. He leaned over and spoke urgently to Akton. When the hubbub that arose over the challenge died away, the King announced, "It is not my will that my ministers do battle with poisoners and murderers. Let the Israelite dog be branded first with the mark of Chemosh, and then sacrificed in the flames to please my Heavenly Father."

Nebo barked a command to the guards, who led Boaz across the open space of the platform to a position just in front of the King. A brazier burned here, the coals glowing only a little more brightly than the branding iron with the circle of Chemosh at the end that lay in the coals. Two of the guards seized Boaz by the arms and forced him to his knees.

Nebo lifted the iron from the coals. "Those Chemosh accepts as a sacrifice," he announced, "he first brands with the holy mark."

"I—I can't look," Orpah whimpered.

Ruth's throat was tight with horror and with pity for Boaz, but she could not take her eyes away from the barbaric scene before her; the nearly naked body of Boaz with sweat glistening upon his torso; the avid look of expectation on the faces of the King, Hedak, and most of the crowd; and finally, the glowing iron of the brand.

Boaz did not flinch as the glowing brand was lowered to his back, although the heat seared his skin even before the hot metal touched it. There was a horrible hissing sound as the iron turned the sweat on his skin to steam and went on to burn into the very flesh. Watching Boaz, Ruth saw perspiration suddenly stand out on his forehead. He did not move or cry out in any way, however, although the pain must have been agonizing.

Boaz spoke as the iron was removed from his flesh. His voice, rumbling through the square, was like the pronouncement of doom. "In the name of the Most High God." It was both prayer and promise. "I swear to avenge this act of treachery and to bring this place to dust."

For an instant there was absolute silence, then Hedak shouted. "Smite down the blasphemer, O Mighty Chemosh! Let him be thrown to the flames!"

The crowd and the King took up the cry, but Boaz's voice rose above them, silencing them once more. His eyes were lifted to Heaven, where the dark, threatening thunderheads massed like a great army marching into battle, and his arms were lifted in supplication.

"God of Isaac and Jacob!" he shouted his prayer to the sky. "As Thou didst in the days of old, give a sign to this heathen people that Moab and their false god shall one day crumble before Thee."

A hush fell over the crowd. Watching Boaz as he defied not only Moab, but its god, in the name of the diety he worshiped, Ruth could not help feeling a surge of pride. Suddenly she was conscious of a loud drumming sound and for an instant thought that the armies of the God of Israel must indeed be marching to rescue Boaz. Then a patter of rain struck his face and the droplets rolled down his face, fulfilling the promise of the clouds that had hung over the assemblage for several hours.

A moan of fear went up from the crowd as a torrent of rain and hail pelted downward upon them, seemingly an answer to Boaz's prayer, as indeed it may have been.

One moment the flames were roaring in the furnace that made up the belly of the great idol, as if eager to appease their hunger with the human body about to be thrown to them as a sacrifice. The next, a torrent of water rolled across the broad head and shoulders of the image as the clouds seemed to open above the square, deluging the crowd and sluicing down to pour into the open furnace. A sudden roar of water turning to steam upon the hot iron drowned out even the drumming of the rain, and a cloud of scalding vapor rolled across the platform upon the King and his court, hiding them from view to Ruth, who stood on the landing at a slightly higher level, and sweeping on to cover the front of the crowd.

When the hot vapor touched his body, Akton screamed with terror and leaped from his throne, running awkwardly across the altar platform in his royal robes, while the jeweled crown tumbled to the stones. He leaped from the platform into the crowd, gibbering with terror engendered by the steam and the terrible roaring of the water upon the hot metal.

Again the lightning flashed and thunder rocked the square while the rain and hail seemed to redouble their furious attack upon the God of Moab. The crowd had been momentarily stunned into immobility by the seeming answer of the Israelite God to Boaz's dramatic appeal. But the King's scream of terror released them. As the steam continued to roll in a suffocating cloud from the fiery maw of Chemosh, a great cry of fear rose from the crowd and they began fighting among themselves to get away from what seemed certain destruction under the fury of Boaz's God.

Ruth was the first to see in this awe-inspiring event an opportunity to save Boaz. If she could only convince the crowd that the Israelite God had indeed intervened to save Boaz's life, there might be a chance to save him during the confusion that reigned everywhere.

"Yahveh is greater than Chemosh!" she shouted. "The Israelite God has answered Boaz! Release him before we are destroyed!"

Grasping desperately at anything that promised to appease the wrath of Yahveh, the crowd instantly took up the cry. Among them could be heard the voice of Akton shouting shrilly, "Release the Israelite! Release the Israelite or we are lost!"

Ruth did not wait to see the effect of her stratagem. Turning to Orpah and Chilion, she said quickly, "I will take Boaz through the passages beneath the temple and let him out of the city through the Priests' Gate."

"What can we do?" Orpah asked.

"Go home and remain there. You know nothing of this."

"But, Ruth——"

She was gone before Orpah could finish, running lightly down the steps to the altar platform. As she ran, she heard the crowd take up the cry that she had begun, shouting. "Release the Israelite! Free him or we are lost!"

A cloud of steam covered the altar platform like a white blanket, but Ruth plunged into it without hesitation. Half blinded by the hot vapor, she sprinted on, bumping into milling bodies, moving almost by instinct toward the spot where she had last seen Boaz. Hands reached out to grasp at her from the cloud, but she twisted away from them, and kept going.

The layer of steam was thinning rapidly over the altar platform, where water cascading down from the great head and shoulders of the god had already overrun the iron furnace, putting out the flames. In the haze Ruth made out Boaz's tall form and seized his hand. "Hurry!" she cried. "We must lose no time."

He stopped to peer at her through the steam, calmer by far than she was, as if he had been confident that just this would happen in answer to his plea.

"It is Ruth!" she said. "Hurry before they realize what happened."

"The King ordered my release. I heard him shout it just now."

"Hedak does not believe in gods or miracles," she cried. "As soon as he can see, he will be coming after us."

Boaz hesitated no longer, but followed as she ran across the platform to a door which she knew from her experience as a temple handmaiden led into one of the dressing rooms used by the dancers. They burst into a room filled with girls in various stages of undress and, amidst screams of surprise and excitement, plunged on through and down a flight of steps.

Now they were in an empty passage and could slacken their pace a little. Both were panting from running and from the excitement of their dramatic dash for freedom.

"Why are you doing this, Ruth?" Boaz asked. "What happens to me is no concern of yours."

"I am Mahlon's wife," she reminded him. "He brought you here with a letter guaranteeing your safety, so it is my duty to save you if I can."

"Where is Mahlon?"

"He was overcome by the shock of what happened to you," she explained. They were moving rapidly through the corridors beneath the temple, speaking in snatches as they ran. "He sits and stares at the wall, weeping and asking God to forgive him for making swords and letting you be taken by Hedak."

As they were approaching a cross corridor Ruth heard the sound of men talking, and drew Boaz against the wall, pressing herself against him. "It is the temple guards," she whispered. "Stay close to the wall and they may not see you."

Flattened against the wall a few feet back of the inter-section, they might have escaped detention had not one of the pair of guards happened to turn his head as he crossed the corridor that Ruth and Boaz were in. "By Chemosh!" he said. "What are these two doing down here?" He had not yet recognized Boaz behind Ruth.

"We are looking for an empty room," Ruth said, slurring the words as if she were drunk.

"Too bad you already have a man." The second guard laughed. "Many rooms will be occupied tonight."

"From the looks of things," the first guard agreed, "these two cannot find one soon enough."

The guards were past the intersection, when one of them suddenly turned. "That man looks familiar!" He started to draw his sword. "It is the Israelite prisoner!"

Boaz's muscles had tensed at the first words of the guard. He thrust Ruth aside now and launched his body at the two Moabites like a battering ram. The one who had recognized Boaz did not have time to draw his sword and the other was so taken by surprise that Boaz bowled him over, smashing his head against the wall in a stunning blow that left him limp and helpless.

The first guard was carried off his feet too, but he managed to roll with the thrust of Boaz's body, lessening its effect. There was no room in the corridor to use the point of his spear, but the heavy shaft was almost as effective as a bludgeon. The handle splintered across Boaz's skull as the guard swung it, and the Israelite chief fell heavily, pinning down his assailant with the sheer inert weight of his body.

The handle of the spear fell almost at Ruth's feet and without hesitation she stooped and picked it up. The guard was already pushing Boaz's body aside, so as to get to his feet and finish him, when Ruth swung the wooden bludgeon with all her strength. Her aim was true and the soldier sank back upon the floor, unconscious.

viii.

On the landing where Ruth had left them Chilion and Orpah could not drag themselves away immediately from the pandemonium still raging in the square. The steam was clearing away a little, but in a wild, unreasoning panic at the wrath of the Israelite God, which they thought had been visited upon them because of Boaz, the Moabites were fighting among themselves. Although momentarily astounded by the unexpected turn of events, Hedak quickly recovered and began to fight his way from the platform to the front of the crowd, where Akton cowered, his royal robes almost torn from his body, and his jeweled crown long since kicked into a corner.

"Come, Orpah," Chilion urged. "Ruth told us to leave at once."

"Where is Ruth?"

Chilion turned and saw his brother in the doorway of the anteroom with a naked sword in his hand. "She told us you were asleep, Mahlon," he cried. "How did you get out of the house without Mother seeing you?"

"Where is Ruth? And Boaz?" Mahlon demanded, his face set and grim.

"She is taking him through the passages to the Priests' Gate," Orpah said. "But she told us not to follow her." Mahlon turned as if he not heard. "Wait, Mahlon!" Chilion cried, catching at his brother's sleeve. "Boaz is free and Ruth will be able to smuggle him from the city without your getting involved."

But Mahlon jerked his sleeve loose and plunged from the room. Chilion hesitated momentarily, then said quickly to Orpah, "Hurry back to the house, dear. I am going after him."

"But, Chilion . . ."

"He is still in a trance. If he meets the guards in the passages under the temple, he may try to fight. And Mahlon is no swordsman."

"Neither are you."

"He may listen to reason if I can get to him and take the sword. At least I can try." Leaving Orpah alone, Chilion followed his brother from the room.

Cursing angrily, Hedak was knocking people right and left as he plowed through the crowd to where Akton cowered in terror. His momentary shock at the seemingly miraculous intervention in Boaz's behalf was now receding. And, contemptuous as he was of gods, the conviction was rapidly crystallizing in Hedak's mind that other than supernatural forces had brought about the dramatic termination of his plans for sacrificing Boaz and whipping the people up to such a frenzy of hate for Israel that they would urge him to make war.

Hedak had barely reached Akton when Nebo appeared at his elbow.

"Where is Boaz?" Hedak demanded.

"When the King ordered his release," Nebo said, "the guards who were holding him ran. I thought I saw a woman with him, but there was so much steam that I could see nothing else."

"It must have been Mahlon's wife, Ruth," Hedak said instantly. "She knows the temple like her own house and would be clever enough to take advantage of this confusion."

"Where could they go? The people are blocking the whole square. Nobody could get through that mob out there without being trampled to death."

"She must be taking him through the passages beneath the temple. The gates are open tonight to let the people out after the coronation. If they get out into the city, Boaz could walk right through them."

Several guards had appeared behind Nebo. "Run through the temple to the city gates," Hedak directed one of them. "Let no one out until Boaz is found." He turned to Nebo and the other guards. "Come with me," he ordered. "We'll see if Boaz's god can still save him from our swords."

Hedak and Nebo had barely entered the maze of corridors beneath the temple when they saw Mahlon trotting ahead of them, with Chilion in pursuit. Nebo lifted his spear to throw it, but Hedak slapped his hand down.

"Hold your weapon," he ordered. "They may lead us to Ruth and Boaz."

Mahlon did not even notice the noise in the corridor behind them made by Hedak, Nebo, and the guards. But Chilion was nearer and heard the rattle of weapons. He glanced back and when he saw the determined faces of the pursuers, his face blanched with fear. "Mahlon!" he shouted frantically to his brother. "Hedak is behind us. Drop your sword."

Mahlon seemed not to hear, however, and plunged on, so Chilion had no choice but to follow, with Hedak, Nebo, and the guards pursuing them both.

Boaz regained consciousness almost at once; he was only slightly stunned by the guard's blow. He looked at the unconscious guards and back to Ruth.

"The spear handle fell at my feet," she said a little tremulously, for it was the first time she had ever wielded a weapon against another human being. "Did—did I hit him too hard?"

"They would have killed us," Boaz said grimly. "Which way do we go now?"

"A passage leads from the end of this main corridor to the garden," Ruth said. "From there we can reach the city wall."

Ruth and Boaz were almost to the end of the corridor when Mahlon suddenly entered it at the end from which they had come. He still carried the sword and at the sight of Boaz and Ruth he stopped, as if uncertain just what to do now. Chilion overtook him. "Hurry, Mahlon," he said. "Drop your sword and we can still escape."

This was the scene that met Hedak's eyes when he and Nebo entered the long corridor with the guards behind them: Ruth and Boaz were far ahead, near the other end, with Mahlon and Chilion less than halfway down the passage, which stretched for several hundred feet. Ruth and Boaz turned the far end of the corridor and disappeared without knowing they were followed.

Chilion saw the Moabites behind them. "Drop your sword," he begged his brother again. "Hedak is almost upon us."

The connection between Hedak's name and the threat to Ruth and Boaz finally sent a ray of logical thought through the semistupor which had gripped Mahlon these last few days. There was no lack of purpose in his face now as he turned to meet the Moabites rushing down the corridor toward him.

"Don't fight them, Mahlon," Chilion begged, knowing how futile it was for him to stand against swordsmen like Hedak and Nebo. But Mahlon did not listen, and Chilion had no choice except to stay beside his brother and face the attackers, even though unarmed. It was then that he saw the second sword under Mahlon's robe and reached over to draw it out.

Startled by this unexpected complication, when his quarry seemed almost within his grasp, Hedak drew up short some ten feet from the two Israelites. "Out of the way, dogs," he snapped, "or you will be killed."

"A sword for the Lord," Mahlon cried, brandishing his weapon, his eyes suddenly glowing feverishly.

Hedak wasted no more time. "Cut him down," he ordered the guards, and leaped aside so they could plunge past to attack the two Israelites.

Neither of the metalsmiths was a swordsman. But the fanatic fire that had burned suddenly in Mahlon's eyes at the sight of Hedak and the guards gave his thrusts an urgency that offset momentarily the skill of the guards. The first man spitted himself upon Mahlon's weapon. When the others drew back, Hedak shouted angrily, "Kill him, or die yourselves," and pushed them forward.

The second wave attacked, two abreast, in the corridor. But now some of the fire that burned in Mahlon seized the usually quiet Chilion, and he ranged himself beside his brother. Sword in hand, he too began to engage the guards. There was no great room for any real display of skill in the narrow space and so their untrained thrusts were almost as effective as the trained sword arms of the soldiers.

Unable to get past the two defenders, and knowing that Ruth and Boaz might be escaping, Hedak raged at the guards, trying to drive them against the swords of the Israelite brothers battling in the corridor. Nebo, however, was more practical. He drew his dagger, a long, thin blade with a heavy handle. Holding it by the point, he sighted carefully at Chilion's broad chest.

The opening Nebo sought came a moment later when the guard who was engaging Chilion in combat stepped back after a brisk thrust and parry. He flipped the knife expertly and the long thin blade of the dagger shot like an arrow driven from a bow toward its target. Chilion saw it the instant before it struck, but could do nothing to divert its course. One moment the weapon was singing through the air; the next, the point found his breast, sinking to the hilt.

Death came almost as soon as the blade struck Chilion's heart. His sword clattered to the floor and, his hands clutching in dying agony at the blade which had taken his life, the younger brother sank to the floor at Mahlon's feet.

"Chilion!" Mahlon cried. Forgetting everything else in a paroxysm of grief, he dropped his sword and knelt to take his brother's body in his arms.

Hedak shouted a triumphant command to the guards and the Moabites rushed over them both toward where Boaz and Ruth had disappeared around the corner at the end of the corridor. Hedak paused only long enough to pick up Mahlon's sword and thrust it into the breast of the man whose skilled hands had forged the sharp steel.

Ruth felt a surge of relief when she and Boaz came to a great door that barred the way. As she had expected, it was not locked, for the priests used the garden a great deal. When both of them put their weight against it, the door creaked open, letting them through. It took only seconds to push it shut again and lock it.

The cool air of the temple garden struck their faces and they leaned, panting, against the door, but they stiffened when the sound of voices came to them through it.

"Up the stairs there," they heard Nebo cry, and knew that he was pointing to a flight of stairs that led upward at the end of the corridor to the levels above. "They must have gone up into the temple itself."

Hedak's voice added jubilantly, "They cannot escape us now." Then the diminishing sound of footsteps and rattling harness told them their pursuers had raced up the steps, sure now that they were almost on their prey.

Ruth took a deep breath. "I thought we were lost for a moment," she admitted.

"The Lord led them another way," Boaz said confidently. "He does ont intend for me to die in Moab."

"Then we must be going on," Ruth said practically. "There is a secret gate at the back of the garden. Only the priests and the temple attendants know of it."

"Ram was right. I once heard him say that some claimed there was a secret gate into Heshbon connected with the temple."

"Who is Ram?"

"One of my men. He lived for many years in Moab and sometimes serves me as a spy. Joseph, my lieutenant, planned to come to Heshbon by way of a passage over the mountains that Ram knows of and wait for me in the caves outside the city."

"Then they can guide you back the same way," Ruth said quickly. The weakest link in her plan had been how to get Boaz safely back to the frontier of Israel. Now that it was solved, she felt a flood of relief.

Boaz shook his head. "I was afraid for them to risk their lives and ordered them not to come."

"Won't your army try to rescue you if you don't return?"

"I expected this to be a trap, so I decided that no one but myself must risk coming to Heshbon. If I am not back in a few days, Eliab and Joseph will return to Bethlehem and raise an army to defend us."

"Would Israel—your army—have a chance?"

"If we can fight in the mountain passes," Boaz said grimly, "our spears are better weapons than swords. Even then the odds are against us," he admitted, "but the Lord saved me tonight. He will fight for us when the time comes."

Ruth shivered a little. "So much fighting. Why can't men want peace?"

"Perhaps they will. When they learn to live by the laws of God and stop making rules of their own, designed to benefit one man more than another."

They had been moving through the temple garden while they were talking and now they came to the wall of the city itself, towering above them. Ruth led the way confidently, however. At the end of a narrow path she stopped before a heavy door so carefully built into the wall that it hardly seemed a door at all but a portion of the wall. There was no handle of any kind and no lock.

Ruth stood on her toes and grasped a small image of

Chemosh located high up on the wall. She tried to turn it, but the image would not budge.

"Let me help you." Boaz took hold of the small image. "Which way does it go?"

"Away from the door," Ruth said. He put his strength to it. For a moment nothing happened, then there was a rumbling sound inside the wall and the great door slowly slid open.

Boaz stepped through but Ruth did not follow. "A path leads from here to the hillside, where there are caves," she said breathlessly. "You can hide there until tomorrow night if you wish; the people shun the place because of the image on the hill."

"And I will shun it too," Boaz said grimly. "I have hunted through the mountains many times. Morning will find me far from here."

"May the Most High bring you safely back to your people, Boaz," Ruth said. "I must go back now, before they suspect how you escaped."

He looked at her with concern. "Will Hedak . . . ?"

"He does not dare molest me," Ruth assured him. "Hedak wants to keep the favor of the Edomite tribes, and my family is very influential among them. Besides, Akton set you free."

"God set me free," Boaz said quietly, "with your help. But why did you risk your life for me, Ruth?"

"I told you. Mahlon is my husband. He was responsible for bringing you here."

"Mahlon was not really responsible for my betrayal. Hedak planned all this to get rid of me before he attacks Israel."

"It was Mahlon's idea to invite an envoy from Israel. And if he had not sent the clay tablet himself, you might not have come."

Boaz shook his head. "I think I would have accepted the invitation anyway, although I suspected Hedak of treachery from the beginning. The chance that I might be able to help Israel was worth risking my life."

"And the chance that I might help save you for Israel was worth the danger to me," Ruth said simply.

"What of Mahlon and Chilion? Will they be safe?"

"They had no part in your escape. Go and warn your people to arm, Boaz, for Hedak means to destroy Israel."

"They will arm," he said grimly, "when I tell them

what has happened. Farewell, Ruth." He turned and strode along the path. Nor did he look back at the city where he had so nearly lost his life or the young woman who had saved it for him.

When Boaz's tall body disappeared in the darkness along the path leading to the caves, Ruth went back into the temple garden and shut the massive gate. Now that the excitement of their flight through the passages under the temple and of Boaz's escape was beginning to wane, she felt a rising sense of apprehension that she could not explain, except perhaps that it had all been too easy so far.

She moved through the garden and opened the door into the temple, stepping in quickly and closing it again, in case someone might be in the corridor. She was on the point of going up the stairway that had led Hedak astray when she heard a groan. Turning quickly, she saw the little pile of bodies on the floor and cried out with alarm. Well before she reached them, she knew that her fears were realized, for Mahlon and Chilion were among the bleeding forms lying on the cold stones of the passage.

Quickly Ruth bent over Mahlon, who was lying on top. At first she thought he was already dead, but as she lifted his head and cradled it against her breast, sobbing her anguish, his eyes fluttered open. At the sight of her a little smile even came to his face.

"Is Boaz safe, Ruth?" he whispered.

"Yes." Her voice broke on a sob. Seeing Chilion's dead body, too, at the bottom of the pile with the soldiers lying around it, she realized what had been happening while she and Boaz were fleeing along these very passages and through the garden to the Priests' Gate, and how dearly had been purchased the time they had needed to escape Hedak.

"You saved him, darling," she whispered then, but did not add what she knew now was true, "with your life."

"God be praised," Mahlon whispered. "Perhaps now He will forgive me for making the swords."

"He will! I know He will!" Ruth cried, and held him tightly against her breast, until a sudden relaxation of his muscles warned her that his spirit had gone to the heaven he had told her about on the mountainside the day he had buried his father, Elimelech.

"Mahlon!" she cried, tears streaming down her face in the agony of grief. "Mahlon! Come back!"

There was no more life in his eyes, but she knew, by the faint smile upon his face as he had died, that Mahlon had been glad to lay down his life for his friend Boaz, and as a penance for his sin in making swords for Moab.

ix.

The ten days during which the small contingent of Israelite soldiers had been waiting at the Place of Refuge for the return of Boaz were almost up. Eliab's face had grown grimmer as the days passed, for with Boaz almost certainly dead, and probably Ram and Joseph as well, the grave responsibility for defending a lukewarm Israel against the attack that now seemed inevitable had fallen on his shoulders

During the afternoon a tall Israelite in dust-stained garments rode into the camp and was taken immediately to the tent of Eliab. The captain greeted him warmly.

"What did you learn, Abiram?" he asked. The newcomer was a member of one of the northern tribes that lived on the border of Moab. In the past he had been able to obtain valuable information through the Moabite families with which the tribe occasionally traded.

"Boaz reached Heshbon safely," Abiram said. "I talked to a man who saw him there."

"And afterward?"

"There was a great celebration in his honor."

"Perhaps the King really did want to talk peace, then."

"If he did, he will talk of it no more," Abiram said harshly. "On the very night of the feast the King died by poison. And Boaz was arrested for the crime."

"Boaz carried no poison. Nor would he kill any man save in battle."

Abiram nodded. "We all know that. The whole thing must have been planned so Zebushar would die and Boaz would be blamed for it."

"Did you learn what happened to him?" Eliab asked anxiously.

"Boaz was to be sacrificed to Chemosh at the coronation of Akton, the new King," Abiram said. "But the man I talked with left Heshbon before the coronation with a load of tools for the northern tribes."

"Then he did not see the sacrifice?"

"No. But it is hard to believe that even Boaz could escape such evil."

Eliab nodded sorrowfully. "Judah will mourn a great leader," he said. "We will sleep here tonight and ride tomorrow to warn the people that we must prepare for war."

"Should we not leave at once?" Abiram asked. "Who can tell when Hedak will strike?"

"Boaz ordered me to remain here for ten days," Eliab said firmly. "And here I remain until the time is up. Come, Abiram, you must be hungry. We will eat and talk of what we must do to arouse Israel to her peril."

The camp was asleep, but Abiram and Eliab were still talking around the fire, vainly searching for some idea that would so fan the feelings of the people into flame that the council would have no choice save to give weapons to the young men and train them for the attack that now seemed inevitable. Eliab's tent was close to the river. Both men heard the sound at the same moment that it reached the ears of the sentry watching the river crossing and the road into Moab.

Eliab surged to his feet, gripping his spear, with Abiram close beside him. They moved quickly and silently to where the sentry stood, staring into the darkness on the other side of the stream. While they watched and listened, the sound came again, the rattle of a small rock dislodged from the path by a horse's hoof.

"Rouse the men," Eliab told the sentry. "But keep them quiet."

A few seconds later the thump of hoofs could be heard distinctly from the other side of the narrow river. "It is one or two men only," Eliab said in a whisper. "We will take them and find out what happened in Moab."

"Maybe they will have news of Boaz." Abiram gripped his own spear.

Tensely they waited, while the Israelite soldiers moved silently into position behind them.

"Take them alive if you can." Eliab passed the whispered order back to the others. "But kill without pity if you must. They are the people who murdered our leader."

Soon three figures on horseback appeared on the opposite bank. One was so tall and familiar that the Israelites
could not fail to recognize him. "It is Boaz!" Eliab
shouted. "Hold your spears!"

The newcomers spurred their horses across the stream,
to be welcomed by those who had given them up for
dead. "Thank God you are safe, Boaz," Eliab cried.
"Abiram came in this afternoon with news that you had
been foully betrayed and would be sacrificed to the
Moabite god. We were riding tomorrow to warn the people
against war."

"We will still leave in the morning." Boaz dismounted
and moved to the fire to warm himself, for the evening
was chill here beside the river. "There will be no peace
with Moab while Hedak lives."

"We heard that Zebushar was dead," Eliab said, "and
that you had been accused of poisoning him."

"My going to Moab was all part of Hedak's plan to
gain complete control of Moab and excite the people
against Israel," Boaz explained. "He killed Zebushar because the King really wanted peace. Now he has set up
a son, Akton, as a puppet."

"Then there will be war?"

"As surely as the sun rises."

"How did you escape, Boaz?" Abiram asked.

"He almost didn't," Joseph said, grinning. "Ram and I
were hiding in the caves outside Heshbon. When we heard
someone coming up the hill, our spears were at Boaz's
throat before we recognized him."

"But your escape from the city," Eliab said. "Surely the
Most High must have favored you with a miracle, Boaz."

Boaz looked across the river into the darkness from
which he had come, toward Moab, where he would have
lost his life but for a woman whose courage was equaled
by her beauty.

"Was it not a miracle?" Eliab asked again. "The people
will believe the Lord fights on our side, if they know He
preserved you to Israel with His own hand."

Boaz turned back to the fire then. "The Lord did indeed favor me with a miracle, Eliab," he said. "The
greatest miracle of all."

Eliab nodded gravely. "He gave you your life. . . . And
returned the Lion of Judah to Israel."

X.

Ruth had never believed that Hedak would dare try to harm her, even though she was sure he suspected something of the part she had played in the escape of Boaz from Heshbon. Her father, Abinoth, had been a leader among the Edomite tribes. And she herself had been invited to the court by Zebushar, mainly because the King was genuinely fond of her, but partly as a gesture of conciliation toward the southern tribes, who were not so warlike as those in the north. Hedak, she knew, would hardly dare to anger them at a time when he needed the support of the people for his projected march westward to the Great Sea.

The forges were not left idle, however. Without Mahlon's skill and knowledge of metalworking no more of the fine swords he had forged could be produced, but any smith could make shields and helmets. Two days after Mahlon's death Nebo brought a burly Moabite smith named Abar into the yard and announced that henceforth the forges would be operated in the name of the King Akton. Once again the fires roared under the blast of the bellows, and the sound of hammers beating out shields, helmets, and metal plates for body armor filled the air.

Ruth did not protest this summary taking over of her husband's property, both because it seemed expedient to let things run as they were, and because all of her time was taken up with caring for Naomi. Since that night of horror months ago now, when she had returned to the house with the news that Mahlon and Chilion had died in the temple with their own swords in their hands, Naomi had been like someone moving in a dream. In a way her reaction was like Mahlon's when he had discovered how Hedak had used him to bring Boaz to Heshbon, where he would be betrayed—a stupor induced by shock and grief.

Most of the day Naomi sat in a corner of the yard, oblivious to what was going on around her, lips moving in whispered prayers to the Most High to let her join her husband and her sons in death. Ruth's own grief was great,

but Naomi's need helped keep her busy, so she was better
off, in a way, than she might have been with nothing to
do but sit and mourn her loss. Besides, Ruth was still
young and, although she had loved Mahlon dearly and
his loss was a constant pain, the resiliency of youth helped
her to recover.

Orpah had never been as close to Naomi as Ruth, and
so was of little help in caring for the older woman. Ruth
was too busy to notice that Orpah soon began to spend
less and less time in the house. If she had, being charitable,
she would have put it down to the other young woman's
need for the companionship of others, which had always
been great, while Ruth had been content with her home
and her family.

Ruth could see that Orpah was troubled, however, when
she stopped beside her in the yard one morning. Ruth
was pounding grain in a stone mortar, there being few
slaves to do the menial work now. "How pretty you look
this morning, Orpah," Ruth said with a smile, pushing
the dark red hair back from her damp forehead with her
arm.

Orpah sat down upon the bench beside Ruth. "Let me
help you."

"I've almost finished. Don't dirty your hands with the
pestle."

"Ruth," Orpah began, and stopped.

"Yes?"

"There is something I must tell you."

Ruth smiled. "Have we not always been like sisters?
What is it?"

"Hedak left this morning to visit the northern tribes.
He is bringing back an army to use against Israel."

Ruth caught her breath. "Are you sure?"

"I learned it from one of his captains."

"But Hedak could have told him to tell you that, thinking we might send word to Israel somehow and stir them
up, giving him an excuse to attack."

Orpah shook her head. "A man speaks truth in the
arms of a woman," she said half defiantly.

Ruth looked down lest Orpah see the shock and surprise in her eyes.

"I am not like you, Ruth," Orpah continued, half

ashamed and half defiant. "No one has ever called me steadfast."

"You must do what your heart tells you to do, Orpah." Ruth put an arm about her. "Did you learn anything else we need to know?"

"When they are ready Hedak plans to accuse all Israelites in Moab of being spies and have them executed."

Ruth caught her breath. "Naomi!"

"She is already marked for death," Orpah agreed. "I pretended to hate her and asked. Hedak will claim that Naomi was responsible for the escape of Boaz."

Ruth turned to look at the pitiful, brooding figure kneeling before the small altar at one side of the courtyard where the family had worshiped. "Our people in Edom do not hate Israelites as they do in Heshbon," she said. "If we went to them Naomi would be safe."

"But would we be allowed to leave the city?"

"We would if we carried an order signed by the King."

"The King!" Orpah laughed. "Akton is a child. He does only what Hedak tells him."

"But Hedak is away," Ruth pointed out. "And as you say, Akton is a child. Tomorrow I will go to him and tell him I want to visit the southern tribes to bind them closer to his kingdom and to bring their soldiers as a wedding present to Hedak. He will let me go when I tell him how proud of him Hedak will be for accomplishing this."

"He might do it. All of Heshbon knows Hedak is anxious to keep the favor of the Edomite tribes. And he did want to marry you once, a long time ago."

"I will seek an audience with Akton in the morning," Ruth said. "Did you learn how long Hedak will be away?"

"A week at least."

"Then we will have time to reach the Edomite tribes before he can return and follow us." She reached up to squeeze Orpah's hand. "You did right in telling me this, dear. It may well save Naomi's life."

"Then you don't hate me for what I did?"

Ruth smiled. "Mahlon taught me that the Most High said, 'I will love thee and bless thee,' to his people. If God can love us, weak as we are, what right have I to hate you, Orpah?"

xi.

The caravan that filed through the gates of Heshbon a few mornings later was a small one. Ruth had possessed only gold enough to buy a few mules, and could not very well sell any of her property to purchase more without arousing suspicion that the three women were leaving Heshbon forever instead of merely taking a brief trip to visit the Edomite tribes.

Naomi rode a mule just behind the burly slave who led the caravan, with Orpah behind her and Ruth near the end where she could watch for stragglers. Only a few house slaves accompanied them, since the larger the caravan the more supplies they must take, depleting Ruth's small store of gold even more. Beneath the stores, the waterskins, and the tents on the back of the mules she carried as many objects of much value and little weight as possible, such as swords, pruning and reaping hooks, and other tools. These, she knew, could be sold at a good price later to buy food and clothing.

They were not molested at the gate leaving the valley, the seal of Chemosh upon the small tablet Akton had given Ruth was quite sufficient to let them through. Beyond the pass Ruth stopped for a moment to look back at the green valley, with its orchards, fields, and herds, and the great shining city in the distance. She felt a sudden pang of homesickness at leaving it, for until her husband had become conscience-stricken about making the swords and had brought Boaz to Heshbon in the hope of achieving peace, she had been very happy. But there was no time to waste now and with a last look at Heshbon and the valley of Moab, she set her gaze westward toward the Jordan and the road that led to Edom.

Several mornings later Ruth came out of the tent she shared with Naomi and Orpah on the journey. They were halfway across the desert wastes and had camped the night before at a small oasis where the road forked. One branch led northward toward the eastern shore of the Sea of Chinnereth and the city of Succoth near where the River Jabbok joined the Jordan. The other road bore

still westward to the Place of Refuge near where the
Jordan tumbled downwards into the sea that knows no life.

Naomi had sat the mule like a statue all the way from
Heshbon, speaking only when spoken to. Once or twice
the day before, however, Ruth had been sure that the
older woman recognized the road along which she and
her family had come to Moab so long ago. And Naomi's
eyes had seemed brighter than Ruth remembered seeing
them since the night Mahlon and Chilion had died.

Ruth's first act when she emerged from the tent each
morning was to look up at the sky, for the weather was
a very important factor in such a journey as this. So far
there had been none of the suddenly swirling sandstorms
that could smother a caravan almost in a moment, cutting
off the very air and burying men, animals, and goods deep
beneath a cairn of sand. But the sky was clear and bright
this morning with none of the brassy look that usually
foretold a day of storms.

Then she looked about her at the camp. And what she
saw sent fear clutching at her heart.

Only one mule remained tethered to a palm near the
small spring, the rest were gone. With them had disappeared the servants and all the food and water save
one small skin. Of the goods she had brought nothing
remained save the clothes they wore and the tent in
which the three women had been sleeping.

This new tragedy, coming upon the heels of Mahlon's
death and the sudden flight from Heshbon to save Naomi,
was like a bludgeon stroke. For a moment Ruth felt like
dropping to the cool grass of the oasis and sobbing, then
with an effort she straightened her shoulders and lifted
the flap of the tent aside.

"Orpah," she called. "Come out here, please."

Orpah put her head through the opening, blinking at
the sunlight. When she saw that only the three of them
remained at the oasis, her eyes filled with a sudden terror.

"What happened, Ruth?" she cried. "Where are the
servants and the mules?"

"The servants stole everything during the night," Ruth
explained. "They must have gone north toward Succoth,
or back to Heshbon."

"What will we do?" Orpah suddenly broke into hysteri-
cal sobbing. "We will die here by ourselves."

The younger woman's helplessness only impressed upon

Ruth more deeply the fact that her own slender shoulders must now bear the burdens of caring for her family. "Our husbands were brave men, Orpah," she said quietly. "We shall be like them." She looked up at the palm trees. "There are dates here, and water, so we will not starve."

"We could stay here until another caravan comes along," Orpah suggested.

Ruth shook her head. "We must not be more than two days' journey from the river crossing. If Hedak should return in the next few days he might send soldiers after us. No, Orpah," she said decisively. "We must go on. Naomi can ride the mule with the waterskin. You and I will have to walk and we will leave the tent behind. You can be picking dates while I get Naomi ready to leave."

Naomi sat in the corner of the tent, her face set in the grim cast of misery that had not left it for months. "The servants have left us, Naomi," Ruth explained as she led her outside. "They took everything except a mule for you to ride and a waterskin, but we will go on."

"Call me not Naomi, but Mara," the older woman said harshly. "For the Almighty has dealt very bitterly with me."

Ruth took her gently by the hand and lifted her to her feet. "Orpah will give you some dates to eat while I fill the waterskin," she said. "We must go on before the sun gets too hot."

And so the forlorn little caravan set out once more westward across the burning wastes of the desert.

Late the following afternoon they staggered over a low hill and saw another road converging upon their trail from the north, with the green belt marking the course of the Jordan barely visible in the distance. The mule upon which Naomi rode was barely able to stagger under her weight and that of the flabby waterskin. They were all half blinded as well by the heat and the dust.

Orpah stumbled on a rock and fell. "Let me die, Ruth," she begged. "Why do you punish us by driving us on?"

Ruth knelt beside the exhausted young woman and lifted her to her feet. A dozen times at least since yesterday Orpah had fallen or Naomi's donkey had wandered off the road, and only Ruth's determined spirit had kept them going. Now she poured both the others a drink from the nearly empty waterskin and gave some to the mule.

She did not drink herself, although her tongue was parched and swollen from thirst, for she did not know for sure what lay between them and the distant green band marking the river.

"It's only a little farther," she said as brightly as she could. "See how the green of the riverbank shows ahead of us."

Orpah lifted her head and stared into the distance. "Look there on the other road, Ruth!" she cried suddenly. "A caravan! We are saved!" And she started running blindly down the road toward a caravan that had just come into sight on the other trail, ignoring Ruth's pleas to stop lest the newcomers might be enemies.

There was nothing Ruth could do except follow with Naomi. When they came to where the two trails met, she found Orpah, surrounded by people from the other caravan, drinking water and laughing hysterically.

"We are saved, Ruth!" she cried. "These are friends from my own tribe among the Edomite people."

The exhausted women were given water and food by the Edomite caravan and room was made for them upon the mules. Thus they covered the last miles to the Place of Refuge and the camping ground for the night in relative luxury.

During the last miles Ruth, riding just behind Naomi, was sure that the older woman recognized this place. As soon as the caravan stopped on the Moabite side of the Jordan, she ran to lift her mother-in-law down from her mule.

"Look, Naomi!" she cried. "There is the river and the Place of Refuge. You can see into Israel."

"Israel!" It was only a whisper, but there was such a gladness in the word that Ruth's eyes filled.

"See," she said. "An Israelite herd feeds across the river, and the herdsmen are encamped there under the trees."

It was only a small herd tended by one family. As Ruth led Naomi down to the stream to bathe her feet in one of the pools among the rocks, a slender young woman with a bright-eyed baby on her hip looked up from where she was filling a water jar across the river.

"Shalom!" Ruth said with a smile.

The young woman looked startled, for, although the Edomites and the Israelites maintained a peaceful relationship, there was little mingling between them. But Ruth's sincerity shone in her eyes and after a moment of hesitation the Israelite woman smiled. "And upon thee be peace, woman of Moab," she replied politely.

Ruth knelt to wash Naomi's feet. "I worship the one true God as you do," she explained. "My husband was of Judah. He was Mahlon, the son of Elimelech."

"I am of the tribe of Judah also," the young mother said. "We come from Bethlehem."

Naomi's eyes had been moving over the flock and the Israelite encampment while Ruth was talking to the herdsman's wife, but she did not speak. "What of Boaz?" Ruth asked the young woman as she dried Naomi's feet. "Did he get safely back to Bethlehem?"

"The Most High preserved Boaz to Israel. This is his flock. We are moving it to Bethelehem so the sheep may eat the straw from the barley harvest and what grain is left by the reapers and gleaners. Where are your husbands?" she added curiously.

"They are dead," Ruth said sadly. "We are all widows now."

"May God be with you on your journeys, O women of great sorrow," the herdsman's wife said, "and turn your weeping into joy."

Ruth helped her mother-in-law to her feet. "I will prepare some food for us, Naomi," she said gently. "The people of the caravan were kind enough to give us supplies and shelter, but we must not be a burden upon them."

Naomi let herself be guided to the tent which their benefactors had lent them. But Ruth noticed that she kept glancing back over her shoulder to where the herdsman's wife was cooking the evening meal over a bed of coals.

Exhausted from the journey, Ruth slept soundly until the noises of camp being broken in the morning awakened her. When she saw that the pallet beside her was empty and the tent flap opened, she got quickly to her feet in alarm. She did not have to look far for Naomi, however. Her mother-in-law was standing on the riverbank looking across to where a plume of smoke rose from the fire of the herdsman's family.

Quickly Ruth went to Naomi and took her by the arm. "We must hurry, Naomi," she said. "Our friends are almost ready to leave."

Naomi turned. Overnight she seemed almost to have become herself again, except for the bitterness in her eyes. There was a look of decision on her face. "I am going back to Israel, Ruth," she said.

"But you have no one there to look after you. The southern tribes are my people and my family is wealthy. We will be safe with them."

"My husband and my sons were buried in a foreign land. But I shall rest in Israel."

Orpah came down the bank of the river from the tent she had shared with a mother and baby of the caravan. "Hurry, Ruth," she called. "Do you want them to leave us?"

"Naomi will not go. She insists on returning to Israel."

"To Israel!" Orpah looked dumfounded. "Why?"

"It is her home. I understand how she feels . . . and we must go with her."

Orpah looked back at the caravan which was now almost ready to depart. A group of men were already dismantling the tent in which Ruth and Naomi had slept, and the young woman who had shared a tent with Orpah was calling to her.

"Go, my daughters, and return each of you to your mother's house," Naomi said gently. "May the Lord deal kindly with you as you have done with the dead and with me. The Lord grant that you may find a home each of you in the house of her husband." She turned quickly to kiss them and her eyes were wet with tears.

"No," Ruth said firmly. "We will go with you to your people, Naomi."

"Turn back, my daughters," Naomi pleaded. "Why will you go with me? Have I yet sons in my womb that may become your husbands?"

Orpah looked at the young Edomite woman with her baby, then back pleadingly to Ruth. "I cannot go to a strange land and live among strange people," she said in a low voice. "Don't ask it of me, please."

"Go on with the caravan, dear," Ruth said, and managed to smile. "We understand."

Orpah hugged her, half weeping in relief and happiness, and embraced Naomi. "May Chemosh—and Yahveh—turn their favor upon both of you," she babbled happily before she ran to join the caravan.

"May you find happiness," Ruth whispered, looking after her.

"Orpah has gone back to her own people, Ruth," Naomi said urgently. "Go after her and leave me here with the herdsman's family. They will see that I reach Bethlehem safely. That is all I want, for I shall soon die in Israel."

Ruth turned and put her arms tenderly around her mother-in-law. "Entreat me not to leave you or to return from following you," she said warmly, the love she bore Naomi shining in her eyes. "For where you go I will go, and where you lodge I will lodge. Your people shall be my people and your God my God. Where you die I will die, and there will I be buried. May the Lord do so to me and more also if even death parts me from you."

Naomi's eyes shone with tears. She held Ruth tightly and did not argue any more. "May God bless thee, O Steadfast One," she said brokenly. "And bring you great happiness still."

BOOK THREE

THE WINNOWING GROUND

So Naomi returned, and Ruth the Moabitess, her daughter-in-law, with her . . . and they came to Bethlehem in the beginning of barley harvest.

RUTH 1:22

i.

IN THE DAYS WHEN THE JUDGES RULED THE TWELVE TRIBES of Israel were no longer united into one people, as they had been under Moses during the long journey from Egypt to the land of Canaan. Not even under the leadership of Joshua had all the tribes fought together, and since then rarely more than four of them had ever acted jointly. Even then it was only for brief periods under the leadership of one of the great national heroes called a Judge or *Shophet*, who guided his particular tribe or coalition through a time of national emergency, only to see them drift apart and grow weak again as the common need for defense became less urgent.

Of the tribes to the south Judah had been the acknowledged leader for several generations. Indeed, but for the leadership of that stalwart rock among the children of Israel, the Hebrews of that region must long ago have been conquered by the enemies who ringed them around, the Moabites to the east and the Philistines to the west. Even in this area isolated strongholds of the heathen still existed, such as the city of Jerusalem only a few miles away, which was still in the hands of descendants of its Jebusite conquerors many generations after the children of Israel had first come into Canaan.

When Boaz sent Joseph and other couriers out after his return to Bethlehem from Moab, requesting a meeting of the long dormant Council of Israel at Bethlehem, it was with no real hope of representation from the northern tribes. These had withdrawn to themselves in the past few generations during which there had been only sporadic wars by minor chieftains against the Israelites. In fact the northern Israelites had so far drifted away from their kinsmen to the south that the two peoples had little in common any longer, save the worship of the one true God, Yahveh, "Whose Name must not be spoken."

Less than a dozen men were gathered around the table in the meeting chamber used by the Council of Elders in Bethlehem when the weather was too inclement for them to use their customary place near the gate under an arbor. Only four of them were from tribes other than Judah, to

which Boaz belonged, and whose official representative
to the Council of Israel was Tob. But all were well fed
and prosperous-looking, for the days of the famine were
over. As after the seven full years predicted by Joseph,
from Pharaoh's dream, whose end had brought the children of Israel into Egypt and eventually into slavery,
the Hebrews were no longer hungry and starving.

Patriarch among the group was Issachar, from the tribe
of that name to the north along the course of the Jordan
and directly opposite the northern part of Moab. Issachar
was over seventy and feeble. With him had come, at
Boaz's request, the hard-bitten, leathery-skinned man
named Abiram who had brought news to Eliab at the
Place of Refuge that Boaz had been taken in Heshbon.
He carried a spear and wore a metal cap upon his head.

Amminidab, representing the tribe of Ephraim, was a
graying but still sturdy man in his fifties. Beside him sat
Eliab of the tribe of Benjamin adjoining Judah to the
north, tall, lean, and about ten years older than Boaz,
a born leader whose dark eyes were usually merry, even
in the heat of battle.

Representing the busy and prosperous city of Bethlehem and the province of Judah was Tob, fleshy and
distinguished-looking in his rich robe, his hair flecked
with silver at the temples. Only his too full lips betrayed
the sensuousness that was his greatest vice after greed. A
handsome man was Tob, until you looked at his eyes
and saw that they were set just a little too close together.

In sharp contrast to the luxurious garb of the other
men Boaz wore the simple harness of a soldier. A short
skirt of tough woolen cloth was girted about his waist
and fell to his muscular knees. His sandals were of thick,
tough leather and laced up his muscular calves with broad
thongs of rawhide. His leather tunic was set with plates
of thin metal like the tunics of the Moabite soldiers,
and a metal cap was upon his head. He carried no weapon
today. His face, although handsome, was set, and there
was a wintry light in his eyes as he finished the account
of his experience in Moab.

"I called you together here," he said in conclusion,
"because we who are in the path of Hedak's army must
stand together or be lost. The land of Moab is a hungry
wolf around which we are clustered like so many sheep."
He paused and looked around the council until his gaze

reached Tob, who colored slightly under the cool scrutiny of his kinsman's eyes.

"My tribe of Judah," Boaz said deliberately then, "is the fattest and foolishest sheep of all."

"Spare us your jests, Boaz," Tob said tartly. "This is a gathering of the Council of Israel, not a drinking bout."

"Well spoken, Tob. By the fattest sheep of all." Boaz turned his back upon Tob, singling the others out in turn.

"The tribe of Issachar is a wary sheep, for it lives near the mountains of Moab and can hear the beat of drums. The tribe of Amminidab is the third, and that of Eliab the fourth. Together we number as many, at least, as the tally of the soldiers of Moab. But can a single sheep fight off a wolf?"

No one spoke for a moment, then Amminidab said heavily, "As you say, Boaz, a wolf will fear to attack a flock, but will devour a single sheep at a time until there are no more. Still, the Moabites have swords. Let us not forget that."

"Forged for them by Mahlon," Tob said caustically, "a kinsman of yours, Boaz."

"You are nearer kin to Elimelech and his sons than I, Tob," Boaz said evenly. "But Mahlon regrets forging swords for Hedak. He tried to make peace between us and Moab."

"And almost cost you your life," Eliab said dryly.

"That was no fault of Mahlon's, and I am sure he will refuse to forge any more swords after what happened. No," Boaz continued, "I fear the weapons of Moab less than I fear the smugness of an Israel that will not prepare to fight."

"How can we fight against swords when we have none ourselves?" Amminidab asked.

"Yes, tell us that," Issachar added.

"Show us a weapon that is stronger," Tob demanded.

"Your spear, Joseph," Boaz said to his young lieutenant, who stood behind him. As Joseph passed the weapon to his commander, all could see how well balanced it was and how careful the workmanship of the shaft. The head showed the hammer marks that were the signs of less skilled metalsmiths, but the point had been sharpened by rubbing on a stone until it was as sharp as a dagger.

"These weapons are stronger than the swords of Moab," Boaz told them. "If you will but give them to us."

"How can spears prevail against swords?" Tob demanded.

"Because we are peaceful people and Hedak will attack us first," Boaz explained. "Then we can choose the ground where we will fight the soldiers of Moab. In narrow defiles spears can transfix marching men from above. And they can be hurled from craggy peaks where swords cannot touch the hurlers."

No one spoke for a moment. It was obvious that Boaz had impressed them at last. Then Issachar said cautiously, "But spears often miss their targets, Boaz."

"If thrown by unskilled hands," Boaz admitted. He turned to his lieutenant. "Show them your skill, Joseph."

Joseph stepped forward and took the spear. He looked around the room, seeking a target, until his eyes lit upon a small skin of wine hanging from a rafter about fifty feet away. It was not much larger than a man's head.

"Watch, scoffers!" Boaz commanded. "Then tell me there are no skilled warriors in Israel."

Joseph threw the spear with an easy, practiced movement. It flew straight and the point pierced the wineskin, spattering the dark red fluid upon the wall.

"Are you convinced now that spears are deadlier weapons than swords and at longer ranges?" Boaz asked.

One by one as his gaze polled them they nodded, except Tob, who only shrugged. "Give me smiths to forge weapons," Boaz pleaded. "And send me young men to train. Do this and I promise that the Moabites will not come close enough to use their swords against us."

Issachar combed his beard with his fingers. "Smiths cost money," he objected. "And our young men will be needed soon for the barley harvest. Perhaps when it is finished and if the yield is good. . . ."

"You cannot wait for the harvest. Abiram!" Boaz called to the leather-skinned man, who sat near Issachar. "Tell them what you have seen."

Abiram stood up and faced the council. "I tend my flocks near the border of Moab. And sometimes I slip across the boundary and listen to the Moabites talking. Then I send word to Boaz of what I hear and see."

"Are you a spy?" Tob asked.

"I am a soldier of the Lord," Abiram said with simple dignity, "against the heathen."

"Tell us what you have heard, Abiram," Eliab prompted.

"Hedak has sent emissaries to the northern tribes of Moab. He promises the young men swords and shields and much booty in Israel when he conquers us, if they will come to Heshbon and join the army he is assembling there."

"Now do you believe we are in danger?" Boaz demanded of the council.

"You were shamed and suffered much in Moab, Boaz," Tob said unctuously. "But would you have us go to war with a powerful nation so that you may have revenge upon Prince Hedak?"

"Revenge? I told you I saw the Moabites preparing for war with my own eyes."

"But we have treaties with Moab that bind each of us not to attack the other."

"Leave your fine home and come with me to the border, Tob," Boaz suggested. "You will see then whether or not the Moabites attack us and what they think of your treaty. Hardly a day passes that some roving band does not cross the border and kill our people."

"But they have never ventured against our cities," Amminidab pointed out.

"The Lord saved Boaz in Heshbon," Tob added. "Surely He will fight again in our behalf if we are attacked. Take care lest hate blind you to reason, Boaz."

"You are the blind ones," Boaz said harshly. "And you will still be braying like jackasses when the Moabites attack you in your sleep." He turned and strode from the council chamber.

Only Eliab among the older men moved to follow. "Don't be too hard on them because their desire for peace blinds them to the danger of losing everything, Boaz," the older man advised as they came out of the meeting place.

"But, united, we would be so strong that no one would dare attack us."

"That is true, but the time is not yet. You are a man of vision, peering always into tomorrow. But we are plain, ordinary mortals, living only for today and leaving tomorrow to the Most Migh."

"So be it, then. I will fight alone."

"You cannot fight alone," Eliab reminded him soberly. "If the Lord of Hosts does not give strength to your arm, you will be swept away like the forest before a fire."

For a long moment Boaz did not speak, then he said quietly, "You are right, Eliab. In my zeal I took too much upon myself. I will go now and pray to God for forgiveness because I pumped myself up with pride, and for guidance in the future."

"We will go together," Eliab said promptly. "Later we can talk about training the young men of my tribe in handling spears."

Inside the council chamber Tob finished addressing the remainder of the group. It was a soothing speech, pointing out how dangerous it would be to offend Moab by arming when they had treaties guaranteeing peace between the two countries. He mentioned the cost of arming, the taxes that would have to be raised, the loss of the young men from the harvest, and the interruption of trade. When he had finished, Issachar stroked his beard with his fingers. "I, too, was like Boaz in my youth," he admitted with some pride. "But the years bring wisdom and cool hot spirits. We will wait and see." And the old men nodded sagely to each other.

Recounting his speech for Adah, his beautiful slave-concubine, as she lay in his arms that night, Tob said worriedly, "But that Boaz. He is like a mad bull at the gate."

Adah laughed softly. "Even the mad bull dies, master," she reminded him. "When a sword is thrust into his heart."

"Hush, Adah," Tob said quickly. "You must not talk like that. Someone might hear you and think I meant harm to Boaz."

"You mean no harm to him, master," she assured him with her lips close to his ear. "But if harm should come . . ."

The next morning Adah took Cheb, the caravan driver, aside when he came to arrange for another load of goods to be carried to Moab. "Boaz is training the young men of Judah to throw spears and buying them weapons out of his own pocket," she told him. "And Eliab is going to send the young men of Benjamin to Boaz for training. I heard them talking of it yesterday in the street."

"Why tell me this?" Cheb asked. "I am not a soldier."

"Your master in Moab is," she reminded him. "If Hedak does not attack Israel soon, it may be too late to keep the other tribes from preparing for war."

"Did you tell Tob that I work for Prince Hedak?" Cheb asked anxiously.

She shook her head. "When Hedak conquers Israel, Tob will make a good ruler. . . ."

"With you as his consort," Cheb suggested slyly, for he knew her driving ambition.

"It has happened before," Adah snapped. "As I said, Tob will make a good ruler, but he has no courage. If he knew you are an agent of Moab, he might give it away. . . . And that mother of yours," she continued. "I heard her screaming something about Moab in the market place yesterday."

Cheb grinned. "Who listens to the madwoman of Bethlehem? Are such not to be ignored by order of the Most High?"

"Shut her up, if you can. We are too near success now to fail because of her ravings."

"Do not fear, beautiful one," Cheb assured her. "I can take care of myself. And I will take your message with me to Moab."

ii.

Ruth and Naomi came in to Bethlehem late one afternoon. The journey across the "land of drought and the shadow of death" had been hard. They had even been forced to sell their remaining mule to a passing caravan to buy food, leaving them the clothes they wore as their only possessions.

"Don't worry, Ruth," Naomi had counseled as they ate the last of their food that morning and spent their last piece of copper for sandals to guard their feet against the rocks. "I have many kinsmen in Bethlehem. Tob, the nearest, is a rich merchant. We will be well taken care of."

Looking now at the waving fields of barley around the town and the green pastures where the flocks and herds grazed, with the tents of the herdsmen pitched under the trees, Ruth felt some of her spirits returning, although they had been sorely tried by the long journey afoot and the heat. Compared to Heshbon, Bethlehem was a mean city indeed and the rocky hills of Judah no match for the

fertile fields of the valley of Moab. But these people,
Ruth knew, worshiped the God Mahlon had taught her
to love. The God who had made a covenant with the children of Israel that if they would obey His commandments, He would love and bless them and show His
mercy to them.

It made little difference, she told herself, if Bethlehem
were little more than a village of mud-walled huts and
dusty streets. Or that the wall surrounding it could be
breached in one thrust by Hedak's battering ram, borne
upon the iron-wheeled chariots forged by the Philistine
smiths on the shores of the Great Sea, and which were
sometimes captured in swift forays westward by Moabite
raiders. The important thing was that these people were
kind and good like Mahlon, Chilion, and Naomi, because
they worshiped the same God.

With every mile nearer to Bethlehem Naomi had brightened a little. Now there was eagerness in her step, even
though she was tired from walking all day on the rocky
path.

"You should be happy, Naomi, at returning to your
own people after so many years," Ruth said with a smile
as they came down the green hillside toward the gate
with the well just outside it. Had Ruth noticed, however,
she would have seen a little farther on, in an angle of
the wall, a pile of stones stained dark in spots. Every
Israelite town had its place of stoning, easily identified
because the rocks were always stained with the blood of
those who had been executed for breaking the stern commandments of their God.

"They are your people, now, Ruth," Naomi reminded
her.

For the first time since they had crossed over the
Jordan, Ruth voiced the fear that had been in her heart.
"But will they receive a Moabite?"

"They will treat you kindly," Naomi said quickly, almost as if she were reassuring herself. "Especially when
I tell them I would have died along the way but for your
courage and strength."

There were no guards at the gate of Bethlehem, Ruth
noted, and people could pass in and out as they chose.
Nor were soldiers in evidence as they would have been at
the gate of any Moabite city.

A few men loitering by the gate glanced casually at the two women, as anyone will at a stranger. Their eyes passed over Naomi's tired and worn countenance without notice, but when they came to Ruth's fresh young beauty, evident even through the dust and her weariness, their gaze quickened. Ruth had seen that look on men's faces many times before and, as they came to the gate, she drew the shawl she wore across her face, leaving only her eyes visible.

Tob's house was well back from the gate in the center of Bethlehem. One of the most luxurious homes in the city, its walls were of stone and mortar. It stood two stories high and the flat roof was surrounded by a parapet, as were many of the houses in Israelite towns.

By day, clothes were often dried on the roof tops, and when Ruth and Naomi approached the house of Tob, they saw a woman moving about above them, taking in some linen cloths that had been hung out to dry. Being a vain man, Tob's table was covered with fine linen, and he often drank from silver goblets.

When Ruth and Naomi stopped before the house, Adah came to the parapet and looked down. Although actually a slave, she dressed better than most of the women in Bethlehem by virtue of her real position as Tob's concubine, and at the sight of Ruth and Naomi's worn and dust-stained garments her lip curled.

"This is the house of Tob, a man of substance," she said importantly. "If you seek alms, go to the courtyard and wait like the other beggars."

Naomi started to turn away, but Ruth put her hand on her mother-in-law's arm and stopped her. "Are you Tob's wife?" she asked Adah courteously.

Adah tossed her head. "Tob has no wife. I am his—his housekeeper. . . . Who are you to question me?" she added, angry at having been forced to admit her menial position.

"This is Naomi, wife of Elimelech," Ruth explained. "Tob is her next of kin."

Adah had been staring at Ruth and the small tattooed mark of Moab upon her forehead. "You are Moabite," she exclaimed. "From what city?"

"Heshbon. I am the widow of Naomi's son, Mahlon." Ruth was tired and not accustomed to being questioned by servants. "Does your master wish his kinswomen to beg for alms in the courtyard?" she asked a little curtly.

Adah recovered from her shock at their being from Heshbon, but her eyes were still wary. If these women knew anything of Cheb's dealings with Moab, it could go bad with the caravan driver. Not that she cared about Cheb. She had agreed to help him with his betrayal of Bethlehem and Judah to Hedak because she hoped that Tob, upon hers and Cheb's recommendation, might be chosen to rule over Judah and perhaps all of Israel when Moab was victorious, as Hedak's vassal. Then she would be raised from the menial status of a slave to that of consort, an alluring prospect indeed for an ambitious young woman.

It would be best, Adah decided quickly, to take these women in and find out what they knew. Then she could make her plans and goad Tob into carrying them out, as she had many times before.

"I will come down and let you in," she called to Ruth and Naomi with some show of courtesy. "My master will be coming home soon. No doubt he will be pleased to see kinswomen who have come from such a long distance."

Adah was waiting outside for Tob when he came home shortly after sundown. He was worried, for word had come that Issachar was yielding to the persuasions of Abiram, who was, of course, a follower of Boaz, and was planning to buy spearheads from the Philistine smiths so that the young men of his tribe could be trained in the arts of war. That, Tob knew, would mean loss of some trade from the tribe of Issachar and money from his pocket.

Adah took her master by the hand and drew him behind a bush.

"Don't be so familliar where people can see, Adah," Tob said pettishly. "You know the women are talking about us already."

"Let them talk! Something important has happened."

"What is it?"

"Two women are here. They came from Moab."

"From Moab? Who are they?"

"The older one is Naomi, wife of Elimelech, the younger is a Moabite."

"Naomi here?" Tob looked as if he were going to faint.

"Much of my land belonged to her husband. I am next of kin so I have been using it, but now . . ."

"Buy the land. It is your right as her kinsman."

Tob wiped sweat from his forehead. "I have no money to buy land, Adah. I am in debt to Boaz already and you still want more jewels." He seized her by the arm. "What shall I do? Naomi can ruin me if she insists that I buy the property. My debtors could have me stoned."

"Take them in," Adah suggested calmly. "Who knows what will happen to them."

"Hush!" Tob looked around fearfully to make sure they were not overheard. "Who did you say the other one was besides Naomi?"

"A Moabite. The widow of one of Naomi's sons."

"A Moabite in my house? What will the council say? Go bring me wine, Adah. Then I will go in and speak to them."

A cup of wine helped Tob regain his composure before he entered the large room downstairs that formed most of the first floor. "Naomi!" he exclaimed, embracing his kinswoman with a great show of cordiality. "Is it really you and not your ghost?"

"It is I, Tob," Naomi said quietly. "You have prospered, I see."

"The business of a merchant is very uncertain," Tob said warily. "I sorrow for you in the death of Elimelech. Where are your sons?"

"Dead. At the hands of Hedak. Their bodies lie in Moab."

Tob lifted plump hands and let them fall. "What can one say? You were warned against going to Moab."

"Had you helped us during the famine," Naomi said bluntly, "we might have stayed in Israel."

Tob looked at her reproachfully. "They were sad days. It seemed that we would all perish."

"I have nothing any more, except the clothes on my back," Naomi told him. "The land that belonged to Elimelech is yours, if you wish to purchase it as next of kin."

"We will talk of that later," Tob said hurriedly, "when you have rested."

"Is your door open to us, then?"

"Of course. I am your kinsman and I know my duty . . . even though times have not been good lately." He looked at Ruth. "Who is this with you?"

"This is Ruth, the widow of Mahlon. She came back home with me."

"She is not of our people," Tob said a little severely.

"She is now."

Ruth raised her head for the first time. Tob's eyes brightened at her beauty and a pleased expression came over his face.

She dropped the shawl from her head, revealing the mark of Chemosh, and uncovering her dark red hair. Tob drew in his breath with a quick sigh at her startling beauty. "Even though I am a Moabite?" she asked deliberately, for she would travel under no false pretense.

Tob licked his full lips. Cheb had spoken of that mark and he remembered now that the women who bore it were priestesses of Chemosh and Ashtar, dedicated to love.

"Does not the Most High command us," he said unctuously, " 'If a stranger sojourn with thee in your land you shall not vex him'? You are welcome, Ruth, for I am next of kin to you as well, since you are the widow of Mahlon."

Ruth did not miss the half leer in his eyes. "I would not want to cause you inconvenience," she said quickly, but Tob cut her off.

"I have plenty of room. It is a large house and I am a lonely old bachelor." He clapped his hands and Adah entered, followed by an old woman. "Take my kinswomen to repair themselves, Adah," he commanded. "And fetch them water for bathing. Give Naomi the room toward the setting sun."

Adah nodded to the servant, who went out with Ruth and Naomi. Tob's eyes followed Ruth's graceful form until the door had closed. "Give the Moabite the room toward the rising sun," he added softly.

Adah started with surprise and shot him an angry look. "That is your room!"

"I shall not use it. At least not for a day or two."

"But she is a Moabite! A heathen! Your room will be defiled."

"I thank the Most High that I am without prejudice." Tob crossed his fingers over his paunch and lifted his eyes piously toward the ceiling. "Completely without prejudice," he repeated, pursing his lips and nodding with satisfaction at his own worthiness.

iii.

Hardly an hour after Tob's house and the town around
it had settled down for the night, Ruth heard a sound
she had been half expecting, the creak of a door being
opened furtively in the darkness. She had not wanted to
leave Naomi, but when Adah had insisted that it was
her master's wish for Ruth to have his own chamber,
she could not refuse without seeming ungracious and un-
appreciative of Tob's kindness in taking them in. Besides,
she had not wanted to jeopardize in any way the haven
Naomi had found in the fine home of her nearest kinsman, for her mother-in-law was old and feeble and needed
food and shelter much worse than did Ruth's strong,
young body.

She had not missed the dawning interest in Tob's eyes,
however, when she had revealed her beauty in order to
leave no doubt in his mind that she was a foreigner in
Judah. And she had almost been able to read his thoughts
when he recognized the mark on her forehead and realized its significance.

The slight creak came again. Straining her eyes into the
darkness, Ruth saw a faint streak of light along the edge
of the door from the lamp burning in the hall outside.
Someone, she knew, had opened the door and was listening now to make sure that she was asleep. Nor was there
any doubt in her mind as to the identity of the visitor.

With a quick movement Tob stepped inside and shut the
door behind him. He carried a small burning candle which
he placed in a holder at one side of the room, illumining
it faintly.

"Leave this room!" Ruth sat up, drawing the covers
about her with one hand. Of necessity this left one lovely
arm and shoulder bare, for she wore only a shift. Anger
and contempt, however, gave her an icy self-possession.

Tob moved toward the couch confidently, as if sure of
his welcome.

"Have you no decency?" Ruth lashed out at him. "I am
a guest in your home."

He sat on the couch near her feet, and when she drew
them up instinctively, he only moved closer. "How beauti-

ful you are," he said hoarsely. "The women of Judah are not like you." He reached out to touch her bare skin, but Ruth drew back quickly.

"Do you want me to rouse the household?" she asked.

Tob shrugged. "Who would hear you? And who would dare come if they did? I am master here."

"Naomi . . ."

"She is too far away. And she is only an old woman." He inched closer. "You women of Moab are famous for your generous natures," he continued ingratiatingly. "That mark on your forehead shows you are dedicated to love; don't deny it."

"I renounced the role of temple priestess when I married Mahlon."

"But you are still a woman." Tob lunged suddenly at her and gripped her shoulders, forcing her back on the couch. His thick wet lips slobbered over her neck and shoulder. Sick with revulsion, Ruth tried to shove him away, but he was stronger and kept pushing her back on the bed until in desperation she raked his face with her nails, drawing blood.

Tob cursed and released her. Ruth used the moment of respite to leap from the bed and run to the chair over which she had hung her worn and threadbare dress. Ever since leaving Heshbon she had carried a small, jeweled dagger—a present from Mahlon—in the pocket of her dress, as a final means of escape, should her situation become completely intolerable. She fumbled for it now, while Tob scrambled from the couch muttering curses under his breath and came toward her.

He was almost upon her, slender and utterly lovely and helpless in the white shift that was her only garment, when she managed to slide the thin, narrow blade from its sheath. Gripping it in her right hand, she worked to slip on her dress with her left

"Touch me again and I will kill you," she warned breathlessly.

Tob stopped, afraid of the knife and the determination in her face. "Do you dare revile me?" he said angrily. "You, a Moabite!"

"I am the widow of your kinsman." Ruth was busy shrugging the dress down over her body. "The laws of the Most High God protect me."

Tob's face cleared as a new thought occurred to him.

"You are my kinswoman. And a woman of spirit as well. I like spirit," he continued in almost a conversational tone. "Intelligence, too. They are excellent qualities in a wife."

"A wife!"

"You have claimed *your* rights. Perhaps I shall claim mine. Under the Law the next of kin can take the widow of his kinsman to wife . . . if he desires."

He moved toward the door as if he were leaving the room, then lunged at her suddenly, snatching at the hand that held the dagger. But Ruth had not let herself be fooled. Before he could seize her hand, she jerked the knife away and the point nicked his wrist, bringing blood.

Tob squealed with pain and seized his wrist, glaring at her in fury. "You!" he snarled. "You Moabite hussy!" Without molesting her further he rushed from the room.

Ruth finished dressing in frantic haste. She drew her shawl over her head and went to the door, the dagger still in her hand in case Tob were waiting outside. But the hall was empty and she crossed it quickly to the room where Naomi was sleeping, and let herself inside. Her entrance awakened Naomi. "What happened, child?" she asked quickly.

"Tob . . . He tried to force me." Ruth was fighting hysteria.

"What a bitterness has come upon two helpless women!" Naomi cried.

"He says he will take me as his wife because he is the next of kin. I should have stayed in Moab, Naomi! The men of Israel are like all the others."

Naomi put her arm around Ruth's shoulders. "Dry your tears, daughter," she said. "Not every man in Judah is like Tob."

Ruth controlled herself with an effort. "These are your people, and the trouble is all over me. I shall flee to Moab, and then you can live in this house in peace."

"There is a better way," Naomi said decisively. "We will leave here tonight."

"But where can we go? Two women alone?"

"We will seek refuge with the beggars and the poor who live outside the walls. Many honest people live in Judah; they will see that we have our rights under the Law."

"That means I must marry Tob. If he wants me."

"Perhaps we can find money to buy the land that belonged to Mahlon. Then you will be free of Tob and can choose your own husband."

"But I still love Mahlon," Ruth protested. "Besides, who would want a Moabite in Israel as a wife?"

"There is a way to solve every problem," Naomi said matter-of-factly as she dressed. "We will take refuge outside the gate tonight while we decide what is best for us to do."

iv.

The town of Bethlehem began to awaken for the day well before dawn. This was the time of the barley harvest and the reapers must be early in the fields. Like any other oriental village the walls were a beehive of huts and hovels built against the mud and stone of the structure itself. In the open doorways of the huts the people who had been sleeping on their mats in the garments they wore in the daytime, not being able to afford a change for the night, began to stir and make ready for the day's work in the fields.

The women bustled about preparing a frugal morning meal for their men, usually a few dried dates and perhaps a cup of goat's milk. After the men had gone to the fields, they would begin the other activities of their daily life, caring for the children, carding and spinning wool, weaving clothing, pounding grain in stone mortars to make the flat cakes that served as bread—all the manifold activities that made up a woman's busy day. There were no servants here, the dwellers in the wall were too poor for that. And, indeed, few in the city could afford them.

When Ruth and Naomi stumbled from Tob's house in the darkness, they had finally found their way through the gate to the common well that furnished water for most of the town. There they sank down exhausted upon a bench under the shelter that covered the well itself, worn out by their long walk the day before and Ruth's harrowing experience in the house of Tob. Completely unnerved by his attempt to force her, Ruth had not become calm until Naomi drew her head down upon her own shoulder and soothed the younger woman into slumber.

A dog scavenging about nuzzled their ankles and

awakened them. Ruth sat up and rubbed her eyes, still half asleep, not recognizing where she was.

Then realization came. "You should not have let me sleep on your shoulder, Naomi," she said in quick reproach. "I know how tired you must be, too."

"You needed rest more than I, after what happened."

"Did he come after us?"

Naomi shook her head. "There are laws in Israel, Ruth, strict laws. Tob will not dare go against them publicly. You need have no more fear of him, unless——"

"Unless he wants me for his wife?" Ruth asked, her eyes widening with fear. "He threatened that last night."

"I know Tob of old," Naomi said quietly. "He is a windbag. If he troubles you we will go before the council and accuse him of lusting after you."

"But he can still claim me as his wife under your law."

"We will worry about that when we come to it," Naomi said. "I did not bring you to Judah to hand you over to such a one as Tob."

Ruth went over to the well and drew water for Naomi. Only when her mother-in-law had drunk did she fill a cup for herself. Then she poured water into a stone basin beside the well, and, removing the rough shawl that had covered her hair and hidden most of her face, bathed her cheeks and her eyes.

Neither of them noticed an old woman approaching the well from one of the hovels in the wall. She was small and wizened, her hair unkempt, and her face still sticky from food she had eaten the night before. She walked with a peculiarly shuffling gait, her eyes darting about while she muttered to herself in a singsong that was unintelligible except for an occasional word. Obviously the woman was insane, a not infrequent sight around the villages where the old and demented were allowed to run loose so long as they caused no particular trouble.

The madwoman was only a few yards away when Ruth raised her face from the basin and started to dry her skin upon the corner of her shawl. When her glittering eyes saw the small circular mark tattooed on Ruth's forehead, her face was suddenly convulsed with fury. Lifting her hands, the fingers with their long dirty nails curved like talons, she advanced upon Ruth ready to claw. "Moabite!" she screeched. "The Moabites cut off the hand of my son Cheb!"

Ruth stepped back, putting her hands up instinctively to protect herself against this hideous creature. But the madwoman's insane fury subsided as quickly as it had arisen. It was replaced by a smile of cunning that showed broken stumps of teeth.

"Now the Moabites are my son's friends," she said, and giggled as if at a secret known only to herself. Still mumbling, she took a cup of water and drank noisily.

A slender young woman had approached the well, carrying a stone crock upon her shoulder. "Go on your way, Ola," she said, much as if she were speaking to a child. The madwoman spat at her but moved away, still babbling to herself.

"She is harmless," the newcomer explained to Ruth and Naomi as she began to draw water to fill her jar. "Her son, Cheb, was tortured by Moabites years ago and his hand was cut off. She has never been the same since. My name is Rachel," she continued politely. "You must be strangers here not to know Ola, the madwoman of Bethlehem."

"We are Israelites," Naomi said. "But we have just returned to Bethlehem after a long absence."

Ruth was busy plaiting her hair into two strands which she wound about her head.

"What of her?" Rachel asked in a low voice. "I can see the mark of Moab upon her forehead."

"She is my daughter. The widow of my son and a comfort to me in my hour of bitterness."

Rachel smiled. "Under the walls of Bethlehem we are neither Moabite nor Israelite, but all poor together. We work and pray, and then we sing and dance joyfully in the sight of the Lord."

"You have spoken well, Rachel," Naomi said. "We are one with you."

A new sound came to Ruth's ears now, a strange sound indeed for this time of the morning, when it was not yet dawn and only the pale softness of the starlight illuminated the hillsides and the fields of waving grain. The faint piping of a flute could be heard, the strumming of a harp, and, intermittently, a shrill blast upon the ram's-horn trumpet called the shofar.

"It is the first day of the harvest," Rachel explained, her eyes brightening. "The reapers are marching to get their tools. Everybody is happy today."

A procession emerged from the gate. First came a group of children preceding the harvesters, led by a small boy who danced as he played the flute. Everyone was gay. It was a sight to raise the spirits and gladden the heart even of the bitter.

Naomi's face brightened and she looked quickly at Ruth, who was putting her shawl over her head once more. "Where there are harvesters," she said, "will there not be gleaners to follow and pick up the grain they leave behind?"

"Oh yes." Rachel picked up her jar. "I am going to glean, but I must hurry home now or I will be late getting into the fields."

"Would you like to go and glean, Ruth?" Naomi asked.

Ruth looked toward the laughing harvesters who were drinking and filling their water jugs at the well. She had not seen people so happy since before Mahlon's death. "Would they let me?" she asked hesitantly.

"All women who are poor or widowed may glean the fields when the reapers are done."

"Even me?"

"Are we not widows?" Naomi's voice was bitter again for the moment. "And are we not poor?"

"Go to the east field," Rachel called to Ruth as she left the well. "Elkan, the overseer, is a good man and will show you how to glean, after he has given the reapers their tools. I will come in a little while and teach you how to separate the chaff from the grain."

"You are very kind." Ruth's face brightened. "I will meet you there." She started in the direction of the distant field, as the reapers moved away toward the small building where the tools were stored. But she stopped when she realized that Naomi had not moved.

"Are you not coming too, Naomi?" she asked.

The older woman shook her head. "I am too old to stoop in the fields, Ruth. Your strong body must be my support now. Go on and I will meet you here in the evening when the work is over."

Ruth hesitated only a moment, then turned toward the field to which Rachel had directed her. As she looked ahead she straightened her shoulders resolutely. She had never done such work as this, but it was a part of the life she had chosen with Naomi, so she would do it. And it was better by far than living in the house of Tob and submitting to his caresses.

The darkness had begun to lighten a little, but it was still not even dawn when Boaz tied his horse to a tree in a shady corner of the east field. From the saddle he took a reaping hook and as he walked along a path at the edge of the field his eyes lifted to the brightness of the morning star in the east, where a few faint rays of light heralding the rising sun were just beginning to show.

It was the time of day he loved most, this period when the starlight seemed brightest just before waning, and when all the world was bathed in a cool and peaceful beauty. At this hour the land, the field, and the sky were most beautiful. The puny troubles of men and quarrels between them seemed futile, and a man could approach near to the God who had painted all this beauty with firm strokes of a divine brush.

This was the time of the year that Boaz liked best, too, the first morning of the barley harvest, when he came early to the fields, not merely because it was a custom, but because he loved the sight of the waving sea of grain before it fell beneath the blades of the reapers. Boaz was not a man of the sword by choice, but a tiller of the soil, and only the need of his people for a leader had forced him to become a soldier. Having put his hand to the sword, however, he gave to the defense of the land he loved his whole strength, save only for a few moments such as this when Boaz the soldier yielded to Boaz the farmer and herdsman.

He was walking slowly along, stopping to shell a head now and then to test the ripeness of the grain, when he noticed the slender figure of a woman standing at the edge of the field, the shawl over her head and the dimness of the starlight hiding her features from view. But there was no mistaking the graceful lines of her body and the sight brought a stab of pain to Boaz's heart.

Tamar had been slender and graceful like this woman. And young, too, as she undoubtedly was. But she had shamed him by choosing the arms of another, the same arms in whose embrace she had died. And since then his heart had been closed to all women.

Ruth was looking into the distance and had not yet seen Boaz. This early morning visit to the fields had taken her back to her girlhood among the tribes of Edom, where there had been just such fields as this and where the morning star shone most brightly just before the dawn.

"Shalom," Boaz said quietly. "Peace be upon thee, my daughter."

Ruth started. She recognized Boaz's voice at once and turned her head away quickly, lest he realize who she was. Partly this was because she was unwilling for him to know she had been reduced to the status of gleaning in the fields, and partly because she could not restrain a momentary feeling of resentment against him for the part he had played in the tragic sequence of events in Moab which had resulted in the death of Mahlon and her own reduction to such poor circumstances.

"Peace be upon thee," she said in muffled tones.

Boaz frowned. There was something familiar about her slender loveliness, he was sure, yet he could not place her among the young women of Bethlehem. "We have a saying, 'The owner of the land should be first in the fields,' " he said. "Others may come after sunrise, but if the master desires increase he will be there before them."

"Did I do wrong in coming before the other women?" Ruth asked in the same low tone.

"It is no reproach to be early." He moved closer, but, sensing his intention, she took a step away from him, so they were no nearer than before. Her face, with only the eyes and the upper part of the nose revealed above her shawl, was a white blur in the dim light. And yet he sensed without seeing her clearly that she was lovely.

"We have another old saying," he began, and stopped.

Ruth did not speak and after a moment he went on, a little hesitantly, "It is, 'Well met by starlight.' May you have good fortune in your gleaning, young woman."

"Are you master here?"

"Yes. They work in my field today." The light was increasing rapidly now, for the dawn was beginning to break. Boaz looked at her shawl and frowned. "I know something of fabrics since I also own flocks and looms. It appears to me that your shawl was woven in Moab."

Ruth caught her breath. "I—I do come from Moab."

"You come from Moab?" he repeated quickly. "Yet you are gleaning in an Israelite field?"

"Is it wrong for me to be here?"

"There are rules concerning the entrance of Moabites

into Israel." He was sure now that he had seen her somewhere before and heard her voice, yet he still could not remember just where. Nor did she help him, for she still kept her head averted and most of her face covered by the shawl.

"Forgive me." Boaz continued, "if I ask you how you came among us."

"I was married in Moab to a man of Israel," Ruth explained. "He died and I came here with the mother of my husband."

"You are here by right as the widow of an Israelite, then. Even our strict laws give refuge to a wife of one of our own people."

The sound of music came to their ears. Boaz looked across the field to where the reapers were coming to begin their work, carrying their tools, with the children still playing, singing, and dancing before them.

"Glean today in my fields, my daughter," he said kindly. "And keep near the men of Boaz. I shall instruct them to respect you and share with you when there is water and parched corn for the harvesters."

"You are very kind."

"Now that there is a trace of sunlight in the east, I can see that the starlight was unfair to you." The words of the compliment were a little awkward on his tongue, but he had been surprised into saying them by her obvious loveliness. And now that he had spoken he was surprised and embarrassed by his own forwardness.

Ruth, too, was startled by his words and for the moment could say nothing. After her experience the night before with Tob this new sign of interest in her by a man made her a little afraid. Yet nothing about Boaz's manner or his speech was in any way offensive, and she sensed that he was altogether different from Tob.

"I—I thank you," she said slowly, "for letting me glean in your fields. And for—what you said."

"Boaz!" a man's voice called across the field. "We are ready to begin when you have reaped the first bundle."

"Coming, Elkan," Boaz called and turned to Ruth again. "Shalom, woman of Moab."

"Shalom," Ruth whispered in his own tongue. When he was a few yards away she turned to watch his tall form until he joined the harvesters. It was thus that Rachel, coming to the field with the women to glean, found her.

"I see you found the right field, Ruth," she called with a smile, and turned to the women who were with her. "Her husband was an Israelite who died in Moab," Rachel explained. "These are Zelda, Miriam, and Anna come to glean with us."

Ruth greeted the women courteously. Two of them spoke kindly to her, but not Zelda, an embittered woman of many years with hostile eyes. "There is little enough grain for us," she snapped. "Why should we share it with a Moabite?"

"Pay no attention to her," Rachel whispered to Ruth. "They say in Bethlehem that she has an asp for a tongue."

But as Ruth gleaned in the fields after the reapers, her heart was heavy. She had not missed the hate for an outsider in Zelda's voice, and after her experience with Tob she knew now that there were many in Israel who did not obey the teachings of the God they professed to serve.

v.

However much Boaz loved the soil, the herds, and the fields, he could not remain long away from his task of preparing the defense of Judah and Israel against the day when the warriors of Moab would strike. Well before noon he stood upon the wall of the town near the gate with Joseph, supervising a group of men who were repairing a breach where the mud had crumbled away from the stones.

"Hedak's army could ride down this wall with their spears alone," he said with a grim look on his face.

Joseph grinned. "Only after they had passed our spears."

Boaz shrugged. "If we killed one with each spear, there would still be enough to conquer Israel." He glanced down at a bent and frail-looking woman who was plodding toward the gate. "Isn't that Naomi, the mother of Mahlon and Chilion?"

Joseph followed his gaze. "It is indeed! I wonder how she came from Moab to Bethlehem."

"Naomi!" Boaz called, jumping down from the wall to embrace her warmly. "Welcome back to Bethlehem. May God bless you."

"God be with you, Boaz," Naomi said. "I was coming to see you." She staggered and would have fallen, but he steadied her and led her to a boulder.

"Sit here," he said. "Where are Mahlon and Chilion?"

"They are dead. In Moab, at the hands of Hedak's soldiers."

"Dead!" Boaz repeated incredulously, then the color drained from his face. "For helping me escape that night?"

"It was the Lord's will," Naomi said sadly. "He punished us for going into Moab, even as you said He would."

For a long moment Boaz did not speak. The news that Naomi's sons were dead was like a blow over the heart, leaving him sick with the knowledge that he must have been responsible, at least in part, for what had happened. Finally he looked up at the sky, very much as he had that day in Heshbon when he invoked the wrath of God against the fires of Chemosh. "I swear to avenge them for you, Naomi," he said. "Moab shall pay for their lives in blood."

"It was the will of God, Boaz," Naomi repeated. "My daughter and I have made a vow to speak no more of it."

"Your daughter?"

"Mahlon's wife, Ruth. She came back to Israel with me."

"Where is she now?" Boaz asked quickly. But he already knew the answer, just as he knew now why the woman in the fields that morning had seemed familiar.

"She is gleaning, so that we may have food."

"You will lack no more, Naomi," Boaz said at once. "Did not Tob take you in? It is his duty as next of kin."

"We left Tob's house in the middle of the night."

"Why?"

"Because my son's widow is faithful to the memory of her husband."

"A woman faithful even to the memory of her husband." Boaz's voice was suddenly harsh. "I find that hard to believe, Naomi. Will you listen to a word of counsel?"

"I will listen," Naomi said politely.

"Send this Moabite back to her people. There have been more border raids lately and some of our men have been killed. The people are bound to hate her and if she stays there may be trouble."

"We left Heshbon because Hedak planned to kill all Israelites," Naomi told him. "He would not have harmed

Ruth, but she came with me because her heart told her to come. When it tells her to go back, let her go back."

"I have nothing against the Moabite woman, Naomi. I only speak to you as a friend."

"The best friend I have in all the world," she told him quietly, "is Ruth, my daughter."

Boaz shrugged. "We will not quarrel about it, for I am a near kinsman and your son saved my life. But I cannot trust a Moabite, after what I know of them."

Naomi looked at him for a long moment before she spoke. "They say you cannot trust any woman, since your wife betrayed you."

The color drained from Boaz's face as if she had struck him. He turned quickly on his heel and strode away. But when he had gone only a few steps, he came back. "I will not leave you without shelter, Naomi," he said. "Do you remember the small house in the wall next to the old wine press?"

"Yes."

"It shall be yours. Use it as long as you wish, you and the Moabite. But I would have thought you had suffered enough at their hands."

"I have suffered at many hands, Boaz," Naomi said quietly. "Perhaps most of all at my own, just as you have done. But Ruth and I thank you for the house."

The women who gleaned talked incessantly as they followed the reapers, picking up the heads of grain that fell to the ground before they could be tied into bundles, and putting them into their aprons. Ruth worked without talking, both because she felt apart from them and because on the few occasions when she did speak, Zelda snapped at her viciously. Rachel, torn between sympathy and her ties to the other woman, tried to make it as easy on Ruth as she could. But it was a futile attempt, and finally Ruth said, "Go glean with your friends, Rachel. They will only dislike you for troubling yourself with me."

Rachel moved away, obviously glad to be relieved of what she had considered her duty. When the Israelite girl approached the other women, Ruth heard Zelda ask angrily, "Why do we let an enemy glean with us? Who knows that she will not poison the water and kill us all?"

"Quiet, Zelda," Rachel cautioned. "She will hear you."

"Let her hear me!" Zelda deliberately raised her voice. "Maybe then she will go back to Moab."

"She is very beautiful," one of the women said. "Did you ever see such hair?"

"Remember Delilah!" Zelda advised acidly. "And watch your husbands. Moabite women are notorious hussies."

Ruth heard every word, but she was too tired from the unaccustomed work even to resent them. Her apron already held twice as much grain as the others because she watched the ground for loose heads and did not waste time talking, but she wondered how much longer she could go on. Only pride and the knowledge that, if she gave up gleaning now, Zelda would exult in having driven her from the field kept her going at all.

"The Most High created the world for the children of Israel." Zelda's sharp tones floated over to her. "Why should a Moabite have our grain?"

Could these be the same righteous people that Mahlon had told her about? Ruth wondered. Could they really be the chosen people of the one true God, Whose pronouncements she had learned to revere as the only really good way of life?

vi.

It was Boaz's custom to go to the fields in the middle of the morning when the harvesters were at work. Joseph rode with him, and as they dismounted at the edge of the field the reapers looked up and wiped sweat from their foreheads.

"The Lord be with you," Boaz said to the reapers. Even as he spoke, his eyes roved over the field seeking one slender figure among the women that was more graceful than all the rest.

"The Lord bless you," the oldest of the reapers said as Boaz walked among them, noticing a dull blade here, a blistered foot there, and instructing the men how to care for them, for he was a kindly and considerate landlord and employer.

Elkan, the overseer, was in an adjoining field. At the sight of Boaz he hurried over to them. He was of middle age with a kind face, but his manner was somewhat worried. "May the labors of your servants find favor in your eyes, O Lion of Judah," he said courteously to his employer.

Boaz smiled. "May the labors of my servants earn their wages."

"May the lion and the lamb lie down in peace together," Joseph said behind them, and the reapers laughed at the joke.

"Does all go well?" Boaz asked.

"With the reapers, yes. But the women who glean are discontented."

"You are letting some extra heads fall as I instructed?"

"The gleaners in your fields earn twice what they do in others." Elkan wiped his brow. "The women are angry because Rachel brought the Moabite to the field. I did not know she was a heathen until Zelda started using that serpent's tongue of hers. Rachel also said you spoke to the Moabite this morning, so I did not want to drive her from the fields until I had talked to you."

"Why do the women quarrel with her?"

"I suspect because she is more beautiful than the others. She covers herself modestly, but she is still gentle to the eye."

"More than gentle, Elkan." Joseph gave a long whistle of appreciation. "She is like a lily, blooming in a mud patch."

The women had come closer while the men were talking and Zelda overheard them. "Gentle on the eye! Zut!" She spat toward Ruth, who had held back at the sight of the men and was some distance behind the others. "First the Moabites murder our men and make us widows. Now they send their women among us as spies to befuddle young fools with their wiles."

"Watch your tongue, Zelda," Boaz said sharply, "lest you sting yourself and die."

Joseph was still looking at Ruth. "Very gentle," he repeated. "Very gentle indeed."

"Hold my horse, Joseph," Boaz commanded. "I will speak to her."

Startled by the sharpness of his tone, Joseph took the reins. Boaz walked across the cut field to where Ruth was picking up some heads of barley, while Elkan remained near the horses talking to Joseph.

Ruth did not look up as Boaz crossed the field to where

she was working, but she knew he was coming. "Why did you not tell me who you were this morning, Ruth?" he asked without a preamble.

She straightened up and staggered a little with weariness. But when he put out a hand to steady her she moved away.

"Maybe because I was too proud to let you know I had come to your fields to glean," she admitted. "Besides, I know how you hate Moabites."

"Any widow has a right to glean after my reapers," he said a little sharply. "Why do you keep on, if you are so proud?"

She smiled a little wanly. "Pride makes a poor show against starvation. And I have more than just myself to think of now."

"Come over and sit on this rock." He took her by the arm. "I was shocked today when Naomi told me Chilion and Mahlon were dead. You said the night I left Heshbon that they were both safe at home."

"They came after us," she explained, "and fought against the guards in the passageway."

"Then they sacrificed themselves so that I could escape?"

"I think Mahlon wanted it that way. It was his way of paying for what he had done in making swords for Hedak."

"I still wish it had been me instead of them. Why did you not go on to your people in the Edomite tribes, Ruth?"

"Naomi wanted to come back to Bethlehem."

"And you came with her of your own will?"

"Yes."

"Why did you do it, Ruth?"

She looked at her feet and the sandals that, although bought only a few days before, were already worn through in places from the barley stubble. "My husband was Naomi's son. I love him and I love her."

"Mahlon has been dead for many months."

"He is not dead in my thoughts or in my memory," she said simply.

Boaz put out his hand as if to touch her, then drew it back before she could notice the gesture. "Did you love him so deeply, then?"

"All that I believe," Ruth said with deep sincerity, "all that I know of good I owe to Mahlon." Her eyes met his and held them. "He was very proud of you, Boaz. He even believed that you have been chosen by God to deliver Israel from the threat of Hedak."

Boaz gave her a startled look. "You did not grow up as an Israelite. How is it that you know so much about our God?"

"Mahlon taught me."

"Did you learn that the Lord is stern and just?"

"Yes."

"And that He gave us the Law and punishes us for breaking His commandments?"

"Yes," she said. "Mahlon taught me also that the Lord once said: *'The stranger that dwelleth with you shall be unto you as one born among you. And thou shalt love him as thyself, for ye were strangers in the land of Egypt.'*"

"I had forgotten that," Boaz admitted. "And you learned all this in Moab?"

"Yes."

"Then you must indeed have loved Mahlon very much."

Ruth's lips curved in a smile and Boaz was startled again by her beauty. "Yes, I do," she said with great feeling. "He still fills my life."

Boaz looked at her for a long moment. Incredulity, admiration, and envy all showed in his face for the moment. Then he turned abruptly away. "Glean where you will," he said harshly, and strode across the field toward Joseph and Elkan.

Ruth stood watching him. The abruptness of his tone had both startled and hurt her, but there was a light of pity and concern in her eyes, for she sensed that he was still a deeply troubled man, and not alone because of the peril of Judah.

Joseph grinned when Boaz came back to where he and the overseer were standing. But at the sight of the bleak look in his friend's face he sobered. "Zelda and the women will try to spite the Moabite woman," Boaz told the overseer. "So do not let her too long out of your sight."

"It will be quieter here if I send her to another field," Elkan suggested.

"She must glean in no other fields but mine," Boaz said sharply. "And charge the young men not to trouble her either."

"That will not be easy," Joseph laughed, but Boaz

gave him a freezing look that erased the merriment from his face.

Ruth was near them now as she came across the field picking up the loose heads of grain. "Stay close to my henchman, Ruth," Boaz called to her. "When you are thirsty, drink of the clear water that my harvesters have drawn."

"Thank you." She bent her head politely in acknowledgment.

"And do not bow to me," he said curtly. "You are in Israel now, not Moab."

vii.

The work upon the wall was finished by late afternoon. As Joseph and Boaz rode through the city on the way home they passed Tob's shop. Like all the others around it, the shop was open to the street, with the wares displayed in piles upon the floor. And, like the other shopkeepers, Tob sat upon a cushion on the small platform at the entrance to the shop. The slave girl, Adah, was at the back where she could keep watch lest a customer secrete under his robe a bolt of cloth or a small tool of iron from the forges of the Philistine smiths and carry it from the shop without paying.

"Peace be upon thee, Boaz," Tob called unctuously from his platform. "Come drink a glass of wine with me as kinsmen should."

Boaz hesitated momentarily, but got down from his horse and went into the shop. From a small box at the back of the platform Tob took three silver cups and set them on the floor beside him and filled them from a bottle wrapped in a damp cloth to keep it cool.

"How goes the training of the young men?" he asked when they had drunk.

"While we wait for spearheads to come from the forges, we cast staves," Boaz said. "But they gain in skill every day."

"Did you know that our kinswoman, Naomi, has returned from Moab?"

"Yes." Boaz frowned. "She also told me they left your house in the middle of the night."

"It was only a slight misunderstanding." Tob licked his lips. "The Moabite called Ruth is truly a delight to the eyes. Her hair is the color of the setting sun. And the skin of her body is soft like down."

"What lies are these?" Boaz demanded savagely. "Her hair you could see. But her body——"

Tob looked hurt. "In the night she sought to beguile me with her hidden beauty. I repulsed her, but ever since she has been like a fever in my mind."

Boaz seized the front of his kinsman's robe. "I will cut your tongue out by the roots if you are lying to me, Tob. I know this woman. She is not what you say."

Tob had been merely bragging, but now he was afraid, for he had never seen Boaz so angry ."I speak truth, Boaz," he gasped. "I swear it."

"Your oath is as false as your word. Recant or—"

"It is as my master says, noble Boaz." Neither of them had noticed Adah come from the shadows at the back of the shop. "I saw him come from the Moabite woman's room that night."

Boaz glared at the slave girl, but he could not accuse her of lying to confirm Tob's story. Her statement had been a voluntary one and Tob had not even asked her to uphold him.

"I do not hold it against the Moabite that she sought to beguile me, Boaz," Tob said hastily. "In fact, I am thinking of exercising my right as next of kin and taking her to wife."

Boaz's fist clenched and it seemed for a moment that he would strike Tob. Then he turned on his heel and, seizing the reins of his horse from the rack before the shop, vaulted into the saddle and galloped down the street.

Naomi was waiting by the well when the reapers came from the field at sundown. The women who had been gleaning followed the men, laughing and bandying pleasantries with them. Behind them plodded the lonely figure of Ruth. She was tired to her very bones and did not even look up until Naomi went to her and took her by the arm. Then she managed to smile wanly and dropped gratefully upon the bench to which Naomi led her.

"What a great evil I did you in letting you come with me to Israel," the older woman said contritely.

"You begged me not to come," Ruth reminded her.

"It is just that I am not accustomed to work like this. And the women hate me because I am not an Israelite."

"They hate you most because you are beautiful."

"Look!" Ruth opened her apron. "I gleaned a whole ephah of barley today."

"Where?"

"In the field of Boaz."

"I saw him by the wall this morning," Naomi said. "He warned me to send you back to Moab."

"I am not surprised," Ruth admitted. "Boaz finds it hard to trust any woman, but I suppose we shouldn't blame him when his wife ran away with a Moabite."

"He is a stubborn fool. But at least he is generous. He gives us food from his field and a house in which to live."

"A house! Where?"

"It is only a little place in the wall beside the old wine press. But it is a house of our own. And now that you have done so well with the gleaning, we will have food and even some oil for the lamp."

"I must thank Boaz when I see him again." Ruth smiled. "Mahlon once said we were like flint and iron—whenever we came together there was fire."

Naomi looked at her keenly. "I wouldn't blame you for hating him."

"I don't hate him, Naomi," Ruth protested. "The future of his people weighs heavily on Boaz's shoulders." Then she added softly, as if to herself, "He was very kind to me in the field this morning, when we met by starlight."

viii.

The sun had barely risen the next morning when Boaz and Joseph rode through the fields where the reapers were busy working, with a line of women gleaning after them. As she had the day before, Ruth was a little behind the other women, alone, searching the ground closely for every barley head that fell from the hands of the reapers when the sharp hooks cut through the stalks.

Joseph noted how Boaz's eyes were drawn to the slender, graceful figure. "It seems wrong, doesn't it?" he asked.

"What seems wrong?"

"So much youth and loveliness. And she is so alone."

"Take care! She makes conquests easily."

"I think Tob and Adah were lying yesterday, Boaz."

"Why should they?"

"I don't know yet. But neither of that pair ever does anything without a purpose. Give me time and I may find out what it is they are up to now."

Boaz frowned, but he did not rebuke Joseph, as the younger man had half expected him to do. Instead he dismounted and walked across the field to Ruth. She did not see him until his shadow fell upon her, then she looked up quickly and started to move away.

"What are you afraid of?" The sharpness in his voice stopped her.

"Nothing. You startled me."

"Have my people been kind to you as I ordered?"

"Yes." The other women had stopped their gleaning to listen, but when they saw Ruth's eyes upon them they quickly gave their attention to the work once more.

"Then you are happy in Israel?" he asked in a lower tone, so the women would not be able to hear.

"Happy?" Her cheeks grew pink with indignation. "Would you be happy if people hated you without reason and accused you falsely?"

"Perhaps they have a reason. Or think they have one."

For a moment Ruth did not speak, but her eyes did not fall before his. "Are you saying that anyone really believes Zelda's stupid idea that I am a spy?"

"You can hardly blame them. You are Moabite and you came here voluntarily when you could have had a life of ease among the Edomite tribes."

"Since you hate all Moabites and all women," she said sharply, "don't you agree with them?"

"My own feelings do not matter, Ruth." There was an odd gentleness in his tone, very much as it had been when they had met by starlight the morning before and when he had not known who she was. "I must think only of the welfare of Israel. The question of whether or not you may stay in Judah is mine to decide. Even if—if I loved you—I would still have to question you and determine why you came to Judah."

"If you could trust any woman, you would know why I came to Judah with Naomi," Ruth said quietly. "As you say, I could have gone back to my people instead of gleaning in the fields and being spit upon by Zelda."

"If Zelda harms you I will——"

"No one can harm me by reviling me, so long as I know in my heart what I am."

"Then why did you come to Bethlehem?"

"For the reason I gave you yesterday. Because I love Naomi and she is the mother of my husband."

The temptation to believe her was strong until he remembered Tob's insinuations and Adah's confirmation.

"No doubt you are an authority on love," he burst out harshly then. "Tob has told me how soft is the skin of your body. He even speaks of marrying you, although why he should escapes me. I seem to remember that Moabite custom does not require it."

Slowly the color drained from Ruth's cheeks. When she spoke her voice was like a whiplash. "And you believed him, of course?"

"He was in your room. Adah saw him come from it."

"I admit that he was there."

"Do you deny that Tob made love to you as he claims he did?"

"You are not the next of kin, Boaz," Ruth said deliberately. "And you are not responsible for either Naomi or me, so you have no right to demand that I deny or affirm anything to you."

"But Tob said——"

"Tob said what he said," Ruth told him scornfully. "If you wish to believe him, then believe him." She jerked out the small dagger she had carried always with her since leaving Heshbon. "But if you are so anxious to learn the truth, ask Tob how he got the cut on his arm. And then see if the point of this dagger does not fit the wound."

The realization that Tob had duped him into believing the worst, because of his instinctive distrust of all women, swept over Boaz with a sudden rush of gladness that the things he had believed of her were not true. He had slept but little last night, torn between his conviction that she was as sincere and virtuous as she seemed to be and Tob's accusation.

"Ruth," he said contritely. "What can I say, except to beg your forgiveness for being a fool?"

It was Ruth's turn to be startled now by the change in his manner, and her anger faded before his apology. "We will speak of it no more," she said gently. "Are there any more questions?"

"I must still determine for the safety of Judah that your coming here will cause no harm."

"And for yourself?"

"I have had no self for many years. My only concern is for the welfare of my people."

"Then I will swear if necessary to the leader of Israel that I am not a spy." She smiled. "But you must decide for yourself, Boaz, whether or not I speak the truth about this and about Tob."

She turned back to her gleaning and so did not see him take a step toward her with his hands oustretched, as if he were going to take hers. He did not touch her, however. Instead he turned back to where Joseph was waiting with the horses, and startled his lieutenant by smiling at his jokes.

The reapers stopped for the noon meal under the shade of a large terebinth tree. Boaz, being a generous landlord, had provided well for his workmen. There were bread, freshly parched barley kernels, cheese, and cold goat meat. Today a real treat had been provided, a large goatskin of wine hanging from a tree, with plenty of earthenware cups from which to drink.

Much laughter and gay talk passed back and forth between the reapers and the women who sat nearby, and much making of rough jokes. One of the gleaners had brought a shepherd's pipe and, while the others ate, he blew a brisk, gay tune.

A few children had come from the city, knowing that after the reapers finished eating, scraps would be left for them. A boy and a small slender girl were dancing to the merry lilt of the pipe. Some workers sang to the music, some kept time, while the younger men frankly eyed the girls.

One group was joking with Yosko, a comical little fellow with bandy legs and a scant beard, who fancied himself very much a ladies' man. Yosko was not a reaper; in fact he was a substantial landowner. But ever since he had happened to visit the fields yesterday and had seen Ruth, he had hung around, staring at her and smiling whenever she happened to look up. She had not encouraged him, but she had not repulsed his interest either, for she saw that Yosko was being made the butt of the reapers' rough humor unwittingly. In a way, she recognized, they were both outcasts, Yosko because of his comical figure, his stringy beard and wizened face, she because she came from another land.

Ruth sat a little distance from the women, eating some food that Yosko had brought her with a great show of consideration. But from where she sat she could still hear Zelda haranguing the others.

"My son was killed by a Moabite," the Israelite woman was saying. "And I say she is a——"

"Hush, Zelda." Rachel's voice cut off the last word, but Ruth knew without being told that it was "spy" or "hussy," Zelda's favorite terms for her.

"I will not hush," Zelda snapped. "And you will know when we have all been betrayed that I spoke the truth. If any of us are alive then," she added darkly.

Desperately unhappy and alone, Ruth stared down at the ground and hoped that the tears smarting behind her eyelids would not begin to flow openly so the others could see.

The musician finished his tune and put up his instruments. "Shoo!" he told the children, scattering them with a flourish of his pipe. The little girl who had been dancing skipped over to where Ruth was sitting and regarded her with the frankly direct, appraising look of childhood until she looked up and smiled.

"My name is Zimma," the child said. "What is yours?"

"Ruth."

"You are pretty. Can I sit in your lap?"

"Of course." Ruth made room for her. "Are you comfortable?"

"Oh yes." Zimma began to examine Ruth's hair, a tendril of which had escaped from beneath the shawl drawn across her forehead. She tried to pull another lock from beneath the shawl and, before Ruth realized what had happened, the fastening came loose and the cloth fell back from her face.

"Oh-h-h," the child screamed suddenly, pointing at the mark of Moab upon Ruth's forehead. "What is that?"

The child's cry turned every eye upon Ruth and the pagan symbol tattooed into her skin. She quickly adjusted the shawl again to hide the symbol, but she could not fail to see the other women nudging each other in shocked self-righteousness, while the whispered word "Moabite" drifted in the hot, still air of midday.

"You had better go now," Ruth said quickly to Zimma, and removed the child gently from her lap. She smiled shakily and patted Zimma's head, then picked up her apron and started toward the field where she had been gleaning.

Boaz arrived for his midday visit to the field in time to witness the incident. He started toward Ruth, but just then Yosko came hopping on his bowed legs over to where he stood, bringing him a cup of wine. The little man was very excited.

"I have never felt so in my life before, Boaz," he babbled. "Perhaps I shall never eat again."

"What's wrong with you?" Boaz asked, grinning at his comical friend.

"She's a goddess." Yosko pointed to Ruth. "She's—she's not mortal, Boaz. I am blinded by her beauty. I'd be willing to give her my north field just to see her smile."

Boaz's face sobered. "Fields are valuable. Think a little longer about that, Yosko."

"I have thought. I've made up my mind and when Yosko makes up his mind it's like a rock. I shall ask her at the winnowing ground. I will take her from whatever man she's with and ask her."

He looked up at Boaz, leaning back on his bandy legs because of his friend's greater height. "But maybe someone else will want her before then. I should ask her now."

"Don't rush things so, Yosko," Boaz advised. "Finish your wine."

"I have no need of wine." Yosko was distraught now, in terror that someone else might ask for Ruth before he could do so. "You use words well, Boaz, but when I try to talk to a woman my tongue is a stone. Please speak to her for me."

"Has she encouraged you, Yosko?"

"She smiled at me. Twice this morning she smiled at me."

"She could do worse at that," Boaz muttered to himself, and a harsh look settled upon his face. "Come with me, Yosko," he said abruptly. "I will speak to her now."

Ruth looked up from her work when the two men approached. "Shalom!" she said quietly.

"This neighbor of mine, Yosko, has something to say

to you," Boaz said abruptly without returning the polite greeting.

"Yes?" Ruth looked at Yosko. The little man's face was white and set. His lips moved, but no sound came from them.

"Can't you tell her what you told me just now, Yosko?" Boaz demanded.

Yosko tried to speak again, but no words came. He shook his head and moved a few steps away, dumbly imploring his friend to speak in his behalf.

Boaz turned to Ruth. "Yosko told me just now," he said, "speaking very earnestly, that you had struck him in the heart."

"I?" Ruth asked, startled.

"Not that he complains of what you have done," he assured her with a note of sarcasm. "He says when he looks at you, it is as if you were a goddess and not mortal. His eyes are blinded by your face."

Soft color flooded into Ruth's cheeks. "Are you—are you merry with wine?" she asked quietly.

Boaz did not speak for a long moment. When he did, his voice and manner had changed completely. "I meant to humiliate you," he admitted. "But you can see that Yosko means no jest, nor do I now."

His eyes met hers and suddenly there were only the two of them in all the world. Little Yosko, only a few feet away and hearing everything, the reapers, the women, and the children—all were forgotten.

"Do you know the miracle a morning star can be when a man has traveled all night in the darkness and thought to himself the miles would never end?" he asked in a voice filled now with wonder. "When of a sudden one star is brighter than all the stars and his heart leaps up because in the east there is a hint of morning?"

Ruth's eyes did not leave his. When she spoke her voice was soft so that only he could hear. "I have traveled on many a dark night."

"And thought you would see no morning star?"

"There has been no morning star for me these many months," she said softly. "Until——"

"Then you know the miracle it can be when it comes. A woman's face, seen suddenly perhaps in passing, maybe in a field by starlight. If it strikes a man dumb, if he cannot speak the words but must only hint at them, perhaps you will forgive. It is not always possible to say what has happened or when it happened."

"There is nothing to forgive." Ruth's eyes were shining. "Nothing to forgive, Boaz."

He stared at her for a long moment, as if even now he could not really believe the truth of her beauty and of what was shining in her eyes. Then he turned away without speaking and strode toward where his horse was tethered, with little Yosko trotting after him.

"Boaz." Yosko plucked at his sleeve. "Do you think she likes me?"

"Some other time I will speak to you of this, Yosko." Boaz shook the little man's hand from his arm.

"But do you think she likes me?"

"You heard what I said," Boaz said harshly. "Some other time."

ix.

The end of the reaping was the signal for a time of celebration, the Festival of the First Fruits. A week later would come another and totally different ceremony upon the cleared open space of hard-packed earth before the grain bins called "the winnowing ground." The celebration of the first fruits was held, however, in a shady park amid the fields where the grain had ripened.

Late in the afternoon people began pouring out of the city toward the park where the festival was to take place. A group of musicians led the procession in a hymn of thanksgiving, accompanying the singers on pipes, timbrels, psalters, the shofar, and other instruments.

Ruth had hesitated to join in the festival, remembering how the women had shunned her in the fields. But Naomi insisted that they go and, as they moved along with the chanting crowd, she could not help being impressed by both the solemnity and the joy of the occasion. Naomi had told her that day in Heshbon. before she and Mahlon were married, of the joy the Israelites found in serving the Lord. Ruth could understand it now because she felt it herself.

An altar of stones had been built at one side of the open space. Upon it a fire was burning and before it stood a patriarchal old man with a flowing beard and a gentle face, the cantor. As he waited, the crowd opened to let a group of children through. One carried a bundle of barley, another some bunches of grapes, a third a young fowl, and the fourth a baby lamb that had only just been born.

The cantor accepted the gifts and placed them upon the altar to be consumed by the flames. First the grain, next the fruits, then the fowl, and finally the lamb; after the ritual killing had been done all were sent up in a smoke of thanksgiving to the Most High. As the smoke of the sacrifice rose in the still air of the afternoon, the cantor led the people in chanting a poem of thanks to God, who had given them these gifts.

"Our hearts rejoice in the Lord; He quickeneth the dry seed in the soft earth; He refresheth the land with rain; He maketh grow the spreading olive; the warm wind of the east is the breath of His nostrils; He bringeth to full ripeness the seed of grass and wine and trees; He spreadeth before man a feast in the land; blessed be the Lord, blessed be His name."

"Let us be joyful in the sight of the Lord for His many blessings," the cantor commanded when the poem was finished. "Let us sing and dance in His praise."

At once the musicians struck up a lively air and the younger people began to dance eagerly upon the close-cropped grass of the park. It was a dance of joy, with much laughing and shouting as the dancers reached out to draw more and more people into the circle. Finally only the old, who sat in a circle around the dancing floor, and a few who were not dancing remained.

Ruth and Naomi stood at one side of the dancing floor. Watching the gaiety of the dancers, Ruth's eyes began to sparkle and, quite unconsciously, her foot started to tap and her body to sway gracefully in the rhythm of the music.

Boaz and Joseph were among those watching the dancers. The young man did not miss Boaz's occasional searching glance over the crowd.

"Looking for someone?" he asked, smiling. "She is over there."

Boaz saw Ruth then and a light of tenderness came into his eyes.

"Are you going to dance?" Joseph asked. "I can see that she would like to by the way her foot is tapping to the music."

"You know I never dance any more," Boaz said. "I have no desire to look like an idiot."

Joseph grinned. "Well, since you often call me one I might as well live up to my name. With your permission." He made an ironical bow to Boaz and threaded his way to where Ruth and Naomi were standing.

"Oh, I couldn't," Ruth said quickly when he held out his hand to her.

"Why not? You are prettier than the lot of them and, I'll wager, a better dancer."

"But——"

Joseph seized her hands before she could resist and drew her among the dancers. And since she really did want to dance, Ruth resisted no more but let the rhythm seize hold of her.

It was a sprightly dance, performed mostly by young couples. Joseph was a graceful dancer and Ruth had been almost a professional in her early role of a priestess in the Temple of Chemosh in Heshbon, so they matched perfectly. Laughing at Joseph's sallies as they whirled about, executing intricate steps that few of the others were skillful enough to try, the two of them made a picture of joyful abandon with nothing of sensuality about it.

Soon the other couples began to drop out, preferring to watch the two who were so obviously more expert than they. Faster and faster the music went, but the handsome pair never missed a beat. Ruth was flushed and happy and by far the loveliest among all the women.

Tob had been standing at the edge of the circle of older people watching, with Adah a few paces behind him, as befitted their outward relationship of master and slave. Now she moved up behind him and said in a low whisper, "Observe how the Moabite bewitches Boaz."

Tob glanced to where Boaz was standing watching the two dancers with a smile on his face. What he saw made him frown with displeasure.

"If Boaz should marry her and have a son," Adah goaded him, "you would no longer be the next of kin."

Tob's scowl deepened and he muttered a curse.

"Besides," Adah continued scornfully, "you desire the

Moabite yourself. Will you remain silent while she bewitched Boaz?"

"You are right," Tob said in sudden decision. He charged
into the open circle where only a few couples were dancing
now, and bore down upon Ruth and Joseph, a picture of
self-righteous indignation with his eyes blazing, his face
beetling red, and his robe flapping about his legs.

"Stop!" he shouted. "Stop this abomination unto the
Lord!" Turning upon Joseph furiously, he demanded, "Will
you help this Moabite cast shame upon the women of
Bethlehem?"

Her cheeks flaming with horror and embarrassment,
Ruth broke loose from Joseph's hand and ran to Naomi,
who put an arm about her daughter-in-law's slender
shoulders.

The musicians had stopped playing at Tob's startling
interruption. Those who were dancing quickly moved away
from the open space, leaving only Joseph to face him.
The crowd itself was uncertain just where to take sides,
but this could not last long. Zelda and the other women
who hated Ruth would not miss this opportunity to stir
them up as soon as they recovered from their own surprise.

Joseph faced Tob without flinching, but it was Boaz
who came to the rescue. Striding into the open circle in
the center of the crowd, he spoke to his kinsman, his
face dark with anger.

"The Most High counsels us to love strangers, Tob," he
said sharply. "Do you dare place yourself above the commandments of God?"

Tob was momentarily taken aback, but the shrill voice
of Zelda came from the crowd. "She is an enemy."

There might have been trouble, even with Boaz defending Ruth, had not Joseph said loudly, with just the right
note of scorn, "Boaz called you a fat sheep more than
once in the council, Tob. But I didn't know until now
that you are really an old ram coveting the prettiest ewe
in the flock."

The crowd roared with delight when Joseph stuck his
fingers up beside his head in a perfect caricature of the
short horns of an old ram and started walking sedately
around the circle leering at the young girls. One of them
caught the spirit of the jest and pretended to leap away.

Suddenly frisky, Joseph kicked up his heels and chased her through the crowd.

Completely outfaced by the delighted shouts of the crowd. Tob stole away, and Boaz signaled to the musicians to begin once more. Some of those around Ruth smiled and spoke jokingly to her. She realized then, with a sudden burst of happiness, that she was more nearly accepted by the people of Bethlehem since the incident than she had been before.

Joseph came back and took Ruth by the hands again. But he did not take her to the dancing floor. Instead he guided her over to where Boaz was standing and put her hands in his. Before either of them realized what he was doing, Joseph ran to the musicians and started to lead them in the simple music of a pastoral dance.

Boaz stood stiffly for a moment holding Ruth's hands. But when she smiled encouragingly and drew him toward the dancers, he did not resist. At first he danced awkwardly, but he was naturally accustomed to the rhythm of the saddle and Ruth was so graceful and lovely that he soon gave himself up to the spirit of the dance as zestfully as did his partner.

Advancing and receding in the simple figure, they touched hands again and again, until the music rose on the last beat and brought them together. All along the line the men were kissing the girls, as was customary at the end of this dance. Boaz hesitated only momentarily, then suddenly seized Ruth and kissed her soundly. When they drew apart, each looked at the other in wonder, dazed and surprised by this thing that had happened to them.

Then the crowd rushed upon them, pretending to pelt them with flowers, as was customary to do with a bride and groom. Boaz realized the meaning of this and was suddenly stiff, but Ruth's eyes were shining and she was obviously very happy at being accepted by the people.

The dancing continued until long after dark. Naomi left early and Boaz walked home with Ruth, holding her hand as they approached the town by a roundabout route through the fields and olive groves.

"Tamar and I were married many years ago at the Festival of the First Fruits," he said thoughtfully. It was the first time his dead wife had been mentioned since

Ruth had flared out at him in Heshbon for criticizing her dancing costume.

"Don't speak of it, if the memory still brings you pain," Ruth said quickly.

"Somehow I want to speak of her now," he said. "She was a woman whose vanity fed upon the admiration of men, and I was busy with my workers, my fields, and my herds, so we grew apart. When I learned that she had left me for the arms of a Moabite lover, I wanted only to kill him and see her stoned as an adulteress at the gates of Bethlehem. But now——"

Ruth did not prompt him, sensing that he must think out in his own way this thing that had been in his heart through the years since she had first seen him.

"Now I am not sure any longer," he admitted. "Perhaps I failed her as much as she did me. It is a difficult thing for a man to understand the heart of a woman."

Ruth smiled. "It is really very simple when a woman loves a man. There's nothing in her heart then but him."

"Ruth." He turned to face her and took both her hands. "When I told you what little Yosko said about you, did you know then that I was speaking for myself?"

"Yes . . . I knew."

"But you said nothing."

"There was nothing I could say."

"You must have known I was in torment away from you. And that the whole world has meaning for me only when I am with you. Tell me you know these things, Ruth, for I must be sure that you feel as I do."

"I will tell you!" Ruth cried, a sudden happiness flooding her soul. "I have been in torment too. Oh, Boaz, Boaz. I have been in such a wild torment that——"

Not waiting for her to finish, his strong arms swept her into a passionate, yet infinitely tender, embrace, and his lips found hers.

Naomi was already lying down when Ruth entered the house. She was not asleep, however, and her quick glance did not miss the flush in Ruth's cheeks, the brightness of her eyes, and the way she moved as if she were walking upon a dream.

"Well," Naomi said. "Did you enjoy the festival?"

"Oh yes! I am happier than I have been since . . ."
Ruth stopped and the rich color left her face, leaving it

marble-pale. Suddenly she threw herself down on the couch beside Naomi, and buried her face in the older woman's breast.

"Why are you weeping, Ruth?" Naomi asked.

"Oh, Naomi! Everything has gone wrong!"

"Come now. Surely not everything."

Ruth lifted a tear-wet face. "I love Boaz. I found out tonight."

"Why shouldn't you?" her mother-in-law said matter-of-factly.

"But it is wrong."

"How?"

"When—when I let myself love Boaz, I am unfaithful to the memory of Mahlon."

Naomi smiled. "Who could speak for my son better than his mother, dear? And I tell you now that even Mahlon could see nothing wrong in your loving the man he honored most."

"Then you approve?"

"Heartily. Both of you have known great unhappiness, and you deserve the happiness you can bring each other. May God bless you both and give you strong sons."

"Tonight when Boaz kissed me," Ruth told her then, "all the sorrow in my heart seemed to break away and fall in pieces at his feet. It was as if I had never felt sorrow, but only the joy I used to know with Mahlon. I even seemed to hear a voice saying, 'Ruth, lift up your eyes. You are a woman again.'"

x.

There was happiness in the hearts of Boaz and Ruth that night, but none in the house of Tob. Adah followed him from the threshing floor and a quarrel began as soon as they were out of the hearing of the crowd, continuing on to a climax in Tob's bedroom where he was preparing for the night.

"I was angry when you tried to force the Moabite woman," Adah lashed out.

"You mean when she tried to beguile me," Tob corrected virtuously.

"You need not lie to me, *master*." Adah spat out the

word contemptuously. "You are not even the ram that Joseph called you, but an old goat."

"Take care!" Tob screamed, beside himself with rage. "You are still a slave, Adah. I can have you whipped."

Adah gave him a withering look. "Suppose I told how you solaced certain women of Bethlehem when their husbands were otherwise occupied?"

"Hush!" Fear replaced Tob's indignation. The penalty for such a deed was death by stoning. "What would you have me do?" he asked in a more placating tone.

"Get rid of the Moabite."

"I could take her as my wife," he said thoughtfully. "Then she could not marry Boaz and raise up sons to cheat me out of the inheritance."

"You can marry her if it comes to the worst," Adah agreed reluctantly. "But try to think of a better way."

"The council meets in a few days. If I were to convince them that we should invoke the old laws against the entry of foreigners into the country, Boaz could not marry her."

"It is a good plan," Adah agreed. "But see that you do not let it fail while drooling over the beauty of the Moabite. Even if you do marry her, you will not enjoy her long. I will see to that myself."

The Council of Elders, which governed the tribe of Judah, met in the large room in Bethlehem where Boaz had addressed the council of Israel upon his return from Moab. Usually they transacted only routine business unless someone guilty of a crime punishable by death was to be judged.

Tob had not made the mistake of openly sponsoring the move by which he sought to keep Boaz from taking Ruth as his wife. For two days he had been busy among the older and less tolerant members of the council, laying the groundwork and sowing seeds of fear in their hearts against Moab. He had to move carefully, however, lest he give further encouragement to Boaz's demand that Judah be armed.

When Nathan, an old and respected elder, rose at the end of the council meeting to introduce what he described as a "special matter," the elders settled back in their seats to listen. Boaz did the same, although he was fidgeting to be about the work of training the young men now that the labors of the harvest were finished and the grain was drying before the winnowing.

Tob was presiding. "What matter do you wish to bring before us, Nathan?" he asked respectfully, giving no hint that he already knew.

"We all know that recently the Lion of Judah was almost taken from among us through the treachery of Moab," Nathan began. "For many years now we have allowed the people of other nations to come and dwell among us, even to own land in spite of the ancient laws against the entry of aliens into Israel and the intermarriage of heathen women with our young men."

Boaz shot Nathan a startled look and glanced quickly at Tob. After the incident at the Festival of the First Fruits he had fully expected Tob to make some move against Ruth. But Tob, as president of the council, exhibited only the judicious consideration of his views that a man of Nathan's age and standing was due, it being an ancient custom in Israel that age and wisdom were synonymous and therefore to be respected.

"It is not unreasonable to believe that some of these heathen would spy upon us if they had a chance and send word back to the countries from which they came," Nathan continued. Several members of the council nodded agreement.

"Why have you just now arrived at this opinion, Nathan?" Boaz asked. "We have allowed others refuge among us for many years and have not invoked the old laws."

Tob had anticipated such a question and had carefully coached the old man in the answer, without letting him know, of course, that he was doing so. "We have only just now begun to train the young men in throwing spears," Nathan pointed out, "and to build up a supply of arms to protect us from attack. Were spies in Judah to reveal these preparations to our enemies, our defenses would be damaged."

"I doubt if we make many moves that Hedak does not know of as soon as we make them," Boaz said. "But I can see your point. What measures do you propose?"

"That we close the borders to all outsiders and invoke the ancient laws against those already here. In a time of danger these are simple enough precautions to take for our safety."

Zadok, another of the elders who had also been coached

by Tob, spoke. "I agree with Nathan," he said. "When the
foreigners come into Israel, they often continue to worship
their own gods and practice their own customs. Soon it
will be accepted among us that some worship the Most
High God, while others bow down to graven images and
false gods. This is worse than a pestilence, for our people
may follow them and drift away from their own God, as
they did while Moses was on the Mount of Sinai."

Boaz shook his head. "I am sure the Most High can
hold His own against heathen gods. My kinsman, Naomi,
and her sons, lived in Moab. Yet they continued to worship
Him."

"We are a unique people," Zadok insisted. "Our God
should be for us alone."

"Would you deny Him to others?" Boaz asked. "Remember that He has counseled us to give shelter to foreigners and to love them as our own people."

"But we are ringed about on all sides by powerful
kingdoms," Zadok objected. "Kingdoms that bow down
to evil and do not let us go into their own lands. Kingdoms
that seek to destroy us and break our faith. Why should
we let their people come into our country when they do
not let us go into theirs?"

"Would you fight their evil by adopting their ways?"
Boaz demanded. "By refusing shelter to those not of our
own people and denying to those who come to us for
refuge the right to learn of the one true God and worship
Him?"

When no one spoke in answer, Boaz continued, "If we
take in a few homeless people from other lands and give
them sanctuary, is it not more likely that the strangers
will turn to our ways than that we will turn to theirs?"

"This is strange talk indeed from one who bears the
brand of Moab on his back," Nathan said.

Tob had not spoken yet, not wanting to let Boaz know
that it was he who had initiated the move to invoke the
old harsh laws. But he saw now that the tide of the argu-
ment was going against him. "It could be that Boaz is
bewitched," he suggested slyly. "I have heard something
to that effect."

"Perhaps my eyes do see clearly for the first time in
many years," Boaz admitted frankly. "They also see that
closing the border and persecuting foreigners in our land

will be an insult that will give Hedak an excuse to attack us."

Zadok and Nathan, the foremost protagonists so far for the proposal to invoke the old laws, looked at one another doubtfully. "I had not thought of that," Nathan admitted.

"Nor I," Zadok agreed.

"Mind you," Boaz continued, "I think the opportunity to show those who come to us that our God is just and merciful is still the most important consideration. That and the fact that we can only lower our own standards if we try to fight evil with evil. We are a peaceful people and want nothing that any nation possesses. If the sword must be drawn, I say let others draw it first. Then we will defend ourselves. But let us keep kindness, justice, and love for one another as our weapons against evil as long as we can. To affront the heathen by invoking the old laws that made so much trouble in Canaan when our people first settled here is neither kind nor just. Nor is it the course I believe the Most High God would have us follow."

"If we do invoke these laws, Boaz," Tob said, making a last attempt to put his kinsman in a bad light, "would you still lead our soldiers in defense of Judah?"

"The defense of the land that God has given us is a part of my duty to Him," Boaz said simply. "Nothing we can do here in this council will change that."

"You have spoken well, Boaz," Nathan said quietly. "I will not vote for any change in the laws."

"Nor I," Zadok agreed. And so it went around the council, with each man supporting Boaz. Tob, recognizing defeat when he saw it, gave in as gracefully as he could, but inside, he was seething with a murderous rage against Boaz for foiling his seemingly foolproof plan.

When the meeting broke up, Boaz walked out with Nathan and Zadok, both of them he knew to be pious and God-fearing, if a little more inclined to caution than he thought proper under the circumstances.

"I am glad you talked us out of taking a foolish and dangerous step in a time of peril, Boaz," Nathan said warmly. "If Tob had not misled me——"

"Was Tob behind this?"

"Why, yes. He talked to me of it for more than an hour yesterday."

"And with me," Zadok agreed. "I will give him a tongue-lashing this very day for misleading me."

"No," Boaz said. "Leave Tob be. This is a matter between us two alone!"

xi.

Having failed in his first course of action, Tob wasted no time in initiating the second, and more attractive one, as far as he was concerned. Ruth left the house by the wine press early to glean in a field that was being reaped some distance from Bethlehem. Before the sun was two hours high there was a knock on the door. Naomi opened it and saw Tob standing outside with two men a few yards behind him.

"What do you want?" she demanded.

"Where is the Moabite? The widow of your son, Mahlon?"

"She is safe from your hands. What do you want with her?"

"I have come to offer her the protection of my house and my couch in marriage."

"I spurn the offer in her name," Naomi said scornfully.

Tob shrugged. "You know the Law, Naomi. I was next of kin to your husband, Elimelech. His property descended to Mahlon, the elder son, so I have the right of next of kin toward Mahlon as well."

"That is true," Naomi said warily.

"If I buy the property that was Elimelech's and Mahlon's," Tob said confidently, "I buy Mahlon's widow as my wife. That, too, is the Law."

"How can you pay for the property?" Naomi demanded. "It is common talk in Bethlehem that you owe everyone. And Boaz the most of all."

"I can make a token payment. Then the Moabite cannot marry until I have finished paying, or until I renounce my claim as next of kin by giving another man my shoe." He grinned at Naomi. "And my shoes will stay on my feet until Ruth removes them at the marriage bed."

Naomi's heart sank. She knew that what Tob said was true under the laws of Israel, laws which every pious follower of the God of Isaac and Jacob obeyed under pain of death.

"So you see I am within my rights, Naomi," Tob continued. Before she realized what he was doing, he had drawn a small bag of coins from his belt. With a quick gesture he tossed the bag to her, and Naomi, without thinking, instinctively caught it.

"You are the witnesses," Tob said loudly to the two men who stood behind him. "Witnesses that I have this day made a token payment upon the property of Elimelech and Mahlon, who are dead. This payment gives only me the right of first kinsman under the Law."

"We are witnesses," the two men said stolidly. "This day we will set the thing in writing before a scribe of the Law."

As Tob turned triumphantly away, Naomi called after him angrily, "You'll be buried in your shoes, Tob. And good riddance it will be."

On that same night in Heshbon, Cheb, the merchant and spy, stood before Prince Hedak in the latter's ornate palace, from which he ruled Moab with an iron hand, using the boy King Akton as a puppet.

"You were not due here for another two weeks at least, Cheb." Hedak frowned his displeasure when the Israelite was ushered in. "How shall I see in Israel with no eyes, not even your treacherous ones?"

"I came to warn you," Cheb said. "You must attack at once."

"At once!" Hedak's face darkened with anger. "Does the jackal tell the lion how to fight?"

"Boaz is preparing Judah for war. And the other tribes are following his lead."

"He began too late." Hedak shrugged. "I will be ready to move in a few more months, when the men from the northern tribes reach Heshbon and finish their training. Then we will engulf Israel as your people claim the Red Sea did the Egyptians. After all, we have swords and Boaz's army has none."

"He has persuaded the Council of Israel that spears can prevail against swords."

"So they can," Hedak admitted. "At a distance."

"Boaz is training the young men in throwing spears,"

Cheb warned. "I saw them as I came along the road from Bethlehem."

"They will be like children throwing sticks," Hedak said scornfully.

"Not so, noble Prince," Cheb dared to say. "He has set up targets shaped like men and horses. They even draw the targets on carts with long ropes so the soldiers can skill themselves in striking a moving object."

"By the fires of Chemosh!" Hedak sat up straight. "That is clever."

"Eliab is training the young men of Benjamin, too," Cheb added. "In the north Abiram is gathering the young men of Issachar and buying spearheads from the Philistine smiths. Boaz drives the smiths of Judah night and day, too, forging two spears and more for every soldier."

"A worthy opponent, this Boaz," Hedak conceded. "But in battle my swords can cut through the shafts of his spears as if they were weeds."

It was Cheb's turn to shrug. "If your men come close enough, yes. But Boaz plans to fight you in the mountain defiles where spears can be thrown safely and swords cannot touch the thrower. His patrols now guard the passes into Israel. The moment you cross the border he will be warned and his warriors will attack you in the mountains before you can reach the plains."

Hedak got to his feet and began to stride up and down the room, obviously perturbed by what Cheb had told him. "If Boaz can choose where he will fight us," he admitted, "his spears will indeed cut us down while our swords are useless. You bring bad news, Cheb."

"I hurried because I knew you would wish to know what is happening. But things are not so bad as they might seem at first glance."

"This is no time for false optimism," Hedak growled. "Chemosh will go with us into battle, but we must win the victory for ourselves."

"There are times when strategy and stealth win battles over superior odds," Cheb reminded him.

Hedak wheeled upon the little man. "Stop talking in riddles! What is it you are trying to say?"

Cheb grinned. "As I said, Boaz is guarding the regular routes into Israel. But there are mountain passes that even the men of Israel do not know of."

Hedak stared at him truculently for a moment, then a

smile broke over his harsh features. "Do you know these passes, Cheb?"

"Like the palm of my hand."

"How is it that you know them when Boaz does not?"

Cheb grinned. "Before you graciously allowed me to bring caravans into Moab, noble Prince, I was a smuggler."

"I remember now. That was how you lost your hand. Tell me," Hedak added. "If I do decide to heed your warning and attack Israel with a smaller force before my preparations for marching to the Great Sea are complete, could you lead us through into the plains of Israel while the guards at the other passes are still watching for our coming?"

"As easily as I travel the regular route between Moab and the Jordan," Cheb assured him. "The chasm of Hezron is wild and rocky, but I know it well, and many others, too."

"By Chemosh!" Hedak cried, his good humor restored now. "You are truly a scoundrel to my liking."

"I can do more," Cheb promised. "No one in Israel, save my mother, who is mad, and a slave woman who helps me, knows I am in your pay. When you are ready to move, I will bring the news to Boaz. He will be so grateful that he will accept my offer to lead his army through a secret pass into Moab."

Hedak went to a chest in the corner of the room and took out a pouch of gold which he threw to Cheb. The caravan driver caught it expertly, even though he had only one good hand. "Refresh yourself with women and with wine," Hedak advised. "We will soon be ready to move against Israel and Boaz."

Naomi met Ruth that evening as she was leaving the field where she had been gleaning. All day the older woman had tried to think of some way to foil Tob's plans to marry Ruth, but at every point her thoughts had run into the stone wall of Tob's rights under the Law. According to it he had fulfilled all the requirements as next of kin when he made the small token payment that morning. Until Tob renounced his claim to the property and to Ruth, she could marry no one else. And since he did, in a sense, own Ruth now, there were hundreds of ways through which he could make life miserable for her. Besides, Naomi had plans of her own to further the budding romance between Ruth and Boaz.

"Is anything wrong?" Ruth asked as Naomi took up one side of the sacklike apron in which the barley was carried.

"Nothing I will not be able to take care of," Naomi said noncommittally.

"They finished the harvesting and I have gleaned enough to last us a month. What will we do after that, Naomi?"

"Boaz will see that there are other things for you to do," Naomi assured her. "There is carding and spinning, and the weaving of cloth. Have you seen him since the festival?"

"He hasn't even been near the fields."

"He may be busy training the young men. Anyway, it is a good sign."

"A good sign?"

"Boaz has distrusted all women for many years, ever since Tamar ran away. Now he finds his love for you stronger than all his hate and prejudice. He will need some time to think out this thing that has happened to him and decide what he must do."

They had approached their small house while talking. As she came into the room that served them as both living and sleeping quarters, Ruth saw the purse.

"Where did the money come from, Naomi?" she cried. "You didn't mention it."

"From Tob."

"What is it for?" Sudden apprehension showed in Ruth's face.

"You know that under the Law the next of kin may buy the property of a man who has died from his widow, and thus exercise the right of kinsman upon the wife of the dead man?"

Ruth nodded, her face white.

"Tob wants you, Ruth. And since he is next of kin of Mahlon he can take you to wife."

"But first he must buy the property," Ruth said quickly. "And you said——"

"I did not think Tob could find the price. And I was right."

"What about this money?"

"I overlooked one thing," Naomi admitted. "The purse is a token payment."

Ruth caught her breath. "Can he——" She stopped, speechless with horror.

Naomi shook her head. "Tob cannot take you into his house until the whole price is paid. He was careful to pay only the tenth part under the Law, as he is required to do, so he must not have the rest of the price at hand. But unless Tob relinquishes his right by giving his shoe to another, you are betrothed to him under the Law."

"No!" Ruth cried. "Oh no!"

"You are safe for the time being, child," Naomi reassured her. "Unless Tob somehow finds the money, and I doubt if he can do that soon."

"Is—isn't Boaz the next of kin after Tob?"

"Yes." Naomi's face brightened. "If by a miracle the lightning should happen to strike that snake Tob." Then she shook her head. "No, it is a sin to wish for the death of even such a one as he. Still," she added, "Tob might give you up for a price, and Boaz is wealthy."

"I am not a cow to be bought and sold," Ruth cried indignantly.

"You are a woman," Naomi reminded her. "Women are owned by the men who take them to wife."

"Without anything to say about it ourselves?"

Naomi smiled. "We may be chattels, Ruth, but women still find ways to make the men they pick out decide to choose them for their wives."

"I could not go to Boaz and ask him to buy the inheritance from Tob," Ruth protested. "He already feels responsible for Mahlon's death, and then he might feel that it was his duty to marry me."

"You love Boaz and he loves you," Naomi pointed out. "He hasn't visited you the past few days, so he may be having trouble making up his mind. It is up to us to help him, Ruth. That is a woman's privilege and duty."

"I cannot trap the man I love into marrying me," Ruth cried. "That would not be honest. Besides he may have decided by now that he does not even want me."

"You would not say that if you had seen his face when you were dancing and after he kissed you." Naomi put an arm about her shoulders. "Leave everything to me, daughter. Your love for me brought you here. Mine for you will see that you find happiness."

Long after Ruth had fallen asleep, Naomi lay awake in the darkness seeking an answer to the problem. When it finally did come, the whole thing was so simple that she laughed aloud.

Ruth stirred on her couch and sat up. "What is it, Naomi?" she asked, rubbing her eyes. "I thought you called."

"I didn't call," Naomi said. "But since you are awake, did you hear anyone say when the winnowing would be?"

Ruth lay back down. "Elkan said the night of the full moon," she murmured sleepily. "I didn't listen because it didn't concern me."

"That is a week from now," Naomi said. In a lower voice she added softly, "But it will concern you, Ruth. It will concern you very much indeed."

xii.

Ruth did not go to the fields the next day, but stayed home with Naomi, helping to scrub the little house until it shone like new. Together she and Naomi went to the market place and sold the portion of grain they would not need, buying food and household goods.

"We are people of property," Ruth said gaily as they entered the house again, carrying their bundles. "A house of our own. Money in our purse for tomorrow. The pots and pans we need. Who could want for more?"

"They are not nearly so fine as the things we had in Heshbon," Naomi reminded her. "Do you ever wish for the old days, Ruth?"

A shadow passed over Ruth's face as she remembered the tired agony in her back and limbs those first few days when she had begun to glean after the reapers. Then the memory of her meeting with Boaz in the starlight that first morning, and the awkwardness of the compliment "well met by starlight" upon his lips came to her and she smiled.

"It was bad at first," she admitted. "But lately it has seemed to me as if Mahlon were near me again. Sometimes I can almost believe I hear his voice."

"I told you I speak for my son. And that he would approve your loving Boaz."

"Do you think Mahlon really knows, Naomi, wherever he is?"

"I am sure he does. The spirit of Elimelech has been with me for lo these many years since he died. Sometimes it was the only thing that kept me going on."

"Then you believe our loved ones really live on after death?"

"You taught me that a long time ago, Ruth. It was before the cave in Moab, the day we were burying Elimelech. Do you remember how you and Orpah came to the grave, bearing food and wine?"

Ruth nodded. "You were very angry. And I don't blame you, now that I know how much you loved your husband."

"No, Ruth, I was the one who was wrong then. I remember you said that in Moab you believed people who died went to a happy place where they could enjoy things that life had not given them. And you could not understand why we grieved for our own loved ones, when we believed they had gone to a heaven where everyone was happy, worshiping God."

"I would like to think that somewhere, wherever he is, Mahlon approves of whatever I do."

"Perhaps many of the things we think only a happenstance are really ways the dead have of looking after those they have loved on earth."

"Mahlon would not want me to marry Tob," Ruth said quickly. "Do you think——"

"Yes, Ruth. In fact, he may already have shown us a way."

The sound of hoofbeats outside sent Ruth to the door. "It is Boaz!" she cried.

"Go out and speak to him," Naomi urged. "I will finish the work."

It was still twilight when Ruth came out of the house to where Boaz was tying the reins to the spreading branches of an olive tree.

"Come see how we have fixed up the house you gave us," she called to him gaily.

"Another time, perhaps," he said. "I must speak to you about something, Ruth."

His clothes were dusty and so was his horse, by which she realized that he must have come directly from the encampment some miles beyond the city, where the soldiers of Judah were being trained. Neither spoke while he guided her to the protection of a clump of trees that shut them off from the sight of the town. When they were thus hidden, Boaz drew her into his arms hungrily.

"The hours away from you have been like days, my beloved," he said. "I would have come before, but yesterday I had to argue before the council. And today I went to the camp early to see how the young men are progressing with the spear throwing."

Ruth smiled. "Did the council listen to you? Joseph told me they never do."

"We were discussing another matter this time, Ruth. One that concerns you."

"Why me?" she asked, startled.

"They were planning to invoke some old stern laws of Israel which forbids shelter to anyone not of our own people by birth and marriage between Israelites and non-Israelites."

Ruth caught her breath as the implications of what he was saying came to her.

"I spoke against it," Boaz assured her, "not just because I love you, Ruth, but because I think we must show others that kindness and justice and love for one another are the best way to live."

"Did they invoke the laws?" Ruth asked quickly.

"No. They listened to my counsels."

"If they had, would you have been forced to obey them?"

He wondered at the odd intensity in her tone.

"Yes. I could not profess to lead my people without abiding by their laws."

"Then whatever love we could have had would have been stolen?"

"Why are you so distraught, Ruth?" He smiled. "Some say stolen love is sweetest."

"But not for you and me, Boaz! If we, if we did that, you could take me, forget me, and put me away."

"Never! I will worship you forever and be yours, Ruth, no matter what happens."

"Even if one day the laws are invoked?"

For a long moment he did not speak, then he said quietly, in a voice from which he could not erase the pain, "As you say, Ruth, neither of us would want a stolen love."

"Then you'd have to send me away, wouldn't you? You

could not come with me. There'd be years of loneliness——"

"And heartbreak for us both," Boaz agreed. "But that will not be."

"You wouldn't need me," she cried almost hysterically. "You're a man and you would forget. But I would remember forever." Suddenly she put her face against his breast and clung to him, sobbing.

"I told you they did not invoke the laws, Ruth. Why are you weeping?"

"Tob made a token payment upon the property of Elimelech and Mahlon today," she explained. "Naomi says I am betrothed to him under the Law."

Boaz drew a deep breath. Now he understood the reason for her concern about what would have happened had the council invoked the old laws. For this was very much the same. Ruth, betrothed or married to Tob—it was the same under the laws of Israel—was as far removed from his arms as she ever could have been, had the council invoked the old laws against foreigners and against intermarriage.

"Tob is the next of kin." Boaz frowned. "But I had not thought of a token payment upon the property."

"There must be some way." She clung to him imploringly. "It is you I love, Boaz. Couldn't you take me away from him?"

"Our laws are very strict, Ruth."

She drew back then, pushing him away. "I hate them! They are unjust! Why must I obey an unjust law?"

"Without laws, Ruth, people would soon become savage bands of robbers."

Her anger at what she considered an injustice was turned now against Boaz, because he upheld it. "Don't you have any mind of your own?" she cried indignantly. "I remember now that you would have even brought Tamar back to be stoned if she had been alive."

"Ruth——"

She jerked away from him. "You can obey the laws! But I will not marry Tob no matter what anyone says. I would kill myself first."

"It would be like death to me to see you taken to wife by Tob," Boaz admitted. At the agony in his voice she could not feel angry at him any longer. "But you must

understand that to an Israelite the Law is above everything else."

"Even above our love?" she whispered.

"Even above that, Ruth," he said slowly as if every
word hurt him to the quick, as indeed it did. "Our love is
from ourselves," he explained. "But the Law is from
God."

She came into his arms again then and they clung together hopelessly, knowing that any further consummation
of their love was denied them.

xiii.

Now that the barley harvest was finished every man in
Judah who could wield a spear was busy training himself against the time when the children of Israel must
again fight for survival. Reports from Boaz's agents in
Moab indicated that Hedak was rapidly preparing an army
for invasion, and everyone realized the urgency of their
preparations.

The training camp north of Bethlehem was much larger
than it had been a week before, for Eliab had come from
the adjoining tribe of Benjamin, bringing a large group
of stalwart young men. Their goatskin tents dotted a
smooth plain among the hills and the smoke of cooking
fires rose into the warm air.

Boaz, Joseph, and Eliab, who was second-in-command
under Boaz of all the forces, were watching a group of
soldiers practicing with their spears. Figures of men and
horses had been drawn on thin cloth with charcoal and
stretched upon rude frames. These were set up at varying
distances from the throwers. Another group was trying
to strike similar targets drawn on low carts by ropes.
One after another the soldiers ran before Boaz, turned
quickly, and threw their spears.

The weeks of training were already beginning to show
results. Most of the weapons transfixed the distant targets
cleanly, but sometimes a nervous thrower would miss
entirely. After one of these Boaz stepped forward and,
with a word to the crestfallen soldier, took up a spear
from a large pile at one side of the area and hefted it,

showing the man just where to seize the shaft so that the heavier iron head was well balanced. With a quick smooth throw he sent the spear flying straight through the air to the most distant target, penetrating it almost in the center.

"Well thrown, Boaz!" Eliab cried admiringly. "You are still the best marksman in all of Israel."

"Joseph grows better every day." Boaz smiled at his young aide. "Soon youth will tell and he will beat me."

"They are all better than last week," Eliab observed.

Boaz looked to the towering eastern mountain range visible in the distance. Somewhere beyond those mountains, he knew, the soldiers of Moab were making ready to march. It was a grim race, with death the lot of the loser. Nor did he delude himself that the odds were not still large against Israel. "Let us hope they will be twice as good two weeks from now," he said soberly. "If we have that much time."

"We will have to return to Bethlehem in a few days," Joseph said.

Since the night when he had learned from Ruth that Tob had officially signaled her out as his betrothed, Boaz had stayed away from the city, knowing that seeing Ruth could only bring unhappiness to both of them. Sometimes, however, he doubted that even the pain of seeing her married to Tob could possibly be any greater than that he felt at the thought that she could never be his. "Why must we go?" he asked. "We have work here and the harvest is finished."

"Have you forgotten the winnowing? Your people will be disappointed if you are not there for the celebration."

"That is true," Boaz admitted. "I have never missed the night of the winnowing. It is the landlord's place to be there." He looked at Joseph. "Eliab will be in command here that night, but someone must ride to inspect the outposts."

"Why did I have to mention it?" Joseph grinned ruefully. "I could have slipped away to the winnowing ground without your knowing it. Now, I must ride half the night inspecting the outposts."

"You will thank me later," Boaz assured him. "Some girl would have crept under your cloak and the next day you would find yourself married."

"At least I would have that night," Joseph said resignedly. "Now I have nothing."

There would have been no thought of going to the winnowing for anyone, however, if they could have known what was happening in the city of Heshbon in Moab that very day.

Hedak had decided to heed Cheb's warning and attack Israel with a smaller army before his main forces were ready for the march to Philistia. In the great square before the Temples of Chemosh and Ashtar the flames roared in the belly of the god. Upon the platform before it stood the boy King Akton of Moab, with Hedak and the high priest of Chemosh. Beside them upon a jeweled platform lay a gleaming sword.

On the square itself the army of Moab was drawn up in battle array. In front of the troops stood a smaller image of Chemosh that was still at least twice a man's height. It was made of wood except for the iron and stone oven in the body, where burned the sacred fires, lit with a brand from the great idol itself. Slaves waited beside the huge wooden wheels of the cart upon which the image rode, and others were ready with the great ropes that were used to pull it. The God of Moab always went before his troops into battle, insuring them victory— or so they believed.

At a sign from Nebo, who stood in front of the army, the trumpeters blew a great blast upon the long, curving, ram's-horn trumpets. Akton turned and lifted the sword from the jeweled pedestal. He moved to Hedak, who knelt to accept the sword, then rose and lifted it high with a flamboyant gesture before thrusting it into the jeweled scabbard buckled about his waist.

"In the name of Chemosh, the all powerful, the all seeing, the Lord of Creation," the boy King intoned, "go forth and with this sword made sacred by my divine father, smite the enemies of Moab. Israel shall fall before you, and victory shall be yours. For the God of Moab, who is over all others, goes before you."

A great roar of approval went up from the army and thousands of uplifted swords flashed in the bright sunlight. Then at a command from Hedak the image of Chemosh rumbled from the square at the head of the army and the troops followed.

All day the threshers had been at work. At one side of the flat open space of hard-packed earth the men sat with their curved wooden flails, beating out the grain from the dried heads with brisk, practiced strokes, and throwing the straw aside. It was lifted by others on wooden forks and carried to round, conical piles that grew higher and higher as the day continued.

On the opposite side of the winnowing ground a group of women were also busy with the grain mixed with chaff, brought to them from beneath the flails of the threshers. They stood at the edge of a large white cloth spread upon the ground and, with the wind at their backs, tossed both grain and chaff into the air. The heavier grains of barley fell to the cloth, but the lighter chaff was blown way by the breeze.

Boaz came in from the camp of the Israelite soldiers at midday and worked with the threshers throughout the afternoon, wielding a flail as skillfully as any of them. Yosko, who was also adept, worked beside him, with the men all around them, and the women busy winnowing at the other side of the ground.

Ruth worked with the women, enduring the constant insults of Zelda and some others in silence. Boaz did not come to greet her, but she had seen his eyes upon her more than once during the afternoon, and her own gaze had been drawn many times to his leonine head and massive shoulders. Although separated by the width of the winnowing ground, each was as conscious of the other as if they had been close together.

Before the threshing was completed, the young women began slipping away to dress for the feast which would take place after darkness had fallen. As Naomi had instructed her, Ruth, too, left just before sundown. When she approached the small house near the wine press, Naomi ran out to seize her arm and hurry her into the house. A large bowl filled with water stood in the center of the room. From it arose the delicate aroma of perfumed oil.

"You worked too late, child," Naomi scolded as Ruth removed the rough clothing she wore while at work. "Now we shall have to rush to get you ready."

The weeks of work had not marred by one iota the lovely perfection of Ruth's body. Had Yosko been able to see her as she knelt in the large bowl and bathed her smooth white skin, he would have felt even more than he already did that she was a goddess. If indeed his eyes had not popped out of their sockets first.

"You will be the most beautiful one there tonight," Naomi assured Ruth happily as she busied herself rubbing the perfumed oil on her skin and brushing her hair.

"But why all this?" Ruth protested. "You haven't told me the reason."

"The winnowing of the grain is the end of the harvest," Naomi explained. "Tonight the people will eat and drink and be gay. Then everyone lies down on the threshing floor under a cloak and sleeps until dawn."

"I still don't understand."

"On every other night of the year the man must choose the woman. But tonight, after the hour of midnight, it is the woman's privilege to choose for herself."

"Do you mean she selects the man she will stay with tonight?"

"Yes."

"Then why am I going? I will certainly not choose Tob, although under your Law I am betrothed to him."

"You must do just as I tell you," Naomi said mysteriously. "Remember you promised me."

"But——"

"When the feasting is over and all are asleep, you must make your way to where Boaz lies, lift up his cloak and lie down there."

"Why?" Ruh asked, frowning.

"As I told you, only tonight in all the year does the woman choose the man. And an old law among my people says that if a woman lies under the cloak of a man in the night, he must buy her as his wife."

Ruth jumped to her feet, horrified. "I will not do it, Naomi. I will not trick him, not even to——"

"You love Boaz, don't you?"

"Yes, but——"

"And he loves you."

"That would be deceiving him——"

"Don't you prefer Boaz's embrace to Tob's?"

Ruth shivered. "Anything is better than that."

"Then you will do as I have planned," Naomi said briskly. "Would you deny me strong grandsons to rear such as yours and Boaz's would be?"

"I will do as you say, Naomi," Ruth agreed hesitantly. "But somehow it doesn't seem right."

"Come along now," her mother-in-law ordered. "I must dress you." She took up a new dress of soft cloth from the couch where she had spread it out. "This will look lovely against your hair, Ruth."

"You must have spent all our money on this dress."

"Not ours, Tob's," Naomi assured her. "I would give much to see his face if ever he learns what his token payment was used for."

xiv.

He could just as well have gone to the winnowing anyway, Joseph thought ruefully as he rode across the darkened plain toward the Israelite camp. About now the feasting would be over and the dancing would be ready to begin. And he, the best dancer in all of Judah, was not there.

The memory of the day when he had danced with Ruth at the Festival of the First Fruits brought a smile to Joseph's lips. When he married, he decided, he would choose just such a wife as Ruth, lovely, graceful, kind, everything a man would want in a bride. Why Boaz had not taken her already he could not understand. Certainly any fool could see the love in her eyes, and Boaz had admitted he loved Ruth in return.

That business about Tob and the token payment now, he thought. It was hard to understand Boaz's reasoning. Tob owed Boaz a lot of money, and if Boaz were to demand payment and Tob could not meet the debt, he would have to satisfy his creditors somehow or be stoned. That was the Law about not paying one's just debts.

But when Joseph had suggested that Tob would be glad enough to give his shoe in return for settling the debt, thus escaping payment and saving his own skin at one stroke, Boaz had stubbornly refused to consider the suggestion. His reason was that it would not be fair to press Tob for payment as a lever to gain something he wanted himself that now belonged to Tob.

Sometimes, Joseph thought wryly, Boaz was too upright for his own good. It was too bad that he, Joseph, was not the one Tob owed instead of Boaz. Tob would get the same consideration at his hands that the merchant would give anyone else, which was exactly none at all.

Joseph had been riding along lost in his thoughts, but when his horse suddenly threw up its head and whinnied softly, he was instantly alert. His mount's action, he knew, meant that there was another horse or horses nearby, and no one was supposed to be riding here except himself.

Joseph looked around him slowly and stiffened when he detected a quick movement behind a clump of trees about a hundred yards away. Tensing the reins and lifting his spear he rode slowly toward the spot where he had seen the movement.

In the shadow of the trees Hedak muttered a curse. He had insisted upon scouting personally the land around the Israelite camp while the section of his army that he considered large enough to throw against the Israelites—outnumbering them over two to one according to Cheb's figures for the strength of Israel—was in camp back in the mountains, but he had not planned for his presence here to be detected yet.

The strategy Hedak and Cheb had worked out in Heshbon was much simpler. A scare produced by Cheb's news that Moab was attacking would send the Israelites marching to the mountain passes. And when the traitorous caravan driver had lured them into the ambush a sudden foray in force by Hedak's troops would destroy the Israelites. That way Hedak would lose few men, leaving his army strong for the march against the northern tribes and the final assault upon the Philistine cities that would move the western border of Moab to the Great Sea and create a huge empire ruled over by himself.

"You told me no one would be out tonight," Hedak whispered angrily to Cheb, who rode with him.

"It is the night of the winnowing, and everyone who can should be at the threshing floor." Cheb peered at Joseph, who was riding toward them. "It is Joseph, Boaz's lieutenant. I know him well."

"If you have betrayed me," Hedak snapped, "I will——"

"Would I betray myself? Put your cloak over your face and we will ride out to meet him."

"My sword point is at your back," Hedak warned ominously as their horses moved out of the shelter of the trees.

Joseph saw them and drew back his spear, tensing the reins to charge, if it came to that. "What business is afoot here?" he demanded.

"It is only Cheb, the one-armed merchant, Joseph." Cheb rode closer with Hedak just behind him. He threw back the hood of his cloak exposing his face. "Surely you recognize me."

"I know you well enough, Cheb," Joseph said curtly. "But who is this with you?"

"Only another merchant." Cheb continued to move closer to Joseph.

"You mean another smuggler, don't you?"

The caravan driver laughed. "We only met here to haggle a bit over prices."

Something about the story sounded wrong to Joseph and suddenly he knew what it was. Although both of the men claimed to be merchants, there was no sign of mules, camels, or a caravan.

"You, there!" He spoke to Hedak. "Uncover your face!"

"He cannot," Cheb said quickly. "His faith forbids it."

The three of them were close together now. Before Cheb or Hedak realized what he was doing, Joseph quickly reached over and jerked the hood away from Hedak's head. He recognized the grim, scarred face of the Moabite chief at once, but astonishment put him off his guard for the moment.

Cheb acted quickly, smashing Joseph on the temple with the heavy metal hook that served him as a left hand. With the same movement he thrust a dagger into the young soldier's back with his right hand. Joseph's body sagged across the horse's neck, and fell to the ground with hardly a groan.

"You fool!" Hedak said furiously. "I would have taken him prisoner."

"So far from the border? It would be like telling Boaz you are attacking." Cheb grinned. "Besides, I can place the body where it will be found tomorrow morning. Boaz will rush to avenge Joseph and I will lead the Israelite army into your trap."

"You may be right," Hedak admitted grudgingly. "Take him, then. And do all that I have charged you, or you will pay with your neck."

"Chemosh must be smiling upon your venture, Prince Hedak," the caravan driver assured his employer. "Surely this is a good omen."

xv.

The workers and their families had gathered around the winnowing ground when Ruth and Naomi found a place at the edge of the crowd. Food and wine were plentiful and the women were dressed in their finest clothes, particularly the younger ones, to whom this was a night of adventure. As the landlord, it was Boaz's duty to open the ceremonies. He stepped to the center of the threshing floor with a wooden flail in his hands and the people grew quiet, waiting for him to speak. When he did his voice was strong and sure:

"It is the custom in our land to give thanks at the harvest time to the God of our fathers, who brought the children of Israel out of bondage in Egypt, and has blessed our lives in this fruitful land. The grapes and the grain are plentiful this year and we shall have an abundance of both wine and bread, so the children of neither the rich nor the poor shall go hungry. We are a small nation, encompassed with enemies, yet in this season we have been allowed to reap a bountiful harvest and press our grapes in peace. Now, let us partake of the things the Lord has given us and sing and dance in His praise."

Food and wine were passed and there was much merriment. When they had finished eating, the leader of the musicians led the people in a hymn of thanksgiving, then the music changed to a stately, formal dance. The older couples rose and treaded the measured, deliberate beat, while the young ones waited impatiently for the livelier tunes that would follow.

Soon the stately dance was completed, and the musicians struck up a lively tune. The young people thronged to the floor to dance. Ruth glanced over to where Boaz was leaning against a post at the other side of the floor. He did not come to where she sat with Naomi, although he must have seen that she was dressed in her best finery tonight for his benefit alone.

The wine was flowing freely and the young people were gay as they danced. Rachel whirled by with a young Israelite. There was much tossing of chaff and the girls' hair was soon flecked with it. Tob and Adah were at one side of the floor, but no one danced with the slave girl because it was well known that she was Tob's concubine and possessed a vile temper as well.

Yosko was dressed in his best, his scant beard trimmed and combed, his thin hair reeking of perfumed oils. He strutted a little as he came across the floor to where Ruth was sitting with Naomi. "Though you are a Moabite woman and I am a man of property," he said a little pompously, "I wish to dance with you."

"I am sorry," Ruth gave him an appealing smile. "Could it be some other time?"

"Before midnight," Yosko said stubbornly, "the woman must dance with the man who asks her. Later, she may choose."

"But I——"

"Dance with Yosko, Ruth," Naomi said.

Ruth looked at her mother-in-law in surprise, but got to her feet. As Yosko was about to lead her out to dance, however, Tob came across the floor and stepped between them.

"I am the next of kin," he said importantly. "She will dance the first dance with me."

Ruth appealed to Naomi. "Does he have this right?"

"I have made the token payment," Tob reminded her. "You are betrothed to me now."

"Yes, Ruth," Naomi admitted reluctantly. "He does."

She did not resist when Tob led her out among the dancers, but she was a different person from the light-hearted young woman who had danced so gaily with Joseph and Boaz at the Festival of the First Fruits. Around them the other couples pressed close together when their bodies touched in the dance but Ruth kept herself stiff. Even to touch Tob was repulsive to her, and she was sure that he had only claimed her to assert his right as kinsman.

Hardly had Tob released Ruth when Yosko was beside her again. "Can we dance, now?" he asked eagerly.

Ruth did not want to hurt the little man's feelings, for at least he had done her the honor of letting her know, through Boaz, that he was in love wth her. But she did not want to dance any more, unless with Boaz. And he had not shown in any way that he intended to ask her.

"I am not a person to be put aside," Yosko reminded her importantly. "I am a man of many fields. And I do you great honor by asking you to dance."

"I know, Yosko," Ruth said. She stood up to go out on the floor with him, but there was another interruption. One of the younger men, seeking to pester Yosko, seized Ruth by the arm and tried to drag her into the press of the dancers.

The little man was quick to defend his rights this time. "She is going to dance with me!" he howled. "She is mine!"

"Send her back to Moab!" Zelda shouted. "She is not wanted here."

The laughing Israelite still held to one of Ruth's arms, while Yosko pulled on the other. Crimson with embarrassment, she could do nothing.

"I shall make her mine!" Yosko shouted. "Even if I have to buy the right of kinsman from Tob."

Zelda leaped in front of Ruth. "Go back to Moab, hussy," she screamed.

"I don't like her clothes," another woman called.

"We will tear them off her, then." Zelda jerked at Ruth's dress. "Strip her and spoil her!"

"Strip her!" the other women chanted. "Spoil her! Tear her clothes!"

Zelda fingers were outstretched to claw Ruth's face. Just then, however, the young Israelite who had started the trouble released her and Ruth put up her hand to defend herself. Wild with rage, Zelda ran into her hand and went staggering back into the crowd screaming that Ruth had struck her. Half blinded by tears of embarrassment and humiliation, Ruth searched for Boaz, mutely imploring him to save her, but he had gone with Elkan to bring out another wineskin for the revelers. He started back at the sound of shouting voices, but Tob stepped into the breach before Boaz could act.

"Do not touch this woman!" he shouted. "She is to be my wife. Keep back! Respect her!"

As president of the Council of Elders, Tob spoke with authority. The hubbub subsided, all except Yosko, who was hopping up and down, a comical figure even in his wrath.

"She is mine!" he yelled. "She is going to dance with me."

"I am the next of kin," Tob said importantly. "No one can take the Moabite from me. No other man can marry her under the Law unless I give him my shoe."

Tob had invoked the Law, and no one dared to go against him publicly. Boaz stopped a few yards away, too, realizing that there was nothing he could do at the moment. He did have presence of mind, however, to call to the musicians and start another tune, and as the people began dancing again, the disturbance over Ruth subsided. When he looked for Ruth, however, she had disappeared into the darkness outside the cleared space of the threshing floor.

Naomi found Ruth in the darkness where she sat upon a rock, weeping hysterically. She put her arm about her daughter-in-law and let the younger woman cry out her unhappiness and humiliation. Finally Ruth raised her head and wiped her eyes. "They were fighting over me like a pack of dogs over a female, Naomi," she said, shuddering again at the memory of it. "Maybe I am what Zelda called me, a hussy."

"Hush, child! You are what you know yourself to be in your heart. And what I know you to be, kind, sincere, and steadfast."

"Boaz didn't even try to help me," Ruth wailed.

"He had gone with Elkan to get more wine, but when they started quarreling he hurried back. He was coming to your help when Tob intervened."

Ruth looked toward the threshing floor. It was past midnight now and the dancing had ended. Men and women were lying on beds of straw, using as covers shawls, blankets, and the flowing cloaks the men wore when riding. Only one torch burned, and it was almost ready to go out.

While she watched, a girl got up quietly and stole over

to where one of the men lay. Quickly lifting up his cloak, she lay down beneath it and he pulled the cloak over her. Ruth saw him take the girl in his arms and kiss her. Presently another young girl did the same and was received with an equally tender welcome. Most of the older people had gone back to the town and their couches, including Tob and Adah.

"It is after midnight," Naomi said. "Each woman is choosing the man under whose cloak she will lie, as is the custom on the night after the winnowing."

Ruth looked to where Boaz lay to one side of the floor in the shadows. He was hardly visible to the others and quite alone. If all this—Tob's lust for her and his making the token payment—had not happened, she and Boaz would be lying in each other's arms tonight beneath his cloak. But everything was wrong now, and there seemed no way that it could be made right.

"See, he lies alone," Naomi said quietly. "It is time for you to go to him."

"But after what happened tonight, if he still wants me he should come to me."

"On this one night of the year the woman must choose," Naomi reminded her.

"I can't go, Naomi! It would be like tricking him."

"Would you spend a lifetime of misery in Tob's arms?"

"No! Oh no!"

"Then you must do as you promised me, Ruth."

"But even if Boaz does want me, he cannot marry me. The Law comes between us."

"Love has been known to laugh at laws," Naomi said practically. "He loves you and you love him. At least this one night will be yours, whatever happens afterward."

Ruth caught her breath at the implication of Naomi's words. Her face was hot in the darkness and her heart was beating fast. "And then?" she asked in a whisper.

"Boaz is an honorable man. He would not rest until he had made Tob give him the shoe. Then all of your troubles would be over."

"But when he speaks what will I say?"

"Let him speak," Naomi advised. "Once you go to him tonight, all the decisions are his. He will make them."

Slowly Ruth got to her feet. She clung to Naomi for a long moment, seeking strength for the step she was about to take. Although surrounded by people, she felt terribly alone as she walked across the threshing floor toward where Boaz lay in the shadows.

At the same moment, some miles away, Cheb was placing the body of Joseph conveniently near the road, where it would easily be found in the morning. With that mission completed he mounted his horse and rode toward Bethlehem, a sly smile upon his lips.

xvi.

When Ruth was a few yards away from where Boaz lay, he sighed and turned in his sleep. She stopped, ready to run away if he awakened, but he did not open his eyes and, after a moment, she moved closer.

Kneeling at Boaz's feet—she could not bring herself to lie down at his side as the other women had done with their lovers—Ruth cautiously lifted the corner of the large cloak with which he had covered himself and crept under it. Boaz did not awaken, for it had been a long, wearying day. She lay there for a while looking up at the stars and presently dropped off to sleep herself.

Perhaps an hour later Boaz stirred and sat up, not knowing what had awakened him. His movement drew the cover off Ruth, and in her sleep she reached out to pull it back over her. Startled by the realization that a woman was sleeping at his feet, Boaz leaned over to see her more closely, hoping, yet hardly daring to believe, that it was really Ruth and not a dream.

"Ruth!" he whispered. "Ruth!"

At the sound of her name she came awake. Suddenly realizing that he had found her there and knew what she had done, Ruth was overcome by a panic of shame and humiliation at having yielded to Naomi's arguments. Without answering him she rolled over quickly and got to her feet. Before Boaz realized her intentions, she was running across the grass beside the threshing floor toward an olive grove that lay between it and the city.

Boaz, too, acted quickly, and caught her in the shadows beyond the threshing floor. "Ruth!" he cried. "Why are you here?"

"Let me go!" she begged. "Please let me go."

"Why were you lying under my cloak?" he asked, voicing the suspicion that had leaped instantly into his mind. "You know what that means, don't you?"

"Yes."

"Were you trying to trick me into breaking the Law so I would have to marry you?"

"Nobody saw us," Ruth burst out, "so you are not compromised."

"But why?" he asked, still holding her arm. "Why did you come under my cloak while I was asleep?"

"It was Naomi's idea," Ruth explained, half in tears now. "Let me go please, Boaz. I won't bother you again."

She managed to jerk away from him and started running away once more, but she was half blinded by tears and tripped before she had gone a dozen feet.

Boaz ran to her and took her hands, lifting her to her feet. Weeping with frustration and humiliation, she tried to pull away again, but he held her tightly.

"Ruth!" At the new note in his voice she lifted a tear-wet face to look at him.

"Y-yes, Boaz."

He released one hand and took her quivering chin in his cupped fingers. Holding her thus, he leaned down and kissed her long and hard, a kiss that drained all the resistance from her, leaving her weak and helpless, with no thought save that she never wanted to be separated from him again.

"If you had tricked me, Ruth," he told, "I would want you still, for always."

She looked at him wide-eyed. "Even when you thought what—what you must have thought, when you found me lying there under your cloak?"

"When you ran away just now, Ruth," he said gently, "I realized at last how much I really love you. No matter what you did or were, I want you for my wife."

She clung to him then, welcoming his lips with her own. "Oh, Boaz, Boaz," she whispered. "Boaz, my beloved."

He held her close for a long sweet moment, then they walked back arm in arm to the place beside the threshing floor where he had left his cloak.

"I remember you told me at the Place of Refuge when we first met that it would be like this, Ruth, and I would one day find a woman I would love so much that what she was or what she did would make no difference."

At the edge of the threshing floor they sat together with their backs against a tree and the cloak over them, content to be together at last.

"Now I can tell you why I came tonight," Ruth said happily.

"You don't need to tell me, Ruth, I am content that you are here."

"But I want you to know, Boaz. Naomi made me promise I would creep under your cloak while you were asleep."

"I must give her my heartfelt thanks tomorrow."

"She said if I spent the night under your cloak, you would make Tob give me up."

"I will speak to Tob tomorrow. He must give me his shoe. What a fool I was not to do it before."

"He will drive a hard bargain," she warned.

Boaz laughed exuberantly. "Even if he beggars me, I will pay it. After tonight you will never leave me again, Ruth. I swear it." He held her close. "When did you first know you loved me?"

"I think it was when you spoke for Yosko about the morning star."

"Mine must have begun that morning when we met in the field by starlight, and I knew you were familiar but could not see your face. I do know that I have not been the same since that day."

"What are we going to do now, Boaz?"

"We will spend the night here together where we found each other," he said decisively. "As you said, neither of us would want a stolen love, so when it is dawn, I will let you go home while I go to the gate and call the elders to witness. Tob shall give me his shoe this very day and we will be wed."

Engrossed in each other, retelling over and over again the story of their love, neither Ruth nor Boaz noticed that Adah, Tob's concubine, had slipped back from Bethlehem and now stood in the shadows nearby, watching them and listening to their voices with a smile of triumph on her lips. Adah had been searching desperately for some way to get Ruth out of Bethlehem, and remove her master's interest at the same time. Now she was sure of success.

In going to Boaz tonight Ruth had played directly into her hands.

Nor was Adah the only human scavenger lurking about the winnowing ground. About two hours after midnight Cheb tied his horse nearby and approached the space where the people were sleeping. He did not let himself be seen, since he was on the lookout for whatever scandal he might learn here to his own profit. His keen eyes saw the slave girl almost at once. He recognized her and moved closer until he could touch her shoulder.

Adah whirled around, muffling an exclamation of surprise.

"Who are you spying upon?" Cheb whispered.

Adah put her finger to her lips for silence and led him well away from the threshing floor before she spoke. "I was watching Boaz and Ruth," she explained. "She lay beneath his cloak tonight."

Cheb whistled. "The Moabite woman is clever. Your master will not like it."

"I am going now to tell him what the Moabite has done. If he accuses her of adultery before the council and we both swear that we saw her lying under Boaz's cloak, she will be stoned and perhaps Boaz with her."

Cheb shook his head. "You forget something, Adah. On this one night of the year much is forgiven, even adultery. I have a better plan. It will keep Boaz busy and also get rid of the Moabite."

"What is it?" she asked eagerly.

"Let us seek out your master, since this concerns him too. I will tell you about it on the way."

Tob was asleep but Adah spent no ceremony in approaching him. Seizing him by the shoulders, she shook him violently. "Wake up, master," she urged. "Wake up."

The merchant turned over and pushed her hand away. But she continued to shake him, and finally he awoke. "What do you want, Adah?" he demanded peevishly. "This is no time to——"

"Ruth and Boaz have spent the night under his cloak at the threshing floor."

"What?" Tob was wide awake now. "What did you say?"

"The Moabite woman went to the threshing floor tonight after the dancing was over. She lay down under

Boaz's cloak and they have been there all night making love."

"But I have made the token payment," Tob said indignantly. "She is mine."

"You wouldn't have thought so if you had seen her tonight."

"Did you see her yourself?" Tob asked.

"With my own eyes. And so did Cheb here."

Tob saw Cheb for the first time. "Will you swear to this?" he demanded.

"If you want me to," Cheb said with a shrug.

"I will accuse the Moabite woman of adultery before the council this very morning," Tob said. "The people will stone her, and Boaz too."

"This is the night of the winnowing," Adah reminded him, "when women are allowed to choose and the laws are not enforced."

Tob muttered a curse. "All Bethlehem will know it tomorrow then. I will be laughed from the city."

"Not if you can prove to the council that she lay with Boaz for a purpose," Cheb said slyly.

"What purpose? Save her own pleasure and to humiliate me?"

"The Moabite was once a priestess in the Temple of Chemosh. She bears the mark and I have seen her dance there at the festivals."

"We know that already."

"But it is well known in Heshbon that Prince Hedak once asked for her as his wife."

"You will swear to this?" Tob asked eagerly. "Before the Council of Elders?"

Cheb nodded. "She is undoubtedly a spy sent to cause trouble between you and Boaz, since you are both her husband's kinsmen and also the most important men in Judah."

"You are a clever one, Cheb," Tob said, flattered, as Cheb had shrewdly surmised he would be, by the fact that Moab, too, realized his importance. "Boaz will look like a fool when I reveal that the Moabite woman is a spy."

"You will do our people a great service by denouncing her," Cheb agreed. "They will realize at last how much wiser your counsels are than those of Boaz."

Tob nodded blandly, rubbing his hands together. This affair was turning out very well. He would punish the woman for daring to choose another man, and he would win a victory over Boaz at the same time.

xvii.

Dawn was just beginning to break when Ruth left Boaz at the edge of the threshing floor and swiftly crossed an olive grove that lay between it and the town. Cheb had been watching them for perhaps a half hour after leaving Tob's house. As she emerged from the grove he came up behind her, moving silently and swiftly.

"Mistress!" he called in a low voice.

Ruth turned quickly. She recognized him at once. "What do you want, Cheb?" she asked. "I must get home before dawn."

"I bring urgent news from Moab. I have just come from there with a caravan."

"From Moab?" Ruth gasped.

"Prince Hedak bade me give you a message."

"I want no word from Hedak!"

Cheb shrugged. "Perhaps the Lion of Judah will be interested in the fact that Hedak sends you messages here in Israel, then. Shall I call him?"

"I have nothing to hide from Boaz or anyone else," Ruth said proudly. "What is this message you say you bring?"

"Prince Hedak bade me tell you that your time of disgrace is over. You may return in honor to Moab. I am to bring you to him."

"You are mad! I will never leave Israel now."

"Why? Because of Boaz, from whose arms you are still warm? Even he cannot protect a spy from the anger of the people."

"A spy!" Ruth caught her breath. Then her eyes narrowed. "Boaz has always said that everything he does in Israel is known to Hedak in a short time. You must be the spy, Cheb. I will denounce you today."

"Who will believe you? When his people learn how you have bewitched Boaz, they will turn against you both.

Besides, who would believe me a spy when I bring news that Hedak is already moving to attack Israel?"

"I must warn Boaz, then," Ruth said quickly.

"Do!" Cheb counseled. "But first tell him how you come by the news. Even Boaz will not be able to keep the people from stoning you to death as a Moabite spy then."

Ruth turned suddenly and ran toward the city, but Cheb made no move to follow her. "You will need help soon," he called after her. "Then you will be sorry you did not listen to the message I brought you."

Dawn was breaking and Naomi was already up when Ruth came into their house. She leaned against the door, gasping for breath, her face pale.

"What happened, Ruth?" Naomi asked quickly. "Did Boaz drive you from him?"

"No."

"Did you do as I said?"

"Yes." Ruth was beginning to get her breath. "I was with Boaz all night."

"What is wrong then?"

"Hedak!" Ruth gasped.

"But he is in Moab."

"A spy of Moab spoke to me as I was coming home. Hedak has sent for me, and he is moving against Israel now."

"Have you spoken to anyone else of this?" Naomi asked quickly.

"Who would believe me, when they all think me a spy already?"

"They will believe me," Naomi said grimly.

Ruth seized Naomi's arms, forgetting her own fears. "Don't, Naomi," she pleaded. "They will say you, too, became a Moabite spy while you lived in Heshbon."

"Boaz knows that is not true."

"When Cheb tells the council that Hedak sent a message to me, not even Boaz will trust me any more."

Naomi was forced to admit that what Ruth said was probably true. The women of Bethlehem and Judah hated her and they would stir up the rest of the people once she was accused of spying. For either of them to mention the alleged message that Cheb had brought from Hedak would be playing into the hands of one like Zelda. At the moment it seemed best for them to remain quiet and see what happened next.

Just after dawn Boaz knocked on Tob's door. Adah answered and ushered him in.

"Tell your master I must see him at once," Boaz said.

"My master has a visitor," Adah said silkily. "But I will tell him the noble Boaz is here." Had he been less concerned with the business that brought him to Tob so early, Boaz might have been warned by the thinly veiled insolence in Adah's manner that something untoward was afoot.

The slave girl disappeared and a few moments later Tob came out. At the almost smug look on his kinsman's face Boaz's eyes narrowed. "I have business with you, Tob," he said. "So pressing that it could not wait."

"And I was on the point of coming to see you about an urgent matter concerning——"

"Let me speak first," Boaz interrupted. "It is soon said. I wish to take Ruth, the widow of Mahlon, as my wife. And I want you, as next of kin, to renounce her so that I can go before the elders and ask permission to marry a foreigner."

Tob rubbed his hands together. "Perhaps you shall have her, my friend. But first you must hear her true history. Then——" He threw open the door. "Come inside. I have a visitor whose story will interest you very much."

Boaz entered the room a little warily. Knowing Tob, he was sure all was not as he would like it to be. He had expected feigned anger and recriminations, followed by a period of bargaining from which Tob would emerge considerably richer than he had been before. At the sight of Cheb, Boaz's eyes narrowed even more. Like many in Bethlehem, he did not trust the wily caravan driver.

"The merchant, Cheb, is known to you, I believe," Tob said unctuously.

"Enough of this play-acting," Boaz snapped. "Of course I know Cheb. Did I not go to Moab with him?"

"So you did," Tob said, pleased. "And you will remember, no doubt, that Cheb brought you a message from Prince Hedak before you went."

"I remember well," Boaz said grimly. "And I wonder

just how much Hedak told him then of how he planned to trap me."

Cheb pretended to be greatly hurt. "You do me a great injustice," he protested. "I drive my caravans and sometimes I carry messages. But I am loyal to Israel and not Moab."

"Can we get on with our business, Tob?" Boaz asked. "I would think a more private place——"

"Cheb has news of great interest," Tob protested, and turned to the caravan driver. "Tell my kinsman what you know of the Moabite, Ruth."

"She is Hedak's woman," Cheb said bluntly.

"What?" Boaz took a threatening step toward Cheb.

"I swear it, noble Boaz," Cheb said quickly. "You must know that she was a temple priestess in Heshbon before she married Mahlon. She bears the mark of Chemosh upon her forehead."

"Ruth renounced pagan gods. She has worshiped only the one true God since her marriage."

"Did you know that Hedak once asked for her as his wife? And that he planned to marry her after the death of Mahlon?"

Boaz was taken aback momentarily by this news, which he had not known before. "Does that necessarily mean she would have married Hedak?" he inquired. "Or that she owes any allegiance to him now?"

Cheb shrugged. "I am a simple man, not a scribe to argue with the Lion of Judah. But if the Moabite woman, Ruth, is what she claims to be, why did Prince Hedak give me a message for her when I left Heshbon a few days ago?"

"What kind of a message?" Boaz demanded.

"He paid me well to tell the woman, Ruth, that he is attacking Israel. And that she should come to join him in the mountains where she would be safe."

"You lie!" Boaz snapped. "Ruth is loyal to Israel."

"Why should I lie? As soon as I reached Bethlehem I came to tell the noble Tob because I knew the council would want to know."

"Of course she will deny it," Tob added. "Cheb tells me he saw her just now in the olive grove outside the city. He gave her the message after he had come to me with the information that Hedak is going to attack Israel, and that the Moabite woman is a spy."

"Confront her with her guilt, Boaz," Cheb urged. "And be swift before she bewitches you completely and drags you to your death as she did the sons of Elimelech."

"What do you mean?"

"Did not Mahlon make swords for Heshbon while she lived with him? And when he would make no more was he not killed?"

"Ruth had nothing to do with that."

"If she does not work for Hedak," Tob asked, "why did she offer herself to you last night? Cheb says Hedak boasted to him of how she would bewitch us both and weaken the defenses of Israel."

Boaz's every instinct argued that these two lied, and that Ruth was everything he had come to know and love in the past few weeks. Yet the structure of guilt they were building up seemed too damning not to be founded upon some modicum of truth. "I should slay you with those lying words on your lips, Cheb," he burst out, as much in pain as in anger.

"Why?" Tob demanded. "Because he told the truth? Must you wait until Hedak has conquered us before you will believe he is attacking, as he sent word to the Moabite woman he is doing? She even spent last night in your arms to keep you away from the army."

The insult was like a whip in Boaz's face. Lashing out in blind anger, he struck Tob, knocking him to the floor. Adah and Cheb drew back, and the caravan driver's fingers stole to the dagger he always carried.

Tob rose on one elbow. His face was pale and he was trembling with anger. "Violence will not make a right out of a wrong, Boaz," he admonished. "You will know we speak truth when you hear that the armies of Moab have crossed our borders."

Boaz advanced upon Cheb, who drew back, ready to draw the dagger.

"If what you say is true," he demanded angrily, "why did Ruth come here to Israel with Naomi?"

"Is she the first spy Moab has sent among us?" Cheb asked, trying to keep the tremor of fear out of his voice. "I warn you, Mahlon and Chilion will not be the only victims of the Moabite woman's evil. Others will follow, and you among them, Boaz. Before the Most High God I swear it."

"She came with Naomi because both you and I are

kinsmen of Elimelech, as well as men of importance in the councils of Judah and Israel," Tob said from the floor. "How better could she carry out Hedak's purpose than through beguiling the both of us and setting us at each other's throats as we are now?"

There was a simple logic to Tob's arguments that Boaz could not deny. His hands dropped to his sides and his old doubts about women flooded upon him, buffeting his love for Ruth and his confidence in her. He was not by any means prepared to believe the tale that Cheb had brought, but he could not throw it off in the face of the caravan driver's story.

Tob scrambled to his feet. "Has your madness passed, Boaz?" he asked a little anxiously. "Or will you smite me again?"

Boaz got control of himself with a tremendous effort. "I shall not smite you again, Tob," he promised. "Unless when I have studied this matter further I find it to be one of your schemes."

"This is no scheme," Tob said virtuously. "Nor is the matter any longer a private one between you and me. It must come before the Council of Elders, where the charges against the Moabite woman shall be made public and she shall be fairly judged."

"Call the council, then," Boaz said. "Ruth will prove that she is innocent."

"She will prove that you are a great fool," Tob sneered. "My heart bleeds for you, kinsman. You have ever been unfortunate in your choice of women."

Boaz turned on his heel and left the room, but he did not go to Ruth's house. Instead he entered the building near the center of the city that served as a tabernacle, as well as for important meetings of the people and their councils. In a few hours, he knew, Ruth would be fighting for her life in this very place, before the people of Judah. Meanwhile he must seek guidance from the God Who had not failed him before, the same God Who had sent the rain in Heshbon and quenched the fires of Chemosh.

"Lord God of Hosts," he prayed on his knees before the altar. "God of Isaac and Jacob who led my people out of bondage in Egypt. Restrain now my rage and give me guidance in my hour of great doubt and need. Give me counsel that I may decide the cause of right. And give me strength to carry out my decision."

Kneeling there, he waited for some sign of favor or decision. None came, however. Instead a picture took shape in his thoughts, the memory of Ruth's face, the tenderness in her eyes and the softness of her lips and her body when he had held her in his arms the previous night. For a moment he was sure this was the sign he sought, a vision of Ruth's gentleness and goodness, sent to assure him that she was everything he still believed her to be in spite of Tob's and Cheb's accusations.

But then the picture faded and was replaced by the face of Tamar, his first wife, who had betrayed him. He saw her body as he had found it that day at the Place of Refuge, lying in the arms of her Moabite lover. Quickly the picture changed before he could deliberately blot it from his thoughts. This time the woman was Ruth again, but it was Hedak whose arms held her.

Sweat poured from Boaz's face as he knelt in agony. "Give me a sign, O God," he begged again. "A sickness has claimed my soul. Give me guidance in my hour of need."

But there was no sign, and finally he got heavily to his feet, a terrible bitterness and resignation in his heart at the knowledge that he must decide this thing without help from any other source.

"Hast Thou forsaken me too?" he said slowly. "Then so be it."

In the chasm of Hezron, less than a day's ride to the east in the wild mountain ranges between Moab and Judah, the Moabite camp was stirring. In the iron belly of the god that always went before the armies in battle the fires were burning brightly in the clear morning air while the priests who accompanied the idol made their morning sacrifices.

Hedak came from his tent and stretched himself while surveying the compact and skilled fighting force under his command. Nebo rode up just then to greet his chief with a smile.

"The men are happy," he reported, "but chafing for battle."

"So am I," Hedak agreed. "Tonight, if all goes according to plan, little Cheb will lead them into our arms like sheep for the shearing. And tomorrow, with Boaz's army destroyed, most of Israel will be defenseless."

xviii.

Ruth was not really surprised when a soldier came for her before the sun was two hours high to take her before the Council of Judah. Ever since she had met Cheb that same morning in the olive grove, and he had given her the incredible message that Hedak wanted her, she had been sure it was all part of some sort of a diabolical scheme whose purpose she could not understand, except that it meant some kind of harm to her.

Naomi followed them and tried to enter the council room, but soldiers barred the door and shoved everyone away. "Let me pass!" she cried. "I must speak to the council."

"No one shall go in until the trial of the Moabite is over," the soldier said stolidly. "Those are Tob's orders."

In the council chamber Cheb was speaking, repeating the story he had told Boaz that morning. He stood before the long table behind which the elders sat, with Boaz near one end and Tob at the other. For this occasion the merchant had relinquished the position of president of the council to Nathan and had taken up that of prosecutor. When Cheb finished he got to his feet.

"You have heard the words of the merchant, Cheb," he said to the council. "The story of how this woman who is called Ruth was sent among us by the Moabites to spy upon us and, even worse, to beguile our men with her charms and sow discord among us."

He glanced toward Adah, who, as a possible witness, was sitting quietly in a corner. Encouraged by her faint nod of approval he went on. "It is your duty now to weigh the evidence and judge the enormity of the crime the Moabite woman has committed."

Tob paused, looking around the room. Ruth had been sitting quietly, her eyes downcast. She had not even lifted them when Boaz took his seat and gave her a smile of encouragement. It had been an evil day when she had crossed the border into Israel with Naomi, she thought, as she listened to the structure of lies being built up against her. And there had been nothing but evil since, save for the short joyful interlude she had known with Boaz.

Now he was one of her judges and, knowing how conscientious and just he was, she realized that he could not but be swayed by the arguments of Cheb and Tob. Her only hope was that the decision would be swift and the execution even swifter, ending this terrible nightmare as soon as possible.

Ruth did not let herself meet Boaz's eyes or look at his face, for she knew that, remembering the bliss she could have known with him had things been different from what they were, she might break down. And she was determined to show these people who had hated and spit upon her that she could go to her death with head proudly erect, even when innocent of the charges against her.

"This woman came among us," Tob continued, "as the widow of an Israelite, claiming refuge and protection, and pretending to worship the one true God. In so doing she placed herself under our laws and became subject to the same punishment as an Israelite would be for breaking them. Her crime is treason, for spying upon us as the agent of an enemy. And the punishment for this crime, if you are content that she is guilty, is death by stoning."

Tob sat down, a satisfied look on his face. The Moabite would pay with her life for daring to spurn him.

"Is the accused not to be allowed to speak in her defense?" Boaz asked. "Have we forgotten under the spell of Tob's oratory that our God has said the stranger among us shall be one of us?"

"The woman may be heard," Nathan said, "if she has aught to say in her behalf."

All eyes went to Ruth, but she did not lift her head. In fact she seemed not to have heard the old man's words.

Boaz's face was a mask of pain. When he spoke his voice was hoarse with emotion. "Speak, Ruth!" he implored. "If you would not have me—and this council—believe these things to be true."

Ruth did not reply at once, but she was only thinking what she should say. Boaz had implored her directly, as much, she realized, to settle the torture in his soul as to let her give her side of the story.

"Is there one here who would believe me?" she asked in a clear, firm voice.

"If what you answer proves you innocent," Boaz assured her, "the council will believe you and you shall go free."

"Suppose only you believe her, Boaz?" Tob asked. "While we do not."

"She shall not die," he said firmly.

"You would have us let her go free of punishment on your word alone?"

"If I am convinced of her innocence," Boaz said. "You shall kill her only after killing me."

"You would mock the Council of Judah?" Tob demanded angrily.

Boaz's face hardened. "You are overly anxious to see this woman die, Tob. Perhaps it would be simpler if this remained a quarrel between us, to be settled in the time-honored way of such quarrels, by swords or spears. Be sure the Lord will give victory to whichever of us is in the right."

Tob paled. The very last thing he wanted was a fight with Boaz.

"It is for the council to decide what is right and what is wrong in regard to this woman, not Boaz or Tob," Nathan said sharply. "Let her speak in her own defense."

Ruth stood up. Her head was erect and her shoulders straight. "I know that my ways and my customs are strange to you," she said. "But my ways were not strange to my Hebrew husband when he took me to be his wife. Nor to his love when he taught me to forsake Chemosh and Ashtar to worship the one true God.

"I came to Israel not to spy upon you, as has been charged, but because my husband had been one of you and because it was no longer safe for his mother to remain in Moab. Yet when Naomi and I sought help from my husband's next of kin, Tob, he came to my couch in the night and sought to force me."

There was a murmur of anger from several members of the council, for her quiet forceful words carried deep conviction.

"It's a lie," Tob squealed. "She sought to beguile me for purposes of her own. Adah is my witness. Let her speak."

Nathan turned to the slave girl. "You may speak, Adah," he said. "But being a slave, you cannot be forced to do so in defense of your master. That is the Law."

"The woman lies," Adah said. "In the night she lured my master to her room by displaying her hidden beauty."

"If Ruth thought to beguile Tob as you claim, Adah,"

Boaz asked, "why did she wound his wrist with a dagger and scratch his face?"

Adah smiled almost pityingly. "The noble Boaz, too, has been fooled by the wiles of the Moabite woman. I saw my master suffer the wounds and scratches from thorns in the yard."

Tob had been listening to Adah's testimony anxiously. Now he leaned back and a satisfied smile came over his face.

"What say you to this, woman of Moab?" Nathan asked, not unkindly.

"They both lie," Ruth said bluntly.

"Why?" Tob squealed. "Why would we lie about such a thing?"

Nathan held up his hand for silence, then nodded for Ruth to continue.

"Tob hates me because I would not lie with him," she explained. "Adah wishes me out of the way because she is Tob's concubine and he once sought me for his wife."

Tob was white with anger and fear. He had hoped the council would not even listen to Ruth before passing sentence, but her calm defense was certain to have some influence upon them, most of whom, like Nathan, were good men and just.

"Will you listen to the slanders of a harlot?" he shouted. "She spent last night under Boaz's cloak. Let her deny it if she can. I have the proof."

"I went to Boaz in the hope that he would buy the right of kinsman from Tob and take me as his wife," Ruth said.

"And I came to Tob's house this very morning to offer him the whole of my fortune, if necessary, so that I may marry the woman I love," Boaz confirmed.

"The Moabite is guilty!" Tob protested. "Why do we listen to lies and slander? Let us cast our vote."

Boaz got to his feet and addressed the council. "I, for one, will not vote unless I know more about why Tob seeks to bring about the death of this woman without a fair hearing before this council." He turned to face his kinsman, who quailed before the anger and indignation in Boaz's gaze. "No doubt you have a reason for your actions, Tob," he continued. "And I am beginning to see what such a reason might be. Tob trades much with Moab through Cheb," Boaz told the council. "I have long wondered why news of what happens in Judah and Israel reaches Hedak almost as quickly as it does me."

Tob was white and trembling with anger and righteous indignation. "Are you accusing me of treason, Boaz?" he demanded.

"Not yet," Boaz said deliberately. "But if I find treason, Tob, you will not live to be stoned by the people." He held up his hands, his fingers clenched. "These two hands at your throat will kill you first."

Nathan, presiding over the council, intervened between the two angry men. "This is no place to air a private quarrel, Boaz," he said sharply. "Or to accuse a respected member of this council of treason without grounds. Take your seat while we listen to the Moabite woman's defense."

Boaz sank back in his chair, but his face was still grim.

"Tob has accused you of being responsible for the death of your husband, Mahlon, who was an Israelite." Nathan spoke directly to Ruth. "What say you to this?"

"My husband died because he loved Israel and tried to make peace between this country and Moab. It was not because of any deed of mine."

"Are you saying that Cheb lies?"

"I am," Ruth said firmly.

"Why should he lie to us?" Tob inquired sarcastically. "He is not a Moabite."

"He is in the pay of Moab," Ruth said.

Tob snorted his disbelief, and several of the council smiled.

"Let her finish," Boaz interposed.

"She can call us all Moabites," Tob said with a shrug. "It will be no greater lie than the rest of her testimony."

Several of the old men around the table nodded agreement.

Nathan turned to Cheb. "Have you ever spoken with this woman before this morning when you gave her the message from Hedak?"

"In Moab many times. In Judah never before today."

"Have you ever spoken to this man?" Nathan asked Ruth.

"Once, in Moab. I paid him to warn Boaz that Hedak was bringing him to Heshbon to betray him."

Boaz suddenly rose, his face set. "You gave me no such message as that, Cheb," he said sharply. "Why?"

"I"—Cheb stumbled for words—"I did not think it meet to do so," he explained, "since I carried a tablet from the King of Moab, and also one from Mahlon, her husband, assuring you of safe conduct."

"I find it easier to believe that you were serving Moab in not bringing me her warning," Boaz countered.

Cheb held up his wrist and jerked off the metal hook, so that all could see the stump where his hand had been severed. "The Moabites robbed me of my hand!" he cried in feigned indignation. "Should I love them for it and spy for them out of gratitude?" He looked around the council. "I will prove my loyalty to Judah and Israel. You all know from the message I brought to the spy here that Hedak will soon march against you. His troops may already be in the mountain passes. Long ago, when I was engaged in smuggling across the border, I learned of hidden paths through the mountains into Moab. Assemble your armies, Boaz, and I will lead them by secret routes so that you may fall upon the armies of Hedak before they can attack Judah."

"Would he make such an offer if he were the spy you claim he is, Boaz?" Tob demanded.

Boaz looked at Cheb searchingly, but the caravan driver met his gaze with brazen confidence. "We will consider your offer, Cheb, when Moab has attacked us," he conceded. "But we will not be the first to take the sword."

There was a chorus of approval from the members of the council. In the lull that followed Nathan asked, "Have you more to say in your defense, Ruth of Moab?"

"Only that I am not a spy. If I were I would have heeded the warning Cheb claims to have brought from Moab and left Bethlehem early this morning to join Hedak."

"And I say this woman is proved a traitor, a murderess, and adulteress," Tob cried. "If we put her to the torture of the stones, she will confess that she plots against us with Hedak. Deny it if you can?" he challenged Ruth.

"Before the Most High God, I do deny it."

"Hear that!" Tob almost screamed to the council. He turned to face Ruth, his eyes blazing. "Blasphemer!" he shouted. "May you be struck down with the words of your sacrilege upon your lips."

"Let us cast our vote and cease this mockery," one of

the members of the council demanded. A chorus of assent came from most of the others.

Ruth knew that she had lost, but she faced her judges proudly, without quailing. When her eyes met the tortured gaze of Boaz, she smiled bravely to show her appreciation of his efforts in her defense, for she knew the battle that was raging within him, the controversy between his love for her, his years of distrust for all women, and the tissue of lies that had been built up here before the council to condemn her.

"Make ready to vote," Nathan told the council, but before he could begin to poll them, a sudden blast from a trumpet sounded outside. A clatter of hoofs was heard, followed by an authoritative hammering upon the door.

"Open!" a man's voice shouted, and at a nod from Nathan one of the guards opened the door.

Eliab strode into the chamber, his face grave with concern. Abiram followed him.

"We are in council, Eliab," Tob protested, but the Israelite captain cut him off.

"Judah is at war!" he announced. "The Moabites under Hedak have attacked, and their whole army is marching against us. Last night Joseph was foully murdered."

Boaz was on his feet before Eliab had finished speaking. "This hearing must rest until I return," he said to Nathan.

"What?" Tob squealed. "This news is enough to damn the Moabite woman ten times over. Throw her to the people to be stoned!"

"I have not heard enough to call her innocent or guilty yet," Boaz insisted. "I go now to lead your armies in the defense of Judah and Israel, but I charge you all to see that I am obeyed in regard to the woman, Ruth. If any one of you takes justice in his hands, I shall punish him myself."

"We know why you protect her," Tob cried. "It is because she gave herself to you last night on the threshing floor."

Before Boaz could answer, Tob turned to the council and the people who had poured into the room in the wake of Eliab and Abiram.

"Why did this pagan, this Moabite harlot, lie in Boaz's arms?" he demanded. "On the very night that her people raided our land and slew our comrade, Joseph? Why on this night of all nights, if not to seduce Boaz from the defense of Israel?"

A roar of anger went up from the people. Some of them even moved toward Ruth threateningly, but Boaz placed himself before her with Abiram at one side and Eliab at the other. Before the naked swords of the two captains, the crowd drew back.

"Hear, O God!" Tob implored dramatically. "Hear how your people have been betrayed by the Moabite harlot!"

Another shout went up from the crowd, but they quieted when Boaz raised his hand for silence. "If I am to lead you, my orders will be obeyed," he said grimly. "This woman will not be harmed until I return. Accept this condition or depose me and name another to lead your armies in my stead."

There was a moment of silence, then Eliab lifted his voice. "Boaz is our leader!" he cried. "I march behind the Lion of Judah for I know the Lord favors him and will give him victory."

"Boaz must lead us!" another voice cried.

"Save us from Moab!" The crowd took it up then, shouting for Boaz.

"I will lead your armies against Moab," he promised. "And if it is God's will we shall triumph. But the woman, Ruth, will not be harmed by any one among you until I return and can look further into this question."

"She is a spy," Tob insisted.

"Someone is a spy," Boaz agreed. "When I return, I intend to find out who it is." He turned to the hard-bitten soldier who had come in with Eliab. "Take four soldiers, Abiram," he directed, "and follow me to the prison near the gate. The walls are thick and with you to guard her Ruth will be safe there until I return."

xix.

"I am sorry you have to remain in prison, Ruth," Boaz said while they waited for the jailer to unlock the door. "But it is the only place where I can be sure you will be safe while I am gone."

"I don't mind," she assured him with a smile. "But for you I would already be dead from the stones."

The jailer opened the door and they could see a heap of rags upon some straw in the corner. "It is the madwoman," the jailer explained.

"What is she doing here?" Boaz demanded.

"Ola was making so much fuss this morning that Cheb told us to lock her up for a while."

"It's all right," Ruth assured Boaz. "I'm not afraid of her."

"Wait outside," Boaz told Abiram and the jailer. When they closed the door he took Ruth in his arms. "I will find the truth of all this, Ruth," he promised, "as soon as I return."

She smiled and touched his cheek gently. "God is just and I am sure the truth will come out. But Israel needs you now. You must go."

"Either Cheb or Tob is lying. I will make them tell the truth if I have to wring their necks with these two hands."

"Don't blame your people. They have been taught to hate Moabites."

"I hated women," he reminded her. "But you showed me how wrong I was. Perhaps together we can teach my people to love others as God commands."

"All I can do now is love you," Ruth said, her eyes shining.

"God be with you, Ruth." He held her tightly for a long moment before he left, closing the door of the jail behind him.

"Farewell, my beloved," she whispered. "May God bring you safely back to me."

Outside Boaz clapped Abiram on the shoulder. "I shall be sorry not to have your stout spear beside me," he said. "But my heart is inside that cell, guard her with your life."

A crowd stood outside the jail, Cheb among them. "You offered just now to lead us into Moab through a secret pass," Boaz called to him. "Can you show us a route that will put us behind the army of Moab so we can fall upon them from the rear when they do not expect us?"

"I will put you in their very midst," Cheb promised, but was careful not to let Boaz see the sudden gleam of satisfaction in his eyes.

"Come along, then," Boaz told him. "There is no time to lose."

Eliab did not miss the note of satisfaction in the caravan driver's voice. Cheb, he decided, would bear watching.

For a long time after Boaz had left, Ruth knelt beside the rough bench that was the only furniture of the cell where she was imprisoned with Ola, praying for Boaz and the success of his defense of Israel. When she finished she looked across to where the madwoman lay curled up like a child on some straw, still sound asleep. There seemed no harm in the poor, demented creature, and with Abiram on guard outside Ruth knew she had nothing to fear, so she lay down upon another pile of straw and closed her eyes. Exhausted from the events of the past day and night, she was soon asleep.

At the camp of the Israelite forces between Bethlehem and the mountain passes into Moab, Boaz sat his horse and looked with approval at the long lines of men drawn up before him. Each carried two spears as well as a shield, and some of the officers also wore swords. Behind the men were long trains of carts and bearers with supplies.

Eliab had alerted the camp and ordered the preparations for marching started before he had ridden to Bethlehem that morning to bring news of the Moabite attack and the death of Joseph. By the time Boaz reached the camp the army was ready to move.

Together Eliab and Boaz galloped along the ranks to the head of the column. When Eliab held up his sword, there was a sudden quiet.

"Men of Israel," Boaz addressed the army. "We go to fight for the defense of our homes and those we love. But we do more than that, for we are a chosen people and the banner of the Most High God goes before us. Let us be brave and strong in battle for the glory of God and of Israel, so that we may show the heathen only He rules the world."

"For the glory of God and of Israel," the men answered in a mighty shout.

At a sign from Boaz the ram's-horn trumpets sounded the call to march and the army of Israel started to move eastward across the plains toward the distant mountains and the battle which would decide for one generation, at least, whether or not the children of Israel would dwell in the place here in this land to which their God had led them from the bondage of Egypt.

Late in the afternoon, with the sun hardly more than an hour above the horizon, the army halted for a short rest. The mountains were very near now and soon they would be entering the passes. Boaz and Eliab were at the head of the broad column of marching men and vehicles, with Cheb just behind them. Boaz sat his horse now, his brooding eyes upon the mountain ranges ahead.

As they had approached closer to the mountain ranges through which Cheb had promised to lead them so that they could fall upon the rear of the Moabite army, Eliab's misgivings about their guide had grown steadily. When they stopped, he moved over beside Boaz and said in a low voice, "I don't like going on after darkness falls. Why not stop for the night here and send scouting parties forward?"

"That would give the Moabites time to get through the passes and onto the plains," Boaz pointed out. "They could cut us to pieces here with their swords and their superiority in numbers."

"They will do the same thing in the passes, in case Cheb leads us into a trap!"

The caravan driver had not failed to note Eliab's growing suspicions. When he moved up close to speak to Boaz, Cheb spurred his horse forward until he could hear what they were saying. Now he jerked off his hook as he had done before the council.

"Does this stump look like I am a traitor, Eliab?" he demanded. "I have waited a long time for revenge upon the Moabites who cut off my hand. Do not cheat me of it now with groundless suspicion."

Boaz looked at Cheb thoughtfully for a moment, then turned to his second-in-command. "I have weighed all the factors here, Eliab," he said quietly. "Cheb may be a traitor. If so, we shall soon know it. But we will go on, since our only hope is to trap Hedak and his army in the narrow defiles where our spears are better weapons than his swords."

"But the risk?"

"The risk is worth taking, for what we can gain. Think you I would knowingly lead you all into a trap?"

"I know better than that," Eliab said loyally.

"It is my duty to take every advantage that we are lucky enough to obtain," Boaz pointed out. "So we will go on in the hope of trapping the enemy."

"Or be trapped ourselves?"

"That is the risk we take," Boaz admitted. "Ride down the line and choose any of the men who have lived in these parts. Send them out ahead and on either side as scouts. I do not propose to be caught napping."

"That is better," Eliab said, and wheeled his horse away.

"And you, Cheb," Boaz said quietly. "Do not flatter yourself that you are fooling me, if you are indeed a traitor. Be sure the Lord will give us victory for our cause is His. Then every man will receive what he deserves."

Cheb turned a little pale, but managed to keep face. "Even Eliab will thank me when I deliver Hedak's army into your hands," he said virtuously. "And be sorry he doubted me."

"I hope so, Cheb," Boaz said in the same quiet voice. "I truly hope so. For what will happen to you if you prove a traitor would be a grievous thing indeed to witness. Your body will be torn limb from limb while you are yet alive, and one part carried to each tribe of Israel, there to be displayed as an example of the fate that awaits traitors. Afterwards the flesh will be torn from your bones and they will be placed over the city gates as a warning forever."

Cheb managed to grin, but his face was a little green as he rode back to his regular position behind the leaders.

Ruth slept part of the day; the rest she spent in prayer. Ola had long since awakened, but she still lay on the straw in the corner, watching Ruth's every move with bright, beady eyes. When Ruth rose from her knees late in the afternoon, she pushed her hair wearily back from her forehead with her arm, exposing the mark of Chemosh tattooed there.

"A Moabite!" the madwoman snarled suddenly. "Kill the Moabite!" She came up from the floor on skinny legs covered with sores, her hands extended like claws, and her eyes burning with the sudden senseless fury of the insane.

Ruth cowered back instinctively from the repulsive apparition, but her momentary revulsion only stimulated the poor mad creature more. Jumping up and down, Ola advanced upon Ruth. "Kill the Moabite!" she screeched. "They cut off my son's hand."

Instinctively Ruth put up her hand to fend off the claws of the madwoman, as she had when Zelda had attacked her at the winnowing ground. In her terror she even forgot that Abiram waited outside on guard with the jailer and would come to protect her if she called.

Ola was almost upon Ruth, when she did something strange, the same thing, Ruth remembered now, that she had done that first morning by the well. The madwoman's whole expression suddenly changed to one of cunning and she smiled, if the grimace exposing toothless sockets in her gums and blackened stumps of teeth could be called that.

"The Moabites are my son's friends now," she crooned in the singsong that so often served her as speech. "They are kind to him."

Ruth was staring at Ola perplexedly, still half expecting her to be seized again by one of those sudden bursts of fury. It was a moment, therefore, before the significance of the words penetrated her mind. When it did she could barely control the sudden shock that went with the realization of what the madwoman seemed to be saying.

With an effort of will Ruth forced herself to be calm. She even managed to smile at the grinning human death's-head that was Ola's face. Somehow, she knew, she had to find out just what the poor woman meant. If it were what she was almost afraid to believe it could be, her worst fears for Boaz would be realized.

"I am of Moab too," she said with a friendly smile. "And I am your son's friend, too."

Ola began to caper about the cell, an expression of fiendish glee upon her face. "When Hedak conquers Judah," she caroled in that sniffling singsong, "we will be rich. Prince Hedak has promised——"

"Hedak," Ruth gasped, unable to restrain a cry of surprise.

The madwoman stopped her capering and a sly look

came into her eyes. "You are of Moab. You should know him," she cackled, and went off into a senseless gale of laughter again.

"Prince Hedak is a great man," Ruth forced herself to say.

The madwoman came closer, dropping her voice to a conspiratorial whisper. "Hedak pays Cheb well," she confided.

Ruth caught her breath. The answer to Cheb's loyalty had been right there all the time, she realized now, if only she could have seen it. Ola had told her the truth that first morning by the well, but Ruth had not known then how to interpret it, since in Moab, as well as in Judah, no one listened to the ravings of the insane.

Sick with horror at what she had just learned, Ruth ran to the cell door and beat upon it with her fists. "Abiram! Abiram!" she cried. "I must speak to you."

The jailer opened the door. Abiram stood just behind him. When he saw Ruth's face he stepped inside quickly and caught her when she swayed and would have fallen.

"What is it?" he asked. His eyes went to the madwoman crouching in the corner, chuckling to herself. "Did Ola strike you?"

"No," Ruth gasped. "No. She just told me that her son Cheb is in the pay of Hedak."

"By the beard of Moses!" Abiram cried. "I have never liked that Cheb."

"Did he go with Boaz?"

"Yes. I heard Cheb promise Boaz to lead the army through a secret pass into Moab, so they can fall upon the Moabites from the rear."

"He is leading them all into a trap!" Ruth cried. "Cheb is a Moabite spy. You must do something to warn Boaz."

Abiram went to the door of the jail. "Isaac!" he shouted to one of the soldiers waiting outside. "Take a fast horse and ride after Boaz. Tell him we have proof Cheb is a traitor and is leading them into a trap."

"Will he—can he get there in time?" Ruth asked.

Abiram shook his head glumly. "Boaz and the army will move fast to get through the passes quickly. And they have many hours' start."

"Do something, then," Ruth implored. "Unless we stop them, Boaz and the whole army will be destroyed."

"We can do nothing," he said bluntly. "Except hope."

"We can pray." She turned back into the cell and dropped to her knees before the bench. "Only God can save them now."

Ruth lifted her eyes to heaven. "God of my beloved and of Israel," she said in a clear, firm voice, knowing now that the only help for Boaz must come from a divine source. "Give Boaz a sign that he and the others may stop before it is too late." She bowed her head then in complete submission to divine judgment. "If it be Thy will . . ."

xx.

As the long column of the Israelite army moved into the foothills, a Moabite scout perched high up among the rocks watched them, counting the columns and estimating the number of men from their size and length. When he had satisfied himself of the number and of the direction they were moving, he ran to where his horse was tied in a pocket among the rocks, mounted it, and galloped down along a crevice hidden from the plains below toward the Moabite camp deep in the mountains. Shortly Hedak would know exactly the number of the Israelite soldiers and the fact that Cheb, as he had promised, was leading his countrymen into an ambush.

In the prison at Bethlehem, Ruth still knelt before the bench, her lips moving in ceaseless prayer to God that Boaz would stop before Cheb led the army into an ambush.

As she prayed, the dying rays of the sun slanted through a small, grated window high up on the wall. They seized hold of her hair, turning it, in the instant before the rays died away, into a living flame.

As dusk began to fall and the mountains towered overhead Boaz's expression grew more and more concerned. Riding beside him, Eliab, too, was grim. "For the last time, Boaz," he said, "I think we should stop and scout ahead before going on."

"You may be right, Eliab," Boaz admitted. "These last

few minutes a voice inside me does seem to be urging me to stop."

"It is the voice of your better judgment. Listen to it."

"I prayed in the tabernacle for a sign from God before we left Bethlehem. But there was none."

"The Most High must be speaking to you now," Eliab urged. "If we——"

"Look!" a soldier shouted suddenly behind them. "The bush there is aflame."

A startled look came into Boaz's eyes and he turned to follow the soldier's pointing finger with his gaze. A reddish bush grew a short distance away and for a moment the dying rays of the sun had enveloped it, making the shrub appear to be in flames. The illusion faded while Boaz watched it, but there was no more indecision in his face now.

"Halt!" he ordered, and held up his sword.

"Thank God!" Eliab said fervently, and signaled the trumpeter to sound the command to rest.

Cheb spurred forward. "Why do you stop?" he asked. "The entrance to the pass lies just ahead."

"We have been given a sign from God," Boaz explained.

"The bush was only lit up for a moment by the sun," Cheb said contemptuously. "See. It looks like any other shrub now."

The bush had indeed lost its fiery glow since the rays of the sun no longer illuminated it, and it was like any other of the hundreds that grew along the way they were following.

"Whatever happened," Boaz said quietly, "it was a sign I needed. Build a fire, Eliab."

He turned to the caravan driver. "We are going to find out before we go any further whether you have been telling the truth, Cheb."

"H-how?"

"With the test of fire."

"The test of fire?" Cheb's face blanched with terror.

"You worship the God of Israel, don't you?"

"Yes. You know I am an Israelite."

"Then you trust the Most High God, as all of us do. If you are telling the truth and not leading us into a trap,

God will not let your hand be burned when you thrust it into the fire."

Eliab had dispatched a soldier to the foot of the column, where a brazier of coals was carried on one of the carts for lighting the cooking fires when they made camp. When the man returned, carrying some coals in a small pot of earthenware, Eliab knelt before a pile of sticks that had been gathered while they were waiting for the coals. Covering the glowing coals with twigs, Eliab blew upon them until a brisk flame appeared and began to consume the wood. Then he added larger twigs and bits of dead brush.

Cheb's eyes darted to his good hand and then to the stump of his left. Suddenly he spurred his horse in an attempt to escape, but Boaz was watching and rapped out an order. Before the spy had gone two horse-lengths, soldiers were at the bridle, holding the animal and dragging Cheb from the saddle. They brought the quivering traitor back to where Boaz stood beside the now briskly burning fire.

"Are you an agent of Hedak, Cheb?" Boaz demanded coldly.

"I am an Israelite," Cheb babbled, "and loyal."

"Then put your hand in the flame."

The spy looked around like a hunted animal, but saw no sympathy upon any of the grim faces about him. Slowly he moved his hand toward the fire, but when the heat began to sear his skin, he jerked it back.

"Thrust you hand into the fire, Cheb," Boaz commanded. "If you have spoken the truth, God will not let you be burned."

Cheb tried again, but at the feel of the heat upon his skin he drew back, his mouth working.

"Hold him, Eliab," Boaz directed, "and force his hand into the flames."

The soldiers who were holding Cheb thrust him toward the fire and Eliab seized his good hand and forced it closer to the flames. Cheb was gibbering with fear, but there was no relenting upon the part of the men who held him. And as if anxious to sear the traitor's flesh, the flames suddenly flared up and seemed to lick out avidly at his hand.

"I lied," Cheb screamed, writhing in the grasp of his captors. "I lied."

"Then you were leading us into a trap?" Boaz asked grimly.

"Yes! Yes! Take my hand from the fire. I will tell you everything."

"Release his hand, Eliab," Boaz commanded. "The rest of you keep hold of him. Now, where is Hedak waiting for us?"

Cheb gasped with relief and jerked his hand back. His eyes darted from one to another of the grim-faced men around him, but he saw nothing that would give him any hope of mercy. Yet, in desperation, he tried to bargain. "Let me go free and I will tell you all I know," he promised.

"We do not bargain with traitors," Boaz said contemptuously. "Put his hand into the fire again, Eliab."

"I will tell all!" Cheb screamed. "Hedak waits to fall upon you in the chasm of Hezron."

"He would have made fools of all of us," Eliab said. "Dead fools . . . if you had not listened to the voice of your better judgment, Boaz."

"Perhaps something higher than mere judgment spoke to me," Boaz admitted. "Take the traitor away but keep a close guard over him. When we return to Judah, the council will determine his fate." He turned to the army. "I came near to destroying you all," he told them humbly, "through listening to a traitor. But God sent a warning to us in time. Hedak waits in the chasm of Hezron, expecting us to march into an ambush. Does any man among you know that region well?"

A rugged-looking man stepped forward from among the ranks of the officers.

"Ram!" Boaz cried warmly. "I should have thought of you at once. You helped deliver me from Heshbon."

Ram grinned at the praise. "I dwelt in this region for many years, Boaz," he said, "and I know the chasm of Hezron well."

"Could the army of Moab have trapped us there?"

"Like a bird with a broken wing. You would have been pinned down, unable to move."

"By the tents of Israel!" Eliab said. "It was a well-baited trap, too. What shall we do, Boaz?"

Boaz smiled for the first time since morning. "In my youth I hunted much, sometimes for lions. Once one of them hunted me instead, almost costing me my life."

"Shall the hunted then become the hunter?" Eliab's leathery face was creased in a smile.

"We shall," Boaz said. "Tell me, Ram, are there paths around the chasm of Hezron by which you could place us above the Moabites?"

Ram nodded. "I have often hunted wild goats among those crags. If you wish, I can put you upon the back of the Moabites before they know you are there."

"You shall be our guide, then. And when victory is ours, the Lord will bless you with great riches."

"But we are still too few to risk surrounding the army of Moab," Eliab objected.

Boaz smiled again. "Have you forgotten Gideon?" he asked. "And the three hundred who put an army of Midianites to rout?"

xxi.

It was after midnight when Ram paused in the darkness and said quietly, "We are at the head of the chasm, Boaz."

Boaz turned to Eliab. "Separate three companies of a hundred men each," he directed. "I will go forward with Ram to see if we can locate the Moabite army. Have each man of the three hundred carry two fagots for torches."

Climbing carefully from rock to rock, Boaz and Ram moved upward along the wall of the chasm until they came out upon a small ledge from which they could look down into it. What they saw brought a smile of satisfaction to Boaz's lips.

The Moabites were encamped in the bottom of the deep cleft in the mountains from which they could fan out up the sides to fall upon the Israelites as they advanced into it, led by Cheb. It was a clever trap, and it would undoubtedly have succeeded had Boaz not learned in time of Cheb's treachery. Now, he thought grimly, the shoe would be on the other foot, or, as he had told Eliab, the hunted would for this night be the hunter. Before morning, if all went well, the idol standing there in the camp of the Moabites, with the fires of Chemosh glowing in its belly, would be overturned and destroyed. And Moab would no longer be a threat to Judah and to Israel.

Boaz and Ram returned by the time Eliab had formed three groups of a hundred men each and loaded them with fagots for torches. Every Israelite was familiar with the thrilling story of Gideon, who, only a few hundred years before, had used this very stratagem against a vastly superior number of Midianites and had triumphed.

"The Moabites are in the bottom of the chasm waiting for us," Boaz reported. "Each group of a hundred will carry several burning torches hidden under empty open jars, so the Moabites cannot see the flames. We will also divide our trumpets among the three groups, saving only a few here to give signals. Ram will lead one group around the Moabite army and block the other end of the chasm. Each of the other two bands of one hundred will locate themselves on a side wall of the chasm. As soon as you reach your stations, set your fagots upright among the rocks ready for lighting from the torches you carry.

"While the torches are being lit," Boaz continued, "others will blow upon the trumpets. When the Moabites move upon us here, trying to escape, you will fall upon them from the three sides, while we block them in at the head of the chasm. Is everything clear?"

The officers who were to lead the groups nodded. "Ram's group will need the most time," Boaz said, "since they must go around the Moabites. When you are ready, Ram, light your torches and sound your trumpet. That will be the signal for the others."

The patrols moved into the darkness with the bundles of fagots, the trumpets, and the burning torches hidden under jars so they would not be seen by the Moabites.

In the chasm Hedak and Nebo were engaged in an earnest conference before the image of Chemosh on its giant wooden wheels. "The outposts reported the Israelites entering the foothills several hours ago," Hedak said. "Where can they be?"

"Perhaps they halted for a rest," Nebo suggested. "Or Cheb may have gone over to the enemy."

Hedak shook his head. "We will conquer Israel anyway and Cheb knows I would burn him alive if he tricked me."

A mutter of thunder sounded above them. Hedak looked up at the sky and frowned. "What a time for a storm," he growled. "If Cheb does not lead them here soon our plans may go wrong. It is hard to fight in darkness and rain."

"Let me take half a hundred men and go forward. If the Israelites are near, I may be able to locate them without being discovered."

"Take them then," Hedak said. "And move fast. The men are getting restive and this thunderstorm is not helping us."

High up in the gorge Boaz waited with Eliab. The main body of the army was drawn up behind them on either side of the narrow defile giving access to the large pocket called the chasm of Hezron, ready to rain down their spears upon the Moabites when Hedak's forces tried to escape from the pocket where they had expected to trap the army of Israel.

Lightning darted across the face of the mountain, illuminating the spears of the soldiers who waited behind the two leaders. And a thunderstorm went rolling through the gorge, echoing and re-echoing on its way.

"The Lord fights for Israel today, Eliab," Boaz said with quiet confidence. "The crash of thunder will drown out the noise made by our men moving to the flanks. Has Ram had time to reach the other end of the chasm yet?"

"He should be there soon. And the others must already be in place. Any moment now we will see the torches."

Lightning flared once more. Boaz was looking down into the chasm, and he stiffened suddenly. "Down there, Eliab," he said quickly, "I saw a small party of Moabite soldiers when the lightning flashed just now."

"I was watching for Ram's signal," Eliab admitted, "so I did not see anything."

"Pass the sword to alert the men," Boaz ordered. Just then a sudden clash of weapons sounded below them as the Moabite party under Nebo met the outer guards of the Israelite army.

Eliab drew his sword and went bounding down across the rocks to take command, but the skirmish was over almost as soon as it began. Nebo had found out what he sought to discover, and quickly ordered his men to retreat.

"Shall we follow them?" Eliab called to Boaz. "It was only a small party."

Boaz was straining his eyes into the darkness. This was the crucial moment, for unless the parties he had sent out gave the signal soon, most of the advantage he had sought to gain would be lost. Even in the narrow gorge that gave access to the pocket in the mountains Hedak's superior forces could still win the battle if they approached in battle order. He had been counting on the realization that they were surrounded by what seemed a vastly superior force to demoralize the Moabites so thoroughly that they would rush for the gorge in panic, and be mowed down by the spears of Israel before they could learn just how small a force opposed them.

"Shall I go after them, Boaz?" Eliab repeated.

"No. Ram should be ready at any moment now."

At the far end of the chasm a trumpet sounded, the notes floating to them faintly across the pocket. Immediately spots of light appeared one after another as the soldiers with Ram ran to light the torches they had wedged into the rocks.

Hardly had the first of the torches burst into flames when trumpets began to blast from the right side of the chasm, to be followed by another breaking out of torches along the wall.

Below, before the idol of Chemosh with its sacred flames, Hedak looked with startled eyes as a veritable forest of flaming torches suddenly appeared behind and to one side of him. Just then, too, Nebo and his band came running back into the camp.

"The Israelites are ahead of us in the gorge," Nebo shouted. He stopped suddenly as the trumpet blasts met his ears.

The sound was drowned out momentarily by a clap of thunder that rolled through the gorge. In the glare of the lightning the Moabite army could be seen behind Hedak, watching the lights on the mountainside apprehensively.

"You fool!" Hedak snapped. "They are not only in front of us, they are behind us and to the left."

Just then trumpets blared on the other flank and lights suddenly sprang into view all along the hillside. A forest of torches burned on three sides of the Moabites now, and they already knew that part of the army of Israel was at the fourth side, in front of them. As Hedak and Nebo stared at each other in bewilderment, a Moabite soldier shouted, "The Israelites surround us! We are lost!"

As the din of trumpets came at them now from four sides, others among the Moabite soldiers began to shout:

"It is an ambush!"

"We have been betrayed!"

"Silence!" Hedak's bellow stopped the near panic. "Chemosh goes before us! Our god will bring us victory."

In a lower voice he said to Nebo, "Our scouts must have lied. The whole of Israel is out against us."

"If we attack, they will wipe us out."

"Would you have me surrender!" Hedak snapped in sudden fury.

"No. Retreat."

"Which way?" Hedak demanded sarcastically. "Downward or upward?"

"That force behind us," Nebo said thoughtfully. "It cannot be very large, or we would have heard them marching around us."

"Then the same thing may be true of the forces on the right and the left," Hedak said quickly. "These Israelites are wily. It may be a trick to make us think they surround us in force."

"How can we be sure?"

Hedak grinned. "There is a way. These people have a strange custom of believing a man's words are true until proved that they are not." He turned to his trumpeter. "Sound the call for a truce."

"A truce?" Nebo echoed unbelievably.

"Only long enough to bring Boaz out where we can see him. When he and his officers appear, charge and kill them all. Without their leaders the Israelites will be like sheep."

The trumpeter lifted his instrument and sent a long blast echoing up the gorge to where Boaz and Eliab stood.

"It is a trick," Boaz said immediately. "Just such a trick as Hedak would think of." He cupped his hands to his mouth and shouted down into the gorge. "The trap you planned for us has closed on you, Hedak. Lay down your swords and come through the gorge file, or we will cut you to pieces."

Hedak answered at once. "Come down and fight us," he challenged. "Together or singly."

"Don't challenge him to single combat, Boaz," Eliab advised. "He will cut you down by trickery and we will be lost."

"We are lost anyway if Hedak has time to discover how thinly spread our forces are. Unless they come to fight us, we must go to fight them. And they outnumber us at least two to one. Believe me, Eliab, this is the better way." Boaz turned to the trumpeter. "Sound the challenge to single combat."

Hedak grinned when the Israelite trumpet rang out the challenge to individual battle. "I thought Boaz would be goaded into fighting me. Now I will kill the Lion of Judah, as I have wanted to do for a long time. . . . Accept," he ordered his own trumpeter, and turned back to Nebo. "Stay behind me while I am fighting Boaz and keep your dagger ready," he directed. "If I do not overcome him early in the fight, throw your blade as you did at the Israelite Chilion as soon as Boaz makes a good target."

Nebo nodded. "And then?"

"The Israelites will be stunned by the death of their leader. If we charge them then, they will break and run. Victory will be ours."

"What about those on the flanks and at the rear?"

"We will take them one at a time, after we have disposed of Boaz and the main part of his army."

Lights appeared at the head of the gorge and Boaz rode into the open space before the god of Moab, with Eliab beside him, at the head of at least a hundred Israelite spearmen. Both the leaders carried long torches which they trust into the ground to illuminate the area where the personal combat would be fought. Eliab bore two spears, Boaz carried sword and spear, and a dagger at his waist.

Hedak and Nebo marked the other side of the square with torches. The entire combat area was now well lighted.

"I gave the challenge, Hedak," Boaz said. "You may have the choice of weapons."

"Sword and dagger," Hedak said confidently, "since you carry a weapon forged by the same hand as mine."

"Agreed."

"Then let us begin." Hedak jerked off the leather jacket he wore, exposing a powerful chest matted with black hair.

"Do not think that I trust you even in single combat," Boaz warned. "Lest your officers or your men be tempted to trick me, I have a warning for you all."

The Moabite chief was momentarily taken aback by the realization that Boaz was expecting treachery. "What kind of warning?" he blustered. "You know that you outnumber you."

"Each man of my army carries two spears, as does Eliab here," Boaz told him. "And there are more waiting to be brought forward when needed. Lest you be tempted to treachery I think it only fair to show you what will happen to him who tries it. Throw, Eliab."

Eliab had been looking about him while Boaz was speaking. It was a macabre enough scene that met his eyes. The Moabite soldiers were clustered behind the huge idol of Chemosh, with Hedak and Nebo out in front of it. Beside the idol a priest was tossing blocks of wood into the furnace that formed the belly of the image, feeding the eternal fires of the Moabite god. As the priest lifted one of the blocks, Eliab rose easily in his saddle and threw a spear. It traveled through the air in a long arc and the point struck squarely in the block, knocking it from the hands of the priest, who jumped aside, startled.

The expression on the priest's face was ludicrous, but nobody laughed. Instead a cry of wonder and of fear came from the soldiers at this exhibition of skill.

"You, Nebo," Boaz called, "remember that Eliab has his spear aimed at your heart. Reach once for that dagger at your belt and the spear will pierce you."

Nebo paled and looked quickly at Hedak. His commander could give him no help, however, for Hedak, too, was beginning to feel the cold, clammy hand of fear.

"Listen, the rest of you!" Eliab called to the Moabite army. "One sign of treachery will bring a hail of spears upon you. Be sure that many will die, and those who lead, first."

"Enough of this mummery," Hedak shouted angrily. "Fight, if you are going to fight, Boaz."

Boaz had shed his own jacket. He faced Hedak now with his sword in one hand and a dagger in the other. Against the Moabite leader's massive ugliness Boaz seemed small, but the sinews of his torso were smooth and rippling contrasted with Hedak's bunched muscles and huge limbs.

The two men advanced toward each other across the open space. As they did, lightning flashed downward, illuminating the squat, massive hideousness of Chemosh and the pallid Moabite soldiers behind the image, while thunder echoed and re-echoed through the gorge.

"Our God fights for His people tonight, Hedak," Boaz cried exultantly. "Remember how He quenched the fires of Chemosh in Heshbon?"

A quick light of fear showed momentarily in Hedak's face before he launched a vicious attack. Boaz parried smoothly, leaping in and out to flick Hedak's broad chest with the point of his blade and bring a sudden spot of red before the Moabite could slash with his dagger.

Hedak fought with bull-like rushes, wielding his sword like a flail, counting on his bulk and strength to beat down Boaz's guard and give him the opening he needed for a fatal thrust. Boaz fought smoothly, giving ground when Hedak rushed, and forcing him back on the recovery that followed. Soon Hedak's chest was spotted with blood and, as the merciless flashing of Boaz's sword continued, the Moabite's lips tightened. Fear began to show in his eyes, in the jerkiness of his movements, and the fury of his rushes.

Boaz recognized Hedak's rising terror and pressed the fight, forcing the Moabite constantly back without giving him a chance to set himself.

"Nebo!" Hedak shouted desperately. But when Nebo's fingers moved toward his dagger, Eliab drew back his spear and the Moabite lieutenant's hand dropped to his side again.

Hedak turned his head to see why Nebo did not throw. His foot slipped and he staggered, falling to his knees. Instantly Boaz's point was at this throat.

"Surrender!" Hedak gasped. "I surrender."

"And your army with you?" Boaz demanded.

"Yes, yes! Only spare me!"

"Drop your weapons," Boaz commanded. When Hedak obeyed, he stepped back to allow the beaten Moabite captain to rise.

Slowly Hedak got to his feet. When he was erect, however, he whirled suddenly and ran toward the image of his god and the army behind it, as if seeking refuge in Chemosh now that he had lost in personal combat.

"Your spear, Eliab," Boaz said calmly.

Eliab tossed the spear and Boaz caught it expertly by the shaft. Hedak was almost to the image now. As he was turning to seek refuge behind it, Boaz lifted the spear and threw it with a smooth, powerful motion, just as he had when teaching soldiers at the camp upon the plains.

Straight and true the spear shot through the air in a smooth arc. Hedak had half turned to pass the image when it struck his body. Driven by Boaz's full strength, the sharp blade plunged entirely through the Moabite captain and into the ground, pinning his writhing body to the earth.

Hedak screamed with agony and clutched at the spear, but not one of the soldiers crouching behind the image of their god went to his aid. They had been stunned both by the failure of Hedak to win the duel with Boaz, and by the ease with which the spear had found its target at such a distance. Facing the winged death that could seek them out before they came to actual battle, with no chance to defend themselves, a paralysis of utter terror had gripped the Moabite army.

"The Lord God of Israel has spoken!" Eliab shouted. "Death to the Moabites!"

"Death to the Moabites!" the Israelite soldiers echoed,

and charged down into the gorge, sending a hail of spears before them, and stabbing at the Moabites who remained on their feet with the second spear that each soldier carried.

Demoralized by the death of their leader and the spears that rained death upon them, the Moabites broke and ran, forgetting even to use their vaunted swords as they sought to get out of this ambush that had become a deathtrap.

The battle was soon over as the Israelites poured down from every side of the gorge upon the luckless army of Moab. Those who were not slain were taken as prisoners, and thousands of weapons and much booty fell to the jubilant soldiers of Israel.

"God has given us a great victory," Boaz told his victorious army when the short battle was finished and they were ready to march back to Bethlehem. "Moab shall threaten us no more." Then with bowed head he led them in a prayer of thanksgiving there on the battlefield to the God who had made victory possible.

xxii.

Late the next afternoon Boaz rode into Bethlehem amid the acclaim of the people. He did not stop to receive their plaudits, however, but went directly to the prison, where he dismounted and opened the door himself.

Ruth was standing in the corner of the cell, looking at the sky through the small, barred window. Word had already come to Bethlehem of the great victory over the Moabite army and Hedak, but she did not know yet what her fate would be. Hearing the door open, she turned and a great happiness shone in her eyes when she saw Boaz standing in the doorway, unharmed.

"Thank God you are safe," she cried, running to meet him.

Boaz took her in his arms, and for a long moment they could only cling together. Finally Ruth said through tears of joy, "My prayer was answered after all. You did stop before Cheb could lead you into a trap."

"Abiram met me at the edge of town and told me how you prayed that God would save me and Israel," he told her. "I know now that it was your voice that spoke to me there on the plains. Hedak is dead and the Moabite army defeated. Now both Moab and Israel can live together in peace."

"This was what Mahlon wanted. Wherever he is, I know he must be glad too."

"I am a fool and a man of straw," he told her. "How can you ever forgive me, Ruth, for listening to Cheb's lies about you."

"Don't speak of them." She shivered. "It is enough that you are safe and we are together."

The crowd gathered at the gates of Bethlehem the next morning cheered wildly as Boaz came through their ranks, holding Ruth with one hand and Naomi with the other. He stepped upon the low platform of the well and held up his hand for silence. When all was quiet he began to speak:

"The gates of Bethlehem were ever proud gates. But we can never call ourselves a proud people until it is known throughout the world of man that we protect the defenseless, the poor, the downtrodden, the innocent."

He reached down and drew Ruth up beside him.

"This is the woman who came to us for refuge, worshiping our God and faithful to her kinsmen. And what would we have done?"

He paused and looked out over the crowd before going on.

"We would have cast her from us, not for any evil we knew against her, but because she was not one of us. And in this matter my guilt was as great as any. Will you forswear her still?"

Elkan, Boaz's overseer, stepped from the crowd. "I welcome Ruth of Moab to Judah," he shouted. "She is one of us now." And the crowd roared assent.

"Where is Tob?" Boaz called.

The merchant had been standing at the edge of the crowd, not taking any part in the celebration. Several of the men seized him now and rushed him up to the platform, where he stood before Boaz, all his pompous air of authority gone.

"I do not hold it against you, Tob," Boaz said, "that you sought to have Ruth punished unjustly as a spy, preferring to believe that you were moved by zeal for the welfare of Israel. As evidence that I have forgiven you, I will this day pay to you the value of the property of Elimelech and of Mahlon, if you will give me your shoe in return, relinquishing your claim as next of kin."

Tob hesitated only momentarily. The faces of the crowd told him what would happen if he refused. Hastily he reached down, removed his right shoe and handed it to Boaz. The crowd laughed as he went hopping back to the place where he had been standing. Adah was not there. Angry at her for getting him into trouble, Tob had reduced her to her proper status, that of a slave.

Boaz turned to the elders and the people. "You are witnesses this day," he said, "that I have bought all that belonged to Elimelech and all that belonged to Chilion and to Mahlon. And I take now Ruth, the widow of Mahlon, to be my wife, to perpetuate the name of the dead in his inheritance, that the name of the dead may not be cut off from among his brethren and from the gate of his native place."

Nathan, as leader of the elders, spoke. "We are witnesses. May the Lord make this woman, who is coming into your house, like Rachel and Leah, who together built up the house of Israel."

A bright ray of sunshine suddenly shone down from among the clouds, making a halo of Ruth's bright hair.

"It is a good omen," Elkan shouted. "God bless Boaz and his wife, Ruth. And make them fruitful."

Naomi turned to embrace Ruth then as the crowd surged up to congratulate them.

> So Boaz took Ruth, and she was his wife;
> and when he went in unto her the Lord gave
> her conception and she bare a son.
> And Naomi took the child and laid it in her
> bosom, and became nurse unto it.
> And the women, her neighbors, gave it a
> name, saying, There is a son born to Naomi;

and they called his name Obed: he is the fa-
ther of Jesse, the father of David.
RUTH 4:13, 16–17

Of this man's seed hath God, according to
his promise, raised unto Israel a Savior, Jesus.
ACTS 13:23